THE
LAST CHOIRBOY

A Novel of Espionage
And Revenge

Zachary Mannheim Book 3

John Hayden

Library of Congress Control Number: Pending
Names: John Hayden
ISBN: (Paperback) 979-8-9858448-0-1
Epub: 979-8-9858448-1-8

Chapter 1

"They're coming."

Computer generated, the voice conveyed urgency. Ignored by the sleeping woman, an algorithm counted five seconds before tripling the volume. The cottage by the bay on Cape Cod reverberated with its demand.

"They're coming…less than two minutes."

Raissa Ribeiro bolted upright, instigating the first in a series of actions to save her life, learn who was responsible for an impending attack, kill or capture the team of attackers, determine the way they'd arrived on Cape Cod and from whence they came. What she would set in motion varied only with the scenario chosen by the opposition and the vagaries of weather.

Everything she would do was the result of Randall Carter's unique genius. Hacker extraordinaire, mad tinkerer with all things digital, and still not twenty-five, Randall had been a temporary roommate/little-brother for the last weeks of the Agency's counter-intelligence operation against Marta Mannheim, Deputy Director of SVR's First Directorate, a principal element of Russia's Intelligence apparatus. Randall predicted how, in a hacker's slanted view, the safety of the person he trusted most could be compromised. Remote servers, where photographs of faces and license plate data were stored, analyzed and subjected to predictive algorithms, made the defensive system work.

Raissa's bedroom was on the first floor in the northeast corner facing the bay. Concurrent with the voice's demands, the security system doused exterior lighting which, under normal circumstances, gave the cottage a warm glow.

Shadowed by Agatha, her eighty-pound black Lab, Raissa examined a massive radar screen set into an interior wall. At 03:00 on a late November night no pip would be expected, yet this radar image was no mistake. A boat nearing the main channel rendered *one if by land and two if by sea* inapplicable; this attack was coming from both directions.

Amongst the fallout at Langley, since an exchange of American and Russian prisoners on the Gleinicke Bridge in Berlin, were the resignations of Dr. Gregory Riley and Randall Carter; Carter was now employed at Riley's consulting firm. In most ways Raissa felt her symbiotic relationship with Greg and Randall was undisturbed. *Most ways* left open a gulf separating good intentions from the road to Hell, paved as it was with human frailty.

Turning from the radar screen, she concentrated on closed circuit video from the two-lane road, broadcast at half-mile intervals. Two cars were visible: At least four armed men, a maximum of eight.

Langley would not be notified.

Local police were unaware; invasion of privacy was the norm in a world where secrets were trivial to create, but hard to preserve.

She scanned cameras and listening devices covering the grounds; less robust cousins proliferated within interior rooms. Attackers could destroy this control panel. In a worst case, the cottage could burn to the ground and its data would survive within a half dozen widely separated server farms. In a final act she activated a separate tap, indistinguishable to the electric, telephone or cable companies, which transmitted one-way messages to Jonathan Chapman at Wide River Boatyard and Lieutenant Tom Nichols of the Massachusetts State Police.

Jonathan and his extended family lived adjacent to the boatyard, a mile south by southeast of the cottage. Nichols and his wife Melissa resided three miles distant, although proximity wasn't critical to actions Tom would trigger, if the need arose. Warned, neither would come to Raissa's immediate rescue.

Raissa and Agatha exited the rear deck without looking back; the cottage, an aged Ferrari, and a fleet of small boats were inanimate. Lessons learned in the aftermath of being burned alive were indelible: Objects could be replaced. Down the stairs she ran through loose sand and a tangle of beach grass. Hand under Agatha's muzzle she delivered the single command the big dog would obey without deviation.

"Go to Jonathan, Aggie. Now." Agatha broke into a loping run.

Waterproof switch activated; she located a handle set into a concrete septic tank installed by Jonathan without permits. As a

Vietnam veteran, having a supermodel/spy as his friend and neighbor served as amusement and intoxication.

Both hands released from the ladder she dropped to the tank's bottom, connected to two-hundred yards of forty-eight-inch corrosion resistant pipe. Half a mile to the bay's opposite shore could almost be walked at low tide, if Raissa was willing to become visible—and shortly thereafter dead.

Wetsuit, hood, gloves, mask and fins hung from hooks above the high-water mark. She crouch-walked through not-yet-flooded sections of pipe. As the saltwater level rose, she fought claustrophobia. Certain death lay behind. Drowning would be avoided, if her last un-submerged breath lasted until her snorkel relieved spasming lungs. Paralytic fear peaked. Fingers clawed concrete to escape the Grim Reaper's engraved invitation. Their renewed acquaintance summoned misery beyond description. Banished with a lungful of cold night air, there wasn't a winner or loser—just détente among perpetual adversaries.

Raissa clung to the perimeter of a large sandbar before easing her head above the surface. Kneeling on the sand before snorkeling another hundred yards, she began to assess permutations and probabilities.

Who provided the boat?

The answer wasn't immediately important, but it would be soon. Triple outboard motors emitted an audible burble from the outer channel where the Harbormaster removed seasonal navigation buoys at the end of October.

Who was at the helm?

Supposition raised Goosebumps under the wetsuit's neoprene. Steady on the proper course, the helmsman was comfortable where an ounce of ill attention meant running aground.

Where was the airplane?

No Russian kill-team—*see where guesses take you, she thought*—flew into Boston or Providence on a commercial flight. So there was a jet on the ground at Hyannis, Nantucket or Martha's Vineyard—unless these attackers were CIA. *Stop attempting to ridicule Langley's involvement*, an insistent voice cackled: Langley had sent two separate contractors to end Raissa's life not so long ago.

A quarter moon painted the bay silver. Remnants of a northwest breeze brushed her left cheek. Time slowed as her fins kicked for the far shoreline. A pounding heart rate subsided, and determination substituted for fear's stagnation. Less than five minutes effort put her amidst the rubble of an ancient seawall. Hands held a Brügger & Thomet Advanced Precision Rifle carrying a Schmidt & Bender scope, fitted with a GRS suppressor, and rated for .338 Lapua Magnum rounds. Left in the waterproof rucksack were more esoteric items: Bricks of new $100s, passports, clothes and sundries.

Forty-two feet long and gleaming white, the boat made a precise ninety degree turn into the Bay's inner channel. At a range of a hundred yards, two men were visible in the deep red glow of its instrument panel. Raissa allowed the bipod to deploy. Scope focused on an older man with chiseled, unshaven, facial features, he stood in front of the companionway. Hands on the wheel to the man's immediate right was Jonathan, wild mane and white beard unmistakable in profile.

An ironic smile creased her lips; the unexpected and improbable were everyday occurrences for a spy who worked off the grid and alone. Opponents were clever. Betrayal was mother's milk. Only a flexible mind, an appetite for risk and acceptance of fate's cruelty would suffice. Long, slow breaths let the situation evolve by inserting herself in Jonathan's head.

Having survived two combat tours in 'Nam, Jonathan was no one's fool, although his physical appearance invited such a comparison from a certain class of dickhead. Jonny was a boatman's boatman, who hadn't stopped the turn to port. Two things would result: Raissa would have a clear shot for precious seconds and the boat would be hard aground within twenty ticks of an unseen clock.

Permutations and probabilities computed, she took the cleft-chinned man with a head shot. Jonathan moved to starboard, inviting her to view the bulkhead as an open field of fire.

How many hostiles? Hostages beyond Jonathan?

Raissa worked the bolt action methodically, emptying the ten-shot clip into the boat's cabin. Hearing a semi-automatic handgun fire repeatedly, she saw Jonathan swing outboard of the helm, then disappear as the boat shuddered to a halt. Its bow sunk further in the muddy bottom with every rotation of three stainless steel propellers.

Ramming a new clip home, Raissa waited. Her cell phone vibrated, which couldn't be a good thing. She answered without speaking.

"Ms. Ribeiro, isn't the evening lovely? Bright stars. A moon. Nantucket over the horizon and Martha's Vineyard hulking in shadow. And you, my dear...no longer a cultural icon, but a frightened fox running from hungry hounds. It's a trifle sad. We'll talk about all of this soon."

"What shall I call you...when we talk?"

"Maximilian is my name. Max to my friends. I've put fresh coffee on the stove in your lovely kitchen. Talking would be to your benefit."

Raissa's purposes weren't served by delay.

"Your boat's stuck in the mud...look East from my deck at nine-hundred yards. By the way...the older gentleman with the cleft chin is drooling blood and brains from a fresh hole in his forehead. Poor Jonathan, my old friend, is dead, but there are always casualties when a fox slashes a chasing dog."

Raissa ended the call, rotated the APR's scope from south to west, and swept the cottage's deck for men intending to launch one or more of her kayaks. The power boat was important to this operation in ways both obvious and oblique; the opposition could only retrieve it using a kayak.

The attacking group totaled eight, but its composition was wrong. Two armed men were inside the cottage in search of weapons, data or Intelligence—one of which was present. On the deck a shorter man held sway over four hostages, arms held above their heads. Yet another male launched a kayak, clambered in and began to paddle. A flare of deep orange seared the darkness as kayak and paddler disintegrated. The odor of burned flesh wafted onto the cottage's deck; it would lessen the confidence of these invaders.

Still as stone, she barely breathed.

An automatic weapon fired a burst at the hostage closest to the explosion. Letting the weight of the weapon be taken by his shoulder and its strap, the shooter's left arm raised a cell phone to his ear.

So Maximilian isn't where he claimed; he's aboard the airplane on Martha's Vineyard. Her cell vibrated a second time.

Ignoring the phone, she worked a solution for the man in her bedroom: Nine-hundred twenty-four yards with zero wind. Dialing down the scope's power, she maintained an optimal field of view. Center mass the target, Raissa's expertise was insufficient to guarantee a head shot at this range. After firing twice, she turned her attention to the man on the porch. In the dead of night, taking fire from an unknown position, any covert veteran would be shaken to the core. If AK-47 man ran, he'd first execute the remaining hostages. Raissa watched him throw the redwood picnic table on edge. From that position, he might, or might not be able to shoot three remaining hostages: Woman, girl and man.

Why don't they run? Amateurs, terror froze them in place.

Powerless to intervene, Raissa devoted her energy towards the remaining attacker, dubbing him the *Fourth Man*.

For a third time the cell vibrated.

Voice cold, she answered. "Two men down at my home, Maximilian. One hostage dead. AK-47 guy, guarding the hostages, is crying behind a table. Cowards, Max, that's who you employed. Why don't you come over? We'll share a coffee. Or are you flying away...keeping your pants pressed and French cuffs clean?"

Jonathan's whisper shocked her. "Shoulder's shot to hell, girl. Long ways off, but I can lay down fire in the table's direction. Won't hit the bastard, but he'll sure as taxes have to move."

Jonny's effort to get close enough must have been Herculean. "Start shooting at five, four..." Raissa centered the scope at the end of the table furthest from Jonathan's one feasible shelter. Gunshots erupted, sighted by a skilled shooter. The second shattered redwood.

Raissa saw a green laser beam dancing on dark wood; this wasn't Jonny. She added an unknown beach shooter to the mix.

The woman and girl hostages hurled themselves over the deck's railing, falling eight feet to sit stunned and helpless. AK-47 man emerged in a crouch, running for the side of the deck away from the handgun and towards the female hostages.

Raissa fired without result.

Two deep booms reverberated from a shotgun. Glass from Raissa's French Doors exploded outwards hurling machine-gun man twelve feet across the deck to lay shredded and bleeding. Tom Nichols emerged, searching for additional targets.

The green laser found the State cop and, as if sentient, vanished.

Within minutes Raissa heard sirens. She couldn't hear Jonathan call to Tom, requesting a medic. She hit redial for the number used by Maximilian.

"Max, I've got north of half a million in my backpack...bricks of nice, colorful hundreds. After tonight I'll be traveling a while. You too, I'd bet. Success has many fathers, after all. Failure not so many. Name a place to meet….pretty much anywhere. A man like you knows things…a girl like me will pay. Whaddya say?"

She heard jet engines spooling for takeoff.

"I admit to being misinformed by my client, Ms. Ribeiro. You would be little trouble to kill, I was told. I've thrown lives away in vanity…it's unlike me. Unfortunately your offer is short a zero. Though I'll look forward to…"

Blossoming due South of Raissa's hidey hole, a fireball devolved into a thousand chunks of burning wreckage. The sky glowed bright before melting to sullen orange, exposing a wing and the forward section of a fuselage floating towards Wasque Shoal and the Muskeget Channel where Nantucket Sound joined the deep Atlantic.

Mundane though the task, she gathered every shell casing. Broke down the weapon. Laced hiking boots on her feet, pulled a tight fitting knit hat onto her head and zippered a parka. Slung fifty pounds of backpack over a shoulder and began to walk. The church, where a battered pickup would be found next to a dumpster, was six miles distant on an efficient routing. An hour and fifteen minutes of serious effort, on a more circumspect route, and she'd be mobile again.

She found herself in agreement with Maximilian, now deceased: The evening's events had been a tragic ruse and Raissa Ribeiro again was a very expensive, well-known pawn. So was the fourth gunman, who, as she counted casualties, was unharmed and desperate to steal a car, boat or bicycle to escape Cape Cod. The Fourth Man, he who'd worn an air of detachment munching a banana in her kitchen, was Raissa's top priority.

***

Tom Nichols handed Cheryl Chapman a glass of water. It was the victims who never saw it coming, whose shell-shocked faces failed to comprehend what happened and what they lost. Her story emerged in fractured bits.

"Dad woke us up, but Laurel and I slowed him down too much. Nothin' else to say, really. Bill Finnegan came barging out of his house and got the shock of his life. Four of them made Dad start

Bill's boat. People shot…I was terrified." Her father was on the way to Falmouth Hospital with stable vital signs.

A second ambulance crew prepped the shotgun victim for transport to Cape Cod Hospital; whether he'd live long enough to benefit was debatable.

Tom leaned over the gurney. "Anything to say?"

The question seemed wasted on a gun-for-hire from who knew where. Glassed over, the wounded man's eyes presaged his words. "Fucking Max. Fucking Choirmaster. They've killed us all. Can you call a priest?"

Tom had no intention of calling anyone, let alone a priest, until he spoke to either Raissa or Jonathan. "Sure, Buddy, you bet."

Chapter 2

Glare from streetlights made identification difficult. Russell Tipton assumed the slight figure was Aydan Fetisov, Senior Counselor at the Embassy of the Russian Federation. Tipton fidgeted with the gun in his overcoat pocket. If the man wasn't Fetisov there'd be no escape.

Fifty yards from Tipton, one hand raised chest high in a coffee drinker's salutation. In the halo of the closest streetlight, Fetisov's gaunt, almost diseased features became apparent. Tipton released the gun, lifting a cramped right hand in a stilted greeting.

Labored breathing marked emotional and physical exertion. Neither man was young, if chronological age was discounted and physical suffering utilized as surrogate measure. Meetings like this brought no excitement. Lying would be an ingrained response to the tribulations of employment by their respective Intelligence services. Neither American nor Russian would employ the truth to escape a quagmire.

Fetisov passed a coated paper cup to Tipton. He spoke Russian.

"Just poured from a thermos in the car, my friend. Made to your liking by a lovely young thing in the Embassy's kitchen." Nothing in these words emulated banter between friends.

Tipton examined the cup as if it might sprout fangs. Sighed while speaking Fetisov's educated Russian in a subdued, possibly sad voice. "Why are there no lovely young things in Russia's political kitchens?"

Fetisov squinted, blaming steam from black coffee. Square eyeglasses, fogged from those vapors, eliminated an accurate examination of his counterpart's ruddy face. Tipton's artificial leg, newest variant of the most advanced technology, must be painful, Fetisov thought as a twinge transited the American's forehead.

"Would it offend you, if I express personal disappointment, Russell?"

Tipton was the creature of Edward Jonas Brantley, Director of the Central Intelligence Agency. Tipton derived stature in the Intelligence community directly from that political umbilical cord. A predilection for artless speech on occasion triumphed over discretion.

"Neither you nor anyone in your nest of vipers has cause to be disappointed or displeased."

Fetisov fit a Turkish cigarette into a yellowed plastic holder. Tip clenched between gapped teeth; his first inclination was to delay.

"I've quit smoking, you know. Now I chew these damnable things until they break...the throwaway society you Americans prefer." Eye contact maintained, the older of the two by thirty years asked the obvious. "If I haven't the right to be disappointed, or even a touch disgruntled, why have I been summoned?"

Tipton considered a range of responses before electing the simplest.

"Because I assumed you'd use a Russian team. And, yes, you executed Maximillian when things went bad...you get high marks for expediency. But there'll have been leaks in Max's proverbial boat...not that those leaks would have resulted from your error. Nevertheless, I wanted to remind you how our acquiescence, our accommodation if you will, included one event...one event only. There can be no second bite at the apple, not on United States soil."

"Our agreement required neutrality from CIA, Russell. There were at least four trained men awaiting Max's team...everyone on the confiscated boat is dead. We recovered one man suffering shotgun wounds...he will die. There may have been a second survivor. Ms. Ribeiro wasn't home as your intelligence claimed. I'd say using a contractor showed foresight, given this betrayal by EJ. It suggests Ms. Ribeiro is, despite fulsome denials, a CIA asset if not an employee. If I'm not permitted disappointment, I'm damned well entitled to displeasure."

"Nothing among your accusations is true. Ms. Ribeiro has no affiliation with CIA. She was in her home last evening...and to describe Max's operation as a blunder would be a breathtaking understatement. They confiscated a boat from a family of four brothers, each a veteran of the Marine Corps, each a decorated combat veteran of Vietnam. Good God, Aydan. Max took one brother and his daughter hostage, leaving three trained men who knew the water and ground better than a Greek who never left the comforts of his jet. One of the brothers recruited a Massachusetts State Police lieutenant…the trooper brought the shotgun. So Max's crew faced five skilled men protecting their families and got slaughtered for their trouble."

Tipton sipped coffee. Moved additional weight onto his flesh and blood leg. Something wasn't exactly right about the Russian's facial response.

"Second survivor, that's what you said…you had someone inside Max's operation who bailed out to save himself. Is he in the Embassy, or somewhere in the New England darkness, bleeding to death, trying to run home to Mother Russia?"

"Even if what you explained is true, where was Raissa? A fatuous, publicity seeking woman whose singular fame amongst the fashion elite are the scars covering her body…how did she avoid Max's attack? Where is she?"

Tipton saw it was time to dial down his rhetoric.

"Who gives a shit, Aydan? Officially, CIA doesn't condone SVR's obsessive determination to eliminate Ms. Ribeiro…though sometimes a small sacrifice is warranted."

Tipton saw a grinding determination in the older man; Aydan wanted more.

"What we know suggests Cobb Chapman phoned to warn her: Cobb is the oldest Chapman brother. Did your inside man report seeing Raissa's dog? Dog and woman…they're inseparable from what I've heard."

"And you know this how, Russell?"

"Because we used our own people, not hired-hands. Your second survivor, SVR's man on the ground…he saw the dog, didn't he? Where?"

Fetisov wouldn't give in, not when dissatisfied. Marta's questions would probe every orifice, every weakness in his explanation. Marta believed Raissa was, could only be, CIA. She wouldn't be pleased with today's outcome.

"I can't say, Russell. I'm not familiar with the identity of this second survivor. Or if he'll continue to survive. When inquiries have been made, we can speak again."

"One bite at this apple, Aydan. You do understand?"

Fetisov winked, turning calmly to walk in the direction from which he'd come.

***

Lt. Nichols held no illusions.

Town police might be slow off the starting blocks, but they'd catch-on quick to a first-rank celebrity landing smack in the middle of a shitstorm. Police on the Vineyard called it celebrity policing; they catered to dozens of the rich and famous. Here on the mainland, in a decidedly lower rent district, there hadn't been a true celebrity since Cyndi Lauper spent a few summers in a house not far from Raissa's cottage.

His own involvement would echo the murder of Gunther Probst. Near on three years ago, Tom Nichols covered for Raissa discovering Probst's body. Trying to remember his original intent, this initial act of kindness sucked him into a pit of dark animus and tangled webs spun by spies, politicians and sycophants attendant to both. In the end he could've sold his story ten times over, but Jonathan, as well as Tom's buddies at the boatyard, would've strung him up from the nearest yardarm.

"Who's going to tell me what's happened?" The loud, insistent voice of the Police Chief gave proof to sporadic telephone complaints about an explosion and shooting by the bay.

Tom used his official tone in calling towards the front of the cottage. "Chief Phillips…Tom Nichols from the State Police. On the back porch."

Maybe ten minutes in the job as Chief of Police, Phillips came from somewhere in Southern New Hampshire. Seemed average by any measure. Was he well intentioned? Tom figured the answer would be in plain view before long.

Phillips' question preceded handshake or smile; it wasn't encouraging. "Where's our most famous resident?"

Nichols was too exhausted to absorb bullshit. "No idea, Chief."

"This a State Police matter?" Dripping with sarcasm, the Chief's chin tilted upwards to delve into Nichols' face.

"Here as a friend of Jonathan and his family."

Phillips elected a haughty tone, disdainful in its application. "Jonathan who, Lieutenant?"

Nichols bit his tongue. Louis Phillips didn't know these folks and didn't care about the horrors of the past several hours.

"Jonathan Chapman owns Wide River Boatyard. Called me…said a group of armed men were outside his home. I got here mostly too late. Shot one guy carrying the old AK-47…about to kill Cheryl Chapman and Laurel Hazen. Cheryl's Jonathan's daughter. Laurel's his granddaughter. Gang stole a boat…made Jonathan bring half of them over here by water. Jonny's got a lot of Swamp Yankee in him. Got his shoulder blowed-up saving his family. Claims everyone on board is dead…boat's in the mud just off the barrier beach. One dead guy in the bedroom. Another in the wreckage of a kayak…didn't go down to look."

"Why not?"

"Triage. Got Jonny in the first ambulance and the shotgun victim in the second. Arranged for Cheryl and Laurel to be taken home to family. First things first…how I do things."

Chief Phillips stared at Lieutenant Nichols, trying to decide if he'd been told GFY. "What's a Swamp Yankee, Lieutenant?"

"Stubborn, frugal, Yankee stock…thought well of in the year-round community down here. Minimal formal education…truckloads of real-life skills. Summer folk laugh, when we occasionally use the term. Sometimes year-rounders shorten it to *Swamper*. Underestimating a Swamper is easy…usually a mistake." Nichols' explanation substituted for elaboration on how Jonny could have bested trained killers.

"Hang around, Lieutenant, okay?"

"Nearly five-thirty, Chief. Haven't slept. On duty at seven. Good luck with this mess."

Nichols needed a shower and a gallon of coffee. The coming day would present more challenging discussions than this one. Louis Phillips was a dick.

***

To search aimlessly for the *Fourth Man* was pointless. Too many back roads, too many backyards made Raissa park next to a fish market on the traffic circle, switch off the lights and leave the engine running. Any driver, going anywhere, would transit this location. The truck's angle would grant a fragment of time during which her eyes and those faces would align.

She shivered; a wet suit wasn't designed for prolonged exposure to frigid temperatures. Traffic wasn't light, nor was it near its peak as the dashboard clock crept towards six. Window rolled down, she settled the APR in the window opening, calibrating the scope for short range.

Passing a supermarket complex, the police car's flashing lights demanded attention. As red and blue strobe-lights entered the circle, she began downloading images, wary of the huge variation in lighting. Headed in her direction, its wasn't returning to Police Headquarters. Too fast and too dark for accurate identification, she glanced at her phone where images from the APR's scope downloaded in real time. The *Fourth Man,* sitting next to the cop, looked more like a college boy, angelic face revealing no emotion.

East towards Hyannis where business openings weren't imminent, or off-Cape to anywhere and everywhere via the Sagamore Bridge— those might have been easier options for Raissa. She withdrew the APR and watched the cop take the third of five spokes of the circle. Hyannis could be crossed out. Town Hall, Dunkin Doughnuts, Otis Air Base, Sagamore Bridge, Boston and the rest of the world beckoned. Her initial plan excluded speaking with Tom Nichols; now there was no choice.

Careful, she admonished herself; when inevitably questioned, Tom will tell the truth. Raissa was wistful for years when there weren't friends to protect.

"Raissa…have you heard about your cottage?" Nichols knew his way around a staged conversation, though Raissa calling from a vulnerable phone on an open line was ludicrous.

"Hey Tom, just had a call from my alarm company. Has anyone found Agatha?"

"The boys found her in the bulrushes by the boatyard." 'Boys' was a euphemism for young men who hung around the boatyard as if it was a clubhouse.

"Any fire damage? Are the cops or fire trucks still there?"

"Look Raissa, this was a full-fledged disaster. Gunmen took Jonny and his family hostage. Firefight ensued. I got here at the end. Lots of shit…too much to explain. Chief Phillips has questions for you…expects your cooperation. Jonny's at Falmouth Hospital…too miserable to talk to anyone. He'll come off the hero…be insufferable for the rest of time. When d'you think you'll get home?" It seemed a reasonable question for a supermodel, who could be found anytime, anywhere in the world in the company of the rich, famous and powerful.

Raissa broke the connection and pushed the accelerator hard. She merged into the traffic circle under the assumption she was following Chief Phillips and male passenger, the unidentified *Fourth Man*. Every instinct, honed by hard won lessons, branded warnings on her brain—*tip of the iceberg, girl…don't get too stupid too soon.* Thirty seconds to search the scope's downloaded images would be the most prudent course. Just as certain, thirty seconds would eliminate catching the Chief of Police.

Pushing seventy on a twisting road, sparse traffic offered hope. Jamming the brakes in front of the Town's sole strip club, a decrepit Oldsmobile cut her off. If there'd been an oncoming vehicle, her maneuver would have put her in service to a higher power than CIA. Swearing like a rock star, she threw the truck into the last turn before Town Hall, screeching to a near halt at the stoplight. Tires screamed as she accelerated up the hill past the doughnut shop, giving it a cursory examination. Settled at sixty-five, nothing of interest would appear for five miles. Past the main runway of Joint Base Otis, she slowed at the stoplight marking the main entrance. Route 6, the MidCape Highway, was less than a minute ahead in the darkness. At an unsustainable speed, she flew by the convoy entrance, barely noticing the parked cruiser, its driver manipulating the heavy chain and padlock securing double-wide gates.

"Dammit," Raissa cursed as the pickup tracked towards oncoming high beams. Brakes feathered, she pulled off onto the sandy shoulder.

A malaise of uncertainty descended. Common enough at a spy's worst times, she lifted her hands from the wheel and forced controlled breathing to take hold. The *Fourth Man*, from an attack on *her* cottage by foreign nationals, was entering a US military base. Less than perfect lighting hindered a solid comparison of a male viewed across nine hundred yards of water to the man sitting in a police cruiser less than two-hundred yards uphill. Preconception was dangerous.

She wanted to believe, ergo they were the same man.

Operational instinct cried out: None of these inputs can be trusted.

She texted Randall: *Attached images…man in my kitchen…passenger in the cruiser. Quick.*

Truck turned around, she glanced at herself in the rearview: Matted hair; dark eye circles; caked salt; covered in black neoprene. Lousy was how she felt. Hairbrush pulled through the worst tangles, Raissa aimed the pickup towards Hyannis and the hospital where Tom's shotgun victim had been taken. In the rearview the police cruiser was no longer visible, and the gates to Otis were closed.

What was real? What had been imagined?

Her secondary phone pinged. Tom Nichols had waited for a quiet moment to text on a burner: *AK-47 Man referred to 'Max' and 'Choirmaster.' Someone using a green laser joined the fray on our side. Hope it helps.*

***

High probability identical. No ID. Searching.

Good boy, Randall. No extraneous information, he focused on the field agent's needs. *Cottage attack failed. Monitor Town cops/Chief. Langley interested?*

Four miles from Exit 6 and the main road to Hyannis, Randall responded. *In progress. Greg?*

Greg Riley would be brought into Raissa's tiny group of insiders, but not when everything was a swirling shamble of guesses and assumptions. Let him sleep. For the foreseeable future, she suspected, sleep would be hard to find and unfulfilling for all of us.

Taking Exit 6 at a sedate speed, the truck was five miles from the hospital nearby Hyannis harbor. Pulling into a strip mall, her Ready Bag held a shabby wig, large, framed glasses and worn-out sweatpants. Slab of faux flab fastened under a parka; mild dissipation surrounded the woman who replaced Raissa.

At the ER triage desk, Raissa allowed her words to drawl; attempts at a native Cape Cod accent would strain credibility. "Police say my nephew here with shotgun pellets all inside him, honey. When can I see him?"

"No gunshot wounds all night, sugar. Three overdoses and a razor slashing…best I can do you for. Anything else, sweetie?" The night nurse began typing entries into her shift report.

THE LAST CHOIRBOY   17

Raissa's tone gained a sharper edge. "Cops still around from the slashing?"

Pushing reading glasses on top of her head, the nurse stared carefully at a woman asking about police. "You got the look of someone don't need attention from the police."

Raissa squeezed out a tear. "Police on the phone told me what I said before. Maybe they took Darryl someplace else?"

Both women looked to their left as the day shift arrived. The clock read 6:52.

With traffic stirring, an odor of desperation permeated her truck. Where could the ambulance have been intercepted, and by whom? As Marstons Mills blended into Centerville, the abandoned ambulance sat empty—off the road, front-end crushed by a tree and the radiator hissing steam.

Tactics changed a second time, never an optimal decision for a woman with secrets, Raissa discarded Hyannis Airport and Boston Logan. Manchester or Hartford were little better, if Langley was involved. A flight from New Haven to Washington Reagan was a time-consuming best among bad options. She pointed the battered pickup towards the Bourne Bridge.

Chapter 3

Road noise was the only sound as the cop car bounced and rattled. Dashboard lights were subservient to the bright laptop screen mounted prominently between driver and passenger.

"Are you my Field Director?"

Elias Thordsen, christened Elijas Halvorsen by his mother and father, was impatient to depart Cape Cod. Angst saturating his question, he fervently wished not to sound virginal.

Louis Phillips watched an object at the side of the road sharpen into a deer. A smallish buck would die in any collision, but unintended consequences would ripple into infinity. Whether this kid—was he old enough to drink?—lasted the night was beyond his mission's scope, or his inclination to give a damn.

"Best not to ask unless you know the answer."

Elias heard a mistake, when a simple thought escaped his mouth. "You sound like a lawyer."

"Do you need a lawyer?" Louis turned, flashing a serious look. "Wherever you're going, it's the truth of your legend that will keep you safe. Invest in every detail. Anything else is a waste of time."

Nervous anger bubbled into silly prattle. "So...Mr. Chief of Police...are you a waste of time?"

"Pick you up, deliver you to the airplane...that's it for me. Don't know who you are, where you're going or what you hope to accomplish. Being Chief of Police is hard enough. Doin' my job."

"Who's the pilot?" Whomever the pilot might be, he/she comprised the weakest link in an overly complex plan, or so his instructor at the Farm claimed when disparaging complicated plans and mercenaries.

Louis Phillips' indignation was common to men and women who, by choice or failure, supported the operational needs and desires of spies. Field Directors lived and died with spies who depended upon them for accurate, insightful data regarding mission status and the spy's survival. If Elias Thordsen survived this day, there'd be time enough to admonish last evening's stupidity. Keep things simple was a Field Director's directive. So, when asked questions irrelevant to the success of any officer's mission, Phillips lied with alacrity.

"No idea. Need to know, you know?"

Elias slumped, staring out the window.

Scrub pines became interspersed with paved roadways. A series of turns were intended to keep the police cruiser away from populated areas. Unsurprised, a single-engine airplane, propeller spinning, erupted from early morning ground fog looked ready to launch down the runway into a glacial breeze from the northeast. Two words chased Thordsen from the cruiser's warmth.

"Good hunting."

Thordsen clambered aboard thinking the plane closer to the junk pile than its prime. "Hi..." he said to the back of a head examining something on the machine's port wing "...sorry to be late." While takeoff could be witnessed by anyone caring enough to look, his trainers all agreed: Butterflies in the belly were normal.

Could fear of this magnitude ever be productive?

She turned to face him.

Crap, she can't be more than sixteen. He blurted, "How old are you?"

"Old enough to fly where you're going."

Her hand advanced the throttle to takeoff position and the two-seat Siai Marchetti SM.1019A was airborne in seconds. Climbing into low clouds, the small aircraft bounced every which way. She adjusted her compass heading, turned hard to starboard until over Nantucket Sound, re-crossed Cape Cod over Eastham and headed out to sea away from commercial traffic.

"What's your name?" Elias watched her right eyebrow twitch.

Over open ocean, she descended to one hundred feet on a heading taking them to Cutler Regional Airport in Maine.

"Aren't we too low?"

She descended to fifty feet.

Spume from curling waves occasionally spattered the windscreen, mocking a bird out of place in a deepening low pressure system. Leaving the Boston/Logan ATC area, she set the tiny aircraft in a climb hoping to get above the weather.

"Why won't you talk to me?"

Climbing was a mistake. She wouldn't have, if ignorant or blind to the fate awaiting Elias Thordsen. Lips pressed thin into a scowl, she flew the damn plane.

Two hours passed in anticipation, when Thordsen watched the altimeter unwind in a blur from twenty thousand feet. Thrown time and again against the restraint of his seatbelt, he asked in a snide tone, "Do you plan to crash into some god forsaken forest? Won't they waive you off?"

"No tower. Pilots make the decisions...we're landing where we're supposed to land."

Forty-foot pine trees the briefing had said. Descending through one hundred feet she couldn't see beyond the nose in windblown snow. At fifty feet, washed-out lights crystallized twenty degrees on her port side.

God, we're going to crash—all Elias could think.

Left wing thrown towards the ground she held her breath, hoping the maneuver wouldn't cartwheel the aircraft into a fatal pinwheel. Never level, they bounced, went airborne and bounced a second time before settling on a gravel surface stabilized with dormant grass under nine inches of fluffy powder.

Cutler Regional was unattended, devoid of activity. Two single engine aircraft, a lone twin and an old helo hunched together against winter's onslaught. She taxied in the direction of lights from pickup trucks signed as property of the United States Navy.

Through an open door, Elias unexpectedly found himself looking back at his non-conversational pilot, face drawn tight with unconquered foreboding.

She tried to think of something that might ease his skyrocketing apprehension. "Hold on tight to who you are. Just who you are...not who you're expected to be or whom you dream of being. No one else matters."

Jumping from the plane, Elias heard a teenager in uniform say, "Get in the truck, sir. I'll be taking you part way."

***

Elias tried to remember Machiasport where blueberries, timber, soft-shell clams, lobster, and the Down East Correctional Facility dominated the economy.

A pleasant woman in her fifties, a Registered Nurse at the minimum-security institution, beeped the horn to jar him out of a brain-freeze. Inside her car, he made no enquiry, choosing instead to sleep.

"Don't doze…few minutes you'll be on the way to Shag Harbor. That's Nova Scotia, if you care to know."

Certain the lobster boat had been baby-blue, he couldn't remember the skipper's name or recall a thing of his physical appearance. Lying by a bucket of fresh bait, tongue thick and head pounding, the needle the nurse jabbed in his neck glowed bright in recollection. Mark of the unexpected and unwelcome, Elias's world was upside down.

***

Craig Hall, POTUS's National Security Advisor and political hatchet-man, was by disposition and governmental brief, a skilled liar with an appreciation for backstabbing irony. Thought brilliant by his boss, considered ruthless by the world in general, Hall appreciated the value of holding firm in a strong wind.

Edward Jonas Brantley, EJ to friends, none of whom were numbered among the government's Intelligence apparatus, was dead. Little more than two years prior, Brantley was confirmed by the full Senate with astonishing bipartisan support. Brantley's background in the State Department made him not at all in the mold of past Directors of CIA ("D/CIA"). Overly abrasive to Beltway power brokers, he'd navigated the pitfalls and inflated egos of the Agency with aplomb.

Craig Hall never knew about Brantley's brain tumor. Who had? It seemed a reasonable question, though asking POTUS would require tact.

"Good afternoon, Mr. President. Brantley died earlier this morning. His oncologist and nurses were present along with his wife and children. Autopsy isn't finished, but nothing funky is likely. No leaks yet. Bet on the evening news having the story…conspiracy theories will abound."

POTUS was more neurotic than on an ordinary day. "His predecessor was assassinated by a Russian spy, Craig. It's not paranoia, if they're really out to get you."

"There'll be tough questions, Mr. President."

"Get a grip...I knew about the tumor when he was appointed. Thought he'd live a year. He gave us two peaceful years without the Agency coming apart at the seams. Rare bird was EJ."

"Who's next, Mr. President?" *Who's next* was the reason for the conversation. The King is dead: Which claimant dared sit on the throne?

"Get me your list, Craig. I'll put out feelers to the House and Senate."

Hall pressed the bounds of familiarity between President and Advisor. "Anyone at Langley a candidate?"

"We'll see what shakes out after the mess this morning." The line went dead.

POTUS' comment reflected realities faced by any President, including soliciting advice from Intelligence Committee Chairmen and prior CIA Directors. Hall's to-do list was instantly re-arranged. Making a single phone call and an illegal U-turn, stomach acid accentuated discontent.

***

Russell Tipton merged onto S. Washington Blvd towards Columbia Pike. Took VA-244/Columbia Pike to the Navy Annex. Turned left onto Air Force Memorial Drive. Found Craig Hall standing by one of three spires arcing two hundred seventy feet into the sky. As he'd done when meeting Fetisov, Tipton withheld his hand. Didn't speak. Tipton's close relationship with EJ Brantley wasn't secret, so Hall would seek a telltale to indicate deception.

Not in the mood for the long game, Hall probed hard. "Let's clear-up one thing...no chance you'll succeed EJ. You called my office. Why?"

Why was so open-ended. Had Fetisov carried out his threat in the aftermath of Brantley's death? Am I to be arrested? Tipton's call to Hall, prior to Brantley's demise, now seemed prescient when he could spin its purpose anew. Seeking to wet his lips, Tipton's mouth was arid.

"Operation *Reformation*...did EJ brief you?"

Hall's expression darkened; this kind of meeting belonged in black and white spy movies. Not that Hall gave a shit about the Agency's precious protocols, Tipton's question leapfrogged four levels of people who would.

"Wrong place, Russell. Wrong time. Go back to the office. Write a draft detailing issues and concerns. Rewrite the damn thing until nothing…not a nit…is missing or ignored. Take a long breath before deciding whether the World, the American Way of Life and your family depend on me being its recipient…instead of Jamie Norris, Jamie's boss, and every other Agency bureaucrat between those gentlemen and myself." Hall jotted an e-mail address on a business card embossed with no more than a phone number. "If you're ready to tear down your entire life, I'll read what you prepare."

Hall stared into an unknown abyss.

"You were a fine soldier, Russell. Now you're a spy who's approaching life like a politician. Get away from me."

***

Listening to the phone ring, Hall found it ironic: Having buried Zachary Mannheim in an unmarked grave, I'll be the one eating dirt during the old man's rebirth.

"Hello Zachary, Craig Hall inviting you to a quiet dinner."

"Being retired, Mr. Hall, I'm no longer at my government's beck and call. What event could have prompted such an unusual invitation, and who would be joining us…if, indeed, you plan on attending?"

"EJ Brantley died this morning." Hall's declarative sentence was issued as a substitute for answers.

"Old news, Mr. Hall, in the workday of the National Security Advisor and confidant of a sitting President"

"There'll be a pass waiting at the White House. Working dinner in the Situation Room at 20:00 this evening. Just you and me. As to the agenda, finding out requires showing up. I'd appreciate you coming."

Mannheim had heard Hall's final sentence turn serious. Neither petulance nor irascibility would suffice in response. "I've never been in the White House, Mr. Hall. Would you be kind enough to request something low in carbohydrates for an ancient spy-hunter?"

***

There'd been no warning for Mannheim, because, like all things digital, tracking a cell phone was fast and accelerating more quickly than commonly understood. Under thirty seconds and she'd have been located. When being discovered meant disaster, using no digital device was the lone defense. Not So Pretty Raissa rang the doorbell as an ordinary person would.

Armed with the .22 Pug revolver used but once with intent, Zachary Mannheim examined his visitor on a flat screen mounted in the dining room. Eyebrow raised, his mind connected dots between dinner at the White House and Raissa Ribeiro's frown.

She blew in with a Nor'easter's ferocity. "I'm famished, Zachary. Shit day, not likely to improve."

Tossing a salad to accompany an omelet, Mannheim arranged a hasty meal while Raissa made tea. As she attacked the food, he witnessed adrenaline fueled hyper-concentration recede.

"Whatever drove you here, Raissa, unpleasant as it must be, has brought me the benefit of your company. I've missed you...Randal and Gregory as well. Do they know you're here?"

She shook her head, gnawing at the last of a buttered scone. "Just you. You'll see through the web to find the spider."

Mannheim examined the wall clock. "Let's put you on the sofa...a power nap while I move your truck around back. Then we'll have an hour before my dinner at the White House."

Her jaw dropped while Mannheim's smile emphasized a cat and its mouth full of dead canary.

***

Mannheim summed up Raissa's twenty-minute monologue.

"Randall's warning system bought enough time for you...and your boatyard friends...to thwart an attack by eight men plus Maximilian, their leader. Maximilian was blown-up on takeoff by parties unknown. One survivor from the attacking group is missing, presumed escaped, aided by the Town's newly hired Police Chief. One hostage dead...identity to be determined. Your friend Jonny suffered a GSW...his family shaken but otherwise undamaged. Lt. Nichols arrived late, made a critical contribution and returned to duty. You, Raissa, first sought the fourth attacker, but abandoned the effort after seeing your *Fourth Man* and the Police Chief enter an active Air National Guard Base. Is that fair?"

"Except for the guy Nichols shot. He cursed Max…whose name and role I already knew…and *Choirmaster*. Maybe *Choirmaster* was Max's client. AK-47 Man vanished…the ambulance transporting him was wrecked and abandoned. No EMTs. No wounded attacker."

"Loose ends abound, my dear, but none adequately serious to bring you here in your current state."

"All of what happened was real, but none of it is relevant. Smoke and mirrors, Zachary, all the participants were puppets…except the *Fourth Man*. Maximilian realized the setup seconds before he was blown to Hell. For me, killing was too easy, too arranged. The *Fourth Man*…he was so young. Hid in the kitchen…out of harm's way. I watched his face in my scope…not frightened, maybe bored. The attack was aimed at Raissa but tilted towards failure by design. Designed to leave the *Fourth Man* a credible and sympathetic victim of Maximilian's incompetence. Designed to further the *Fourth Man's* participation in some larger plan. Designed by *Choirmaster*, maybe?"

Raissa, having switched from coffee to beer, took a long pull from the bottle. "Who's doing what to whom, Zachary? That's why I'm here. Because you believe in shadows…because you're a dues paying member of the Shadow-hunters club."

"Did *Choirmaster* strike a chord? Some long-forgotten enemy?"

"No." Raissa was falling victim to the kind of exhaustion only a true haven allowed.

"What type of shooter uses a green laser gun-sight?"

"Hard to generalize, but discounting temperature variations and durability, the best prefer green to red."

"Otis and Hyannis are the only jet airports on the Cape, is that correct?"

"That's right, but lots of grass fields where single engine aircraft operate."

"I've got to leave…the bedroom off the kitchen doubles as a safe room. Steel door, concrete walls, separate ventilation, a small armory under the floorboards. Close the door, punch 1984 to set the locks and alarms. You'll see me on the monitor, when I return."

Chapter 4

"Good evening, Mr. Hall. Was it a sign of confidence, or was it haste which made the Marines impose such a cursory search?"

Hall held zero intention of being baited.

"Lots of descriptors have been applied to you, Zachary...some kind, some quite the opposite. None ever made you a threat to this government. Food's hot. We can eat and talk."

Hall wasn't sorry for hastening Mannheim's departure from Chief of Counterintelligence ("Chief/CIC") at Langley: Expedience had demanded a sacrificial lamb.

Mannheim's recommendations caused heartburn for politicians indifferent to blood spilled by the nation's best. Mind like a razor, EJ Brantley and men like Russell Tipton had been spawned from a single episode of carnage—CIA's Director dead by an Agency drone, targeted by an Agency Officer wrongly accused of dismembering her child. Witch-hunt resembled a cozy dinner party more than the frenzied search for scapegoats and assassins. Sturm und Drang faded, as it routinely did when long knives dripped onto French linen at Georgetown soirees. Craig Hall was abandoned to clean the mess. Until this morning, when EJ Brantley's passing lanced a boil whose pestilence smelled of festering infection.

Mannheim forked a second bite of lamb; chewed slowly, aware of Hall's delay and indecision; stabbed a carrot, adding half a new potato to the fork. Allowed the National Security Advisor to stew until tender. Craig Hall was tied in an identical knot to the one shared by Raissa Ribeiro. Neither operated in ignorance, each preferred offense to defense. Neither was schooled in the art of moving freely in the absence of light.

Hall, a both feet kind of fellow, jumped in. "*Operation Reformation*, Zachary...heard of it?"

Mannheim paused to dredge catalogues of memory. "No."

"No files to check, or sycophants to telephone?"

"I have no knowledge, past or present, of *Operation Reformation.*"

"Neither do I, Zachary. It's the reason you're eating in the White House."

Mannheim swallowed, used his napkin, then asked the question hanging over the table. "Who has frightened you, Mr. Hall...and by what method?"

Hall bent over and hissed the words. "This is where you excuse yourself, thank me for a tour of the White House and never return, if jumping into the breach, or over a cliff, is unappealing."

Mannheim assessed their age differential. Wondered whether Craig Hall had ever been a street fighter in the literal sense. Decided what his price would be and began a negotiation destined to remain verbal yet binding.

"Not so long ago, you were the blunt instrument whose blow sent me packing from Langley..." Mannheim paused to ascertain Hall's level of patience "...so pardon me for looking before I leap. On the assumption you want me to enumerate the risks and identify the players involved in *Operation Reformation*, and further assuming you reserve the option to destroy the operation and its authors, what would be my brief? Whom may I rely upon? What are my budget limitations? Whom will counsel and direct me? What will the Intelligence Committees be told, if a bad odor reaches their nostrils? Will there be a rope I can knot...to hang onto my undervalued life? Or will you kick away the chair to watch me hang, when it's suits you? How will you react should our situations reverse, and I hold significant leverage over you or the President? Surely, without lying too extravagantly, you can answer these concerns without breaking security or obtuse promises made in too much haste."

"I can recruit someone else."

"True enough, Mr. Hall, though no suitable name comes to mind. No one from the Agency will do, because you can't know whose allegiance can be massaged, purchased or otherwise assured. Not a private security company...they shoot first without discrimination. Perhaps someone from the military, though your popularity at the Pentagon is in decline. Someone from the Bureau might be viable, though counterintelligence isn't their strongest suit, and they drip information like a leaky whore. You selected me as your dinner partner. Answer as you think best, leave evaluation to me."

"Define the scope of the threat, if a threat exists, be it political or physical. Identify the players, be they American, foreign or both. Develop a strategy to eliminate the threat. Use any resources or assets you wish, in your discretion…you'll find account information in the file here next to me." Hall pushed it within Mannheim's reach. "Don't even consider identifying the assets you utilize, employ or coerce. My only defense in this situation…is denial."

Mannheim interrupted. "You mean deniability for the President…you'll be sacrificed, if this becomes a media circus."

"Yes, I acknowledge those rules apply to both of us."

Mannheim nodded assent. "So someone not named Hall must become the unwilling, high profile face of my investigation should it unwind? I've been fried and re-fried on earlier occasions…re-heating my carcass won't satisfy hungry dogs. Who will you nominate?"

"Congressman Emile Wright is well suited…both Mr. and Mrs. Wright have avoided incarceration under Zachary Mannheim's wing. They'll cooperate with little enthusiasm but cooperate they will."

"So…I conduct myself as I see fit, until my efforts embarrass the Administration, or there's a spectacular public failure?"

Hall wasn't accustomed to being interrogated. Answering Mannheim's question in a blank monotone, his objective infused words with finality.

"Should you come to believe I can be leveraged to do or say anything against the President's interests, think your options through several times."

Mannheim wouldn't agree to Hall's limitation. "Should the President's interests conflict with the nation's interests, I'd ask you to do the same, Mr. Hall. Other than that, we've reached an understanding. Tell me all of whatever little you profess to know. All of it, please, without personal or political edits."

***

Elias failed to notice the signs of hypothermia.

Confused by the cacophony of mechanical noises, screeching sounds drove him to distraction: High pitched protests of steel cable, stainless steel floor plates and tubular steel safety railings all stressed to their limits; throbbing bass from strained diesel engines; and staccato percussion from screamed instructions, insults and threats.

Squadrons of sea birds swept over him. More than one attacked his scalp, bare shoulders, back and chest. Unable to resist, an oblique corner of his brain pondered why he was nude. Blood drained onto his lips. Hunger was no part of his reaction.

Men who wore white crash helmets moved with purpose near where he sat.

Sounds and smells of fish, struggling against inevitable death, invaded Elias's psychotic dream state. Fish were here to save him, or so he thought.

In a moment of lucidity he struggled to rise, opposed by the rolling and pitching deck. He screamed into an unforgiving gale, "Where is the Captain? How can I kill Choirmaster without clothes?"

Consciousness waned. Elias felt two sets of hands dig into his armpits. Tossed without ceremony on the floor of an unidentifiable room, crowded with different types of equipment and tools, he faded in and out of reality. Eyes open, or so he believed, it was a black hole where three men stared with open malevolence. Elias recognized Stefan Korsakov from SVR's Directorate S.

Stefan Korsakov was not on board a stinking factory ship as a reward. Was not any kind of medical man. Besides his current misery, possessed no experience with the effects of severe cold. Memories of his encounter with CIA consisted of multiple layers of emotional scar tissue. Korsakov survived his encounter with Zachary Mannheim but hadn't prospered. Ricin poisoning left him physically debilitated and mentally overwhelmed, navigating each day a Herculean effort. To the ship's doctor, a native of the Czech Republic, he spoke Russian.

"If he dies, you, and possibly the Captain, will be hacked into bait. When will he be coherent?"

The young Third Officer stifled a laugh. "The *Oleg Shakirov* is a trawler…there is no need for bait."

Korsakov, in search of the doctor's stash of dark rum, tried to discern whether Elias' torture was prescribed by the trawler's Captain, in a fit of rebellion, or by Marta Mannheim.

"Doctor…?"

Speaking English while taking Elias's temperature, the doctor's hands shook at the idea of sharp knives and bait.

"We fish cold water. Work on the decks is the worst job…at the onset of mild hypothermia the men shiver and suffer mental confusion. In moderate hypothermia shivering ceases while confusion increases. Severe hypothermia induces a paradoxical compulsion to undress as well as increased risk of heart stoppage. This man's core temperature was 92°F, when he arrived in the surgery. We employed extracorporeal membrane oxygenation…the machine removes blood from the body, removes carbon dioxide and oxygenates red blood cells. He has better than a fifty percent chance to live twenty-four hours."

Korsakov used the speed dial function of his satellite phone. Reserves of willpower drained by a migraine; Elias's death was impossible to contemplate.

***

Four corpses decorated Mannheim's foyer and kitchen.

No leap of intuition required, when he exited from the kitchen door the expected was confirmed: Raissa's truck was gone, her departure informed by necessity and critical to Zachary's subsequent actions.

Zachary allowed loneliness to flood the threat center of his brain, acknowledging the familiar enemy while granting it unfettered access to heart and soul. Isolation, reclusiveness and mistrust must be subdued to steel the mind and firm the hand of an out-of-practice Spy-hunter.

Detective Arthur Scolen wasn't shocked by the late hour: Murder cops were a hardened lot.

"Nice to hear your voice, Zachary. Who's dead this time?"

Scolen laughed at his black humor, having assisted Mannheim on other occasions with both the dead and dying.

"I had my first ever dinner at the White House this evening, Arthur…" Mannheim's opening statement provided a fulsome warning "…how about you and Trudy joining me for a Brandy to hear about it?"

Civic duty performed, focused on DNA and fingerprints Mannheim removed any sign of Raissa's presence. A woman in her position would've been cautious, but perhaps not cautious enough for the examination to come: Two dead Eastern Europeans and an equal number of Federal Agents couldn't and wouldn't be swept under the rug. Indeed, Zachary intended to shine a spotlight on these events, but not a spotlight held by CIA, FBI or anyone reporting to Craig Hall.

Scolen arrived without benefit of lights and sirens, bringing with him the County's top forensic team and his partner, Digger Jaerlyn. Having searched the re-built home top to bottom, and conferred with Digger and the lab rats, Arthur drank coffee from a thermos in his unmarked Dodge. Watched Zachary Mannheim sip green tea from an oversized mug.

"Time of death was between eight and ten. When did you get home?"

Mannheim believed in telling the truth. Answering Scolen's questions wasn't precisely the same thing. "Within a minute or two of calling you, Arthur."

"What'd you do in those couple of minutes?"

"Besides feeling sorry about the shambles made of my home?"

Scolen squinted from the steaming brew. Considered whether retirement had softened Mannheim. "Sorry. Bad enough to have it bombed. Now this. Touch anything? Move the bodies to get a better look? Anything like that? Gotta ask."

"By the book, Arthur, I did nothing to contaminate or alter the scene of these killings."

"Anything kinky gonna show up? Drugs, girlfriend, boyfriend, classified documents, blueprints of the latest drone, freezer full of body parts?"

Scolen winked, scoffing at the very idea.

"Ordinary items for an ordinary man living in retirement or forced exile if you prefer the raw version...that's all they'll find."

"Alibi?"

"As I mentioned, Arthur, dinner at the White House. Logged in by the Secret Service. Logged out. Home those two minute before I called you."

"Dinner with whom at the White House?"

"For public consumption...or for your use as lead Detective?"

"No distinction, Zachary. Unless you're somehow covered by the invisible cloak of *National Security*. You really still retired?"

Mannheim smiled in appreciation. Arthur Scolen was recording their conversation, as required in high profile killings.

"Yes, Arthur...still retired. I had dinner with Craig Hall, National Security Advisor to POTUS. He'd offered a tour of the Situation

Room and the Oval Office, when I left CIA. Called yesterday, a little later than expected, to make good."

"Any reason for two Feds to be in your house? Mr. Hall wouldn't have invited you to dinner then sent scallywags to intrude on your civil rights?"

"No reason I know of Arthur." Mannheim resisted asking where kill-shots originated.

"Looks like the Feds died first. Nine mil Grach. Never even turned to defend themselves from the look of things. Bulgarians were next. Larger caliber slugs. Very nasty exit wounds. You don't own a sniper rifle, do you?"

"There's a Pug revolver." This answer discounted the forensic team finding the lead-lined armory beneath the safe room's concrete floor.

"Where would the .22 be found?"

"Behind the front door alarm panel...combination safe was a gift from my priest." A small detail omitted, the gun had been provided by Raissa, years ago, at a moment of abject necessity.

Scolen frowned. The referenced priest would be Timothy Timilty, ex-Jesuit, considered by FBI to be a hired killer. "The gun was a gift...or the safe?"

"The safe...the gun's provenance has a slightly checkered past. I used it to shoot a Russian spy, who survived and returned home."

"You'll give up the weapon, if asked?"

"Of course."

Scolen's next question came quickly and from left field. "Where's Raissa Ribeiro, Zachary?"

Scolen's warning left a reverberating puzzle.

"I haven't the slightest idea, Arthur." Would Arthur pursue, demanding elucidation of an uninformative truth?

"It's on Network news...kidnapping with people killed near Raissa's home on Cape Cod. Woman has an uncanny knack for headlines...good or bad apparently make no difference. Apparently she wasn't home. Thought for sure she'd have checked-in...told her old friend Zachary she was okay."

"I'm an old, ex-Agency employee, Arthur. Not the sort to be a close contact with a super-model. Raissa is a meteor...Zachary a dray horse. Never the twain shall meet."

"So it's a puzzle? Two Feds killed by two Bulgarians…in Zachary's house. Then the Bulgarians get whacked by a party or parties unknown…also in your house. Seems like lots of folk have keys, Zachary. Maybe it was the plumber, or the electrician. Or the cabinet guys. Would you say that's possible?"

"All the tradesmen were vetted by the Agency. Langley would have that information."

"Feds will be here like a tidal wave, when they get wind of this. You're not asking us poor County cousins to withhold notification?"

"Certainly not, Arthur. There are families who need to know, who'll need support. My sympathies are with those families."

Scolen reached a hand into his suit pocket, flicking off the recorder. "Thanks Zachary, having you on the record might keep me afloat amongst the tsunami of bullshit."

"No Arthur, it's me who thanks you. Even with a suitable explanation of my whereabouts, over excited FBI agents would sooner take me into custody than leave me free."

"White House gonna back you up?"

"Excellent question. Depends on whether my host and dinner partner sent the dead Feds, the dead Bulgarians…or caused both to arrive at the same time."

Scolen whistled in amazement. "Seriously…what's going on, Zachary?"

"Some of the most powerful men in government are very anxious. Afraid of what, I don't know. Not yet."

"So you're working off-book for the White House?"

"If I've been imprisoned by this afternoon, then no."

Mannheim watched the County Detective drive away, perhaps ten minutes before the dam would break and rational, considered, thought would be muffled. On a cell customized for him by Randall Carter, he sent an encrypted message to Raissa: *Quebec City…Rue de Balzac 31…Stefan Korsakov's hideaway…use Randall…text ASAP if Korsakov materializes.*

Digger Jaerlyn spoke as he approached. "Better get ready, Mr. Mannheim. We'll hear the sirens."

"No matter Detective Jaerlyn…" Mannheim was calm and showed it "…que sera, my boy."

"You told me once…SVR is Russia's external intelligence agency. *Directorate S* is all about illegal intelligence: Preparing and planting agents; conducting terror missions; sabotage in foreign countries; biological espionage; recruitment of foreign citizens. *Zaslon*...SVR's elite killers, right? You figure the Bulgarians were subcontractors?"

Mannheim thought it useful to answer. Digger was bright and might pass along misinformation to the Bureau.

"Blunt instruments, Digger...would have been the Bulgarians. But if Marta's anger with me remains uncontrollable Zaslon will be discovered lurking in the weeds, when the Bulgarians' movements are examined thoroughly enough."

Digger grinned. "Goddam Russians don't advertise their hard men. You told me once...Zaslon are experienced, speak several languages and their back stories are bulletproof. Chase ghosts... something constructive for the Federales to do."

***

Raissa wouldn't transit metro New York City, so elected a route through Harrisburg, joining I-81 towards Scranton, Binghamton, on to the St. Lawrence Seaway, Montreal and Quebec City. A cover story for *Raissa's* cancellation of a rare appearance was concocted on a call to Clark Ludlow, her business manager.

Kill-shots were fired before she escaped sleep's grasp and within seconds of the Bulgarians' entry. Two Feds dead within those same seconds; saving them hadn't been feasible. For a woman with her skills, retribution on the Bulgarians fell silent and quick. In an artificial world of tire noise and the heater's raspy fan, she let implications from four deaths expand and contract. In the narrowest interpretation, two disparate groups sought her extinction. In wider context, from a dying man's slip of the tongue, *Operation Reformation* was a wisp of smoke informed by guesses and given an indistinguishable silhouette by snatches of intuition and contradictory events. Facts were few: Maximilian was blown from the sky; Bulgarians were sent to kill FBI Agents without a chance to tell the tale; a small-town Police Chief delivered a killer to a US Military Base; a professional cleanup crew removed the living witness from an ambulance.

Zachary thinks there's a Russian connection. Is he paranoid? Deranged? God knows: If he's either of those things, there's no hope at all.

Memory fresh despite elapsed time, what she said more than two years ago, when they left an employer/employee relationship behind, irony slapped Raissa in the face. *No, Zachary,* she'd said, speaking of Raissa executing Mannheim's wife's spy-daughter, *you concocted a convoluted truth…an unsoiled, clinical truth…a truth without Mexican drug gangs, helicopters, threats, blood spatter, a dead fetus, millions of dollars in bribes, faked photographs, heartache, and guilt. You're a man who's never known that special darkness, when all is noise, fear and blood. Crawling out of that black hole…I've cajoled, threatened, negotiated, prostituted and killed my way out…you feel unclean for escaping.*

Now here we are again: Mannheim eating dinner at the White House—me doing his janitorial chores. Me driving to Quebec City to find an SVR hard man beaten into mental and physical mush by Zachary Mannheim. How had Zachary answered that long ago night? *You'd think my grotesque anger would have come from Marta leaving me. Did I love her…turns out I can't remember. Silly of me. Turns out my anger is for Emily; Emily who wasn't my child. Seems I'm fed up…consumed by cruel injustice. I'm prepared to bathe in blood, including my own, to sate this horrible anger. I simply don't have the skill. I'd fail…and that would be worse. I will finish…with Raissa's participation or without. I have become the devil I've so long chased.* You play God, she'd countered, but don't enjoy it? *I employ my best judgment, frequently pray for forgiveness and have zero expectation of receiving it in this or any other world.* How do you govern yourself? How do you say no to the voice that sends me to kill, or die trying?" *I have little admiration or affection for the voice you refer to. It must surely belong to a wretchedly unhappy man, who no longer believes in humanity prevailing over brutality. Going forward, I will resist anger with every fiber of my being. You have my word.*

Raissa felt old on the inside, acknowledging death's scythe as a fearful monster. Radio tuned to anything but news, she re-arranged her driving position for the long haul.

Chapter 5

Old fashioned technique, the gloved fist soaked in water slammed Elias's abdomen.

Korsakov lost count of how many blows the kid's body, hanging by its arms, endured. With the smallest movement of his eyes, the bull-like sailor stopped and wiped his arms and face with a towel. Korsakov found a vein, inserted the hypodermic and patted Elias on the cheek.

"Just a few more days, kiddo. Suffer now…live later, if things go your way. Couple of thousand miles before we drop you. Marta will be with us soon. Maybe day after tomorrow." Wearing an expression of sympathy, Korsakov inquired with sincerity, "Voice seem okay?"

Elias felt his face flush from the drug cocktail. Vision blurry, he attempted to center Korsakov's face between dots racing across his eyeballs. Spoke in little more than a murmur.

"He shouldn't have broken my rib. No one can be a soloist with a broken rib."

***

Mannheim pressed a button on his phone; inspected how the front yard was bathed in high intensity light.

"Hold your badge up high, Digger my boy. Wouldn't want you shot to pieces again so soon…especially by the good-guys."

The lead SUV rolled to a stop. Four others following suit, disgorging a dozen members of an FBI tactical team. Zachary entwined his fingers on top of his head.

"Deputy Assistant Director Tisdale, how nice of the Counterterrorism Division to come out so late."

"Take your hands off your head, Zachary, you look silly." Right hand jammed in a pocket, annoyed by the artificial daylight, suspicious of a well-known CIA alumnus, Wade Tisdale turned to Digger Jaerlyn.

"You're the local cop."

Digger provided the basics. "Detective Digger Jaerlyn, Fairfax County. My partner's lead on this case...Arthur Scolen. Left a couple of minutes ago."

"Yeah, I know. Scolen texted me his preliminary interview with Mr. Mannheim." Pointed finger aimed at Zachary, Tisdale showed Digger his best smirk. "Mannheim under arrest?"

"No."

"Planning on arresting him?"

"Nope."

"Then toodle on back where you came from, son. We'll be taking Mr. Mannheim with us."

Approached by one of the tactical team, Tisdale leaned over to hear the agent whisper, "Door's locked...break it down?"

Tisdale's voice sounded weary. "Open the door, Zachary. Postponing the inevitable isn't helpful. Isn't cute, either. Not the almighty Agency's Counterintelligence Czar anymore, are you? Senior citizen is all."

Mannheim's interests wouldn't be served by exchanging insults or demanding to be addressed by other than his given name.

"As an ordinary citizen I have certain rights, Director Tisdale. Those rights protect my person and home. Under what authority do you wish to enter? How will you compel me to accompany you, and to where would you take me?"

Tisdale stared at Mannheim without answering. Not a stupid man by any stretch, his next words were telling. "Turn off the lights...and any other electronic goodies."

"No, I don't think so, Mr. Director...we're live streaming now. I rather think an audience enhances a citizen's rights...wouldn't you agree?"

Tisdale made two hand signals to his team.

Mannheim was unhurried even as an agent wielding a battering ram approached the front door. "The Agency installed a few enhancements during the reconstruction of my humble abode. Seems they're concerned with losing my long institutional memory."

Tisdale shouted at the door. "Chris, stop. Gimme a second." Examining Mannheim, he added, "What are we talking about?"

"Defending my person and home from security breaches is the Agency's business, Mr. Director. Authorized by D/CIA Brantley, now deceased. I'd think breaking in and conducting an unauthorized search would be frowned upon, absent the endorsement of the Acting D/CIA, whomever might be resident in the seventh floor's finest office suite."

Tisdale assessed options and probabilities. "Break it down, Chris. Use caution inside."

Mahogany, inset in a steel frame embedded in concrete, resisted.

Tisdale's phone chirped. FBI's senior counterterrorism executive listened without a word.

A television truck arrived replete with satellite dish, camera technician and female reporter.

Mannheim turned his phone's screen towards Tisdale, who watched himself watching the screen.

"That's enough, Chris." Tisdale's voice was pained. "Pack it in. Take the guys back to the office. Leave the forensics crew."

Mannheim pressed a different key on his phone. Darkness ensued, momentarily concealing three men from the camera's prying eye. "Can I offer you coffee in my kitchen, Mr. Director?"

Coffee and orders from on high in hand, Tisdale entered the lists to joust as best he could. "You have a flair for the dramatic, Zachary. What is it you're hiding…and who are you hiding it from?"

"Yes, Mr. Director, those are the correct questions to ask. From my perspective, your questions are out of sequence. I'll do my best to answer anything that concerns you, if you allow my few preliminary questions. Will you indulge me?"

Tisdale's anger at Mannheim's disregard for two dead FBI agents bubbled to the surface.

"Why would you want to embarrass the Bureau…live streaming our investigation to the entire fucking world…disrespecting those dead men. Endangering my people. What could have been so damnably important, unless you were involved in those shootings?"

Obstreperous tenacity was the tool to win the day. "Who telephoned you, Mr. Tisdale? What they said isn't important…just a single name will do."

Tisdale's rebellion against orders reached limits imposed by self-preservation.

"Congressman Emile Wright, Chairman of the House Select Committee on Intelligence, was conferenced in with several FBI senior executives. I won't give you their names, as your microphones must still be active."

"No such thing is true, sir. An invitation into my home isn't trivial, not that your colleagues identities are important. The fact they were together with regard to this matter is critical."

During the phone call in question, Tisdale had been instructed to listen carefully and not impede Mannheim's movements or communications. Other than those guidelines, he was to utilize his judgment in regards the shootings at Mannheim's home.

"What *matter* are we discussing, because my interests are purely the killing of two good agents…husbands and fathers both?"

"This home was recently bombed…burned to the ground by an agent of Russia's SVR. You might have seen the media coverage. Are you familiar with SVR?"

Tisdale knew what he didn't know. "Not like you."

It was time to draw Tisdale in, to make him feel included.

"My wife, Marta, is second in command of SVR, which includes a group of highly skilled assassins identified as Zaslon. Zaslon would have sent the Bulgarians here tonight. I was designated for death, Mr. Tisdale…not your agents. Who sent your people? For what purpose were they in my home?"

"You aren't retired?"

"I most certainly am retired, which seems lost on my wife…lost in a past where she methodically tallies wins and losses in a very private war. Most recently she suffered a most serious loss. Marta won't allow me to ride gently into the sunset. I tell you these things, known to less than a dozen people in government, including POTUS, so I can again ask…who sent your people and why?"

Tisdale was dumbstruck and unable to easily let go of Mannheim's revelation.

"How could you have been CIA's Chief of Counterintelligence with a wife high up in Russian Intelligence? Weren't you impossibly compromised?"

"Ask Congressman Wright, Director Tisdale, as I'd expect you to do. Right this instant, I'd appreciate a sharing of information from the Bureau."

Tisdale had legitimate cause for worry, because what he knew, or at the least suspected, wasn't complimentary to himself, his superiors and the Bureau's Director.

"It's not clear yet how those agents wound up in your kitchen. Worse, I haven't located hard copy of their orders."

Manna from Heaven this was. "Possibly a breach of the Bureau's digital security?"

"Hacked? Hasn't been ruled out." Tisdale gagged while speaking, his immediate future clouded by the thought of what a successful hacker could have accomplished.

"Odds, Director Tisdale, favor a hack originating with Zaslon. The Agency's best estimate suggests several hundred experienced operatives, each speaking several languages and having backgrounds in secret units of the Russian military. SVR agents are always legal immigrants, including scientists and other professionals. Those in American law enforcement, like yourself, will remember Aldrich Hazen Ames, Harold James Nicholson, Earl Edwin Pitts, Robert Philip Hanssen and George Trofimoff…SVR agents all. Finding Zaslon will be difficult."

"You're assuming Zaslon eliminated the Bulgarians."

"Yes, unless someone at the Bureau, or elsewhere in government, sent your agents…hired the Bulgarians…and paid a third party to clean up the mess. Wouldn't be the first time, would it, Mr. Director?"

"And if I find Zachary Mannheim complicit in any way?"

"Then you, or someone you trust, will have made a grave error. While you haven't an acceptable security clearance, Mr. Grover Norris may elaborate on trusting my words and actions. I am retired, Director Tisdale, but not yet deaf, dumb or blind. My past, like your own, looms large on the horizon. Now, if there's nothing more you need to know, the hour is late and my efforts merely beginning."

"Give me somewhere to start looking."

"David Nazarian works for Phyllis Martell, Chief of Counterintelligence at Langley. Ask him for assistance. Don't use my name…David's cooperation will be identical with or without it."

"Can my forensic team examine your home?"

"Any pertinent data has been collected by Detective Scolen's team. There's nothing else to find. Trust me on this. Good night to you, Mr. Director."

Mannheim watched a slump shouldered FBI Assistant Director cross the lawn to his SUV. Tisdale should have been better prepared.

***

The worldwide Intelligence community resembled other insular groups with a narrow focus. Like rumors among teenage girls, the drumbeat of its underground communication was frightening, accurate and as fast as Internet providers allowed. Greg Riley, PhD in more than one technical area, and former technical guru at CIA, woke before two in the morning to read David Nazarian's quizzical text: *Has the FBI been hacked?*

Showered, dressed and arrived at his office, Riley found Randall Carter deep in concentration impeded by starvation. "Coffee and doughnuts, Randall. Take a minute…the world won't end while you fill me in."

Randall didn't agree. In fact he believed accelerated keystrokes were the medicine to prevent the world burning down. Without looking up from multiple flatscreens, he wolfed two crullers.

"How'd you know?"

Riley sipped tea, puzzling his way through the primary screen's data. Half a minute went by before he responded. "Nazarian called. Four men were shot to death at Mannheim's home last night. Two FBI. Two unknowns…likely Bulgarian." Riley hesitated, wanting to keep the discussion centered. "FBI can't explain how or why their guys were in Mannheim's home. Nobody's admitting anything, but one theory says the Bureau's been hacked." Riley could see Randall was way beyond disproving that theory.

"No one attacked the Bureau, not last night. Most recent attempt was more than a week ago…and it failed. Before that…some non-critical data was compromised three weeks earlier."

Riley appreciated Randall's love of layered logic. Emotion rarely entered an algorithm's equations or the coding of its solution. "Money exchanged? Bearer bonds, stock, Real Estate, some other consideration to family? Payments to women other than wives? Maybe indirectly through other Bureau personnel?"

Mouth full, the young genius' head shook in the negative.

"Neither agent?"

"You think I'd check-out just one of them? There's no footprint older than twenty years on either of those two. Not that's genuine. Not anywhere." Randall's face broke into a satisfied smile. "Come on, Greg…"

"*The truth is rarely pure and never simple*…Oscar Wilde, dear Randall, a man not well known in hacking circles."

"Is he a crazy Irishman like you?"

"So, one or both Feds was a sleeper? So the order to go to Mannheim's home came in-person…jeez, meeting their contact was a high-risk proposition."

"Or they used a dead drop."

"Or were supposed to wind up dead…and undeniably wound-up dead. Should give us pause." Riley noted a temporary slowing in Randall's keystrokes. "You track their movements from earlier?"

"Most of the time the senior agent's phone was powered down."

"So, we suggest a critical search…from birth canal to coffin…to Nazarian. Somewhere along that timeline, there'll be a blip. Gonna take a lot of man-hours."

Randall's eyes glowed with affirmation, while his hands jammed another cruller into his mouth. Suddenly pointing at a third screen, he said, "Mr. Mannheim's using his trackable phone." When an algorithm decoded the numbers, the message was an address. "Does he want you or me?"

Riley was halfway to the door, when the unstated portion of Mannheim's message kicked in. "Collate recent movements of everyone on Mannheim's old master-list. Send'em when you've got'em."

***

Zachary's fingers fumbled with the phone's keyboard: Randall's encryption functioned best in text mode. Raissa would receive a double encoded message, requiring her to utilize a specific book to decode the data. Although unavoidable the resultant time delay made matters worse. When finally in the clear, the message would read: *Feds seeking your statement; Are you injured?*

Examining the pump shotgun on the passenger seat, he used the rearview mirror to back-down the driveway. Under perpetual renovation, Pentagon Mall was a hubbub of activity during business hours. In deep shadow at the entrance to the parking garage, Mannheim called-out.

"Over here, Gregory."

"Good to see you, Mr. Mannheim. Been nearly a year." Keeping small talk to a minimum was the goal of both men.

"What have you heard about last evening, Gregory?"

"Four dead at your home. Two FBI Agents. Two Bulgarians. Arthur Scolen caught the case with Digger. Rumor has it you were uncooperative with the Federal government's representatives." Riley stopped short of extraneous commentary. "How can I help?"

"How about yesterday morning?"

Face hidden by darkness, Riley's embarrassment would have proved he withheld information. "The attack on Raissa's cottage...Randall's gear performed as per specification. Raissa wasn't caught unaware. News has been sketchy. No recent comms from Raissa. Nothing on the grid about where she's gone to ground."

"Did she offer details?"

"No, sir. Randall identified certain participants...local Police Chief was one of those."

Mannheim nodded vague interest, then changed topics. "How long did the seventh floor hide Brantley's inability to function?"

Mannheim and Riley were men who'd experienced high stress situations and the inevitable mess left behind. Greg's presence, in and of itself, assured the truthfulness of his answers.

"Probably nine months...the last three or four his condition was common knowledge at Langley...and to anyone else with an ounce of persistence."

"So how long before his death, if I'd been persistent?"

"Sixty days or a little less...the media liked EJ. No one wanted to look like a vulture awaiting a meal."

"Anyone who needed to know would have known?"

"Yes, sir."

"White House?"

"Yes."

"Pentagon?"

"Yes."

"Committees?"

"Likely, yes."

"Who is Russell Tipton?"

"Special Projects Director working out of Director Brantley's office. Former decorated military…lost a leg in the sand box. Very close to Brantley. Not so close to anyone else. Bit of an enigma."

"Your personal opinion, Dr. Riley…do you think well of Mr. Tipton?"

"Haven't met him, sir."

"Mr. Tipton is trusted, if not liked at Langley…would you say that's accurate?"

"I'd say the jury's out on both counts. Assuming the jury has any evidence beyond jealousy and career advancement."

"Is Tipton married?

"Yes, married twelve years to the former Verity Lindley of Huntsville. Two children. They suffer the usual strains of a workaholic husband; he sometimes drinks too much. Is it related to losing the leg…who could blame him? If booze is more than an occasional problem, no one's willing to say so."

"Workaholic like you, Gregory, like damn near everyone in our business…it's why handing-off the baton is healthy and critical to long term success."

Riley let the older man's wry humor pass.

"Turning to Congressman Wright…what's the present status of his marriage?"

"Mrs. Carol Wright has, based on our continuous surveillance of her phones, negotiated an open marriage with the congressman. Her prior affair with the Russian, Stefan Korsakov, seemed to whet her appetites."

Mannheim frowned at Riley's intimation. "Ongoing relationships at the Russian Embassy?"

"Not that we've seen. Wealthy hedge-fund types are in vogue."

"Video?"

"No, sir. Strictly based on data from her phone. And the man's phone, if he uses it while in her company." Anticipating the next question, Greg texted Randall for her phone's current location. "She's at home tonight. Or at least her phones are home."

"Refresh my memory…the money comes from her family, not his?"

"Oil field equipment. She inherited the business and sold it." Checking his phone, he added, "Mid-seven figures."

Mannheim nodded, now disinterested in Carol Wright's money. "Does she add or subtract phones as part of a routine?"

"Not always...sometimes upgrades her registered phone or buys a burner. No discernable pattern."

"So, we're never certain of her whereabouts."

"No absolutes, just a preponderance of evidence. Mrs. Wright doesn't leave home without a phone. Sometimes it isn't her registered number, but it's still a phone and we're able to identify it upon first use. We haven't employed field staff for the tracking we do for you. Randall's algorithms are constantly upgraded. Targets aren't aware of our interest. Government agencies are a minimum of two steps behind...partly because they don't want to know what we're doing, when not working for them."

Mannheim wouldn't pretend to understand Randall's genius or methods. Nor would he challenge their effectiveness. It was the limitations of Randall's algorithms, and the ability of an equally clever opponent to take advantage, which pressed on his mind.

"Where is Emile Wright?"

Riley paged down to examine Randall's data. "FBI building, where he's been since the shootings at your home." Riley debated answering an unasked question. "Would you like Tipton's current location?"

"Russell Tipton hasn't yet arrived on my watch-list, Gregory. Are you and Randall exercising independent judgment?"

"To anticipate future requirements sometimes requires initiative. Tipton's outside Congressman Wright's home. Phone hasn't moved in over two hours."

Mannheim clapped Riley's shoulder in approval and turned away. Under the impetus of something forgotten, he asked, "How often has Tipton visited Wright's Street?"

Pausing to text specifics of the question to Randall, Riley repeated, "Not before tonight."

"Thank you, Gregory. Suggest Randall increase his level of personal caution...ill wind and all that."

Chapter 6

Raissa admitted the longer, more obscure route wasn't a mistake, and blaming Mannheim for her quagmire was neither practical nor warranted. In the near term, she would decide between the logistics of dumping the pickup versus crossing the Canadian border as a *Person of Interest.*

Four phone calls resulted in exiting I-81 to Wellesley Island, New York. Thousand Islands Country Club entered into GPS, a local smuggler, referred by a trusted chain of stringers, would take her across the border by water. Several miles from the agreed upon meeting place, Not So Pretty Raissa parked in the appointed salvage yard. APR wrapped in a blanket, platinum curls buzz cut, wearing tight jeans and a floppy sweater she slid an FNP9 into the pocket of an un-zipped parka. Cheap sunglasses, no lipstick or makeup and the ubiquitous knit hat completed her fourth transformation in twenty-four hours. A Canadian passport identifying her as Paula Walker occupied a rear pocket. The US passport of Michaela Wallace, who'd died an innocent in 2009, would be burned to ash at the first prudent opportunity.

Alone by the roadside, worrying was pointless.

***

Mannheim elected Columbia Pike to Washington Blvd and the Key Bridge: Georgetown would be deserted this time of night. For what he needed done, there were too few choices and too little time: Arthur Scolen had no jurisdiction and Henry Stackhouse, a DC Metro detective, outlived his informal Agency relationship. Besides, he accepted while dialing David Nazarian, the tighter the circle the better for our collective health.

"Good evening, Mr. Nazarian, you aren't busy, are you?"

"Haven't been to bed, thanks to you."

Mannheim settled his priorities. "Russell Tipton is outside Congressman Wright's home, where Carol Wright may be entertaining a guest…co-ordinates on your phone. Emile Wright is in the Hoover Building with the big boys. Roust Tipton…emphasize the importance of not interfering with CIC's interests. Then a deep dive into the backgrounds of the unfortunate FBI agents…birth to death, David, nothing less."

An empty driveway selected and monopolized without permission, Mannheim benefitted from a clear view of Emile and Carol Wright's white brick townhouse. Light from a rear, ground floor window, amongst an otherwise darkened façade, provided the heightened allure of a quick look. Hunger was met with a dietary bar of questionable composition. Restraint and perseverance would be their own reward, because Tipton wasn't waiting and watching without foreknowledge of Mrs. Wright's visitor.

A car entered the street from the opposite direction. Edging forward, its motion ceased eight cars from a maroon SUV nestled against the opposite curb. Nazarian exited to approach the driver's side window. Parabolic antenna aimed at Tipton's lowered window, Zachary listened without distortion.

"Mr. Tipton, I'm David Nazarian from CIC…Ms. Martell's Deputy. You're in the middle of an active surveillance zone. Move out of the area, please."

Tipton intended his condescending tone. "CIC can jerkoff somewhere else. I'm here on a Special Project for the Director."

"There isn't a Director, Mr. Tipton, and no Special Project takes priority over a CIC investigation without prior arrangements, which you don't have. Drive away, sir, or my next call will be to the Night Duty Officer. I don't want that…you don't want that."

"Make your call. I'll get what I need by knocking on the damn door." Tipton attempted to open the driver's door against the resistance of Nazarian's leg.

"Keep on keepin' on, Mr. Tipton. I'll stand here exercising my First Amendment rights."

Tipton threatened, "You'd prevent a senior officer from exposing a security breach?"

"You're the one invading a congressman's front walk bleating about a security breach. I'm the CIC officer you should've told your story to. Ready to listen, if you'd like. Sure as your bare ass is hangin' out a fifth story window, we won't do it here."

Tipton managed a deep breath; there was nothing left to accomplish here. Dignity restored, he concentrated on his prosthesis. Without uttering another syllable, he pulled away from the curb heading West and then Southwest towards his Condo near Nationals Park.

Nazarian contemplated whether to knock on Wright's door. Telephoned Mannheim unaware of their proximity. "Tipton's been rousted…he's not happy. Anything else before I start on the dead FBI agents?"

"Thank you for your efforts, David. Brief Phyllis, when she's got adequate time to hear you out. We three ought to have dinner one evening soon." Mannheim unscrewed a thermos to sip black coffee. Carol Wright's guest, or guests, would emerge sooner or later.

Jolted from a semi-comatose reverie by a barely risen winter sun, blinded by the certainty all was lost, a Senior Citizen's need of sleep destroyed a prized opportunity. Mannheim strained against a charge into Carol Wright's kitchen with absurd demands and moralistic accusations at the ready. Eyes wiped of crust, the front door opened exposing a well-dressed, contented, Craig Hall.

Mannheim felt the metaphorical earth move under his feet.

Every line of methodical inquiry needed a starting point, and prior to this moment Zachary's had been dinner at the White House with a man of immense power. Now blurred lines scrawled every which way across a crooked canvas viewed through the broken prism of a long lens. Without a benchmark to rely upon when disoriented, wounded or in disbelief of persons who appeared reliable and truthful, Hall's knowledge of *Operation Reformation* seemed based in quicksand.

Given Craig Hall's satisfied expression, informed by the flame of a cigarette lighter, Mannheim's efforts would be difficult, dangerous and entangle those he sought to leave in peaceful ignorance.

He rang Phyllis Martell's cell and was directed to voicemail.

***

Apparent it was; shitty circumstances had taken a turn for the worse.

Hands bound behind the back of a woolen shirt, legs shackled with clanking chain, Elias's wrong-sized shoes shuffled along the deck towards the stern. Salt spray driven by a twenty-knot northwest wind diminished his vision. Swollen slits of eyes shielded, he noticed nets wound onto their huge drum and a dearth of crew tending their needs. Meager concentration extended; a shape towed astern at a hundred meters was easily identified.

"Surely an American faggot...a singer of church songs...a *soloist* even...can sail an itsy-bitsy boat alone?"

Derision issued in Russian, from the sailor who'd beaten him, continued a blind assumption Elias could neither speak nor understand the language. Brutally clubbed across the shoulders, Elias went down in agony, left leg torn open across razor sharp ice which protruded from steel rigging. Blood spurted, coagulating rapidly in a mass of frozen crystals. Pain and logic blunted by frenetic anticipation, he turned his head towards Korsakov.

"Marta arrived on the sloop?"

"Marta isn't coming."

Elias Thordsen slumped in defeat, finality hitting harder than any blow he'd endured.

"Why not?"

Korsakov dropped to a knee. "*Forever is composed of nows* said your American poet, Emily Dickinson. Before morning Kazimir will kill you or you will kill him. I tell you, boy, we are all subject to fate. Summon disregard of its ferocity or die in despair. Marta knows this. I know this. You must learn for yourself."

Oleg Shakirov's diesel sounds died away. Twin searchlights lit the sloped stern revealing an inflatable skiff powered by an outboard motor. Kazimir waited, pitiless eyes glaring at Elias, sea bag slung over the shoulder of a woolen pea coat, laughing as he revved the motor in anticipation.

Transfixed, Elias turned to find Korsakov's absence replaced by two uniformed guards, AK-74s at the ready. The closest prodded Elias towards the small boat, colored orange for safety.

Muscles constricted around masses of contusions on an icy, pitching ramp, when the inflatable turned away from the trawler's stern towards a different kind of floating prison. Elias concluded the sloop's hull was an appropriate color: Black as death. Approaching the sloop, concern deepened when forced to prevent the towrope, cast off from *Oleg Shakirov,* fouling the outboard's propeller.

Transferring themselves, small boat to large, would be no trivial task. Elias watched the big man glance at a cresting wave. Face caught by its froth, he shook off water like a big hound, casting a look at Elias which confirmed the parity of their introspection. Five-foot swells worsened; an unwelcome shift in the wind's direction and intensity felt on Elias's cheek.

Could Kazimir trip and fall overboard?

Speaking English for the first time, Kazimir yelled, "Hey, soloist, drag yourself from here..." pointing at Elias's seat "...to there..." pointing at the deck of the sloop "...on your own. I'll be too busy to babysit. And wouldn't help you, if I could." Familiar laughter punctuated the sailor's prediction of future events.

"My leg shackles..."

"Drown yourself...save me the trouble."

In one fluid motion Kazimir veered the inflatable into the sloop, grabbed a stainless-steel stanchion with one hand while searching for a cleat with the other. In defiance of his bulk, Kazimir swung a leg over the sailboat's gunwale, pulled himself into the cockpit nearby the large, polished wheel and looked back in disgust.

"Come on you little prick...when the mainsail is set, I'll cut you loose."

Arms wrapped around himself in feckless cowardice, Elias tested the chain's twenty percent increase to his body weight.

A lifetime living by the sea helped him ignore two waves before, at the third's apex, he stretched legs and arms upwards to assist a two-handed grip. Strained from hours of torture, both arms contracted in paralytic cramps. Animal desperation drove legs to whip shackles and feet upward and over the wire railing. Elias hung half inboard half outboard, entangled among shackles, stanchions and wire. Not strong enough to swing shackled legs a second time, he slithered headfirst, hand over hand, towards the teak deck. Legs, mid-section and upper body rejoined, he collapsed in momentary refuge.

Lights erupted in the rigging, ruining Elias's night vision but aiding Kazimir as the Russian began to winch the mainsail skyward.

An old wooden boat, forty feet in length, she was well kept. Surveying critical parts, Elias saw mast and brightwork varnished to a deep shine, winches and cleats chromed and polished, and multiple braided nylon lines stored in readiness. No self-steering vane gear apparent, an electric powered autopilot was unlikely. Self-steering would have freed Kazimir to walk the boat to tend sails, navigate, cook, eat, and rest out of the weather. Traveling day and night, he could have eliminated the constant battle between fatigue and boredom. Without self-steering the difficulties in Kazimir's task— killing me and returning to Mother Russia—multiplied. Sleepless by the helm for days on end would be the most innocuous of his troubles.

Why not shoot me here on the deck? Orders from Marta provided an answer. Which led Elias to consider: Where are we? Neither a GPS nor radar antenna could be located above the spotlight's blinding glare.

Kazimir's voice interrupted. "Hey shitbird, crawl down to the cabin and find a berth. In the morning, if I'm feeling charitable, you'll get training as a helmsman."

Unsure whether Kazimir's words were a hallucination, Elias failed to speak. Fingernails dug into teak, he dragged an unresponsive lower body into the main cabin and the refuge of a sleeping bag.

Woken by a wooden boat's moans, a porthole revealed dark clouds and pelting rain. Arms and legs returned to a semblance of normalcy, he examined instrumentation mounted in a fiberglass cabinet: A dropping barometer; wind velocity of Force 7; and steady green lights on the panel of an autopilot.

"Shit." Murmured in understatement, green lights were the worst news. Kazimir's delay in ending Elias's life was down to whim or psychopathic humor.

Elias shuddered. Is it feasible to kill a man six inches taller, fifty pounds heavier and more capable of brutality than myself? Training lessons, thought foolish at the time, flooded his mind. A grisly tribute to the macabre, their bag of tricks included crushing nerves behind the head, slashing the windpipe, an icepick or knitting needle in the heart, and compromising large arteries with a knife or razor blade. Implementation sounded trivial in a classroom. For the inexperienced assassin, a club was the instructor's weapon of choice. Ludicrous these lessons were, meant for better men in vastly different circumstances.

Where was Kazimir?

Across the salon Elias saw the V-berth in the bow, where a rumpled sleeping bag and a sailor's tote left no doubt as to the Russian's location.

Wreck the Gyro Unit of the autopilot, he told himself. Wreck it how, or with what?

Three minutes passed evaluating the practicality of strategies and tactics. Artificial confidence, as dangerous as the real thing, pumped through Elias's body. Knurled brass fasteners, rotated counterclockwise with thumb and forefinger, revealed a neat bundle of wiring and one item he'd prayed to find: The autopilot's siren alarm. Not designed to defeat sabotage, it remained silent when its power feed from the batteries was ripped off the positive terminal. Done with the easy part, unwilling to delay or wallow in terror, Elias powered the autopilot off. Not thirty seconds would pass before the sloop yawed wildly without the autopilot controlling her rudder.

Elias's all or nothing gamble bet Kazimir's reactions would be slowed after a night without sleep.

Press and hold the correct combination of softkeys, Elias told himself, until the power-up sequence was complete. Running on factory defaults, the device was useless without calibration. Inside the sleeping bag Elias closed his eyes to feign sleep.

Without warning the sloop slewed to starboard, then heeled over accompanied by a loud ripping sound. Elias, rolled against the curve of the hull, resisted the urge to save the sloop from serious damage.

At the hatch accompanied by a swirl of green water, Kazimir shouted. "Get your worthless ass up here."

Weakened legs burdened by chains, Elias pulled himself onto a deck where the starboard rail was awash. Jib in tatters, it dragged the boat off course and impaired the sloop's ability to right herself. Not yet in real danger, the graceful old girl would soon be overmatched.

Turning his head towards the helm, Kazimir's face told Elias the truth: It was Kazimir who was overmatched against the North Atlantic.

Handhold affirmed; Elias's sullen voice shouted. "I'm here as you commanded."

All Kazimir's remnants of humanity vanished. "Out to the bow...pull the fucking sail back onboard."

Again he hung upside down; a side of beef to be butchered into a meal. Elias rebelled. "I can't, not with my legs chained."

"I'll shoot you where you stand."

"Go ahead...I'll die of a gunshot. The sea won't forgive your incompetence. You'll die drowning and terrified...swallowing seawater will seem a blessing. I've sailed all my life...two-man crossing of the Pacific when I was fifteen. You go... cut the jib away, don't fight to haul it out of the water. I'll steady her close into the wind. Reef the mainsail on your way back...we'll take shifts at the helm, if the autopilot can't be re-programmed."

"You ruined the autopilot?" Kazimir stood, raised the semi-automatic pistol and fired.

Bullet noise consumed by the storm, Elias managed not to flinch. Unafraid, he offered an olive branch. "Look at the screen...lights are green. Power must've blipped. Software's messed up...I didn't do a damn thing. Half an hour before two pumps won't keep up. We'll sink slow. Or sink fast if a pump's motor burns-out. Get rid of the jib and we're a sailing vessel again."

Kazimir fired a second time. "I'll put a round in your crotch."

Dug into a ten-foot wall of water, the bow shuddered before it recovered, sluicing a fresh deluge of saltwater towards the cockpit and helm.

"Don't slip," Elias yelled. "I can't save you."

Kazimir looked down.

His anxiety provided Elias with opportunity. "You can have my vest."

Goaded by ego, the big Russian would never accept aid from a lesser man. "Get out to the damn bow. Go slow...the chains won't bother you. Cut the sail away like you said. Reef the mainsail. Then we'll see."

"Maybe you're afraid to go forward...you could hook on a safety tether."

Kazimir had refused a life vest. There were no signs of offshore safety equipment. Enveloped in a bad circumstance, the Russian failed to monitor the sloop's heading. Another wave struck at an oblique angle. Lifted to its crest, the sloop rolled and slid away. Mast nearly parallel with the trough, deck canted to a serious angle, Kazimir's hold on the wheel weakened. Legs and feet washed away by four feet of boiling ocean, hanging by one hand above the abyss, paralyzed by conflicted emotions, the Russian could do nothing.

Backwash flooded the cabin hatchway. Sheltered by the cabin's housing, Elias wouldn't fall overboard, but acquired a nasty bruise and tasted blood running down his left cheek.

Slower recovery noticeable, the sloop righted herself.

Kazimir regained his footing.

Elias sensed their time would soon expire. "Bring her into the wind. I'll try to start the diesel. We can heave-to…give us a chance."

Badly shaken, Kazimir recognized a simple truth. "Still have to cut away the jib. Fully reef the mainsail. I'll remove your shackles." Kazimir fought the wheel and rudder.

Elias saw the next large wave beyond two smaller ones. "Hard to port. Do it now." Praying the rudder cables wouldn't snap, he could only watch the Russian apply brute strength to the task.

Gasping for breath, the Russian capitulated. "Come here, I'll remove the shackles. Then we'll heave-to."

In different circumstances, Elias would've laughed. "Throw the Makarov in the sea."

"I could kill you barehanded."

"Thirty seconds we'll be awash…won't matter what you do."

In a decision made in haste, the Russian abandoned the wheel, grabbed the port railing and moved forward hand-over-hand.

Almost lost in the wind's howl, Elias heard, "Take the wheel, soloist. I'd rather deal with sails than you unshackled."

Buckled at the knees, a large wave drove the Russian to the deck. Correct in her alignment, the sloop took no water as the bow pitched upwards to the sky and the wave passed underneath.

Elias saw the wheel spin crazily in the wave's aftermath. Hurling himself he scrambled ten feet, pulling himself erect without losing the boat.

Leaning into the wind, the Russian bypassed reefing the mainsail.

Good decision was Elias's thought, observing Kazimir lock his feet around the forestay, then lean outboard to hack at the jib's remnants.

Kazimir cut on the rise and hunkered tight to the deck as she plunged. Twenty minutes hard labor expended; her starboard side lifted as the underwater impediment vanished. Exhausted yet elated the Russian stood triumphant, hand welded to the forestay's wire.

Thunder caused Kazimir to look up. Arm raised to block thunderous snow blowing sideways, the sloop handled better. Kazimir scurried for the cockpit's safety.

Elias spun the wheel hard to starboard.

Starboard gunwale under water as she heeled, anywhere on deck was unsafe. Powered by gale force winds, the boom accelerated through its arc as the sloop turned one hundred eighty degrees, running straight downwind. Kazimir saw a blur of aluminum and white canvas as the boom caught his chest. Carried until man and boom were jerked to a halt by fully extended rigging, the Russian fought to breathe. Hands clawed for a grip on ropes or pulleys with only the North Atlantic beneath him.

Kazimir dropped into the cold North Atlantic. In an instant he caught hold of the thick tow line which earlier held the sloop behind *Oleg Shakirov*. Survival instinct strong, he wove it around his right arm. When the sloop surfed down the steep backside of waves, he became almost weightless. In the trough, as she slowed, the Russian sank beneath the surface.

Kazimir shouted his hatred for the skinny boy who killed him. "We'll meet again soloist. Sing your songs and keep an eye behind you."

Elias kept the wind at his stern for half an hour of a roller-coaster ride. He'd managed the single thing his oldest instructor at the Farm advised: *Kill without pleasure.*

Chapter 7

Nothing special to look at, the approaching aluminum johnboat was past its prime, but its operator was young. Possibly too young for the task at hand and watery miles still to be covered. Bow crunched against a rocky bottom, the girl spoke with the demeanor of a long-time trader in human cargo.

"Toss your passport into the boat."

"What's your name, dear?" Like a favorite Aunt might inquire, not an iota of suspicion came with Raissa's question.

"Don't need my name, just toss the passport." Feet dancing without benefit of music, the girl's eyes swiveled in mistrust.

"I'm Paula, is that Retreat Island over there?"

Pointing over her shoulder, the girl said, "Yup. Eleven miles from Mallorytown Landing...after you give me your passport."

"Can you show me the route on my GPS?"

"No GPS. Just me. You'll never find Mallorytown if you shoot me...and my daddy's a real good shot with his deer rifle."

No emotion—either the girl wasn't as advertised or daddy was bloodless, risking his daughter's life for a thousand dollars. Raissa decided to accede to the kid's demand. Tossing one of many passports in its waterproof sleeve, she said, "Sounds like you and daddy have done this before."

Examining the document, the girl responded, "Enough to know you're not some random Canadian called Paula Walker. You're some American in deep shit...daddy says you're probably a Wall Street scammer running from the cops."

"Shall I get aboard?"

"How much you got in the backpack?"

"Enough to pay for our arrangement."

"Toss the backpack in the boat."

Raissa's nerves began to frazzle so standing still wasn't the easiest thing. Counting on the vest to protect her chest and abdomen meant daddy, if daddy was real, needed a head shot.

"You plan on taking my money...leave me in a shallow grave?" Raissa took three steps towards the boat without incident. "Or are we renegotiating the fare?"

"Ten thousand, or he'll blow your left knee into bits of bone."

"Or you're a talented and greedy actress."

Semi-automatic emerged from the parka, Raissa shot the girl while diving and rolling as a heavy caliber round struck a tree behind her head. She'd seen the muzzle flash out on the water. She calculated a firing solution three hundred yards on a line extended behind where the girl sat whimpering. Raissa's scope scanned ink-black water for a man with a deer rifle—without a result.

The man's deep, ageless, voice demanded, "Don't much care whether the kid lives or dies...she's not mine. Take the boat, leave the backpack. Got a Barrett M82...blow big fat holes in your escape from the U S of A."

Odds against her on the rise, Raissa shrugged the backpack onto the ground and raised her arm to show the gold-film wrapping a brick of $100s. "All I've got in the world." Brick tossed sideways, she added, "Let me take my stuff, I'm never going home."

If a smuggler got a chance at $400,000, he'd take it every time. If this guy's here to end Raissa, he'll want everything. Smuggler or professional, neither the boat's engine nor my vest will survive against a semi-automatic .50 caliber rifle with a range of two thousand yards.

"Don't dump the girl anywhere near here."

Jamming the outboard into reverse, the GPS on Raissa's phone showed North/Northeast at an initial heading of thirty degrees. She watched him aim a spotlight at the shiny, golden, brick. "Damn," she said under her breath, the .50 Cal was exactly three hundred yards from where Raissa had stood.

Tremors started in her hands, wound their way into the armpits and back down to the bottom of her spine. Three other times in recent years she made similar wagers and won; in the spotlight's brilliance, she saw a figure bend over to grab the Brick. When a small explosion lit the sky, relief flooded Raissa's brain: Betting on greed was always a smart play.

A through-and-through to her right lung would be the girl's souvenir of a bad night's work. Raissa asked, "Who was he?"

Slinging the words through gritted teeth, she said, "Stepfather."

Raissa thought *Liar*, but said, "Where should I drop you?"

"Oughta kill me, if you got any sense at all. He'd have left you for the animals."

Raissa lapsed into silence, concentrating on navigating a strange waterway. Half a mile from where the boat would be abandoned, she eased it into a grassy bank and woke the girl.

"The injection I gave you…antibiotics and pain killer. You need a hospital. I called Brockville General…wait here for the ambulance." Phone raised for the camera App, there was no humor in Raissa's voice said, "Smile for your mug shot."

An hour later Raissa opened the hood of a battered Trans-Am to find keys hidden under the air filter's cover. A faster road forsaken, she'd settled onto Thousand Oaks Parkway for the six-hour trip to Quebec City, when Randall Carter texted: *Photo identified as Leanne Crowder, CIA, NCS Special Operations. Advise.*

Raissa responded: *Confirm Crowder GSW victim Brockville General, Ontario, Canada; transmit Crowder's current orders; ID Crowder's Field Director; copy all to Mannheim by hand.*

If she'd blown-up an Agency Field Director, repercussions would be inevitable, and, in a headless Agency might be defined by an excess of pragmatism. As minutes stretched to hours without Randall's response, pragmatism seemed a poor relative of retribution.

***

Settled in a leather chair, in Grover Norris' office, Mannheim waited for either Grover, or his son Jamie, to speak. Whether political calculation or embarrassment caused their mutual silence mattered not at all; information in-hand required justification.

"Let's be clear, gentlemen, both things cannot be true. Either Craig Hall invited me to the White House to establish a back-channel investigation, or he did not. If he did, your silence suggests you've both been cut out of the loop on, at least, this one set of circumstances. If he didn't, I invented the young woman whose photograph sits before you. If he didn't, why would Leanne Crowder, listed as a serving officer in NCS, have inserted herself into an illegal border crossing from the US to Canada…and wound up with a gunshot wound for her trouble. Enlighten me, please, for in Mr. Hall's world this may be the first thread in an intricate design."

Grover Norris, former D/CIA, current Managing Partner of an investment bank, and long-established confidant of POTUS, saw his influence deteriorate during the ascendancy of EJ Brantley. With Brantley's burial, contestants for leadership at Langley would be sharpening knives and greasing skids. Whether Craig Hall's role as ringmaster of the circus was real or imagined, his recruitment of Zachary Mannheim demonstrated an emotional state near panic. On the negative side of the ledger, Mannheim wore the stink of independence and arrogance. On the positive side was the man's incontrovertible record of success.

Grover hesitated, then chose a compromise. "You've given us too thin a book, Zach. What is the scope of your assignment? Who was crossing into Canada, and why? Who shot Ms. Crowder? Where are all the actors now, as we sit with at least my thumb up my ass."

Grover looked at his son, inviting participation.

Outside his father's professional sphere for the first time, admitting what Jamie Norris, Deputy Director/NCS, knew and didn't know was unappealing on many levels.

"Leanne Crowder appears on NCS' organization chart, but she's a ghost. Worked exclusively for Brantley. More to your point, Mr. Mannheim, she takes operational orders from Tipton. I'd guess Brantley's death hasn't changed that relationship."

Allowing himself a thin smile at Jamie Norris' use of *relationship*, Mannheim asked, "What are Ms. Crowder's particular skills?"

Jamie answered, "She flies hither and yon."

"Come now, Jamie, I need more than *hither and yon*. Infiltration and exfiltration? Fixed wing and helo? Multi-engine? Jets?"

"Infiltration and exfiltration, fixed wing, single engine, bad weather and/or night operations…she's reported to be highly skilled and a daredevil. Her file suggests no field experience, no weapons expertise, and no record as an analyst…although I could speculate Crowder's file is a farce…in the same way Raissa's file is a farce."

"So as a working theory, Leanne Crowder's raison d'etre is killing people Russell Tipton wants dead." Mannheim looked first at Jamie and then Grover for dissent. Seeing none, he carefully moved to a more sensitive subject. "Does Mr. Tipton's file confirm his routine use of Ms. Crowder's skills?"

Jamie was quick with a denial. "I've never seen his file. Don't know anyone who has seen it."

"Thank you, Jamie, for your candor. As an aside, how old is Ms. Crowder?"

Jamie anticipated Mannheim's follow-ups. "Twenty-three, but she easily passes for younger or older as the situation warrants. No family. No attachments. No discernible digital footprint. No known digital skill."

Zachary focused again on the elder Norris. "Does Craig Hall's ship leak, Grover? Would you think my presence at the White House brought me under significant surveillance?"

"I think we've gone far enough without some reciprocity. Trust us or don't, but I'm done with this one-sided chit-chat."

Mannheim rose, extending his hand to Grover.

"I do plan to trust you, Grover. Maintaining my agreement with Mr. Hall permits me latitude in performing due diligence. Should I become dissatisfied with the parameters of that agreement, it will be better for all parties to part with as little animus as possible. Right now, however, my priority is not endangering either of your ability to be truthful about this conversation."

Under the assumption his every movement, text, telephone conversation and e-mail was being surveilled by NSA, their Russian counterparts, and possibly other interested parties, Mannheim left the Norris males to enter a Georgetown watering hole. His large fingers texted clumsily: *Jean-Louis—Dinner at your home sounds wonderful. See you tonight.*

A multi-billionaire banker, if there was a man free of the incestuous nature of Intelligence gathering, Jean-Louis Michani might qualify. Often accused of being a shill for Mossad, Jean-Louis, his daughter Nasha and her now fatherless children had become irregular company for meals at Mannheim's home. In this case Zachary's text served as a cutout: When Jean-Louis or Nasha forwarded the message to a phone encrypted by Randall Carter, the underlying instruction became the digital equivalent of a One-Time Pad.

***

Randall didn't understand why a meeting involving Zachary Mannheim would be conducted in public. With no regard for this confusion, an encrypted text sent to Congressman Emile Wright was straightforward: *Congressman Wright — Please join me at the Vietnam Memorial at 1500 hours tomorrow. Regards, Zachary Mannheim.* Incredulous at Mannheim's inexplicable, formal texting style, a second encrypted text was sent to an unidentified phone: *0800 breakfast.*

Having long since moved to more formidable problems, Randall was caught off balance when Greg Riley and Zachary Mannheim entered the office shortly after he finished a large pizza. He stifled a yawn while his current and former bosses settled in the conference room.

Mannheim was direct. "Randall, I come bearing bad news. My home has been under surveillance at least since the attack on Raissa's cottage. The Agency, or more specifically a faction within the Agency, is either the perpetrator of said surveillance or the recipient of same. Whichever it proves to be, a young officer named Leanne Crowder intercepted Raissa at the Canadian border. Posing as the exfiltration agent Raissa expected, Ms. Crowder and an unnamed male accomplice attempted extortion under the threat of violence. Ms. Crowder was shot. Her accomplice is deceased. Raissa has not re-established communication. What I need from you, my young friend, is an explanation…how did this happen, who is responsible and how do we bring confidence back to the workings of our tiny cabal? I suggest we start with your assurance that this conversation…the one we're having right now…is secure."

Greg Riley slid a note across the table to Randall: *If you're uncertain, keep up the conversation and we'll use pen and paper.*

Randall's face blended horror and guilt. Underneath Greg's note, he appended: *Give me ten minutes.* Returning in seven, he gave a thumbs-up and dove-in to Mannheim's anti-surveillance issues.

"What rooms were you in with Raissa?"

Mannheim reflected before answering. "Living room and kitchen."

Riley jumped in. "Never the safe room?"

Neither Greg nor Randall enjoyed need-to-know when it came to the death of two FBI agents and two Bulgarian hard-men. Absolute ignorance would preserve their innocence.

"Never."

Randall typed command after command on a laptop labeled ZM– Air Wall. "I have to head over to your house to interrogate the security system…think it's safe?"

"Let's not presume anything, my boy." Mannheim dialed his cell and spoke quietly. "Detective Scolen, could you send Digger over to Dr. Riley's office?" Nodding at something Scolen said, he added, "Yes Arthur, a few things have popped into memory. Tell young Digger lights and sirens would be helpful."

***

Video showed Digger Jaerlyn at reception.

Mannheim left the conference room to save everyone the embarrassment of a spy-hunter's paranoia.

"Digger, we have incontrovertible evidence Zaslon has been watching and listening. A Russian, who we'll call the party of the first part, gave stolen intelligence, either directly or through a convoluted back channel, to someone at Langley. CIA, as party of the second part, upon receiving the information assigned an officer to interdict a party of the third part crossing into Canada near Wellesley Island, New York. The Agency officer was shot and may have already been released from treatment at a local hospital."

"Didn't hear any names in that fairytale. Doesn't sound like fodder for a local murder cop."

"Possibly what was seen and heard at my home is the first cousin of the execution style deaths of two FBI agents and a brace of Bulgarians. Would that suggest anything interesting to a Fairfax County detective?"

"First I'd wonder how fortress Mannheim was bugged."

"Exactly my thought, Digger, and the rationale for you protecting Randall while he sorts through any breaches in electronic security. If there have been breaches, the implications are depressing…I've relied heavily upon Randall's superiority over opponents." Taken by gloom, Mannheim added, "Every man has his Waterloo, after all. Short-sighted of me to ignore such a possibility." A defeated smile accentuated Mannheim's conclusion. "If there hasn't been a breakdown on our digital side, the opposition has committed massive human resources…following every single person who comes and goes from my home. If that kind of surveillance operation dates to the killing of four men, think who's been caught in the Russian web."

"Russians tailing Feebs is more than bizarre."

"Possibly an enterprising detective could find footprints left by the Russian Bear."

"And…"

"Deputy Assistant Director Tisdale would find such a Russian intrusion of great interest, wouldn't you think?"

Digger jumped two steps further. "Bet you Arthur knows who at the *Post* or *Times* would be interested in Russians, Bulgarians, dead FBI agents and mysteries surrounding CIA Counter-Intelligence."

"Precisely my boy. Civic minded policing is always in fashion."

"You're betting we'll find the mother lode."

"I'm betting on you, Detective Jaerlyn, which is as far as my eyes see into the future."

***

Greg Riley, after listening more than an hour, was content with whatever portion of the truth Mannheim told. "Craig Hall, if he's having a sexual relationship with Emile Wright's wife, is balanced on one leg too close to the cliff."

"Sex and taxes…cheating on a spouse or one's democratic tithe is a strong gravitational pull for the powerful." Mannheim waited for Riley to bring up the nub of their discussion.

"What's your working theory on *Reformation*?"

"At the moment you, Randall, and I are blind squirrels scratching through fallen leaves hoping for chocolate covered acorns. We are overrun with oddities; each could be a trap, or a misdirection intended to run out our clock. To be sure there is a countdown, otherwise Marta wouldn't have sacrificed the FBI/Zaslon agents."

Discussing Marta's involvement was a can of worms Riley had no choice but to open. "Which means *Reformation* is Russian, authored by Marta."

"Half correct, I'd think…*Reformation* is certainly Russian. Is Marta, or someone else in the Bear's shadow, responsible for *Reformation's* goals? Who knows? There are too many simultaneous equations to solve. To reduce those unknowns, I'd like you and Randall to identify every officer at Langley who, like Ms. Crowder, claims an esoteric skill set…and who reported exclusively to D/CIA Brantley while he was alive. We'll assume such officers are currently seconded to Russell Tipton. Where are they, Gregory? What are they doing? Without this information, we blind squirrels are nothing more than rats dining on slow-acting poison."

***

By itself the absence of invasive listening devices and cameras wasn't important in Randall's inspection. Of significance was the status of motion activated cameras and listening devices he built and installed to capture real or ethereal intruders on the property or inside Mannheim's home. Essentially dumb, their design delivered captured A/V to an offsite storage facility in real time. Data transmitted couldn't be retrieved without possessing the physical storage devices, and their location was known only to Mannheim. While Randall found the design cumbersome and less secure than other methodologies could have provided, it suited the mistrustful nature of Zachary Mannheim. Need-to-know was a hallmark of the man, and no other human met that standard.

Randall called to Digger Jaerlyn. "All set, Detective, I'm ready to leave when you are." Randall would've questioned Digger's role in Mannheim's unofficial crew but had no such authority.

Digger wouldn't sugar coat what he'd found. "Next door to the garage, is the camera in the tree yours?"

Randall was instantly defensive. "There aren't any cameras, mine or otherwise. Show me."

Examination of the massive oak through Digger's night-vision scope took less than a minute; a purple light mounted on a miniature plastic housing provided its own narrative. Yes, it was a camera. No, it wasn't sophisticated. Motion sensitive, it started and stopped based on that parameter, recorded video accessible to anyone with the password from anywhere within fifty yards.

"It's not on Mannheim's property…captures a limited area around the garage. Not very effective."

Digger had witnessed how genius could be subject to blind spots. "Depends on what it saw. Depends on how many other cameras are linked to it. Download what you can, Randall, I'll have a look around."

After watching less than a minute of pirated video, Digger briefed Arthur Scolen, then dropped Randall back at Riley's office. His phone turned from 11:59 to midnight as he returned to Mannheim's home where Scolen and Deputy Assistant Director Tisdale waited.

"Where you been, Detective?" Not at all welcoming, Tisdale pointed to the trees. "Why should I give a shit?"

Digger enlarged the video on his tablet, then handed it to Scolen.

"Three short bursts from two cameras. First is a week ago, second three days ago, third from the day of the shootings." Scolen and Tisdale watched the videos several times before Digger's snide tone intruded. "Prowling around a citizen's home…dead or alive, not the best look for your Agents."

Tisdale bit his tongue.

Arthur Scolen wouldn't participate in a pissing contest.

"These cameras don't belong to Zachary Mannheim, Mr. Director. We're trying to cooperate with your investigation, but I'm in a tough spot. Who sent your Agents, why did they scout Mannheim's home so long before they were killed in his kitchen?"

Wade Tisdale recognized when a Fairfax cop was in a real bind. "How long before we read all about it?"

"Not tomorrow, unless Mannheim sees the video. I'll show it to my Chief the day after."

"Mannheim knows about these other cameras?"

Scolen never missed a beat. "Highly motivated and not stupid, when would you think he'll catch on?"

Chapter 8

Face wrapped in a scarf, stomping slush off her boots inside Toolbox Café, Phyllis Martell found Mannheim in the last booth opposite the deli counter. Patrons scanned as she approached, the majority wore military uniforms. In a seat facing away from the crowded room, her voice gave no indication of curiosity.

"Crappy morning."

Zachary felt competence radiate from her demeanor. A demonstration of pride in her professional growth would be regrettable; he'd caused her to be wounded, figuratively and literally, along the way. He spoke in a reserved tone.

"Who would you consider the leading candidates for D/CIA?"

Coat folded, she examined the steaming coffee mug. "Glad for the coffee. As for the new D/CIA...it's unlikely I'll know until the President's appointment goes public."

Her face altered by acquired stoicism, Mannheim saw a new resilience burdened by distaste for all things political. "Hasn't it ever been thus." Watching her prior expression soften, he added, "Despite being a spy-hunter, you'd be entitled to three guesses, Phyllis. How about Russell Tipton?"

An indifferent moan escaped over the mug. "What game are we playing, Mr. Mannheim? You and I haven't spoken since Berlin. You're retired. I'm doing your old job the way I think best."

Not what he expected, or desired, her dismissal of collegiality conveyed a different kind of opportunity. Phone slid across the table, he urged, "Press *Send*, Ms. Martell. Ask the President's National Security Advisor whether I'm out of line."

Phyllis's white knuckles were a sign of anger. When Craig Hall answered, a burst of profanity greeted her. "Fuck all Zachary, what now...we agreed your judgment would prevail."

Martell responded, "Excuse me, Mr. Hall, I'm Phyllis Martell from CIC/Langley, sitting with Mr. Mannheim. Does he have authority to question and/or direct my actions?"

"Are you kidding?"

"No sir, in the absence of a D/CIA I'm asking for clarification."

"Decide for yourself. Have a good day, Ms. Martell."

Turning back to Mannheim, she dismissed the idea of being recorded and answered without missing a beat. "Tipton won't get a sniff."

With one unequivocal response, Mannheim moved on. "Jamie Norris?"

"Wouldn't get his father's vote today. Ten years from now, maybe."

"Does Grover still get a vote?"

"Veto seems a better description."

"Emile Wright?"

Martell stared hard at a man who arrived with more inside information than she would ever possess. "He'd be a good choice, which probably eliminates him."

"What's the condition of the Congressman's marriage?"

Martell's answer needed to be crafted with care; she'd been taught the skill by Zachary himself. "Congressman Wright's marriage hasn't been an issue at CIC since you retired."

Emile Wright, once upon the miserable episode which cost Mannheim his job, proved easy to lead astray, too quick to act, and too inexpert to properly analyze raw Intelligence. "Would you trust Congressman Wright to put Country before the Agency or himself?"

"Jesus, Mary and Joseph...I can't name five people at Langley, never mind Congressional Committees, who would pass such a test."

"Congressman Wright spent considerable time at FBI headquarters following the murder of their Agents in my home. Has he made his bed with the Hooverites?"

All of this—coffee at a military hangout, burner phones which dialed the National Security Advisor and open questions about the nature of Congressman Wright's relationship with the Bureau—made Phyllis jittery.

"Wright treats CIC with professionalism. I don't sense his fingers on the scale, but he's a newbie. When he gets comfortable, there may be new rules."

The House Subcommittee on Terrorism, HUMINT, Analysis, and Counterintelligence had been led by Congressman Rupert Jones Perry for over sixteen years. Mannheim's on-again off-again relationship with Perry soured with discovery of the former Chairman's illegal proclivities. Wright's succession would prove either benefit or disaster; Mannheim could not guess which.

"I ran into Mr. Nazarian the other evening. Would you say he's fully recovered from his injuries or…?"

Raising her hand to stop Mannheim, she said, "You were right about David…he's been a terrific Deputy. His background as a field officer is indispensable. I give him almost total freedom in carrying-out CIC investigations." Pushing barely touched coffee aside, she grabbed her coat. Eye contact maintained a second too long, she said, "Like I said, crappy morning."

***

At the Vietnam Memorial, 15:00 hours found Mannheim staring at Panel 03E of its black stone. Of more than 58,000 names on the Wall, he'd attended one funeral, in 1965. Tears suppressed, he witnessed Emile Wright, of Texas's 19th, approach without an overcoat.

"Good afternoon, Congressman, I appreciate you making time."

Wright's composure strained, his tone remained neutral. "Friends in high places, Mr. Mannheim, make you a man not to be ignored. Or detained for questioning by the Bureau, though your holier than thou superiority should've kept your ass out of custody."

"Perspective is everything, Congressman. Today you see things from a lofty perch, forgetting how it felt to be faced with a charge of Treason. To be an effective Chairman Wright, seeing the world through one narrow lens will not serve you well. Does effectiveness remain important in a world where facts have become a matter of opinion?"

"Still charming as a rattlesnake, Zachary."

Mannheim conceded Wright's accusation. Evidence of betrayal was first and foremost in his mind. "Have any of my highly placed friends spoken to you directly?"

"Didn't have to. I got the message."

"From whom, Congressman…the messenger is important."

Wright looked ready to explode. "My wife, if you must know."

"Odd way to hear sensitive information, don't you think? Has your wife become a member of the Intelligence Community?"

Wright bemusement was apparent. "In her own way, yes."

Mannheim pressed harder, despite the risks. "Trading sex for information is more traditional than unique. Who is your wife's source as it relates to my friends in high places and killings at my home?"

An air of anguish added a ring of truth. "I don't know who told her or why she bothered to tell me."

Mannheim's relief palpable, recruiting Emile Wright might still be accomplished. "What theory do the Bureau bigwigs believe most viable?"

"*Bulgarian bad-guys…whether human traffickers or heroin salesmen seeking long planned retribution against a retired CIA spymaster…were killed in tragic gun duel with FBI Agents, who perished doing their sworn duty.* Some form of that story would've been boiled into a two-paragraph press release…until the latest pile of horseshit was discovered. As of an hour ago, when time-stamped video of those Agents snooping around your home became public, the Bureau has gone quiet. The video will be on the evening news. It's on-line now." Wright held out his phone to Mannheim.

An abashed grimace gave Zachary away. "Thank you, Congressman, I've seen it."

"So, I'm here to play jackass."

"Here to do your job, if you've still got a combat soldier's stomach."

Mannheim regretted his loss of temper. At least he hadn't shoved Carol Wright's cuckolding of her husband up his nose; both of us are familiar with marital betrayal.

Each man remained a prisoner of misgivings about the other.

Unable to penetrate Mannheim's poker face, Wright surrendered to a sense of foreboding. "Does my job involve Carol?"

"Much is unknown about your wife's admirers, Congressman. Given Mrs. Wright suffered no penalty for her dalliance with Korsakov, she seems to be encouraging her pigeons home to roost."

Showing resistance, Wright said, "Why is it you lecturing me about the responsibilities of my job? You don't own an official seat at the table, or do you?"

"Because I've been given a broad mandate to dispose of a potential threat to our nation's security. Because for spies, lies well sold are a badge of merit. Because there's the possibility I am, or will shortly become, expendable. You remember the feeling, Congressman, of being sacrificed to the whim of the Top Brass? Beyond bare bones, which I can't yet share with you, the game has proceeded without me, without you, for some length of time. We, if there's to be a cooperative effort, need to chip away at our Gordian Knot of ignorance."

"I'd be entirely in conflict with the Subcommittee's responsibilities."

Wright's demeanor had become so negative Zachary's mind began to spin an exit strategy. "That's for you to manage, Mr. Wright. I won't appear before the Subcommittee under any circumstance."

In Mannheim's right ear, Nazarian's voice expressed a warning.

"Text me, Emile, with whatever decision you make…take an hour or two, but not longer."

"You want a human to sacrifice, if things go wrong?"

Mannheim rose to peer down at a conflicted husband. "I want a man of honor to join me in sacrifice, if everyone around us is dead."

***

Hum from the safe-room's treadmill provided the monotonic sound he craved. Two hundred calories burned in thirty minutes; he would expend a further two hundred in the next twenty. Four hundred fifty calories were Mannheim's target, together with giving up a late-in-life passion for pizza and beer. Focused on Congressman Wright's behavior, he applied the test of Original Sin: Fear of exposure was the driving force behind every double agent's daily life. A loyal foreign agent might dread death or prison, but not a double agent. It was egotism, or some amalgam, which made provocateurs both successful and mistake prone. Emile Wright surely was a long-suffering husband; he was not a mole, a double agent or any traitor's nom de guerre.

Mannheim panted with increased effort while he considered pieces on a cerebral chessboard.

Could EJ Brantley's fatal illness have covered a disavowed agenda, when poisoned by a loyal Bishop? Has a man with one leg inherited an ill wind, or does he seek a parachute? Would a Bishop break his vow of celibacy with a commoner, or is her on-the-make veneer vainglorious? Could the Bulgarian pawns have expected dollars, rubles or an FBI get-out-of-jail-free card? Analogy stretched to its breaking-point, Ms. Crowder seemed more Squire than Knight. She wasn't within a mile of Raissa's skill or daring. Then there was the issue of the *Fourth Man*, about whom nothing was known except his rescue by a Police Chief. Field Directors at Langley specialized in rescues like the one benefiting the *Fourth Man*.

Lather of sweat toweled-off, Mannheim dialed Nazarian. "David, we'll be departing Manassas Regional in ninety minutes."

***

In the hubbub of boarding their Lear 60, there was no opportunity for conversation. At thirty-eight thousand feet for a fifty-eight minute flight, Mannheim brought his companion up to date.

Nazarian's question was straightforward. "Who could *Choirmaster* be?"

"Cart before the horse, David. If we scurry about, trying to guess the opposition's identity…we'll miss the bit-players and character actors under our nose."

"Climb the ladder, learning as we go…focus today on the local cop delivering the *Fourth Man* to Otis."

"Police Chief's name is Louis Phillips. Identify yourself and tell him to meet us at Raissa's cottage."

***

Mannheim circled Raissa's precious cottage, stopping to survey the rear deck with its bullet-pocked shingles and shattered sliding doors. Covered in durable plastic sheeting, like bandages on bleeding wounds, the cottage gave off the smell of decomposition. Across the Bay from where intruders first went aground, then perished at Raissa's hand, Mannheim heard Nazarian's voice from the street.

"He's here. Brought backup."

Mannheim wouldn't enter Raissa's home, so stood in defiance against the biting northwest wind. As Phillips approached with two deputies, Nazarian spoke.

"Just you, Mr. Phillips."

Phillips spit contempt. "My town, my rules." Disdain aimed at Mannheim, he added, "They kicked your ass to the curb. Who are you to order local law enforcement around?"

Mannheim remained implacable.

Nazarian answered. "CIC has broad authority, Mr. Phillips. Have you spoken to Jamie Norris? Or Russell Tipton? A good Field Director knows how to evaluate risk."

"Don't need any help to jail you two for property invasion." Both Deputies drew their weapons. Phillips dialed his cell phone. Mannheim turned away to observe a seagull, the first of his answers about Phillips received in full.

Nazarian remained in-character as bad-cop. "None of your three phones will function, Mr. Phillips. Technology has moved along, you know. We're not armed...the live broadcast of this chat is what should worry you. FBI is at the traffic circle...where you were photographed hauling a terrorist to Otis' back door. Won't be Mr. Mannheim or myself in a cell tonight."

"Bullshit. CIC hasn't read-in any Boston Fed." To his lead Deputy, Phillips said, "Take'em away, Ricky."

Mannheim thought their situation ludicrous, but sillier circumstances were known to turn-out tragic. "Not Boston, Mr. Phillips, but in a display of inter-agency cooperation Deputy Assistant Director Wade Tisdale awaits Mr. Nazarian's request. Director Tisdale has questions, when CIC finishes. Send your lads home, we can talk in David's car."

Deflated and beside himself, Phillips waved his Deputies away. Diminished by the ambient temperature, he climbed into the back seat. Nazarian started the engine to generate heat.

Mannheim instructed, "Please David, the cold will sharpen our wits."

Nazarian eyed Phillips while pointing at one in a sheaf of photos. "There were four attackers at Ms. Ribeiro's home. Were you to extract all four, or only this kid?"

Phillips' face turned angry. "Give'em here." After careful examination of Raissa's photos, he claimed, "High as a kite on heroin. Nothing to do with Ribeiro or her boatyard buffoons. Get me an attorney."

Nazarian used a plain-spoken tone. "Louis...you're a terrorist, planted well in advance as Police Chief. Making it so was not easy or without political complexities...all to abet an operation by foreign nationals aimed at killing or capturing an American citizen and Agency asset. You'll get a lawyer someday, but not today or several hundred tomorrows. Christ man, you're a Field Director...you know better than to play common criminal with me."

"Get rid of Mannheim."

With a diligent eye on Phillips, Mannheim was inclined to believe the man played a limited role: Extract the *Fourth Man* and deliver him to a waiting airplane. Inclination, however, was too low a bar to make policy or grant clemency.

"Seventeen years at the Agency, Mr. Phillips. Numerous Field Agents counted on your reliability...you've never lost one. Out of the blue you accept an assignment without proper briefing or written orders...any Field Director given such an assignment would have raised a dozen red flags. Give David and I our due...something is far amiss about this operation. Tell us about your misgivings and how they were resolved."

"I received a valid, verbal order. I did my job."

"No misgivings?" Mannheim didn't care about misgivings. Phillips had claimed his actions were authorized and, therefore, valid.

"None."

"Who issued the verbal order?"

Imitating Mannheim's earlier claim, Phillips spat the words, "Neither of you are cleared to hear my answer."

"Are you an ideologue or zealot, Mr. Phillips? Field Directors are normally a practical lot."

"How about you, Mannheim? Whose ideology are you pushing?"

Speaking into his phone, Manheim's voice sounded annoyed. "Good afternoon, Jamie. Mr. Phillips has contributed what he can and admitted what is incontrovertible. Send the Langley security boys. David and I will wait."

Nazarian and Phillips were marked by looks of astonishment for entirely different reasons.

***

Without the panache of a Gulfstream, the Lear offered more comfort than its two passengers could use. Having grabbed a beer, David Nazarian offered one to Zachary Mannheim. "How much does Jamie Norris know?"

"Less than he'd like, David, not enough to be targeted by Zaslon."

"Like me."

"Absolutely. I'd estimate your demise, if it comes, will precede my own by a matter of hours not days."

"Where does Phyllis fit?"

"Still carrying a torch?"

"Not the way you meant it."

"Phyllis is, as much as possible for the Chief of CIC, sitting this one out. Her choice, not mine. You'll have independence...she'll try not to interfere."

"You never offered me a choice."

Zachary smiled without warmth. "Because you, David, are an irretrievable addict. You aren't reduced to a puddle of tears, when faced with a hard thing. I delude myself we share more than one admirable trait."

"So, what did we learn from Phillips?"

Mannheim reclined his thickly upholstered, navy blue, leather seat. Settled-in he said, "Most significantly, he confirmed more than one Agency employee has been assigned to *Operation Reformation*. To climb your metaphorical ladder, we need to chat with Ms. Crowder ASAP. Without doubt outside contractors have been involved...we should establish whether the cameras aimed at my property were purchased and installed privately or installed after purchase by SVR or other parties. Phillips insertion as Police Chief demonstrates the opposition timeframe has been up and running months, perhaps as much as a year or more...which leaves room for D/CIA Brantley to have been *Reformation's* sponsor. Leaves us the puzzle of Russell Tipton. Tipton isn't Phillips, not in their ability to defend themselves, and must be treated with great care. At least for now."

Nazarian looked chagrined. "It's you, me and some part-timers...against SVR and their American friends? All so Marta can extract thirty pounds of flesh from a man she's seen once in forty years."

Mannheim enjoyed David's double entendre, although losing weight had nothing to do with any woman.

"In the demolition business, David, small charges of explosive, placed with precision, bring down massive structures. Our challenge is to decide which structure is corroded beyond resurrection and which grown fat and complacent."

His phone vibrated, drawing attention away from David. Mannheim read the text twice, and then a third time. Cursed the truth of inadequate resources. Dialed Jamie Norris.

"Jamie, I wanted to thank you for your assistance with Phillips…and lean on you again to locate Ms. Leanne Crowder, who has exited her Canadian hospital against the advice of attending physicians, headed for points unknown."

Silence filled the phone as Mannheim allowed Norris to think his options through.

Still suffering mild embarrassment at not knowing anything of Crowder's self-discharge, Norris asked, "Do we know if she's made a report to keep Langley in the loop?"

"She's spoken several times from a hospital phone to a burner located in the District."

Jamie would like to have cursed, but asked in a civil tone, "Tipton?"

"Not unless Mr. Tipton has moved into the Russian Embassy."

Not entirely true, Mannheim considered his allegation a productive simplification.

Chapter 9

Mannheim watched Greg Riley work via the scientist's lapel camera.

Law enforcement scrutiny always a concern, Wright's verbal authorization would prove insufficient to avoid media attention. Mannheim remembered how installation of electronics went sideways on a prominent, earlier, occasion.

Carol Wright wouldn't cause an interruption; she was enjoying a suburban shopping engagement with another congressional wife. Nazarian's loose surveillance of the twosome was ordered in an excess of caution.

A vibration on his phone made for an unwelcome distraction. The text from an unrecognized number read: *Consulate in Quebec City unable to accommodate requested date.*

Mannheim took one deep breath after another until calm saturated his mind. Whom to send? Who would Raissa agree to liaise with?

When he'd been Chief of CIC, specialized personnel by the dozen were dispatched around the country, or the globe, without a second thought. Barely able to muster five names, all of whom were overtaxed, no other decision was viable: He'd go himself.

Checking Riley's progress, he spoke into the headset's microphone. "How much longer, Gregory?"

"Problem?"

"Something's come up."

"Just the Master Bedroom."

"Pack it up, Gregory. I won't leave you alone and hung out-to-dry...and cannot stay."

Riley appreciated how Mannheim's humanity could, on occasion, rear its head. "David can cover my backside. Check-in later and we'll get you setup with the A/V feeds."

"Gregory, are Randall's bees alive and, if so, could Randall deliver a half-dozen quarts of honey to Manassas Regional ASAP?"

In a tired voice Greg responded, "I'll arrange everything."

Pointing the car towards I-95S, Mannheim tallied the charges for two charter flights in less than forty-eight hours. *When Craig Hall's black money turns to dust, something quite worse than prison will greet my arrival.*

***

Mannheim paced in front of a guard station overarched by the stone columns and walls of *La Citadelle de Québec*. At 21:30, a taxi stopped, and he entered.

"Château Frontenac s'il vous plaît."

Entering the landmark without luggage, he passed the *Wine and Cheese Bar* on a circuitous route to a side door. Steeply downhill, he walked ten minutes before flagging a cruising taxi.

"*Bar Le Sacrilège*, 447 Rue Saint-Jean."

Mannheim allowed himself to be seated in an L-shaped church pew where broken tiles set in epoxy covered the tabletop and ancient brick walls rose to a high ceiling. *Mactavish Trou du Diable* sounded suitable, paired with ham and cheese without bread. When the middle-aged, overtly gaudy prostitute joined him, he summoned the waiter.

Snuggled together, Zachary whispered, "Leanne Crowder left the hospital, clearly not healed or fully operational. She's held more than one lengthy conversation with someone at the Russian Embassy. Ms. Crowder, who is a licensed pilot, works for Jamie Norris but serves Russell Tipton. Infiltration/Exfiltration is her day job, like haute couture is yours. We must conclude Stefan Korsakov is expecting you."

"Korsakov hasn't made an appearance."

Whether Raissa was certain, or not, ugly thoughts invaded Mannheim's mind. "With apologies in advance, could you have missed him?"

"No," was her emphatic response.

"Then Miss Leanne Crowder has made a rational assumption Raissa is here in Quebec City…to be followed by an irrational attempt to remove Raissa from the game."

In character, she nibbled at his ear. "Maybe Crowder's got somewhere to be other than Quebec and can't take time to heal. I'm familiar with how punishing yourself for the Operation feels."

"I agree. You shot her in a lung...she didn't leave her hospital bed for a social dilly-dally." Waving for the waiter, he pondered out loud, "Where does that leave my pal Stefan?" Glancing up, he requested, "Two espressos, please."

Raissa agreed. "Maybe nowhere. Maybe on his sailboat."

"Marta won't pass on a second bite at Raissa's apple...and Crowder can't hunt you relying on one operative lung." Mannheim sat up straight. "There's a team in place or on the way, and Korsakov its leader. No suave Maximilian. No hired bruisers. Stefan has been told to redeem himself or die trying. Ms. Crowder's job is to verify results for her American sponsors."

Raissa disliked the idea of a full-on fight on the opponent's home ground. Without full preparation, it was a choice made by fools.

Guiding his lady-of-the-evening by an elbow, Mannheim tossed two CA$ twenties on the table. On the street, a black SUV's door opened.

"These gentlemen from CSIS have collected all your things. My charter will fly wherever you direct. I'll deal with Ms. Crowder and Stefan." Mind suddenly flooded; he adopted a jaunty persona. "Have a good flight."

Raissa couldn't help herself. "Raissa rests on the sideline while Zachary rolls the devil's dice?"

"We'll each experience something new."

From the front seat of the SUV, a hand offered Mannheim a stainless-steel briefcase. "From your airplane, sir, as requested."

***

Pierre Tremblay shook Mannheim's hand from the taxi's driver-seat.

"Greg didn't explain too much. Told me we'd need small anti-personnel devices with remote detonation capabilities. I've got suppressed semi-automatics for each of us, and a long-gun with excellent coverage of the apartment where your asset has been staying...as well as the front windows and roof of the target condo."

"The long-gun is CSIS?"

"Trusted colleagues and old friends are best for these jobs."

Mannheim trusted Gregory Riley explicitly, so challenged no further. "I've brought some of Greg's toys...they'll provide autonomous intelligence on the opposition."

Pierre's incredulity showed. "You have drones operating in Canadian air space?"

Mannheim opened the shiny, stainless, briefcase to expose six battery-powered, winged devices less than four inches in any dimension.

Literally amazed, Pierre said, "Autonomous drones...these don't look like they'll fly. Whose are these?"

"Let's say they're not mine, Mr. Tremblay, and be grateful we have them."

"Can they be recovered?"

"No. When the battery expires, they self-combust."

"So, our first chance is our last? And you still think it's tonight."

Mannheim had bet the farm, so answered, "Yes."

"Full video?"

"Three hundred sixty degrees looking down from one hundred to three hundred feet."

"Do they work in urban environments?"

"One can hope."

***

Shortly after midnight, Randall's instructions arrived.

Step by step Zachary entered estimates of grid coordinates, estimated building heights, time of day, weather conditions and launch variables.

A tethered goat named Mannheim departed alone and afraid from Raissa's rented apartment. A ten-minute march to a mini mart brought him near a full-scale breakdown. Rummaging through shelves as if on an everyday errand, stopped near the cash register, he examined his phone. Screen and hand shaking, fingers ripped open cello-wrap protecting chocolate fudge cookies.

Sugar would never have been the solution.

Zachary Mannheim wasn't a field agent and couldn't subdue qualms eating away at his stomach. Had Pierre placed charges at the top and bottom of front and rear stairways? How could flying insects talk to each other thousands of times a second; assign and overlap search patterns; reach conclusions about the validity of targets; and alter tactics in a micro-second? Was Pierre's sniper awake?

Something was bound to go wrong. Sugar be damned, he wolfed a second cookie.

Legs forced to move, the gun's weight made him lopsided. He crossed the street and rounded a corner so Korsakov's condo would be on his right. Opposite him, a woman walked a white Poodle on a slack leash. Zachary kept pace with the dog-walking twosome, imagining he heard the high-pitched whine of Riley's creatures. Lights glowed through curtains in Korsakov's living room. Mannheim's heart rate skyrocketed. Guilt accompanied heartburn.

His earpiece crackled: *Targets acquired.*

Two round blips outside Korsakov's condo were matched by four others, five blocks north.

"Six total?"

Pierre responded, "Affirmative."

Square blips erupted in the screen's upper left quadrant. "Two vehicles?"

"Affirmative."

Marta literally wanted Raissa disemboweled, not dead on a cold slab; that's why they're using two vehicles and so many men. Given Marta's most recent failure, taking Raissa alive would severely stress the SVR team. Seeing Vehicle Two turn away, Mannheim re-calculated Vehicle One's threat: two in front, two in back, one of whom will be Korsakov.

"Three guns in Vehicle One, plus one non-combatant."

"Roger."

Amateurish to remind Pierre and his Canadians of danger, Mannheim didn't care. "No crazy risks. Confirm." When he heard a dog bark, the woman and canine had turned east out of sight. Except for two Russians, the street was empty.

Four muffled explosions, accompanied by muted screams carried on a breath of wind, tore tranquility to shreds. Aided by an exact time of entry from the drones, remote detonation had been clinical. No fire alarms rang-out where four battered Russians hoped for rescue and rapid medical attention.

Eyes drawn towards unseen havoc, the closest Russian staggered, buckled and fell. In a shallow doorway, the second Russian fired at

Mannheim, when, with the back of his head missing courtesy of a sniper's bullet, he crumpled. Mannheim crossed the road to examine two bodies which didn't look Russian and could easily be Chechen.

Why not deploy front-line SVR agents? Intellect better than emotion, an earlier pattern remained Marta's choice: Mercenaries on Cape Cod, Bulgarians in my home, and now Chechens in Canada.

Vehicle One's blip moved at high speed, one right-hand turn and three blocks from Mannheim's location.

He heard the sniper's composed voice. "Vehicle One fifteen seconds out."

Kneeling in blood and brains, the absurdity of wearing a suit and tie produced a plaintive laugh. *Das is furchtbar*, he thought.

Arrogance had betrayed him. Four angry guns, not three, would arrive, because neither Stefan Korsakov nor Leanne Crowder was in Quebec City this night. Semi-automatic raised, he waited.

Tires squealed; blue smoke rose as brakes worked at their limit. Four doors opened in a synchronized ballet. At the right front, an automatic weapon sprayed 5.45×39mm cartridges in Zachary's direction; four rounds drove Mannheim backwards and onto his right side as one of his 9mm rounds impacted the right-front Chechen's diaphragm. The driver was driven to the ground by a sniper's round, and in rapid succession two additional sniper rounds caused the last Chechens to fall in a heap.

Zachary acknowledged good fortune. Bruised from two impacts on Level IV armor, bleeding from one bullet through fat around his belly and another in his left thigh, he cursed Korsakov: three bullet-wounds in forty years at the Agency, each attributable to that smarmy bastard.

His earpiece erupted. "Move. Move. Move. Vehicle two approaching behind me. I've no shot, repeat no shot."

Mannheim stared at the slow-motion approach of life's conclusion.

Pierre emptied a clip from behind a parked car; Vehicle Two never faltered.

At what Mannheim guessed was three hundred yards, Vehicle Two shuddered and bucked to the left. Steam and metal parts spewed from its engine. Zachary lay dumbstruck as armor piercing shells shattered the interior.

Realization arrived.

A guess proved accurate as horrible impacts resumed with a fresh ten round clip of armor-piercing ammunition loaded into Raissa's custom-made rifle.

Silence blanketed the street.

Mannheim spoke softly to men he barely knew. "Go now. Go quickly. Thank you and safe home."

Far from any hoped-for outcome, belt cinched above the thigh wound to quell blood loss and the semi-automatic handgun wiped clean, he dialed 911 to report a shooting and request an ambulance. Unable to stand, Zachary pushed himself into a sitting position as a swarm of six fireflies fluttered towards the pavement.

Startled by the dog's tongue, Zachary tried to clear away the fog of war. Focused on the woman holding the leash, recognition settled somewhere between neutrality and submission.

Marta Hinrich Mannheim displayed no humor. "Will no one rid me of this meddlesome husband?"

Zachary strained to sit further upright. "Shouldn't you misquote a Czar, or at least some poetic oligarch…instead of an amoral, 12th century British King?"

"Always the smartass…bleeding and diminished, clever words are your weapon of choice. Can you see the long strings attaching poor Zachary to his puppeteer?"

"Where is my friend Stefan, Marta? How is he these days?"

Prodding the entry wound with her shoe, she watched his face contort in pain. "On his way to Hell, husband, like fathers who kill their children."

"You should find a way to let go, Marta. Beatrice is your daughter…not mine."

"*Was* my daughter, you bastard, until Zachary fucking Mannheim ordered his girl-child disemboweled in the Mexican desert by a Brazilian whore."

"Beatrice is very much alive, as you well know. Seven years in Limbo, Marta…the penance you accepted. I'm damaged goods, thrown away by politicians and laughed-at by newly minted Intelligence gurus. I wonder if you're not far behind. Your lord and master in the Kremlin cares nothing about Beatrice but surely worries over Marta's all-consuming obsession."

Face suffused with rage, Marta Hinrich Mannheim fought for self-control. "Beatrice is dead. Killing you is something I can arrange on a whim but won't while you cling stubbornly to this…" Marta waved her arms to encompass the dead and dying "…morbid belief Vladimir Putin wishes your country ill."

"Are you enjoying young Leanne's company? It's tragic you need a surrogate for Beatrice."

"So far out of the loop, husband…so sad. The competition is over. Two years away from the game, you've lost more than fat around your middle."

Children's games—tit for tat. Remorse filled his head before the words could escape his mouth.

"Forget Beatrice, Marta. Fear the Choirmaster."

Zachary watched her mask slip. Behind faded vitriol resided a monstrosity.

***

When the ambulance arrived and police cordoned off two crime scenes, Raissa allowed concentration to ease. Breaking-down the rifle and assuring she would leave neither DNA nor physical evidence behind, she asked: Why not kill Marta? Pushing regret away, the voice in her head said: *You've been right, girl, Crowder has somewhere important to be and is on her way.*

Raissa watched Mannheim loaded onto a gurney. Leaving the rooftop, she dialed. "Hey kid, wake up. Gotta perform miracles."

Randall Carter never misread Raissa's work voice. "Ready."

"Mannheim cashed chits with CSIS tonight. Find out whom he talked to and give that contact to Nazarian. I need the following…ready, Randall?"

"Go."

"First, unofficial protection for Mannheim at whatever hospital they've taken him to…he's been shot. Second, for every corporate jet at *Jean Lesage International* within the past three days, I need the owner or who purchased the charter, where it came from, and any flight plans or manifests filed for where it went or is going. It's okay to hack any individual or any government department, Canadian or US. It's okay to grease palms or break legs…find the right jet. Third, get me the official whereabouts of Leanne Crowder…then start looking for Crowder's real location, Randall, because no one wants her found. Got it?"

Randall had a hundred questions, but experience told him more than one clock was ticking. "Answers ASAP."

***

Raissa texted Mannheim's charter pilots to stand-down until further notice.

Then she began the hike to a mid-level business hotel off *Rue St. Louis*. Disapproval at the front desk over her tawdry backpack—*does Madame need help with any other luggage*—and the lateness of the hour, she'd made an immutable impression on the hotel's late shift employees. A gloved hand manipulated the keycard, and, even with such a robust first line of defense, nothing in the cookie-cutter room was touched. Randall's update of cellphone encryption noted, she pressed one digit and waited to hear her Business Manager's sleepy voice.

Clarke Ludlow's British accent sounded miffed. "It's very late in New York, Raissa. Is the sun up where you are?"

"Listen up, Clarke. Quebec City...you must have a contact, so arrange a meet-and-greet for lunch tomorrow. Photos wearing the owner's clothes...Raissa looking thrilled...that sort of thing. One hour maximum. Send along an attorney with the appropriate connections, prepared for hostilities with the locals. Have the Gulfstream at the airport no later than 14:00...on standby till I arrive. Got all that?"

Ludlow was overpaid for infrequent impositions caused by the high intensity life of Raissa, celebrity super-model. "Will this be gratis?" he asked.

"I've met a lovely Quebecois I'd love to please, so yes, assure the owner that my fee is being waived."

Time checked, there was none to waste; Marta by now would have volunteered information to the police about a female carrying a sniper rifle. Given that Mannheim was either in surgery, or possessed of adequate wits to deny involvement, tonight's slaughter in the streets was incentive enough for police to authorize a wide area search. Wig and faux-flab removed—to be deposited in the icemaker near the elevators—she pulled a Montreal Canadian's ball-cap low over her forehead. Ordered an Uber at the hotel's rear delivery entrance. Handing the driver US$50 for a one km trip assuaged potential irritation.

"*Le Château Frontenac*, please. I'm sorry for the trouble, but my boyfriend's a pig."

She saw the driver glance in the mirror. Nothing he'd say to cops would suggest the badly dressed, frizzy haired, woman who checked-in and paid cash fifteen minutes earlier.

***

Alone at the front desk, the Frontenac's young Assistant Manager never missed a beat. "Ms. Ribeiro..." Openly flustered, she looked around for a celebrity's posse "...are you alone this evening?"

"Alone and utterly exhausted. Did my reservation make it into your system?"

Tapping on her keyboard, she cooed, "I love everything you wear."

Raissa's laugh conspiratorial, she said, "You mean everything I wear in the magazines."

Glancing up, the young woman wore embarrassment in multiple colors. "I don't see a reservation, but I have a lovely selection of rooms."

Reading the nametag, Raissa said, "How about you choose for me, Elaine?" Moments later, keycard in hand, there was an opportunity to harvest goodwill. "I'm doing a small appearance tomorrow. Please come; you'll have a good time. Give me your cell, I'll text you the address and time."

Showered and beginning to shake-off the night's chaos, Randall's text was unwelcome: *No hospital security until morning. Too many aircraft-too many flights-can you narrow by destination? Crowder officially on vacation-no location. Nazarian arriving Quebec City ETA 08:30. Advise.* Raissa tapped: *Go to bed. Be ready no later than 06:30...then try Turkey, Finland, Denmark, Norway, Sweden and the UK. Countries bordering Russia are our best start.*

Desperate for sleep, it was the backpack and its contents that gave her pause. Celebrity was one thing, accompanied as it was with allowances for alcohol, sex and drugs. Carrying a sniper rifle, handgun and hundreds of thousands in cash was something else altogether.

***

Perched on a promontory overlooking the St. Lawrence River, Quebec City's Old Town would, when pre-dawn sleet relinquished its grip, appear as froth from a fairy tale: Silver church spires towering over rows of 18th and 19th century stone merchants' houses; a traditional German Christmas Market; and horse-drawn carriages clip-clopping down cobblestone streets.

In the shadow of Château Frontenac's pretentious turrets and towers, Raissa bit off half an energy bar, tightened the anorak's hood and re-assembled her route. Headed northwest on Rue des Carrières, her first target was Rue Saint Louis where a quick left and right put her on Rue du Trésor. Stopping to window shop, notice was taken of the building where her meet-and-greet had been arranged for noon. A circular transit of Cathedral Notre-Dame de Quebec convinced her she wasn't being tailed. Within minutes at a fast pace, she entered Mannheim's hospital. Shift change imminent, she pushed open his door ahead of a self-imposed timetable. Heavy backpack shed onto the room's sole chair; she observed the sleeping man's left leg encased in bandages.

When Mannheim responded to her presence, she said, "How long till you're back on that leg?"

Rueful smile in place, a hoarse voice carried Zachary's admission, "Without your intervention I'd be dead. Is that why you stayed...to prove a point?"

"No time for proving points. Could have killed Marta, but that would have been selfish. I feel her...like the wicked witch...searching for me."

Mannheim's eyebrows rose at a rare personal utterance from a consummate professional. "She can't be certain."

"No, she's not certain...but she's left people behind to have a thorough look round. Haven't seen them yet, but they're here." Seeing his brain working, she offered a status report. "Security's been arranged...I'll wait with you till they show up. David's flight gets in at 08:30. Randall's tracking private jets going back three days. One left within an hour of your chat with Marta...filed a flight plan to Moscow. No sign of Crowder, but we know she prefers an ancient single-engine job with a range substantially less than a thousand miles. If Marta's operation is outside North America, Ms. Crowder needs more capable transport."

Coughing sent a spasm of pain through his body. Mannheim reached for a water glass. "Find Crowder…she'll take us the rest of the way."

Raissa recognized the unique cough attendant to broken ribs. "How many?"

"Two on the left. Two on the right. I'm a man who prefers symmetry."

Too much sympathy was a bad thing. "Got to get up and move no matter the pain." Reaching out with her left hand, Raissa held his tightly. "Where did you say Korsakov kept his yawl?"

"Kaleiçi Marina in Antalya…though the nationalistic climate in Turkey isn't favorable to yacht owners."

***

Raissa figured eight to ten minutes to reach the combination train/bus station. Quebec City's morning commute was ramping up, and within seconds she'd have to choose between a more pleasant route through a park or sticking with city streets. Jogging towards *Rue Saint Nicholas*, her unencrypted phone vibrated. Turned to reduce the eastern sun's glare, a woman twenty yards behind reversed direction.

"Stupid girl…" she said under her breath "…damn those hospital cameras." Adrenaline production rose from negligible to frenetic. Is it just the single woman, with reinforcements on the way? Or have they cobbled together a snatch-and-grab? *Wait it out, Raissa, until you can breathe.*

Looking down, the text read: *On the ground – Eduardo.* Just this dollop of good news kick-started priorities: Be unpredictable; be quick; spend money before blood. Backpack shrugged off, extra-large sunglasses went on her face and the semi-automatic into the rear waistband of old, faded blue jeans. All thought of the train station's bag storage abandoned, she hustled in her original direction. On *Rue Vallière* a plate-glass showroom emerged from memory. Inside double doors she removed her hood and shades, shook out platinum hair and politely asked a man dressed head to toe in black biker's gear, "Know anyone who'd ride me to the airport?"

He allotted less than a few seconds to look her up and down: Hiking boots, nice ass, winter parka and a pretty face. "Know plenty of fellas happy to ride you."

How much testosterone is too much? she wondered in passing. Don't make a mess of a minor transaction, girl. "Twenty-minute ride, right now...five hundred US. Twenty minutes riding me would cost more than your dirty little mind could comprehend."

"Show me the money."

Counting five hundred from her stash, she said, "Show me the money...you an old movie buff?"

Seeing the semi-automatic in hand, his intended crudity was rearranged. "Julien..." he shouted "...get your bike." To Raissa, his voice retreated into meek atonement. "Through the door on the left, Miss."

"You'll need a helmet," was all a badly shaven youngster said in response to her arrival.

"I gave your boss five hundred, Julien. You get a hundred bonus for every minute under twenty."

"Where to?"

"Wherever private jets are parked."

***

Showered and dressed, she consumed quiche cooked in the Gulfstream's galley and drank real coffee. Contemplated cancelling the meet and greet. Pros and cons jumped at her like berserk popcorn escaping an overheated pot: Yes, scheduling an event had been too hasty, particularly if the woman who'd done a one-eighty was the opposition; yes, she hadn't been in the public eye since her home was attacked—slack granted by a hungry media wouldn't last; no, it wasn't good for a super-model to schedule and cancel within twelve hours— fame was fleeting under the white-hot fever of social media; yes, Marta returned to Moscow, which could mean her team-in-place is emboldened enough for a massacre.

Enough paralysis by analysis.

For the third time, she examined Nazarian's text: *CSIS has pulled Mannheim's support...hurt feelings, I guess. Service de police de la Ville de Québec is seeking a female witness to last night's carnage. Description of female varies: young, blonde and beautiful (likely Marta's claim) or middle-aged hooker (seen with Mannheim who was found wounded at the scene). See you 12:00 hours.*

She texted Randall: *Come on genius, where's Crowder?*

As she entered the jet's main cabin from the bedroom, a tall man of fifty in an impeccable double-breasted suit greeted her. "Mademoiselle Ribeiro, it's a great pleasure to be in your service. My name is Adrian Vaillant."

All business, Raissa would encourage no small talk. "How do you know Clarke Ludlow?"

"My firm has offices in Montreal, Toronto and Quebec City. We are under retainer to Clarke's firm in New York for all of Eastern Canada."

"I've scheduled a little affair today. Whether the host has adequate permits, or any other requirements is unknown. Clarke's recent text suggested a crowd of two hundred plus media. Do you foresee problems?"

"Rue du Trésor is well suited for such an event, and there's been well-placed advance publicity on morning television. I've spoken to a few friends…with the mayor's wife planning to attend, things should go well."

"There's no entry stamp on my passport, Mr. Vaillant."

"Where did you cross into Canada?"

"Memory's a bit foggy."

Vaillant's expression never quavered. "Where did you stay last night?"

"Château Frontenac."

"Perhaps the front desk will remember you?"

"Yes, I think so."

"Then don't worry, Ms. Ribeiro. I'll be nearby throughout your event."

Raissa called-out, "Eduardo, my backpack's locked in the stateroom closet. Everything else…handle as usual. See you in a few hours."

***

Half an hour into *Un événement de mode avec Raissa*, the egalitarian crowd was enthralled. Enjoying complimentary wine, fruit and cheese at four informal table-bars, as well as raffles of merchandise modeled by Raissa, applause grew for each successive ensemble. Walking informally through the gathering, she stopped to share a thank-you-for-coming with adults and fashion tips with youngsters.

Two television crews had come and gone with the party still at full volume.

***

Nazarian had photographed the crowd from different angles. Sent directly to Randall in Virginia, facial recognition identified attendees in real time. Raissa caught a look of consternation on David's face, then heard Greg Riley's voice in her earpiece. Without missing a beat, she whirled the outfit's skirt and strutted towards the changing area.

"Say again, Greg."

"CIC is here in my office to interview Randall. He's away on a few days of vacation…God knows where…but who are these guys? Anyone at CIC should know we're Agency contractors…vetted and cleared."

"Hang on, Greg. Back in a second."

Nazarian switched to a different channel so he and Raissa could see Randall's photos and text: *Woman is Russian Consulate Montreal; Adrian Vaillant represents Russian oil interests.*

Back to Greg Riley she said, "News to me, Greg. I'll get David to call Phyllis and get back to you."

Stuck without options, Raissa texted Randall: *Location?* Impatient, she stared at the phone until it delivered: *Beer and breeze.* Okay, he's at my cottage where, if undamaged by gunfire, all the electronics he'd ever need were available. She answered: *Don't get sunburned.*

With three additional changes scheduled, Raissa checked her appearance in a mirror and went back to work. Behind an effervescent smile, she located the Russian woman and Vaillant; the attorney was texting, and the Consular representative's demeanor screamed boredom. Nazarian's thumbs were flying. Was the Russian woman SVR? Would she know where Crowder went? Does it matter, if an SUV full of Chechens is on the way? As for Vaillant, money bought an attorney's loyalty.

Speaking to the gathering, she told them, "We planned two more raffle gifts, but I've got a better idea. How about two of you gals come up here…I'll turn you into models for our finale."

Hands flew into the air.

Nazarian positioned himself between Vaillant and the exit.

Raissa pointed at the Russian woman. "You're my size. I've got something lovely for you." Seeing the woman's flight reflex, Raissa raised her voice above the din. "She's shy ladies...don't let her out the door. We need an adult to offset..." Raissa finger came to rest on Elaine, Château Frontenac's late-shift front desk manager "...this terrific member of the younger crowd."

In the changing area's privacy, Raissa told Elaine, "Pick anything you like from the rack...you can bring it back for tailoring, if it doesn't fit." Turning to the Russian, she offered appreciation. "Thanks for being a good sport. What's your name...so I can introduce you?"

Making a scene was never a spy's first choice, particularly when her cover had evaporated. Playing shy, she mumbled, "Marina is my name."

"Marta is such a pretty name."

Spitting knives from her eyes, the Russian maintained composure. "No, my name is Marina, not Marta."

Side-by-side the threesome preened and rotated, Raissa providing running commentary on fabric, fit and colors. On the dot of the hour, she issued copious thanks while disappearing to cheers and applause.

Nazarian weaved his way through the dispersing crowd, catching-up with an anxious Vaillant. "Who should we be expecting, Counselor...police or true hard men?"

"Get out of my way."

Nazarian's fist moved with ill intent. "I'm not a nice man, Counselor, and you shouldn't be concerned with what you've been promised or how you've been threatened. Worry about me, because I'm right in front of you. Nothing else will matter, if you're dead."

"This is outrageous."

"Too true. Be still and patient...we'll see what transpires."

Dressed as she'd been upon arrival, Raissa watched Vaillant and Nazarian cheek by jowl, looking content. At the curb, Marina from the Russian Embassy waited as a chauffeur opened a limousine's rear door.

A dark sedan disgorged occupants who made their way inside. "Ms. Ribeiro, we're detectives with *Service de police de la Ville de Québec*. We'd like you to accompany us for questioning."

Standing tall, she pointed at Vaillant. "Talk to my attorney."

"Je suis Avocat Adrian Vaillant…is Ms. Ribeiro under arrest?"

"She should cooperate…we'll decide about charges."

"Ms. Ribeiro is an internationally known celebrity, here promoting local business. I've been with her since the plane landed and will vouch for her impeccable behavior."

"Stand aside, Avocat Vaillant. Ms. Ribeiro, come with us."

Nazarian raised his camera, catching a facial shot of both men. "Are you boys certain about interrogating Ms. Ribeiro? Why don't we start with your badges?"

Raissa took a healthy step backwards, as dyspepsia became evident on the closer detective's face.

"None of this is your concern," said a faltering thespian.

For Nazarian, their footwear raised an indictment; no Quebec City cop would wear such crap shoes. With a quick look at Randall's response, he pushed them further.

"Maybe you should have said *Sûreté du Québec*, where you both worked until fired as Agents Provocateurs. Climb back in the sewer, before real cops arrive."

A slight movement in the second man's arm brought an instant reaction from Raissa. Aimed at his head, the hand holding her weapon never trembled. "Do it…I'll let you get the gun in your hand, then put one round in each eye."

Nazarian grabbed Vaillant's wrist as two fake cops backed out. Offered the attorney advice with a wry grin. "Playing both sides can be a big fucking risk, when the super-model knows how to shoot."

Chapter 10

Nazarian departed on Mannheim's chartered Lear. Unable to raise Phyllis Martell prior to departure, CIC's sudden interest in Randall Carter seemed more ominous.

Raissa found Zachary aboard her Gulfstream, asleep in the stateroom. "Eduardo," she sked, "do we have a flight-plan?"

Careful with his words, the pilot answered. "The gentleman in your stateroom instructed me to file for Antalya. We're fueled and have a takeoff slot in twenty-five minutes. Winds are reasonable for a mid-morning arrival. Meals are stowed...let me know when you'd like to eat. There'll be plenty of time to sleep."

"When did my guest arrive?"

"Very soon after you left. Explained he needed a nap."

"Say anything else?"

"Said he would soon have to *get up and move no matter the pain*."

***

When the plane's engines altered pitch for its descent, Mannheim's phone proclaimed 09:48, which was two o'clock in the morning for an old man's sore and stiff body. After shaking off sleep, the full import of where he was, where they were going and what was yet to be accomplished chased him off the bed.

Wrapped in a blanket, curled-up on a seat reclined flat, Raissa felt Zachary loom over her.

"On the ground in twenty minutes." He handed her a steaming mug. "Bullets can be helpful in knocking rust off a fossil."

"Looks like sleep helped too."

Mannheim was being patronized. She meant well and he valued the intention. "Marta believes *Reformation* is beyond the point of no return, believes her campaign to diminish her enemies so advanced as to render us irrelevant."

"You two had quite a conversation."

"When husband and wife carry enmity, words are often a pretense…but not here. Two excerpts are illustrative: *Killing you is something I can arrange on a whim but won't while you cling to the morbid idea Vladimir Putin wishes your country ill.* When tired of our talk, she ended it with understatement: *So far out of the loop, husband. The competition is over. Two years away, you've lost more than fat around your middle.* I was unable to resist having the last three words: *Fear the Choirmaster.* A shot in the dark, Marta's face betrayed the truth…there's a battle for supremacy within Russian Intelligence."

Raissa considered Zachary's theory in light of recent events. "Have you communicated with David or Greg since you came onboard?"

"Tell me, Raissa."

"CIC sent a team to collect Randall. Phyllis is unavailable…Randall's in hiding at my cottage, doing the best he can. At my little fashion show, two ex-agents from *Sûreté du Québec* tried to arrest me…and the Russian Consulate sent a woman to watch. Marta may believe we're distracted or diminished, but in no way has the *Reformation* crew backed-off."

Photos of two ragtag French-Canadian ex-cops, and the SVR woman named Marina, brought Mannheim no recognition.

As the Gulfstream banked hard to the left, Eduardo's voice came through the intercom. "On the ground in five minutes."

Raissa asked, "Why come all this way to see Korsakov's boat?"

"I don't think we'll see the boat, and Turkey isn't charming any longer. Once autocratic rule takes hold, everyone's a spy and everyone is spied upon. What was loaded on the boat…who sailed it away?" Distracted a moment, he looked back at Raissa. "Wouldn't it be best for a celebrity like Raissa to remain on the aircraft?"

"Not what you were thinking."

"I was hoping your boatyard friends would adopt Randall for the duration. But putting them in the crosshairs a second time is something I cannot condone." Tires screeched as they hit the runway. Engines reversed to slow their speed. "Perhaps your friends could assist Randall to reach Michani's estate in Great Falls."

"I'll talk to Jonny…you check-out Korsakov's boat and talk with Jean-Louis."

Mannheim felt the need to reassure her. "I'm getting the hang of pushing pain aside. Being productive is the best medicine."

***

In the Non-Turkish Passport line, Stanley Benson's US passport was examined without drama: Mannheim let crutches tell their story. Passing through the 'Nothing to Declare' line, a Turkish soldier demanded the crutches be examined for explosives.

On their surface Antalya and Kaleiçi Marina were made for postcards: Old buildings, cobbled streets, restaurants and bars overlooking the marina. Underneath was another matter. Five hundred klicks from Incirlik, the strategic NATO Air Base within spitting distance of Syria, Antalya was less welcoming of American expatriates, military personnel, and spies. An American passport no longer rewarded its holder with immunity.

Ensconced at a table overlooking the marina, second Turkish coffee gone cold, Benson/Mannheim was lost in thought as he shifted to a chair exposed to the December sun. Two hours had flown. What knowledge he gained made an unimpressive list: Korsakov's yawl sailed away weeks ago.

Middle-aged, a man emerged from a car less than fifteen meters away; he wore a suit tailored in Moscow. Zachary dredged the name and its context from a bad, years-ago, memory: *Sokoloff, you've left diplomacy for the crusty existence as a spy. What have you done with poor, emaciated Stefan and his rainy-day fund?*

One glimpse of Sokoloff's companion drove him to examine a high bluff where sun reflected off Nasir and Laura Akkoyan's roof. Nasir, an engineer with thirty-years service at Incirlik and twenty years supplemental employment with CIC, disappeared five months ago. Laura hired attorneys, investigators and politicians to free her husband. Thomas, their only child, came home from Boston University to help his mother.

Why is Sokoloff, one of Marta's mid-level apparatchiks, in Antalya today?

Laura's coiffed hair and peach lipstick presented discordant notes. Holding Sokoloff's hand struck Mannheim wrong on so many levels. Questions related to the couple's relationship vanished as they eased themselves aboard a sixty-foot sloop.

So, Stefan found himself a newer, larger sailboat to replace the one dispatched to serve Mother Russia. A minute lengthened into forty-five; a less complimentary suspicion gained traction.

Post-coital exhibits of affection on parade, Zachary's disdain for Laura Akkoyan deepened. As their car departed, Mannheim felt the burden of impending tasks. Not a serious sailor, let alone a one-legged pirate, boarding Korsakov's new sloop would require a Herculean effort. To carry away drugs or cash, if they were present, would be farcical. To defend himself against Russian, Bulgarian, or Chechen agents—or a Turkish rug salesman—would hardly be feasible.

Right leg and foot lowered onto the sloop's main deck, he grabbed a wire stay supporting the mast. Near disaster, he maintained a fierce hold. At a turtle's pace he slid to a sitting position. Bound by a spy-hunter's determination, he shed one crutch and utilized the other to navigate the companionway to the interior. Reconnaissance indicated nothing of interest in the galley/salon or staterooms. Sail locker and engine room unreachable, he opened and closed drawers at the navigation desk in a mindless sequence.

Questions which needed answers came into focus. Have mother and son spirited Stefan's treasure away? Has Laura's Russian boyfriend promised to save Nasir? What do mother and son know of Korsakov's departed yawl?

In the third drawer of a bank of four Mannheim discovered a Makorov 9mm pistol, grip wrapped in electrical tape. No field agent would be without a suppressor, so he rummaged high and low to find it. Checked the clip, threaded-on the suppressor, racked the slide and deposited the gun on the chart table. Attention turned to a cabinet door; the interior was filled with a collection of concealed components. He touched the GPS' heat sink and found it still warm. Why would Sokoloff delay a sexual dalliance to use GPS?

Mannheim's texted Riley: *Marine GPS may have Intel. Advise.* Half a minute passed before Greg's sleep-filled voice responded.

"Yes, Gregory, my time is short. What do I remove...is it a memory card, a chipset...how will I be certain?"

"Take it all. Rip off the cables, dismount secondary units. Bring it...or send it."

Riley's instructions were elegant in their simplicity but sweat stung Zachary's eyes as he splintered custom paneling in lieu of risking the

GPS' innards. Cables were the easy bit; he tossed them in a supermarket carryall. Six screws held a plastic housing where the GPS' brain would be located. Guts of the electronics exposed; Mannheim's stomach flip-flopped; a series of wires protruded from a miniaturized explosive device. He re-dialed Riley.

"Small plastic charge. Wires covered by a metal cap. What do I do?"

"It's not concealed?"

"In plain sight."

"No owner wants his yacht blown-up, so we'll assume it's purpose is theft deterrence."

"I'm dealing with Russians, Gregory. Assassination is forever among their motives."

"Get off the yacht."

"I can't do that."

Riley realized argument would be futile. "Tools?"

"Just the basics...what's the likely damage?"

Riley ignored the question. "What size is the explosive?"

Mannheim's concentration wandered. "How far away is safe? Will I get a warning?"

"I don't know. Get away from the damn thing."

Zachary convinced himself: Korsakov, weasel though the Russian would always be, wouldn't trust his life to an erratic deterrent.

"Gregory, if it becomes necessary instruct Raissa to get the Gulfstream off the ground super-quick." Silence provided affirmation. "I've sent you a photo with my hand as a measure of dimensions. Talk me through disarming this thing."

Less than half his tasks complete, Mannheim and a carryall occupied a taxi to Laura and Nasir's home. Zachary held no illusion of being welcomed.

Laura met him in the drive. "You nervy bastard, come to pick over the bones?"

"I was fired without ceremony two years ago, Laura. Nothing of my former position remains. I can't help Nasir but would very much like to say hello to Thomas, if only for a minute."

"So my neighbors can line up to betray us?"

"I'm here on private business. If you want Thomas to leave Turkey in safety, it has to be this afternoon."

"He won't leave his mother."

"Does he approve of his mother's lover?"

Laura's ethereal voice wasn't intended for Mannheim. "It *would* be less worrisome, if my precious son was away from here."

"Is Thomas home?"

"Don't paint false pictures for the boy...you could at least tell him the truth."

"Give me his number...he can tell me where to meet."

Back in the taxi, his worst fear refused to fade: Has Laura informed Russian or Turkish Intelligence of Zachary Mannheim's whereabouts?

Crutches propelled his body in a pendulum-like motion along the harbor's stone and concrete breakwater. Underneath a navigational light tower, Thomas cast a lure into a placid Mediterranean.

Facing the open sea, Mannheim began. "Your mother worries."

"They confiscated our Turkish passports...our US passports are blacklisted. We can't get out unless they say so."

An inquiry about the specific *they* was counterproductive. "Will you return to BU?"

Thomas's rod bent in half, and then went slack. "Dammit, that fish could've been dinner." He let seconds pass, then completed his appraisal. "Mom texted...you want something. We need money for food, petty bribes and protection. Lots of money."

Laura and Thomas weren't the first members of the Agency's extended family to be abandoned. Still, guilt made Zachary pliant. "How much would make a difference?"

"Ten thousand might keep us afloat six months." Coldly calculated by a kid, Mannheim's hopes dropped further.

"Are you familiar with a forty-foot yawl named *ESPION*? Owned by a Russian named Stefan Korsakov...nasty sort of fellow you'd remember. Boat departed Antalya four to eight weeks ago. Maybe you saw what was loaded, or discovered the identity of her skipper?"

"Mom said CIA shit-canned you. Why would you care about Korsakov's boat?" Thomas radiated resentment. "What's wrong with your leg?"

Last backlog of sympathy expired, Zachary said, "Ran into friends of Korsakov. Did you see who was aboard ESPION?"

"Two Russians I'd never seen before." Too quick and smooth, Thomas's lie had been rehearsed. "Told you all I know."

"It's business, Thomas. Korsakov owes a great deal of money. Your assistance would merit a share."

Climbing down from his perch on jagged rocks, Thomas Akkoyan marched half a mile across the harbor towards the Marina without another word.

Zachary observed the boy's arrival. Twenty minutes passed before Thomas' ability to outwait him became plausible. Arrived back at the marina, leg aching from exertion, he found a bench in the shade

When Sokoloff and Laura approached the sloop with a large pushcart, he pulled himself erect. Whether Laura or Thomas had warned the Russian was irrelevant: Sokoloff wouldn't have returned except for treasure.

The sloop rocked gently when he lowered himself on deck. Arranged in modest comfort on the gunwale, Mannheim's kept his eyes on the companionway.

Thomas emerged, face expectant.

Mannheim saw Laura in the salon, unable to choose between lover and son.

Sokoloff searched for a Makarov that wasn't there.

"What can you tell me, Thomas? If I don't find Korsakov, his boat, or his money, there's no reason for me to help."

"Nothing was loaded…stuff was unloaded."

"What kind of stuff?"

"Packages wrapped in heavy plastic film, like drugs in movies."

Mannheim's opinion of Thomas's pre-packaged spiel brought world-weary heartache. "Maybe bricks of cash?" He doubted the college lad appreciated his layer of derision. "Who took the cache away?"

"No one took anything away." Thomas Akkoyan's defiance was a multi-colored bruise brought on by events he couldn't control.

Incredulous, Mannheim wasn't prepared to brace Thomas with a direct accusation. "You're saying Korsakov's treasure didn't leave with ESPION?"

"Not what I'm saying." Glaring at wrecked cabinetry and voicing an incorrect assumption, Thomas insisted, "He raped her…" Voice sullen, fighting off tears, he insisted, "…he must have raped her."

Crocodile tears shed too easily, thought Zachary: Young Thomas knew better and was complicit in hiding his mother's dirty linen. Mannheim rolled his eyes and raised his voice.

"Sokoloff, come up here. Laura, you come too."

Sight-line altered by sliding further astern, he said, "Dammit Thomas, what else...cell phone, e-mails, diary, notes, hieroglyphics, any goddam thing Korsakov kept private...anything you stole while he was off with Sokoloff running errands. Think harder."

Laura and her Russian boyfriend stared at him with palpable malice. Sokoloff's words were half-hearted bravado. "I am authorized to assist Mrs. Akkoyan's efforts to repatriate her husband. Why would a castoff spy break-in to my colleague's yacht? Turkish prisons are full of spy scum."

"You heard Thomas accuse you of raping his mother...but you and I know better. Korsakov seduces vulnerable women to gain advantage...Sokoloff trades hollow promises for sex. Have you told Laura how Nasir died, how your future together is governed by Marta's whim? Does your pillow talk contain anything but empty vows, made just before you ejaculate?"

Sokoloff seemed to fumble for a weapon which wouldn't alter the inevitable. Korsakov's suppressed Makarov fired twice. Sokoloff's head drooped to examine drooling chest wounds. Blood pooled on a polished teak and holly deck.

In the same moment Laura Akkoyan feigned one-part horror with three-parts practicality. "How will I ransom Nasir?"

Mannheim looked at Thomas. "See if he had a weapon. Use your thumb and little finger when you hold it up." Conflict ruled Zachary Mannheim: Necessity was neither excuse nor absolution.

Laura's tone expressed disbelief. "Who is Marta? Does Dmitri have another woman?"

"When you first slept with Sokoloff, did you allow yourself to believe it was about Nasir? Turkey is dangerous...any day you could be evicted or imprisoned on a whim. Sokoloff made promises that couldn't be real, but you began to enjoy his deceit. Too bad you brought Thomas into your wreckage." Turning on Thomas with a fury, Mannheim demanded, "Trade for your life, boy. You've seen what your mother's bullshit has bought."

Thomas was numb.

"It's not worth leaving either of you alive, if you won't help. Clear?"

Thomas' epiphany burned bright. "What you want is under a tarp in the engine room." Like a puppy waiting for approval, he lacked a dripping tongue. Zachary remembered why field agents drove him mad.

"Laura, sit there and stay still. Thomas, retrieve it."

"I want half."

"Half of what, son?" Shoreline examined for signs of police or Russians; Mannheim's raw nerves abated.

***

Thomas heaved a red sports-bag emblazoned with white stars and crescents up one step after another until it sat by the sloop's compass binnacle.

"Nearly three million Euros...Korsakov's retirement fund."

"What else, Thomas...tell me something I'll believe. There's no one but me to rely on." Mannheim unzipped the bag to confirm Thomas' claim. Wasting another minute wasn't on his agenda.

"They talked all the time about ice...how cold it would be where Korsakov was going in ESPION. Korsakov was agitated...more than once he told Sokoloff he wouldn't be back."

Mannheim couldn't think Thomas's claims through to any kind of conclusion. It would be dark in two hours, and he wanted to be in and out of Adana on route to Cape Cod. Hefting the Makarov, Zachary issued terse instructions.

"Find Sokoloff's car keys. Put my carry-all and the sports-bag in the cart." Turned to Laura, her stupor at Sokoloff's death had begun to wear off. "At the airport Laura, you and your ill-gotten cash will be listed on the manifest for my jet...our flight plan will be filed for Adana, so there's no question of clearing customs. Hire a porter with one hundred Euros in hand. Find General Aviation and act like you belong on a private jet...you'll have no trouble. Thomas and I will wait in the car. When you text from the plane, I'll follow. If we're allowed to depart, I'll call Thomas with further instructions. If you screw up, I'll turn you over to the authorities. There are airport officials whose loyalties are fluid...and you'll be a big fish with three million Euros in your luggage. Do you understand?"

Laura's dull expression was a bad sign. "What if they open the bag?"

"They'll see Sokoloff's underwear, shirts, suits and shoes." They might find the Makarov wrapped in the dirty underwear, he thought.

"If they look further, tell them your boyfriend is a high-ranking Russian diplomat. Tell them you work for CIA. Tell them any damn thing that comes to mind. Above the fray is how you behave…polite, but snotty. Entitled to board your fifty-million-dollar Gulfstream with your luggage untouched."

Chapter 11

Antalya Airport security meant cameras and security personnel on patrol.

"Thomas, get your mother a baggage cart."

Mannheim added a final instruction for Laura. "Don't lift the sports-bag; it weighs seventy pounds. Don't carry it or move it. If you were a billionaire, you'd never think of doing such a thing. Play the part, Laura. Play it for all its worth to your son."

Following wheelchair signage, Mannheim directed Thomas into a space providing perfect field of vision to monitor Laura's progress.

***

Adana Airport's single runway afforded views of a much smaller facility than Antalya. Gulfstream parked at the far end of a terminal equal in size to Hyannis on Cape Cod, Zachary awaited Thomas' arrival on a domestic flight. As the cabin door unfolded for Laura Akkoyan's exit, Mannheim gave Laura a final piece of advice.

"Colonel Phillip Cooper is Incirlik's Wing Commander. When you and Thomas arrive at the gate, tell security Col. Cooper is expecting you. If some other officer shows up, ask again for Cooper. One way or the other, he'll get you back to the States."

A little too excited, she said, "What if they ask about the bag?"

"Don't be concerned, you're not taking the bag."

"I need money...we have nothing."

"Nasir has family. They'll help with renting or selling the house...you can call them when you're safe under Col. Cooper's protection. Thomas has my number. When you get back home, we'll talk about how to get you settled."

Laura Akkoyan deployed a last threat. "Someone will pay for my story: American woman's Turkish husband, employed by CIA, killed by the Turks. Former CIA executive executes Russian diplomat after stealing millions in Russian government funds. Threatened with imprisonment should the woman go to the media. Mother and son spirited out of Turkey by Air Force Colonel." Hands on hips, she burned a final bridge. "Fuck you, Zachary. Thomas and I will fend for ourselves."

***

When the Gulfstream lifted off for their ten plus hour flight to Hyannis, it was 11:00 hours Washington time, 19:00 hours in Adana. Raissa opened the door from the stateroom, where she'd listened but not been seen.

"You owe me a new truck, Zachary. Mine's gone through the crusher by now...I was fond of that truck. Can I subtract the price from Korsakov's treasure?" Turning serious, she pointed at his leg. "Let me have a look at that. More antibiotics I think. Fresh bandages." Raissa listened as Zachary summarized what they learned in Antalya.

When she finished, he switched topics. "You said Lt. Nichols is transporting Randall...how?"

"Borrowed the boatyard's flatbed. Jonny's brother, Chubb, is riding shotgun to split the driving. Did you speak directly to Michani?"

"You'll remember Nasha lost her husband in Rio. My peripheral involvement kept Nasha from a similar fate. She'll meet them at the estate's main gate."

"Is Michani Mossad?"

"Michani rarely needs Mossad—Mossad is circumspect in begging his facilitation."

"Does Michani have a similar relationship with Langley?"

"A hundred times no."

"But he enjoys a cozy relationship with Zachary Mannheim."

"Once upon a time, I blackmailed Jean-Louis. We both learned things in the process."

"Well...that's interesting."

"Now you've exhausted a wounded man, let me sleep."

***

Mannheim woke to the vibration of his encrypted phone. "Hello David, where are you?"

"Food court at the Pentagon Mall, with Phyllis. FBI is looking for you. Air Force Major at Incirlik says you've been accused of shooting a Russian diplomat...says you disappeared with a pile of cash belonging to an American woman named Akkoyan."

"You said an Air Force Major, correct?"

"Major William Bryce."

"Deputy Assistant Director Tisdale is on the attack, I presume?"

"Bingo."

"Does he know where to find me?"

"He's looking...don't know how hard."

"Has Phyllis said why CIC wants Randall?"

"No."

"Are you still her Deputy?"

Nazarian chuckled. "One day at a time."

Limping the short distance from stateroom bed to cabin chair, a myriad of political oddities swirled through his mind. A half empty bag of cashews pushed aside, ordering tasks led to a gentle hand on Raissa's sleeping shoulder.

Awake in an instant, hand tightened on a semi-automatic, she inquired, "Too early to be landing?"

"I asked Eduardo if we could land at Reykjavik."

Raissa's raised eyebrow required elaboration.

"Laura Akkoyan is keeping her promise...and a former ally at FBI is stirring the pot."

Returning from the cockpit, Raissa made coffee in the galley. "So Zachary Mannheim, who lived decades in the shadows to protect brothers-in-arms, will be thrown into the bright light of day on a whim."

"Deputy Assistant Director Tisdale exemplifies Phaedrus who once claimed *an alliance with a powerful person is never completely safe.*"

***

Mannheim carried an orange backpack on his lap as a wheelchair assisted him aboard Icelandair arriving Boston at 18:35 hours.

Backpack bulging with clothes and irrelevancies, he wore a second-hand parka and purple hat while navigating Boston's Logan

Airport. Bedlam prevailed in baggage claim as a tall stoic stood in the taxi queue. Federal agents never expected crutches or bright-colored clothing a spy-hunter would never wear. After clearing the Ted Williams Tunnel, he dialed Wade Tisdale on his personal phone.

"Good afternoon, Director Tisdale. Rumor has it you'd like to share coffee and conversation."

"Where the hell are you, Zachary?"

"Private citizens aren't required to keep the FBI abreast of their movements."

"You were booked on a flight to Boston…plane landed thirty minutes ago. Change your plans?"

"What's on your mind, Wade?"

"Wife of an Agency employee…husband's Turkish, she's American…is making a lot of accusatory noise. She'll do the morning shows tomorrow. Your quiet life in retirement stands to take a hit."

"Free country, Wade, where no one wins a pissing contest with the media. Still interested in coffee?"

"Okay if I come by your house."

"How about 22:30?"

Dropped by taxi at Bedford-Hanscom Airport, the flight back to Washington from an obscure airport in Massachusetts would draw sparse attention.

***

Mannheim exited the last in a string of taxis at 22:12 hours.

Leaning on a Mercedes limo, the slight figure of Aydan Fetisov blew cigarette smoke downwind of his chauffer and the weapon held with confidence in the man's hand.

"You've gone too far, Zachary. Murder and mayhem on two continents will not stand."

"Speak up Counselor Fetisov. Stand at your full height, because Russia's cameras have been hacked by Langley and my own video broadcasts in real time. Make your threats so the Internet can offer sympathy to the Russian people. Or come in for coffee…Director Tisdale will be here in minutes, but then you were listening when we arranged our meeting. Either way, it would be polite if your associate puts his gun away."

Fetisov glanced up and down the street, the level of his anxiety revealed.

"Yes, my dear Fetisov, your fears are well-founded. At such close range, no laser is required. If you prefer, a lovely green dot could dance on your chest?"

"You are no longer the man I once held in high esteem."

"Give my best to Mrs. Akkoyan. It would make better television, if you returned Nasir from his grave to be autopsied."

"Marta will avenge Sokoloff."

Marta's reprieve in Quebec wasn't mentioned. Fetisov being a chameleon raised questions for Mannheim: Which Russian was in another Russian's pocket?

Inserting sand into the Russian oyster, Mannheim inquired, "Will Choirmaster have a say in my demise?"

***

"Were you listening, Wade…I certainly hope so."

Mannheim wanted nothing more than a long, hot shower and ten hours of sleep, but to ignore or dismiss Wade Tisdale would be counterproductive.

"I didn't expect Fetisov to be involved."

"In our previous talk you learned about my wife's private war against her husband. We shared a mutual concern regarding the backgrounds of two murdered FBI agents…which, by now, has blossomed into a nightmare for the Bureau. When it becomes public…the Bureau rolled over and played dead, while Marta's sleepers infected its ranks…current leadership will be burned at the stake. With that in mind, Aydan Fetisov is the Kremlin's man and a long-term survivor. He was in my driveway to assay the fear in my eyes, to gather crumbs of information which reveal what my masters know of a high profile SVR operation. Fetisov is uncomfortable dancing on the head of a pin…lets you and I not waste time doing a slow waltz."

Tisdale couldn't resist. "Where are your Friends-in-High-Places? Any chance they've hung you out to dry?"

"Abandoned by my masters, if such a circumstance comes to pass, will hasten your own fall from grace and a bullet in your brain. Three recent opportunities presented Marta with an opportunity to eradicate her spouse. Two I thwarted. One ended with Marta standing over me, gun in hand, unencumbered by witnesses. She never relented…I'm alive the way a bull is alive: Lanced by Picadors, weakened and bleeding, too stubborn to hear the crowd cheer for the Matador."

Mannheim went to the sink and poured his coffee down the drain. "What do you want, Wade? It's late in the game."

"How long have you known Laura Akkoyan?"

"Enough prattle…you've got Nasir Akkoyan's file inside your coat."

"She says you executed a Russian named Sokoloff. True?"

"No, and I'd wager she hasn't offered a shred of evidence."

"You think she killed Sokoloff?"

"I doubt it. He seduced her after Nasir's death…all her chips were invested in Sokoloff."

"Do you know a Major William Bryce, at Incirlik?"

"Laura and her son would have been arrested by Turkish Intelligence, on behalf of SVR, within hours of Sokoloff's death. I sent her to Incirlik's Commanding Officer, Col. Phillip Cooper…knowing he'd make every effort to get Americans out of harm's way. Apparently, it didn't work out."

"She claims you stole every cent the family had."

"Sokoloff worked with another Russian, Stefan Korsakov. I've interrogated Korsakov…he owned bolt holes all over the world. Maintained accounts to fund his last weeks on the run, when Marta tired of him. Sokoloff would've been no different. Since Laura Akkoyan was screwing Sokoloff, she'd be the one to have found his money. Nasir Akkoyan was a loyal employee of the USAF and CIA. He's dead because the US and Russian governments let him die. Like they'll let you and I die, if need be."

Mannheim saw Tisdale weigh the pros and cons of possible actions: Would he straddle the fence?

"Just to be clear…you're implying those dead FBI agents, who it seems could've been SVR sleepers, as well as the Bulgarians, Korsakov, Sokoloff and unknown individuals are part of an SVR Op that's secret enough to terminate its operatives."

"Yes."

"Laura Akkoyan…she SVR?"

"Doubtful, because she'd serve no purpose."

"What's the goal of Marta's Op?"

"I don't have an ounce of hard data."

"Speculate."

"I won't do that."

"Are you getting anywhere?"

"Yes."

"If I was inclined to lend a hand, what would you suggest?"

"Tonight you witnessed Counselor Fetisov threaten a former Agency executive. I've wondered whether Mr. Russell Tipton, a former protégé of D/CIA Brantley, has had a similar visit. Tipton may be adrift on the winds of change. Perhaps you'd inquire?"

"Gentle pressure?"

"Nothing accusatory, but other than that…"

In the middle of speaking, Manheim's secure phone pinged from Nazarian: *Check video from Wright's home. On the way there.*

Head shaking in disbelief, Zachary said to Tisdale, "I think you should look at this with me."

Together they watched someone enter the Wright's kitchen through an unlocked rear door. Gender indeterminate, wearing the latest intruder's uniform of sneakers, trousers, hoodie and ball cap—all in black—holding a semi-automatic fitted with suppressor, the interloper moved as a professional would. As if an adversary could appear out of nowhere, each stair tread was measured before trusting it. Turned towards the master bedroom, Mannheim and Tisdale saw the intruder's arm rise and weapon recoil. From the bathroom a man appeared, dripping wet wrapped in a towel.

"Shit," said Tisdale. "That's…"

"Yes, it is," replied Mannheim. "Get your car, Wade."

"We calling Metro Police?"

"Let's not lose our balance or our minds, Mr. Director. Congressman Wright approved the video installation, and a CIC officer is less than a minute away. We can reappraise on route."

A last precaution caused Mannheim to deposit the orange backpack, with its electronic cargo, in his safe room.

Nazarian's follow-up was direct: *Mrs. Wright DOA. Craig Hall one in the chest. Where r u?"*

Tisdale looked confused and determined, if those emotions were compatible, so Mannheim let minutes pass in contemplation before he found a landmark: *Five minutes.*

"Turn off the flashing lights, Wade. Better if we park some distance away."

Chapter 12

Elias Thordsen found instructions for either outcome: His death or Kazimir's. He memorized Marta's bullet-points designed to assure safe completion of his travel.

Provisions were neatly packaged: Teabags; sugar; powdered milk; chocolate bars; canned stew; canned soup; bottled water; medical kit; soap; matches; flares; satellite phone; cash in three currencies; diesel fuel adequate for three-hundred nautical miles; and a detailed route to follow, marked on a series of nautical charts.

During a rare break in the weather, Elias grew bleary-eyed staring at those charts; weighed potential discovery against making up time lost fighting against contrary winds. Despite mental gymnastics and a willingness to rationalize, he was hopelessly behind schedule. A final decision made, relief flooded his body; he would make for the Faroe Islands, two-hundred nautical miles over the horizon. From the Faroes, he would take the Tórshavn ferry to Hirtshals, Denmark; Hirtshals ferry to Larvik, Norway; Larvik by car to Trondheim. Fifty-four hours would be lost—more than two entire days after reaching the Faroes.

"No, it doesn't work," he moaned. "I'll have to risk a commercial flight."

***

To the trained eyes of Tisdale and Mannheim, not one item was out-of-place on the first floor: the assailant knew where to find Carol Wright and Craig Hall.

Mannheim called upstairs to Nazarian. "Who have you alerted, David?"

Nazarian appeared halfway down the stairs. Wearing gloves, he stared at Tisdale. "No one, not yet."

Formality unexpected, Mannheim asked, "Director Tisdale, do you wish to take charge of the scene?"

"You've got something in mind, Zachary…easier if you tell me before I step any deeper in the shit."

"David…evidence left by the shooter?"

Nazarian shook his head.

"Carol Wright still breathing?"

"No."

"Is Mr. Hall alive or dead?"

"Alive…pressure on the wound with a bath towel. Needs medical attention yesterday."

"Would you suggest 911, Director Tisdale?"

Tisdale understood: Mannheim held no official position. "If this is SVR, no. Not if there's a rational alternative."

Zachary dialed while texting Wright's address on his other cell. "Gunshot to the chest…I've no one else to turn to."

Nasha Poynter's response was immediate. "Gavriel and I will be there ASAP."

Tisdale was two steps ahead. "How long?"

Zachary gave a best-case answer. "Twenty minutes."

Looking at Nazarian, Tisdale's voice conveyed ambiguity. "Has NSA Hall got twenty minutes?"

"Why not look for yourself?"

Tisdale returned snark in kind. "Can't have the National Security Advisor die while we pick our noses."

Mannheim discarded shoes, limped to the stairs and began to climb. Finger pointed at Nazarian, he instructed, "Stay where you are."

Inside a woman's bedroom where no signs of a husband were apparent, a sea of white carpet, bed linens and curtains were disturbed only by her black hair, alabaster skin and a pool of blood. Carol Wright had been shot in her left chest—through the heart.

An open bathroom door was smeared with the National Security Advisor's blood in the early stages of coagulation. To a non-existent observer Mannheim appeared transfixed by the drip of the man's vital fluid onto the junction of white rug and Carrera marble. Mannheim's face remained steady, while his eyes examined condensation on the glass shower surround, towels strewn every which way, the bidet faucet leaking, and its sink covered in blood. All these details were subsumed by the bath towel pressed against Craig Hall's chest and abdomen.

More than one thing can be true, he reminded himself. Feigned disinterest marked his inquisition.

"I've arranged private, confidential treatment, which means hanging-on another half an hour...or I can call the White House and summon Hell's storm troopers."

Irony inhabited Hall's voice. "Didn't think we'd reach an impasse between the nation, POTUS and self-interest so soon."

"You should've stopped at *didn't think*. So shall we postpone a soulful reckoning, or expose your sins to the klieg lights?"

"Let's buy time."

"No matter what rabbits emerge from my hat, forensics will tell a sorry tale."

"Tomorrow or the next day...another fucking lifetime."

Mannheim observed Hall's attempt at a deep breath and offered a sybaritic shrug. Instincts developed over decades screamed: *Craig Hall never told you the truth.*

"So be it, Mr. Hall. Reinforcements are on the way."

Hall's voice soured. "Met your expectations, have I?"

Mannheim turned away, texting Randall: *Media know? Where are Tipton, Martell, Grover and Fetisov?*

As Mannheim's mental clock sent out a warning, the return text arrived: *All home.* Zachary wondered how soon he'd regret every minute of this evening.

"David, give Director Tisdale a clean cell phone. Director Tisdale...call the cavalry, it's time to report Mrs. Wright's shooting. Limit what you say...you're making a report based on a confidential source's information."

To Nazarian, who sat in expectation, he said, "Time for you to go, David. Call Phyllis whenever you choose. Restrict what you tell her to what you absolutely know as fact...not a crumb of what you think or heard."

To a confused Wade Tisdale, Zachary offered, "Best if you wait in your car, Wade, we can't have you seen. There'll be two SUVs coming for Mr. Hall. I'd be grateful if you followed."

After Nazarian's and Tisdale's departure, Mannheim stared at the unlocked kitchen door until Nasha Poynter, accompanied by Gavriel Rabin, entered.

"Thank you, Nasha."

Extending his hand to the rugged Israeli, his tone was professional. "Gavriel, your patient is upstairs." Rabin, expression set in disapproval, and two qualified EMTs moved with alacrity.

With Hall loaded, Nasha was purposeful. "Where are your crutches, Zachary? Don't be dense, I know you've been shot so a comprehensive examination is on the docket." Watching Mannheim's features twist into a knot, she stated the obvious. "Young Randall's a thinking-man's professional...we're all impressed."

"So, a retired spy-hunter, betrayed by his star-student, is taken against his will by a Lebanese Intelligence operative and a Mossad hard-man...shame on you both."

From Gavriel's SUV, with no attempt to shield his phone, Mannheim texted Congressman Wright: *Bad news arriving. Hold-on tight. Don't mention cameras, let others find them. Dump your SIM and phone separately.* Instructions for Randall were brief: *Immobilize cameras after sending one copy of every original pixel to the attached address. No other copies. Render local memory un-useable following transmission.*

Randall's response appeared: *Done. Software rendered inoperable w/o multi-level, regenerating, encrypted key.*

Nasha asked, "If I guessed those cameras are installed in Congressman Wright's home, and the copy gives you leverage over the National Security Advisor, would I be far off the mark?"

"I've been led round and round by my nose...and grown tired of feeling dizzy." Reaching for Nasha's hand, he changed the subject, "Is your Papa well?"

Nasha suppressed a laugh. "How could he not be thrilled? After years of resistance, I've surrendered from bull-headed defiance...Papa's words not mine...and joined him at the bank."

Mannheim returned her earlier rhetorical question. "Would I be off the mark in assuming the current atmosphere made the bank a better fortress than the Lebanese Embassy."

"There is no fortress strong enough, when hatred triumphs over civility."

"You and the children are American citizens...will you consider Britain or Israel, if things get worse?"

Exasperated, Nasha said, "And you Zachary, are you planning a return to your parents' Germany? Andrew was British. Jean-Louis is a Jew. I'm Arab American...my children are American, despite having a practicing Muslim for a mother." She recognized Zachary's sympathies: He knows my history; knows why I joined Papa at the bank; knows how hard it's been to lose a husband; and knows how wealth manipulates perceptions. "Listen to me sound barking mad…this crazy woman values your friendship beyond all doubt."

Zachary injected, "You must have questions."

"Tell me how Director Tisdale wound up a member of your underground network."

"Wade planned to arrest me, when my home was used as a killing ground. When Randall shone a light on his dead agents, he accepted the truth: FBI was infiltrated by SVR. Unlike most, the implications weren't lost on Director Tisdale. And here we are…two old fools, fingers in the dike hoping the tide doesn't rise."

"What tide, Zachary?"

"When you hear some of my theories…promise not to have me taken away in a straight-jacket."

***

Mannheim's answer to Tisdale's unasked question was direct. "Multi-billionaire bankers with health issues, a philanthropic nature, Diplomatic Immunity, rumored ties to Mossad, and an estate lacking for nothing might be expected to have an on-site surgical suite equal to a teaching hospital."

Within the radiology suite, Craig Hall's surgeon explained his patient's post-operative status to Director Wade Tisdale, of the FBI's Counterterrorism Division.

"Mr. Hall would have been better served with less delay, but that's no surprise. If you look at the film, the bullet's path is clear: Entered the right chest near the centerline, impacted a rib with fragmentation of bone, deflected further right and upward to exit. Lots of damage along the way, though not fatal. Gun was a garden variety 9mm; fragments of the bullet are in this sample bottle. His condition is serious, but stable. I'll look in tomorrow."

Tisdale asked, "Are you affiliated with Israel's Embassy, Doctor?"

"Yes."

"Military officer, perhaps?"

With a pleasant voice, the surgeon demurred. "Mr. Michani's home is an extension of the Embassy. I apologize Director Tisdale, but you've exhausted my ability to answer."

***

Jean-Louis Michani, his adopted daughter Nasha Poynter and Grover Norris listened as the second of three medical professionals lectured Mannheim.

"You've badly abused the work they did in Quebec. What we've done may seem trivial, but don't let anaesthesia fool you. There were two significant bone injuries...one will require a plate with screws should your current disregard continue. As it is, you'll be miserable for a few days, and will regret declining pain medication."

Mannheim plead guilty. "Mea culpa, doctor. In meager defense, pain sharpens the mind when others wish you harm."

Settled in Jean-Louis' office, Michani's housekeeper delivered coffee, tea, whiskey and a variety of sandwiches.

Grover spoke first. "Craig Hall was shtupping Carol Wright?" Sensitive to unpleasant interactions with Michani's daughter, he began to atone. "My apology..."

Nasha laughed. "Don't apologize Grover, I learned all the variations in the Lebanese army...even the Yiddish ones."

Mannheim wouldn't confess to planting cameras. "I think presumption is worth less than speculation. Mrs. Wright and Mr. Hall's motives and loyalties are and may forever remain unclear."

Angry and impatient, Grover wouldn't let go. "Didn't Craig Hall drag you out of retirement because no one in the Intelligence apparatus was trustworthy? Now you say the dumb bastard, himself, is under suspicion."

Wade Tisdale knew Grover Norris by reputation: Arrogant, self-centered, wealthy, loyal confidant of POTUS and not easily moved off established views. As an intercession, he gave a status summary.

"Let me assure you, Mr. Norris, there are Russians and their surrogates swarming over an SVR Op called *Reformation*. Before last night the body count approached two dozen...all on the Russian side...all eliminated by *Reformation's* authors as cleanup. While we talk, events have muddied the water. Carol Wright was more than cozy with Russian bad boys, so killing her might make sense...but why on earth would SVR target the National Security Advisor? Craig Hall could be acting for POTUS; acting for himself; in the Kremlin's pocket; in some other pocket; or in multiple pockets. CIA officers, FBI agents, and third parties may be acting outside their authority to enhance the probability of *Reformation's* success. And in the interest of saving unproductive questions, Zachary hasn't identified *Reformation's* goals."

Jean-Louis interjected. "Men who believe they know *who*, but demonstrably do not know *what, when* or *why*, are doomed to be thought paranoid and/or deranged. Mr. Mannheim, focus on *Reformation's* possible purpose?"

Grover lifted a glass of Scotch in mock salute. "Zach doesn't play well with others. Prefers to mix his potions in private, while breaking every goddam rule, or law, necessary to get a result. Craig Hall fired him, and old Zach never wrote an Exposé or appeared on Cable News to dig up a bunch of smelly political cadavers. Faced with a choice between Craig Hall and Zachary Mannheim, only an idiot picks the political hatchet-artist. Tell us what's making you crazy, Zach."

Everyone turned to Zachary Mannheim, unfamiliar with defending theories which were closer to castles-in-the-air.

"You all are aware of my wife's role in Russian Intelligence. Marta's long-term strategy involves weakening US Intelligence capabilities via targeted assassination...old news some would claim, but still important. Marta believes I ordered the execution of her daughter, a ruthless SVR agent, as retribution for her mother's many sins...an accusation which is untrue."

Gavriel Rabin jumped in. "No shortage of gossip about Beatrice Hinrich Mannheim's execution. Your successor at CIC believes Randall Carter, your hacker friend, is off the reservation if not out of his mind."

"Mr. Rabin is correct as to historical gossip surrounding Marta, her daughter Beatrice and myself. To borrow another man's wisdom: *Truth is one thing...gossip shows where people's hearts lie.* Marta's heart was broken by her own actions. Mistakes stain her every living moment. As for Randall, he's a private citizen with all the rights and privileges attached thereto."

Rabin's wry smile indicated disbelief.

Nasha hoped to rein-in confrontation. "How does Marta connect to *Reformation?*"

"One working theory presupposes a power struggle between Marta and someone code-named *Choirmaster*...where CIA is an active participant. In this scenario, the Agency intends to assist Marta's assassination of *Choirmaster*. Dates, times and personnel are in-place, and the clock is near midnight. SVR's involvement will vaporize, leaving CIA's unequivocal murder of a high-ranking Russian official with all the blowback attached thereto."

Rabin's attitude acted as Jean-Louis' inquisitor. "How did you learn of CIA's participation?"

"Two sources, one an Agency Field Director now being detained, the second an Agency field officer assigned to *Reformation* as the assassin."

"Names?"

"Mr. Rabin, your need to know is non-existent."

Rabin snapped. "My employer is harboring a presidential advisor, who may be a murderer...which makes you a criminal threatening to tar the Michani family with the same brush. You're a pathetic conspiracy theorist."

Cold as ice, Zachary's disclosure would be news to Jean-Louis but a raw lesion for Rabin.

"Absent Diplomatic Immunity, Gavriel Rabin would have been found guilty of conspiracy to murder the third highest ranking officer in CIA, Fulton Bennett. I possess video which would have destroyed this family." Mannheim's anger rose. "Where was your rabid concern for the Michani family, when Nasha's home was invaded? Her brother, Yusef, and I killed four Hezbollah terrorists bent on sacrificing Nasha, Miriam and Brad to their lunacy. Holier than thou doesn't suit a Mossad hard man, Mr. Rabin." With a cleansing breath, Zachary took a new course. "Call the police, Mr. Rabin, suggest Director Tisdale abandon his current course of action, or do anything Jean-Louis instructs. Mossad sheds blood on Israel's account without second thoughts or moral accounting. Not from my mouth will you hear the names of Agency officers misused by Langley and/or the White House."

Jean-Louis maintained an accusatory glare at Gavriel Rabin while he spoke.

"Nasha offered sanctuary to Mr. Carter, and extended shelter to Mr. Hall and you, Zachary. Our family will honor Nasha's commitment so long as she deems it in our interests. Mr. Carter may continue his occupation of the cottage. Mr. Hall may recuperate day to day in the medical facility. I assume you, Mr. Mannheim, will return home as soon as practicable. Now the morning light and another taxing day approaches. None of us have slept, so please excuse me."

In Michani's grand foyer, Grover Norris wore a satisfied smirk. "Nicely done, Zach. Mossad bastard was enjoying himself."

Wade Tisdale nodded assent.

"Grover, could you sniff the air in the White House?" Seeing Randall approach, Zachary urged him to pay attention. "Get what you need to come home with me...we'll take the GPS memory apart bit by bit."

Randall countered, "Why not use the cottage?"

"The stench of duplicity makes me nauseous." Zachary's harsh words irretrievable, Nasha's footsteps made him turn. "Guests shouldn't cause trouble in your home, Nasha, I apologize."

"Uncertainty makes fools of us all." She hooked her arm around his shoulder. "Come now, there're beds for you all in the cottage. The bathrooms have toiletries. Better than being exposed to the media hounds."

Tisdale preferred three hours sleep at his wife's side.

***

Four individual suites with private bath proved a Michani *cottage* to be a misnomer. After less than three hours sleep, Zachary and Nasha drank tea while Randall recovered the most recent map plots from Korsakov's GPS.

Nasha asked, "Are there no dates on the files, Randall?"

Randall's social skills were unrefined, especially around women. "Uh, there would have been...might have been, I mean, except..."

"Someone corrupted the dates and times."

"Yes, Mrs. Poynter. It won't screw-up what I'm doing but takes time to reconstruct."

Nasha touched Zachary's hand, lowered her voice and turned serious. "You can't think Gavriel would..." Unable to find the right words, she reassured him of her friendship with a warm smile.

"Mr. Rabin took me by surprise...it was never my intent to pick at old scabs. Forgive me."

"Gavriel serves at my father's pleasure...not the other way round. Jean-Louis isn't Mossad and has no role in the Israeli government. He's a businessman, grandfather and father...in that order. He's old school, not easily taken for a simpleton. Chapter and verse is what he'll dig out from Gavriel about Bennett's murder. Papa will never forgive Gavriel for abandoning the children and I to Hezbollah's thugs, though not for an instant did I blame my childhood guardian."

"Your father is correct in one thing, Nasha...your guests have become more burden than blessing on his home."

Randall didn't know how to interrupt, so blurted, "Five viable routings...all terminate at the same co-ordinates." Randall reset the screen to show Antalya, several intermediate course changes, and a terminus in the North Atlantic Ocean more than a thousand miles from any land mass.

Looking at Zachary, a single alternative remained. Nasha said, "Korsakov's sloop met another ship."

Looking pleased, Randall responded, "Now I need to find that ship."

Nasha, the former Intelligence analyst, asked the relevant question. "How."

"Korsakov is SVR...so we look for a Russian vessel." Randall pointed at the screen. "First we interrogate Vessel Monitoring Systems operated by entities like NOAA or the European Fisheries Commission. Russian factory ships fish in a huge swath of the Atlantic...fifty miles off Cape Cod to the North Atlantic west of Ireland and east of Iceland...even further north into the Norwegian Sea and beyond. VMS database is maintained in real time, so we should get what we need. If not, I'll search known reconnaissance vessels...military spy ships often masquerade as civilian trawlers."

Mannheim sipped his tea. "All well and good, Randall...unless Korsakov's rendezvous was with a Russian sub."

"Then we borrow data from SURTASS LFA, a long-range, all-weather, sonar system. USNS *Impeccable* operates the original LFA system."

Mannheim interjected, "Perhaps we shouldn't burden Nasha with technical details."

Nasha wondered aloud. "Will the Admirals approve you borrowing their precious data?"

Mannheim thought the search for Korsakov in good hands. "Good day to you both, I'm going back to bed."

Nasha answered, "Lucky you. Papa left for his plane before God awoke...I'll be at the bank, if you boys need anything."

Chapter 13

The murder of a Congressman's wife dominated the morning news.

Pleased not to see Mannheim's name on television, Raissa watched politicians and political operatives feast on hearsay and innuendo.

She texted Randall: *List of flights?*

His reply was succinct: *Working.*

Something left her cold: Where was Randall the Smartass or Randall the Nerve-wracked? She tried a different tack: *ATC personnel at Otis?* Nothing—the cursor blinked in robotic rhythm. Why? Michani's estate wasn't impenetrable, but it wasn't anyone's idea of an easy target. She texted Tom Nichols: *Everything go well on your trip?*

Raissa lacked a relationship with either Phyllis Martell or Nasha Poynter. Suspicious of Martell's recent behavior towards Zachary, she texted Nazarian: *Randall compromised. Zachary's status unknown. Probe Michani's perimeter. I'll call Nasha Poynter.*

World turned upside down, Nazarian drowned consternation in immediacy: *On site less than an hour. I'll call - ask for Mannheim.*

When Raissa requested Nasha's office, a super-model's name recognition opened the door. "Good morning, this is Nasha Poynter."

Aware of an open line's risks, there wasn't a viable option. "Good morning, Mrs. Poynter, my name is Raissa Ribeiro. Sorry to interrupt, but I'm concerned about Mr. Carter."

Nasha took seconds to sort through what might've happened. "Why?"

"A text from his phone...Randall didn't write it."

Last night Gavriel and Zachary exchanged ugly accusations; unfortunate possibilities bloomed in Nasha's mind. "What can I do?"

Raissa heard Nasha Poynter's sincerity. "Where was Mannheim last night?"

Apprehension suffused Nasha's response. "Bedroom next to Randall."

Raissa was too familiar with the calculus of betrayal. "Please don't intercede, Mrs. Poynter." Estimating travel time, she added, "I can be in your office in forty-five minutes…we can talk it through."

Raissa, dressed in pants, blouse, leather bomber and running shoes, entered Michani Bank to a palpable stir. Met by Nasha, they entered a small conference room.

"This room is safe, Ms. Ribeiro."

"Safe from Mossad?"

Nasha's expression never varied. "The bank pays both sides…hackers to invade and defenders to defeat them. Our clients won't stand for anything less." Allowing a thin smile, Nasha added, "Though you and I know hackers have an edge in this kind of conflict."

"Have you seen Randall or Zachary this morning?"

"Not since dawn." Nasha wouldn't discuss the prior evening's events.

Raissa needed a different approach. "By now you've heard Zachary's theories. Could SVR have breached your father's home?"

"You want to know whether Gavriel Rabin would bite my father's hand."

Raissa's phone beckoned: *Gate insecure. Two down near house. Thoughts?* A fatalist by habit, she knew whatever had been done was irretrievable.

"Excuse me," she said to Nasha, "I need to answer a text." She tapped: *Back off…ETA 30.* "I'm asking whether, in an end game, Rabin serves Israel or your father. If you're in any way uncertain, please let me see for myself. Mannheim's elimination would clear the last hurdle for SVR and *Reformation*. Randall's skills would be critical to counter-balance Marta's advantage in resources."

"Zachary admires you, Ms. Ribeiro, are you a serving officer?"

Here was the crux: Credential myself when nothing short of the truth will do. "No. I'm an asset."

"Paid, I presume…under Jamie Norris' flag."

"Not today."

"What are you today?"

"Zachary's friend and ally in all things. I hope it's a relationship we share."

Nasha thought friend and ally an apt description, given her own history with Zachary Mannheim. "I'll call for the car."

***

Electric motors short circuited, Nazarian shoved heavy steel gates aside to let the limo enter. Pushed the gates shut and climbed into the front seat.

"No vehicles. Two IDF kids will wake up embarrassed. Haven't gone near any buildings. Is your father at home, Mrs. Poynter?"

"No, he left hours ago."

Raissa added, "Who else should be in the main house?"

Nasha found it too easy to regain a spy's suspicion, evaluation and calculation of acceptable losses. "Chef, housekeeper, groundskeeper and one physician's assistant this time of day. My children go to private school, where security is tight. How close do you want to be?"

Raissa nodded at David, who spoke to the chauffeur. "Roll up to the cottage…two hundred yards from the front door. What's in the trunk?"

Nasha responded. "Jericho 9 mils and IMI assault rifles."

Raissa tightened her laces. "Vests?"

The chauffeur, whose breast pocket nametag said *Phil*, shook his head as the limo came to a stop.

"David…lend me your Glock." Silent signal exchanged as he handed over the weapon, Raissa said, "Take the rear with Nasha. Pop the trunk, Phil, then take the front fender. Nasha…is there a basement? How many bedrooms? Weapons other than what Gavriel carries?"

"No basement, three bedrooms, Gavriel carries a Desert Eagle."

A fraction of a second after the trunk opened, Raissa moved to the right, aimed the Glock at Phil—just as the chauffeur's semi-automatic came into position. Two rounds impacted his chest where, if he wore a vest as she assumed, ribs would be broken.

Watching him gasp for breath, she warned, "Don't say something you'll regret, Phil."

The chauffer wobbled and fell over. His words showed defiance. "I will tell you nothing."

David retrieved Phil's weapon.

Raissa confirmed what Nazarian inferred. "No clips in the trunk...had to be wearing his vest." Running for the cottage door, she intended to substitute logic for chaos.

Front door open, Gavriel Rabin's innocence, or redundancy, was evidenced by the dart in the back of his neck. Had Michani's guardians been granted mercy, or left alive to claim innocence?

None of three bedrooms occupied, Raissa noted Mannheim's leg wound dripped a blood-trail on the carpet. Randall's devices were missing, which brought a smile. Somewhere far away, on a dozen different servers, backups would be protected by backups.

Raissa wanted video and sound, but Randall always set digital traps. She'd never find the cameras, so tried the simplest trick— hiding in plain sight. Television tuned to channel 3, well-fitted balaclavas masked identities, night vision goggles made intruders look badass, black clothing was pro-forma, and similar physical characteristics told Raissa nothing about a team anticipating no opposition after Rabin and his soldiers were anaesthetized. Near both the door, and the end of the video feed, arrogance or purpose exposed their faces.

Raissa sensed an elaborate rearrangement of reality. "Come take a look."

Nasha's response was immediate. "Benjamin Aaronson..." She pointed at one of the men on the screen "...works at the Embassy. Definitely Mossad." Defensive, she said, "There's no reason for this. Papa will never forgive an invasion of his home." Mind jumbled, she sat before anger subsumed tact. "Who the hell does Martell think she is...joining Aaronson to invade an Annex to Israel's Embassy. Three Embassy security officers drugged. Two American citizens taken by force. What a clusterfuck."

Raissa suggested, "David, reach out to Martell, see what's on her mind." His equivocation obvious, she demanded, "Spit it out, David, what's wrong...besides everything?"

"Craig Hall..." Nazarian hesitated, searching for the right words "...the man's a riddle. Gets shot after sex with Wright's wife. Chooses surgery at a private clinic instead of a hospital. Why take the worst option for survival? Why risk bleeding-out on the Parkway or in a SUV belonging to a famous banker? You'd think it would be all about the humiliation from an all-world sex and murder scandal. Hall knows who did what to whom is gonna hit the media sooner than later. Maybe this is an exercise in deception to alter perceptions. Maybe more about who witnessed what? About whom would be credible in a courtroom testifying against POTUS' National Security Advisor? Muddy the events around Carol Wright's death. Make Mannheim into an unreliable witness. With Mannheim discredited, Tisdale and Nazarian's unauthorized presence at the murder scene make us easy targets for character assassination...or criminal prosecution."

"Call Phyllis, David...after this she knows you're on different sides." Touching Nasha's arm Raissa added, "Let's see what's happened in the main house."

Video showed, and Michani's employees described being gathered in the kitchen and watched over by one man, who never spoke. Each employee agreed; the man wasn't interested in Mr. Michani, or a wounded patient receiving care in the surgical suite.

Nasha needed certainty. "No one searched the house?" Seeing them shake their heads, she asked her question a different way. "Could one of the other intruders have searched without you knowing?"

Frightened faces gave an identical negative response.

Without useful answers, Raissa suggested to Nasha, "Best we check on your patient."

To a casual observer, Craig Hall would've seemed disoriented or unconcerned by the arrival of two visitors.

Raissa stood at the bottom of the bed reading his medical chart.

With her vast experience with Lebanese Intelligence, Nasha knew how to tag-team an interrogation. "How are you feeling this morning, Mr. Hall?"

"Like a truck hit me."

"Everyone taking good care of you?"

Hall's sense of entitlement wasn't damaged by the bullet. "Your staff has been wonderful."

Raissa's role was bad cop. "Aren't you going to say hello, Craig? You spread enough shit about me after the Russian prisoner exchange in Berlin...or has two years eased your sociopathic mind?" Raissa approached Hall's left side, near his monitors and IV drip.

"You've thrived, Raissa. Professionals like us move on to whatever's next."

Nasha picked-up the narrative. "Surprised to see me, Mr. Hall? I wouldn't have thought they'd leave me alive after killing three members of the Israeli Defense Forces…" She let the lie sink in "…on top of kidnapping Zachary Mannheim and Randall Carter. I'd have killed every man and woman on the estate…in for a penny in for a pound."

Diminished by anaesthesia and surgery, Hall's face was blank. Then blank was replaced by discomfort as Raissa Ribeiro fiddled with a syringe.

"I haven't…"

Nasha interrupted, vehemence punctuating each word. "You chose my father's home as a sanctuary…why would POTUS' National Security Adviser be left in peace. Shouldn't Craig Hall have been the prize, not a toothless old spy and a twenty-something nobody?"

Feral self-regard dominated Craig Hall's response. "Mannheim works for me. I gave him complete autonomy."

Raissa laughed. "Holy shit, Batman, you need better writers. You gave Mannheim a patriotic enema. Sent him off as a sacrificial lamb. *Reformation* is about to happen and, voila, Zachary disappears as if by magic."

Nasha leaned over and placed her hand on Hall's chest. "If I choose, no one will find your corpse, bleached in the desert sun after you rot to death. But they won't blame me, Mr. Hall. Once you disappear, blame will rain on your legacy in buckets. Craig Hall, the perfect villain, because that's what he truly was. Will POTUS mourn the passing of a womanizing murderer? Or, in the wake of *Reformation*, will he say good riddance to a rabid conspiracy theorist?"

Raissa caught Hall's attention, when she partly emptied the syringe into the IV line.

Emotions bounced like pinballs, leaving Hall almost too diminished to speak. "You're killing me?"

"Small bubbles will block capillaries in your big brain. They'll cause severe pain, neurological damage and paralysis…rarely death."

One pinball clanged off a dozen different outcomes, leaving Hall desperate. "Stop, please, I'm begging you."

"Begging doesn't make much impression, when you've been burned alive. Try harder to impress me." Raissa's thumb depressed the plunger further.

Nasha spoke across Craig Hall's torso to Raissa. "Notice how his approval of torture strictly applies to others?"

Hall's hands covered his ears. Tears ran down his cheeks. Submission arrived with near inaudible lies. "Mossad...some faction of zealots who believe SVR and their Kremlin sponsors will annihilate Palestinians, Saudis, the whole fucking lot."

Raissa's thumb pushed harder. "What part does Craig Hall play?"

Reaching for the IV on the back of his left hand, he pleaded, "Stop. Just stop."

Raissa swatted his right hand away like she would an insect.

"I sent a starving fox to kill a fat bear. It's called geopolitics...Mannheim understood."

Nasha banged her fist on Hall's chest as she screamed, "You starved the fox while feeding the bear."

Cringing and whimpering Hall said, "Yes, but the goddam fox proved resourceful."

Raissa was bored. "Fuck your wilderness analogies...who's *Choirmaster*?"

"I don't know and don't care."

"What does POTUS get in return for CIA doing SVR's wet work?"

Nasha's sardonic laugh preceded the truth. "He doesn't give a shit about who gets what, as long as the Kremlin nutjobs are placated."

"Does POTUS really know...better yet, how did he authorize what you, Brantley and Tipton are doing?"

Hall's eyes glassed over. Face covered in sweat, blood-pressure monitor beeping, lies wouldn't suffice. "No president authorizes this stuff...wink and a nod is eloquence."

Raissa felt bile rise. Shaking her head in disgust, she managed to say, "Your boss is a coward. You're a worm."

Hall felt a massive headache getting worse: Is it my imagination, or brain damage from an embolism? "My boss is an idiot...not the same thing."

"Who's running *Reformation* at CIA?"

Hubris arose out of habit. "For Christ's sake, that's not much of a secret."

Raissa asked, "Grover Norris?" Hall grimaced. "Phyllis Martell?" Hall's grin belonged to a court jester. "Russell Tipton, then?"

Hall became animated. "Only after that shitbird Brantley died. Last of the Choirboys, EJ was. *Can't we all just get along? Catching flies with honey.* Stupid bastard."

"Who killed Carol Wright? Why would he shoot you…were you surprised?"

Ignore Carol Wright, Hall told himself. He answered part of the question to cover a separate deflection. "Not *he…she*. Stood over me quite some time before pulling the trigger."

Nasha asked with faux innocence, "So Mr. Hall…what shall we do with you? Or better yet, what would Zachary Mannheim do with you?"

Last mental resources summoned; he told a gratuitous lie with conviction. "Zachary is dead by now, so he doesn't count. Would've been dead hours ago, if not for Mossad's reverence for Mrs. Poynter's father." Because Hall believed delay an all-purpose elixir, he suggested, "See who survives the Christmas season. Keep me where I am…what have you got to lose?"

Raissa toyed with a cell phone, noticed upon arrival. "Who brought this?"

Hall saw escape and a path to glory. Revived he spoke too soon. "I could tell you it was the chauffeur, but that's Gavriel Rabin's phone. Jealous, I'd say, Mrs. Poynter. Gavriel believes he'll be your next husband."

***

Raissa and Nazarian half listened to Nasha's phone calls. Handpicked people were on the way to replace Gavriel and his two soldiers. Aaronson would be on the next El Al flight to Tel Aviv. The chauffeur was in custody at the Israeli Embassy.

Jean-Louis Michani issued strong diplomatic protests to the Israeli Prime Minister and the American Director of National Intelligence. All parties agreed to keep the day's incidents out of the media, if possible.

Raissa asked Nazarian the lone question which mattered. "Did Phyllis provide their location?"

"First she threatened me with disciplinary action. Then suspended me, with pay. After I offered a private viewing of Randall's video, she offered a meeting on neutral ground. We get Zachary and

Randall…Phyllis gets the original video file. Bullshit…it's all bullshit."

Raissa agreed. "The video could be delivered to every journalist in the country…so you told her to release Mannheim and Randall."

"Exactly. She wanted a few days to save face but didn't fight too hard. Phyllis has lost her way."

"Are you still Deputy Chief/CIC?"

"If Randall releases the video to the media, or if Grover Norris hears the truth of what's happened, Chief/CIC might be more plausible." Examining his phone, a text from Greg Riley confirmed Randall's arrival. Reaching Mannheim, he listened then told Raissa, "We're invited for breakfast…the invitation was rhetorical. How does the old man keep his cool?"

"He's just like you and I, David. He keeps fear at bay by filling his mind with probabilities, permutations and outcomes based on data and cold calculation. No different than a spy who relies on drink or drugs, someday Zachary will think himself to death."

***

"My deepest sympathy, Congressman Wright, from one man who's lost a spouse to another."

Mannheim's reference wasn't lost on Congressman Emile Wright. "Lost to the same disease, I'd wager." Wright downed his bourbon. "Do you know who killed her?"

"Yes, I've got a reasonable theory about whom…but the greater puzzle is why was Carol murdered? Right now I wouldn't hazard a guess."

"You *could* guess…but won't?"

"That's accurate."

"I told you before Carol was killed …I'm in…what's next?"

"I'd suggest an emergency meeting of the Subcommittee with the following witnesses called to testify: Russell Tipton, Phyllis Martell and Jamie Norris. Witnesses should be placed under oath and warned of the Subcommittee's intention to pursue criminal prosecution in the event of perjured testimony. For security purposes, attendees should be restricted to Members. A video record should be made and sealed. The Chair should personally pursue a line of questions in their entirety prior to entertaining questions from other Members."

"Which of those three is our target?"

"Mr. Tipton is a Person of Interest. Ms. Martell is seriously compromised. Mr. Norris the Younger possesses information we need. Jamie is loath to provide it to a non-Agency employee like myself."

"How soon we all forget."

"My ego has never been a problem, Congressman. Can you corral your rambunctious mischief makers?"

"Even Lester Morgan won't piss on a grieving husband, whom he'll soon be lobbying from the outside looking in. Tomorrow morning soon enough?"

***

After limping along a painful four-mile trek beginning at Russia's Embassy, down Wisconsin Avenue to 28th St., through Rock Creek Park to Ohio Drive, Mannheim watched Fetisov fit a Turkish cigarette into a yellowed plastic holder.

Fetisov honored their agreement as to security; if he hadn't, during those four miles a security team would have revealed itself. Their absence was indicative, not dispositive; with knowledge of the destination, security could have established a position in advance. Mannheim thought not; the exhibition in my driveway had been theater signaling an interest in open communication.

Both sides of the street were comfortable for the Aydan Fetisovs and Craig Halls of the world.

"Zachary, did you enjoy our walk? Better than the damnable treadmill for your weight. Better than these Turkish cigarettes are for my lungs. I am alone...you are alone. Why am I here?"

Abundance of caution explained Mannheim's tentative movement. "May I reach in my pocket for a phone?" Under Fetisov's silent approval, two edited videos played in succession.

"Would you play them a second time, please?" After watching frame by frame, Fetisov commented. "Your editing captures the important bits...provided nothing of a critical nature has been omitted. Not that I'm making such an accusation."

"My purpose is to put our knowledge of events on even footing. Carol Wright's murder, seen on the first video, is known to the FBI. Ms. Leanne Crowder will be declared a rogue CIA officer and a fugitive from justice, which should make her participation in *Reformation* clumsy, unproductive, and embarrassing for Marta. If Ms. Crowder's murderous intent was instigated within your embassy, a quiet admission could lessen tensions. As to the more recent incident, your corrupted Israelis' activity was too impulsive. I have arranged their return to Israel's embassy for whatever disposition is deemed appropriate. Mr. Michani's influence within the Israeli coalition should quell future hysteria from splinter groups."

"Rumors abound, my dear Zachary. I try not to play the fool."

"Let me assist, if I can."

Fetisov hadn't expected such an offer. "Mr. Craig Hall...he recently passed away?"

"Mr. Hall was shot, possibly by Ms. Crowder. Young and under pressure to depart the Wright's home, Ms. Crowder failed to acquire proof-of-death, which may have led to misguided rumors. As it happens, I arrived in time to staunch the wound and call for emergency medical attention. Mr. Hall is well enough after surgery to be an irritant in my efforts to absolve Aydan Fetisov from blame. Mr. Hall is inclined towards an eye for an eye...more specifically your eye...and has made preliminary plans in that regard. Were I a betting man, I'd wager Brazilian blondes make you skittish?"

Shaken to his core, Fetisov considered whether this discussion could take another path. "You, Zachary, have recently been spared by Marta. My death would hasten your own, an altogether avoidable escalation."

"Perhaps so, but my death would remain speculative even after you'd gone to eternal bliss, no longer to benefit from nonsensical tit for tat. What other rumors need we discuss?"

"Some say your departed Director Brantley initiated *Reformation* in talks with Marta. Others say Brantley is alive."

Mannheim guffawed. "Old news, my friend. Brantley's death will be confirmed when, later today, his casket is exhumed. Besides, Marta may not survive numerous character flaws. What else?"

"Your protégé, Ms. Martell...I hear she became an acolyte of Director Brantley."

"Did you not watch the video? Phyllis is a well-trained, cautious woman. Counterintelligence wears on its practitioners, and she's no exception. Mr. Hall is well satisfied with Ms. Martell's performance, in particular her restitution of my freedom. Unless you'd like to discuss Marta's plans for the Christmas holidays, I can't think of any further rumors needing resolution."

Fetisov was well prepared. "Christmas isn't my favorite time of year, Zachary...all pomp and circumstance, puppet shows, carolers in the streets, bloody commercial street markets and priests demanding tithes in the name of Baby Jesus's birth. Give me Easter, when the Cherry Blossoms are in bloom and old men such as ourselves have weathered another winter. I bid you goodnight."

With the entire discussion recorded, Mannheim watched the Russian disappear, limp accentuated for Zachary's benefit. He counted on Fetisov's cellphone having performed an identical task.

When Greg Riley came on the line, Mannheim was terse. "I sent you the audio."

Riley responded. "It cries out for interpretation."

"Ms. Crowder never flew overseas from Quebec City; she returned to DC and was present at the murder of Carol Wright. Given Crowder's limited physical status, I'd say *Reformation* isn't chock full of Major League hitters." Mannheim paused, electing to omit a kernel of speculation not fully germinated. "Neither was Marta present on the flight leaving Quebec for Moscow; she flew to *Reformation's* location. Randall should use the following search parameters, tweaked as he sees fit: Northern European countries with cities hosting televised, high-tone concerts in churches. Pre-Christmas, Greg, means the next few days. Conflate those concerts with flight patterns he already identified."

"Is Fetisov a target?"

"Not if he told the truth. Not unless it suits our needs."

One last question burned bright. "Why nothing about Russell Tipton?"

"Tipton never mattered and still doesn't matter. We don't need Fetisov to hurry Mr. Tipton's elimination, because tomorrow morning at 08:00 hours, EJ Brantley's orphan spy is going to testify as to the Agency's staffing of *Reformation*."

Riley saw the obvious next move. "Randall needs to find Martell's phone. Who gets the data?"

Mannheim's thoughts jumped into the near-term future, when *Reformation* would be over but its aftermath still seething. "Not David...not Raissa. Emphasize that to Randall, the boy tends to send her copies of everything. Send the location, or locations if there's more than one phone, to me alone."

Chapter 14

Elias Thordsen's flight from Lorvik landed on-time.

Located on the south shore of Trondheim Fjord, at the mouth of the river Nidelva, Trondheim's principal claims to fame were technology-oriented institutions of no interest to Elias. Trodheim's Nidaros Cathedral—locus of *Reformation's* operational intentions—was his destination. Through all the tests, travails and physical suffering, his arrival coincided with the Op's schedule.

Would his voice hold up?

Moving through Værnes International Airport, after collecting Kazimir's backpack from baggage claim, he searched for a horde of young Americans and their college choirs. Mingled among the boisterous group, he drank-in the innocence of their enthusiasm.

How and when to meet his Russian contact remained clouded. Korsakov had told him— *Enjoy being young, let Marta's people reach-out to you*. Clothes which stunk of weeks at sea stood in the way of anything like self-indulgence.

***

"Good morning to all of you. My name is Göran Berglund…I'm the conductor and artistic director of the Cathedral's Boys Choir, Norway's oldest with nine-hundred years of tradition here in Nidaros. Next to me is Isabelle Almgren, conductor and artistic director of the Cathedral's Girls' Choir. Our repertoire for the Christmas Concert will be chosen from major works for choir and soloists."

Göran Berglund fit Elias's mental image of *Choirmaster*. Physically fit, mid-forties, well spoken with an affinity for violence covered by a pleasant exterior. Could Berglund be Marta's man? He felt a hand grab his shoulder.

Berglund's baritone broadcast disapproval. "You're Thordsen...been through a meat grinder by the looks of you."

Stunned, Elias's eyes fixed on the Western Façade. At the center of the *Rose Window,* a red panel symbolized the Day of Judgment. It was Judgment Day Elias felt affinity for. *Tell them something near the truth*—the advice of trainers at The Farm.

"My passion is singing, but sailing runs deep in my family. When I was accepted for your Christmas program, the North Atlantic solo was too big a temptation. Gale force winds for weeks on end, broken gear, battered mind and body...made port in the Faroes. I'm headed for the shops to buy some suitable clothes."

Berglund not only didn't release Elias's shoulder, but a vise-like grip squeezed harder.

"I came under a lot of pressure when it came to your selection. Two high-ranking faculty from Yale's School of Music sent recommendations. Both U.S. Senators from New York did as well...and there was the letter from Norway's Prime Minister." Berglund's hand dropped away. "It's not like you won the *Giordani,* or any competition which would get you noticed in Norway. How did an unaccomplished beginner manage to arrive with fantastical stories of sea demons? Can you sing, Mr. Thordsen, and, if you can't, why are you here?"

Elias relied upon verifiable facts, as well as an on-line presence adjusted by the cyber-spooks at Langley.

"My family is wealthy. Sometimes, no matter how much I protest, my grandfather makes phone calls. Mostly those calls get results. But I can sing...in rehearsal I'll prove that."

Berglund rolled his eyes. "Where is your primo passaggio?"

Elias didn't hesitate. "D4, more or less."

"Second passaggio?"

"G4."

"So you consider yourself a leggiero?"

"No, Mr. Berglund, in classical categorization I consider myself a lyrical tenor. I can generally access C3-D4."

Wheeling away from Elias, Göran Berglund tossed incredulity over his shoulder. "We shall see, Mr. Thordsen, whether you sing better than you sail."

***

Sipping tea after a circuit of the mall, Elias met her examination by staring back. Not beautiful, she wasn't a typical Nordic blonde babe. In a guessing game of contrivance, he decided she was the product of a Thai woman who married a Norwegian. Long black hair fell over the corner of a striking face. Heat spread across his face, when her lips changed into a smile.

Crossing to his table, self-confidence not sex oozed from her gait. With aristocratic bearing at odds with employment in a mall, she could have been seventeen or twenty-seven. Three fingers on each hand were adorned with golden rings, none of which could be taken for a wedding band.

"I saw you in the men's department. You should have bought something…it's possible you're the worst dressed man in Trondheim." Pulling out a chair, she laughed at Elias's reaction. "Am I too brazen? Does your girlfriend in America let you dress like a homeless person?"

Not wanting to admit there wasn't a girlfriend, he countered with an accusation. "So you followed me?"

"I didn't follow you. I didn't not follow you. The Great Buddha says, *Do not dwell in the past, do not dream of the future, concentrate the mind on the present moment.* That's how I live my life."

Gravity doubled his weight, constraining Elias's movements. Pulled in every direction, soon he would be drawn and quartered. Which side was she on, if paranoia could be believed? "Buddha's words cut both ways: *A woman of the world is anxious to exhibit her form…even when represented as a picture, she desires to captivate…and rob men of their steadfast heart.* Are you a woman of the world?"

Wearing an expression of sympathy, she said, "I am a Norwegian woman who sees you are, maybe, suffering the beginnings of SAD."

"So I'm wretchedly dressed and borderline depressed…thank you Dr. Suzanne Freud."

Reaching across the table with her left hand, she held his right in a firm grip. "My name isn't Suzanne, it's Kirstin…SAD is short for *Seasonal Affective Disorder*, a Winter depression effecting those who live in Nordic countries. The main symptoms are fatigue, cravings for sugar, feelings of sadness, a loss of self-esteem and avoidance of social and physical contact. You're here for the Christmas concerts at the Cathedral...maybe it's actual darkness making you feel the way you do."

In a delayed reaction, he demanded, "How do you know I'm here for the Christmas concerts?"

Rolling big, dark, eyes, she withdrew her hand. "How do you think?" Mockery of the kindest sort, she said, "You've got the bewildered, exhausted look we see from choir-members unprepared for four hours of half-light and twenty hours of darkness. There are lots of ways to make your visit more fun."

"Rehearsals take-up most of the day."

"I don't want to sound preachy but get out in the fresh air and exercise...darkness in Norway is playtime, just the same as if it was light. Streets are alive with people not fazed by the darkness or the snow...the full moon in the northern sky is a second sun. If you look up, there are the Northern Lights."

Elias began to lower his guard. Aware how much could be at risk, resistance made him say, "So where do *you* go to feel alive in the dark?"

"That's easy...I go to the beach."

Uncontrollable laughter encouraged lukewarm coffee to drain out his nose. Bent over with a napkin, he recovered to say, "Sure...what a great idea. Boots, parka, snow pants...perfect ensemble for a beach party in the dead of winter. How could you be my fashion consultant?"

"Bonfires on the beach, cooking fires, bright coals in the fireplace, candles in windowsills...I can show you, if you'd like. There's a big gala at Korsvika Beach...fire everywhere, music, wine, lots of people our age." With a warm expression and a voice inviting imagination, she said, "Afterwards you'll see window lamps in every house. Welcome Candles in small dishes nestle in the snow by front doors. Perhaps because the sun can't be seen, fire often makes strangers into lovers."

She took him to *Zara* on *Norde gate*, where Elias spent cash found in the sloop's supplies like a drunken sailor. New everything, from boots to hat, made him nostalgic for college shopping with his mother. Euphoria was his drug of choice when they entered *Egon*

Søndre for dinner. I might be drunk, he allowed, but it was not from *Akvavit*.

Floating away on a hot-air balloon wasn't improbable, but in a parallel existence he was distraught. *Reformation* had imposed a monastic existence to survive the North Sea. A spy could choose, he'd been told at the Farm, among three distractions: Women, drugs and alcohol. He remembered the cruel punch line best—a spy dies quick with women and drugs, stick with alcohol for a slow death.

***

Near an hour's walk to *Korsvika*, she said, as they crossed the *River Nidelva*.

She kissed him for the first time on *Thaulowkaia*.

He saw signs for *Trenerys Gate, Jarlsborgveien*, and *General Von Hovens vei*, before the ocean's tang blended with smoke from a dozen fires. Rocks and sand littered with blankets, picnic baskets, and jury-rigged bars, kids of all ages danced.

Close to Kirstin, they talked about nothing of consequence in between kisses and a deepening sexual attraction.

Twice an older couple fixated on Kirstin and Elias. When he returned their gaze, they called to three boys kicking a soccer ball and departed. Moments later, Kirstin pulled Elias into her arms and held him tight.

Above swarming sparks, the night sky was ink black. Elias surrendered to the moment.

***

Woken by a text, Elias straightened up in the demonic darkness of Norway's winter. Naked and cold, rumpled sheets brought total disorientation.

Commiseration with long dead spies struck Elias like a hammer. Will I be shot in a woman's bed? Ennui made sadness too familiar, too laughable: I'm a caricature, brought to grief by fatuous self-deception. He switched-on the bedside lamp.

His phone declared: *Kristiansten Fortress, Restaurant Kommandanten 18:00.*

***

Harried and hurried, wet hair freezing, Elias expected Göran Berglund to dress him down. Scrambled into position with other soloists, apprehension became reality.

"Good morning everyone…and a particular welcome to Mr. Elias Thordsen after his evening with a Norwegian lass at a beach bonfire. Come join the Cathedral Boys, Mr. Thordsen…we'll begin with *Bethlehem Down* by *Peter Warlock*. Do you know it?"

Risking additional wrath, Elias elected an impertinent response. "*Warlock* wrote the work in 1927 for a holiday drinking binge. I'll try not to embarrass your Boys."

Except for an occasional shoe shuffling over stone floors, hush fell over the Cathedral. Berglund raised his arms to gain the entire Choir's attention. In three minutes forty-two seconds of triumph, silence was restored. Berglund advanced upon Elias like a wolf would a meal.

"Competent, Mr. Thordsen. What do you think of *Hodie Christus Natus Est*?"

"*Poulenc* wasn't exactly a serious composer, but his *Four motets for Christmastide*, of which *Hodie Christus Natus Est* is the fourth, is a joy. I prefer the Latin version to the English."

Handing Elias sheet music, Berglund declared victory. "Then we'll do the Latin. You begin Mr. Thordsen, and I'll have the chorus join you along the way…we'll call it an experiment."

When the organ's last note faded, spontaneous applause erupted. Berglund accepted their verdict. "Well done, Nidaros Boys Choir. Well done, Mr. Thordsen. I think we'll polish your effort and insert it in our program. What would you think about Mozart's *Laudate Dominum* for your featured solo?"

"Better piece for a woman," said Elias. "Or a really talented Boy. A challenge is healthy, however, and I'll trust your judgment."

***

A long rehearsal day provided time in contemplation of his mission's status. Is the method of assassination mine to invent? When will the target arrive? Where in the Cathedral will he be located? Is *Reformation* doomed by long odds and duplicitous allies?

Elias's doubts recalled his family's expectations and remonstrations. Scarred by the Vietnam War, his father reacted with ill will to Russell Tipton's recruitment of his only living son. Sullen and silent, Henrik depreciated a one-legged spy's call to patriotism. Daughter of a spy, Mom showed deference to CIA's representative.

"A real opportunity to move Russia away from the ambitions of current leadership," Tipton claimed. "*Reformation* will prevent rabid nationalism from consuming Russia's Intelligence Agencies."

Henrik rose to leave the room.

"Why are Elias's qualifications unique, Mr. Tipton?" She would've preferred to say, *what kind of operative are you, spewing bullshit to adults who know better?*

***

Elias left Nidaros to its medieval darkness. A little more than a kilometer via the *Old Town Bridge*, fifteen minutes would see him enter *Restaurant Kommandanten*.

He turned onto *Gamle Bybru,* the peculiar *Old Town Bridge* in plain view. Built after the great fire of 1681, its location served as strategic access between Trondheim and *Kristiansten Fortress.* Carved gates from the 1861 reconstruction were replicas; they wouldn't save today's spy, if retreat became a last resort. At a fast walk *Kristiansten*, a freestanding fort, loomed over him. In a steady climb, he sympathized with soldiers ordered to cross an uphill field of fire from the four-story tower. Set at an oblique angle to an attacking force, topography and geometry gave protection to its defenders.

Close enough to see a shadow move atop the wall, reflex drove him to the ground. Stomach cramps twisted his gut. Fantasy banished, he entered *Restaurant Kommandanten*. In a cramped private room, a woman sat stone-faced, a glass of white wine extended towards him like a handgun. "Sit Mr. Thordsen, we're nearing the finish and all you think of is your penis."

Chapter 15

A cold front lingered, making humans miserable and pavement treacherous to walk.

Mannheim stood in a deserted corner of a public park in Arlington, VA where, dependent upon economic fate, a man could buy a magnificent Cuban cigar or nothing more appealing than a three-day old donut. Patience rewarded, a battery-powered taxi pulled into the curb; Emile Wright and David Nazarian emerged.

Ringtone seemingly twice as loud as normal, Mannheim recognized the number. He greeted Randall Carter without pleasantries. "Will he hear me?"

"Keep it short."

"Discovery would be unfortunate, Randall. Be precise."

"Twenty seconds maximum."

"Someday my boy, if I discover you've invented these restrictions out of thin air, I'll have your toys confiscated. How about video from the Chairman's phone?"

"It'll stream live, a little blurry at times, to the phone numbers you included in your text."

Ending the call, Zachary wondered whether encryption mattered an iota.

Briefcase and coffee in hand, Wright approached. "Why the last-minute emergency?"

"An old man worries, Emile. I wanted to remind us…most of today will be mind-numbing detail…politicians speaking to each other for their personal interests without consideration of the outcome. You, Emile, will come upon some immovable obstacle which resists every verbal and mental effort. David and I have arranged to put my voice in your ear, for a few seconds of reassurance, when our collective goal is at risk. No one will know…the technical details are beyond mere mortals and its implementation illegal. Place this thin wire close by your ear, with the little thingy on the end touching your skin. Then listen…you can't talk. Text David's cellphone and you'll hear me ASAP. That's it in a nutshell."

"You think I'm going to blow it?"

"Not in the least, but, if your Congressional cohorts frustrate you, we'll be there for encouragement." Placing his hand lightly on Wright's arm, he added. "Place your phone's camera where it can see the witnesses."

Congressman Emile Wright re-entered the taxi with Nazarian; the weight of the world was uncomfortable upon his shoulders.

Earmuffs added to a winter parka, Zachary walked four miles to an occasional hidey-hole. He would watch and listen to the closed session of the Subcommittee without risking discovery. Nazarian would do the same from a parking garage near the Capitol. Zachary wouldn't dwell on an altered reality faced by spies in the age of amoral technology: Adapt or die always applied to fuzzy moral aspects of Intelligence gathering.

***

The Subcommittee's full membership took their seats, each eager to witness their Chairman's reaction to the murder of his wife. Looking down at a small gathering of witnesses, Emile Wright gaveled the hearing open.

"Just a reminder…provided the Subcommittee's goals can be achieved, we'll continue our tradition of informality. One exception…today's testimony will be under oath."

Mumbling among Members went un-noticed as each witness was placed under legal jeopardy. Legal caveat aside, Wright proceeded to illustrate plain language would rule the day.

"Can anyone from Langley tell us where Ms. Martell might be? Mr. Norris, you're the ranking Agency executive. Help me out…can CIC justify blowing-off the Subcommittee?"

Contempt of Congress wouldn't apply in Phyllis Martell's absence, but contempt of her career was on the table. Jamie leaned over to speak into the microphone.

"Mr. Chairman, there was no communication between Ms. Martell and me regarding attendance this morning."

"All right, Asst. Director Norris. Ian Riddick still runs Internal Security…right?"

"Yes."

"Phone Riddick...tell him to locate Ms. Martell and bring her down here. We'll move on while we wait."

Wright altered his demeanor to address Wade Tisdale.

"Director Tisdale, we appreciate the Bureau's Counterterrorism Division sparing you this morning. Let's begin with the evening of my wife's murder...were you present in my home after Carol's death?"

Tisdale allowed murmurs of shock to subside. He wouldn't lie under any circumstance, so relied upon questions that wouldn't elicit worrisome responses.

"Yes, Mr. Chairman. Protocol requires certain personnel attend crime scenes related to government officials who hold sensitive positions."

"Did you examine my wife's body?"

"No sir, I did not. My role was...please forgive me for an insensitive response...and remains counter-terrorism elements of Mrs. Wright's assassination."

Chairman Wright paused for Tisdale's word to sink-in among Members. "Assassination...not a break-in gone wrong, not a passionate dispute between lovers, not a husband seeking redress for a wife's indiscretions? How can you know?"

"Unedited video from your home's security cameras told me so."

Commotion among Members rose to a crescendo. Wright banged his gavel twice. "Let's stay focused. Time enough for thorough analysis and wild-ass speculation when Director Tisdale completes his testimony."

Lester Morgan, of Florida's 4th, Vice Chairman of the Subcommittee, virulent antagonist of Zachary Mannheim and soon to be K-street lobbyist, issued a strident demand.

"Damn well time for every Member to know when you, Mr. Chairman, came to hear these revelations. Damn well time to know if you're a suspect in your wife's murder. Damn well time to know if you're a treasonous bastard."

Focused on Mannheim's instructions to behave as a professional whatever the circumstance, Chairman Wright maintained a modicum of civility. "With appreciation for the concerns expressed by my Honorable Friend from Florida, we'll continue the witness's testimony."

Faced with the hardest question he would ever ask, his voice broke. "Director Tisdale, does this video identify the person who shot my wife?"

Here was the rub for Wade Tisdale: Mannheim worried over the difference between what Tisdale *absolutely knew* and what he *absolutely believed* based on Wright's security cameras and Mannheim's meeting with Aydan Fetisov. Distinctions which, in this instance, restricted the wiggle room of an honest man. Tisdale sipped tepid water to lubricate dry vocal cords.

"Circumstances surrounding Carol Wright's death are complex and remain fluid this early in the investigation. Ms. Leanne Crowder, a serving officer at Langley, is a Person of Interest. Ms. Crowder, whose whereabouts are unknown, serves in NCS under Mr. Norris..." Tisdale pointed at Norris the Younger "...but apparently has been seconded for most of her service to Mr. Tipton. The Bureau is actively seeking to interview Ms. Crowder."

Chairman Wright stuck to a prosecutor's methods. "To be clear, Director Tisdale, the Crowder woman's presence in my home has been confirmed by my security video?"

Finesse not Wade Tisdale's strongest trait, he'd debated how much to say and how to say it.

"Mr. Chairman, your security video makes it crystal clear...Carol Wright was shot in her bed. Ms. Crowder's identification relied upon forensic detail and interviews with several Persons of Interest. Among those interviewed were senior officials of foreign governments."

"Would Russia be among those governments, Mr. Director?"

"Yes."

"You have video and audio supporting the Bureau's conclusions?"

"Yes."

"Again to be clear, the Counterterrorism Division of the Bureau has verified both audio and video evidence related to Ms. Crowder's presence during the assassination of my wife?"

"Yes."

"When will this Subcommittee get to view the Bureau's evidence?"

Finally a question to which Tisdale could give a definitive response. "The Bureau doesn't release evidence until an investigation is complete. Today's testimony from Mr. Tipton, Mr. Norris and Ms.

Martell may assist in furthering our investigation, so I'll defer a comprehensive answer at this time."

"Thank you, Director Tisdale. The Subcommittee would appreciate you remaining with us until all witnesses have been heard."

Vice Chairman Morgan's request to question Tisdale dismissed, the Chairman moved-on.

"Mr. Norris…what is Ms. Crowder's location, current assignment, and, if Ms. Crowder assassinated Carol Wright, under what operational orders would she have done so?"

Zachary was certain: Jamie would select what he considered the truth, counting on his father's influence at the White House to defuse and deflect attempts at censure.

Voice strong, Jamie Norris kept his testimony simple. "Director Tisdale's earlier testimony was based in part upon my statement to the Bureau. D/CIA Brantley assigned Ms. Crowder to the Office of Special Projects under the direction of Mr. Russell Tipton. At no time did she report to NCS. As Deputy Director of NCS I have no knowledge of her location or current assignment. If Ms. Crowder assassinated Carol Wright, I don't know why or who authorized such a kill-order."

Wright raised his voice to suggest guilt by association. "So you were satisfied to be deaf, dumb and blind while Tipton sent Crowder to kill my wife?"

"Chain of Command, Mr. Chairman…surely your tours of duty in Afghanistan illustrated how it operates. While Brantley was alive, Tipton refused to answer questions regarding the Office of Special Projects. After Brantley passed away, Tipton stonewalled. Absent a new D/CIA, I could not, and still cannot compel Tipton's cooperation. Accuse me of weakness if it eases grief, but you would be wrong. Anyone at Langley whose head wasn't buried in the sand knew Tipton ran an assassination program designed by Brantley. Whether authorized by the White House in writing, or not, I won't learn in this lifetime. You, Mr. Chairman, and this Subcommittee should have known. If you didn't know, how could such a thing have occurred? Phyllis Martell viewed Tipton's operations as acceptable, perhaps admirable. I wouldn't be stunned to learn CIC actively supported Tipton's assassination operations."

"You're accusing this Subcommittee of tacit approval?"

"With no apology, I accused the Subcommittee of mistaking a quacking duck, armed with an automatic weapon, for something more benign."

Wright sat stunned, perplexed and disinterested in following any prepared script. "How should we have seen through Mr. Brantley's veneer?"

"Mr. Brantley's public persona and his professional writings illustrated a conflict which, though ignored during the process of his confirmation, didn't go unnoticed within Western Intelligence Communities. Perhaps the House and Senate Intelligence Committees should have probed more deeply."

Wright challenged Jamie. "Where were you, Mr. Norris? Why didn't you throw yourself in front of Brantley's train?

Zachary felt a mixture of sympathy and righteousness as Jamie's balloon deflated.

"How easy it must be to make me sound deaf, dumb and blind with respect to your wife's murder. How hard is it to imagine the outcry, when Brantley's bona fides as a man of peace were challenged? Politicians from both political aisles elevated Brantley to sainthood."

Wright leaned back to regain equilibrium. Poured a second glass of water. Fought despair, let go of blind anger, took a large breath and tacked away from destructive questions.

"Who is Ms. Martell's Deputy Chief at CIC?"

Norris answered with reluctance, eager to confront the accusations of cowardice made against him. "Mr. David Nazarian…as of close of business yesterday."

Lester Morgan laughed out loud. "Nazarian again…a buffoon. One of Mannheim's acolytes. Played a big part in Brantley's predecessor getting blown to pieces by one of our own drones."

Off-script and staggered, Wright forged ahead. "We'll worry about Mr. Nazarian and Ms. Martell's positions at a subsequent meeting." Without a fresh breath, he dove into Tipton's interrogation seeking one piece of information above all else.

"Mr. Tipton…was Ms. Leanne Crowder, at D/CIA Brantley's verbal direction, assigned to the Office of Special Projects under your direction?"

Russell Tipton knew this day would come: Brantley hadn't disclosed his illness or the arc of the disease. Having lost a leg defending the United States, Tipton would stand erect to defend orders received and his implementation of those orders.

"Yes sir, you are correct."

"What is the primary operational purpose of the Office of Special Projects?"

"To carry-out the orders of the Director of Central Intelligence, whatever they may be in whatever manner required."

"So…you ran a black-ops assassination unit within the Agency?"

"Sir, I refer you to my previous answer."

Wright thought it appropriate to delve into Tipton's professionalism. "You're proud to have served D/CIA Brantley…you believed in the goals Director Brantley set. Is that an accurate statement?"

"Yes, sir, it surely is."

"Was your input sought by Brantley, when distinct operations were debated and planned?"

"Director Brantley had little military experience, or familiarity with CIA methods and practices. He encouraged open discussion about pending operations."

"Was the recent effort by Russian Intelligence to assassinate Ms. Raissa Ribeiro, a US citizen and Agency contractor, supported in the field by the Office of Special Projects?"

Tipton saw no reason not to answer. "Yes, sir."

"Who negotiated this cooperative arrangement?"

"D/CIA Brantley, before his death."

"You supported Brantley's decision and provided manpower and resources as the Op required?"

"Yes, sir."

"Under your authority from Brantley, you re-assigned NCS Field Director Louis Phillips to support an Agency officer working with the Russian assault team. Mr. Phillips was inserted as Police Chief of Ms. Ribeiro's resident municipality to implement his role. Is that correct."

"Yes, sir. Mr. Phillips' performance was exemplary, despite the failure of the joint mission."

"Is the aforementioned Ms. Crowder one of the officers who supported the Russian attempt on Ms. Ribeiro's life?"

"Yes, sir."

"How many NCS field officers were, directly or indirectly, assigned to this joint effort?"

"One in addition to Ms. Crowder."

"Who is that officer?"

"Operational security prevents me revealing an officer's identity while that officer remains in the field."

"What is this officer's current location?"

"Same answer, sir…operational security prevents me answering."

"Mr. Tipton, are you aware the Agency is prohibited from operating in the United States?"

"I believe there are exceptions, sir. Director Brantley informed me this specific operation had been cleared by the White House."

Wright moved on with no recognition of simmering Congressional bombast. "Has CIC provided support to this joint CIA-Russian operation?"

"Yes, sir. Ms. Martell personally provided support to Director Brantley, although the details of that support weren't shared with me by Director Brantley."

"What is Ms. Martell's current location?"

Tipton waffled. "I don't have Ms. Martell's precise location, sir."

"How do you contact Field Officers working this joint CIA-Russian operation?"

"This operation has gone silent, sir, in compliance with mission protocol. No contact. No termination."

"Is Mr. Phillips the Field Director for any element of this joint CIA-Russian operation?"

"Mr. Phillips is currently being detained at Langley."

"Who is the current Field Director?"

"Each Field Officer is acting on their own initiative."

"Is *No contact, No termination* routine Agency policy?"

"Only if authorized by D/CIA." This time it was Tipton who felt sweat bead in his armpits.

Wright wanted Tipton further out on a limb before firing-up the chainsaw. "You supported Russian Intelligence killing Ms. Ribeiro. Why?"

"Director Brantley negotiated an arrangement with the Russians…they would be allowed a single attempt to eliminate Ms. Ribeiro on American soil; CIA, via the Office of Special Projects, would be allowed a similar attempt to eliminate a high-level Russian Intelligence operative on neutral soil."

"Is Mr. Petr Sillin...codename *Choirmaster*, rumored to be the Russian President's *Rasputin* in matters of Intelligence...the high-level Russian Intelligence operative to be eliminated?"

Tipton gagged: How could the Subcommittee know *Reformation's* target? "I can't say, Mr. Chairman."

Nazarian heard Mannheim's voice in his ear. "David, it's time. I'll suggest Emile ask if *Reformation's* objective is located in Norway."

Wright felt the vibration, listened and changed course. "Mr. Tipton, did you order Ms. Crowder to assassinate my wife, Carol Wright?"

Spine straight and rigid, a position Tipton assumed at times of duress, he answered, "No."

"So Ms. Crowder acted alone in the assassination of a Congressman's wife on US soil. How can that be condoned, when Ms. Crowder could have requested your guidance and orders? Where is Ms. Crowder right this minute?"

"Operational security..."

"Stop talking, Mr. Tipton, before you say something you'll regret every day until you're executed for treason. There is no D/CIA...CIA's Deputy Director has never heard of *Reformation*. Your pet project died with Brantley. There is no ongoing Operational Security for *Reformation*. You will answer my questions directly. Is *Reformation* operational in any other country besides Norway?"

Nerves rebounded in scattershot fashion while facial muscles remained constant. The mention of treason caused a wrestling-match with the concept of truth. "No, sir. Just Norway." Tipton's labored breathing, audible through the microphone on the witness table, was a signpost for Congressman Wright.

"Would it be reasonable to assume Crowder, Martell and your mystery agent are in Norway?"

"I couldn't..."

Wright interrupted with a disgusted laugh.

"Do you expect the Subcommittee to believe your management of *Reformation* is based upon orders from a dead man? Or has Russell Tipton soldiered-on without moral or intellectual curiosity? Tell me I've lost my mind...admit you're insane. Tell me something to mitigate this disaster."

Tipton summoned a long-prepared rebuttal. "I'm not insane, Congressman Wright. My orders were legally issued by D/CIA Brantley and remain in effect. Those orders haven't been countermanded by any legal authority...not by DD/CIA, not by POTUS. *Reformation* remains authorized and its Field Officers will complete their mission."

Tipton had been given a clear opportunity to invoke the name *Craig Hall* and refused.

Wright looked around at the Subcommittee; not one Member wished to touch a third-rail capable of electrocuting POTUS, House and Senate Intelligence Committees, the Agency and governments from Washington to Moscow.

Wright wouldn't give members of the Subcommittee this opportunity to go fishing, although fishing would inevitably come later. "Director Tisdale, what would you recommend?"

"I suggest a fifteen-minute break, Mr. Chairman. There are too many issues raised by Mr. Tipton's testimony, including his underlying conduct, which may result in charges being filed, a mental health examination being sought, or both. If you grant a break, Mr. Chairman, I'll consult DOJ colleagues and return a definitive recommendation."

***

Wright's gavel sounded more ominous, when he called the Subcommittee back into session. With the hearing pregnant with competing interests, its members would be anxious to regain the comforts of their offices and staff.

"Director Tisdale, what is the Bureau's recommendation?"

"Mr. Chairman, the Bureau and DOJ require time to consider Mr. Tipton's testimony in greater detail. It's our interim recommendation for CIA to place Mr. Tipton in protective custody. I've informed Mr. Norris verbally, so with the Subcommittee's concurrence, Mr. Tipton can be transported as NCS determines appropriate. Beyond that recommendation, *Reformation* is a matter falling under the purview of CIA. The Bureau will coordinate with and assist the Agency in every way possible."

Having lost a quorum, Wright wouldn't open the hearing to general questions. "Mr. Norris, have you located Ms. Martell?"

"According to her office, Ms. Martell is away from Langley on official business. Her itinerary began at Incirlik AB and includes Copenhagen as well as the Shetland and Faroe Islands. She checked-in from Copenhagen yesterday."

"Mr. Norris, it would seem the ball is in your court. If *Reformation's* intent is as described by Mr. Tipton, we can't allow CIA to become an unwitting iron fist in Russia's internal affairs. The Subcommittee will expect regular briefings and will convene as you require until this bizarre travesty is dealt with."

***

In Greg Riley's conference room, Zachary Mannheim disdained pizza in favor of salad. Antsy to be underway, years of experience made patience no easier to sustain. Examining the faces awaiting Randall's conclusions, Jamie Norris was ill at ease; Grover Norris' legendary temper simmered; David Nazarian was sullen; and Raissa Ribeiro, connected by satellite, listened in unflappable silence.

Grover, present as the White House's unofficial representative, spoke to Mannheim. "How do you know Craig Hall was Brantley's rabbi?"

Loathe to tell Grover the truth, Zachary responded. "Hall had been regularly intimate with Emile Wright's wife for a minimum of six months."

"That makes Hall stupid, not a double-agent. It makes Wright a gutless wimp."

Zachary appreciated Grover's mammoth hypocrisy—a self-proclaimed lothario who never served in harm's way, calling Emile Wright gutless.

"No one said Craig Hall was a double, Grover. He was the go-between…POTUS to Hall to Brantley to Tipton. When Brantley died, Hall shorted the circuits…left Tipton without the first idea how to proceed. Whatever terms had been in effect, Brantley's death erased them. Poor befuddled Tipton marched forward more out of habit than determination. Or in an alternative universe, a resourceful Tipton took the best deal available from SVR. Marta would have known of Brantley's death, would have smelled Tipton's weakness in a microsecond. It's possible field officers on both sides have no clue…after all, we sit here having been co-equal in ignorance."

Ignorance, Grover Norris knew from hard lessons, could and almost always did result in the worst outcome. Turning to his son, he questioned with a mixture of disbelief and disdain.

"You turned Langley upside down...and the best information at-hand hasn't identified Tipton's Agent-in-place? How many candidates are out in the hinterlands?"

Jamie had grown tired of indiscriminate bullshit. "Couple of dozen...it's been bloody hard to whittle it down. Field officers don't live a punch-in, punch-out existence...you don't need to be reminded of that. Coordination of data from Field Directors, Human Resources, Travel and Security doesn't lend itself to speedy results. It's why we agreed to Randall's combination of CIA's data with travel to Scandinavia in general and Norway in particular." Unable to resist poking his father's ego, he added, "You of all people, Grover, should know better...secret operations are drawn-up to stay secret."

As Grover's mouth opened to issue a rebuke, excitement leaked from Randall's voice. "There's not a single Agency officer who isn't where he or she is supposed to be...except Leanne Crowder, who travelled under an alternate identity and arrived in Oslo a few hours ago. Crowder has no arrangements for further travel, which suggests there's a plane on standby and Crowder won't file a flight plan."

Grover cut Randall off. "Spit it out...I don't give a fuck about every spy, just the one we have to kill."

"I expanded the parameters of the search...American citizens under the age of thirty-five, who transited any of the airports established by Mr. Mannheim. Then used other criteria to narrow my list to a single name: Elias Thordsen, whose current location is Trondheim. No record exists of him leaving the United States...first time he shows up is a ferry from the Faroe Islands. On your screens are family details, education background as well as hotel information in Trondheim. His cover is as a soloist in the annual Christmas Choral Concerts sponsored by Nidaros Cathedral. Petr Sillin is a fan of choral music."

Grover dead-panned, "How many laws did you break to bring us this news?"

Randall's face maintained an attitude of indifference.

Grover feigned congeniality. "Where are you located, son?"

Zachary pointed to the screen's lower left corner where a time stamp showed a five-hour difference from Washington.

Randall never hesitated. "Europe…using air-gapped machines untraceable to Langley." His answer was a lie, which never fazed Randall Carter.

Chapter 16

Preoccupied with details from the conference call, need-to-know trumped emotional reinforcement. Entering the passenger's side of Greg Riley's Porsche, Mannheim took note of the new car smell.

"Is your new toy safe, Gregory?"

Greg looked askance. "Absolutely."

"Randall knows were calling him back?"

Greg responded with caution. "What do we need to clear up?"

"My list begins with Elias Thordsen. Are you familiar with Henrik Halvorsen?" Zachary watched Riley's mental search. "Never mind, Greg. Henrik Halvorsen made a pile of money in the late seventies and early eighties...imagine a financial genius with outsized integrity. Not many of those around today. Henrik married Mariah Ackerly...any bells? He'd be seventy-five, so she's mid-fifties."

Riley's face brightened with recollection. "Mariah Ackerly...double-agent. Worked for MI-6 and Langley but got exposed by the Russians. Something about missile guidance radar?" Cautious, he turned to Mannheim for what might be revealed. "Did you know her well?"

"Yes, I knew her but only a bit." With no desire to drag-out history, Zachary added, "Marta knew her very well."

"Reprisal seems a stretch, when it puts your son at risk."

"I agree, Gregory, but betrayal and revenge are the oldest and most unpredictable ingredients among friends turned enemies."

"What will you do?"

"I'd prefer to leave them alone. Henrik isn't in the best of health..." Mannheim sighed "...and Mariah is prickly at best. Nevertheless, it's a thread which must be pulled."

Riley thought better of pulling threads from Mannheim's un-healed marital wounds. "So what's number two?"

In a cocktail of ferocity and melancholy, Mannheim's voice wavered.

"Must we attach our entire supply of credulity to Russell Tipton? Can there, truly, be no other person, in or out of government, with sway over *Reformation*? Suspension of disbelief is inadequate, wouldn't you think Gregory? I'm inclined to look close to home. Grover Norris has a long history with our president. Craig Hall struggles to separate the occupant from the Oval Office. Wright's video, if it should become public, will end Hall's usefulness to POTUS. So who would be more likely than Grover, drinking from a cauldron of jealousy, intelligence and hubris, to foster a grand strike against Russia's Intelligence apparatus?"

Riley raised an eyebrow. "Killing *Choirmaster*...would Petr Sillin's death be that big a deal?"

"What if Petr Sillin and Marta Hinrich both died at the hand of CIA, in Nidaros Cathedral, on television, during a concert of Christmas music?"

"If that's *Reformation's* true remit, I'd say Zachary Mannheim, Randall Carter, Raissa Ribeiro and David Nazarian would also be on *Reformation's* short-list for elimination."

"Just so, Gregory, as long as your name is included with the other four. Where's Randall today?"

"Living and working at Jonathan Chapman's boatyard. Randall needs familiarity to perform at his best."

Gregory stopped the car in the Pentagon's North Parking lot, easily reached from the George Washington Parkway in the direction of Reagan National Airport. A dozen different questions were inherent in what he said next.

"Where else can we put him?"

Mannheim had considered this matter of contention. Randall's brilliance was the lynchpin to any hope for a plan not fully formulated, yet fraught with high risk in every permutation.

"Ask our most flexible and unexpected assets, Gregory. Talk to Jonathan and Lt. Nichols in person...don't go home, nine hours in your new toy should get you to Cape Cod. Explain the options. Explain our concerns. Come up with secure options for all the people on Cape Cod we need to provide for."

"How about David?"

"He'll be with me." Reaching for his phone, Mannheim confirmed the requested video's arrival. "Another thing Gregory...lets you and I watch every frame exported from Congressman Wright's home. We'll look for anomalies, beginning the moment cameras came on-line till the video was terminated."

***

Elias exited *Restaurant Kommandanten* into heavy snow. For better or worse, he was adjusting to Marta's ability to see and hear everything. Kirstin's polluted interest in Elias, more than worthy of suspicion considering Marta's rebuke, saddened him. How could he, or even should he, probe her apparent affection to incinerate doubt. How could he flail against false exposure—any spy's ultimate burden?

On a circuitous route along the outer walls, the earlier shadow transformed into a solitary figure standing in stark relief against a black canon. He wanted to run but couldn't summon control over helpless legs.

The figure addressed him by name. "Elias, it's Phyllis Martel from CIC Langley. We need to talk."

Windblown sleet narrowed Elias's eyes to slits. CIC's Chief wouldn't be alone. His months long mission would end here, incomplete. His response sounded absurd even to Elias.

"What do you want?"

"To help."

She walked towards him, tangled hair blowing every which way despite a fur muff covering her ears. Just out of reach, jitters made her stop.

"Let's get coffee. I can't feel my fingers."

Surrender was easier than anticipated. "Not in the restaurant, Marta's there."

Phyllis fought against suspicion and doubt. "How many with her?"

"I don't know."

"Let's walk, there're lots of places in town." His brain struggled to re-boot.

As they exited the carpark, three figures entered a vehicle; Elias heard the engine come to life. Worse than all his terrors was the reminder of cold-war videos—searchlights targeting escapees at the Berlin Wall. He glanced at their headlights, then back at Martell.

"Your security team?"

"I'm alone." Phyllis's unease enlightened the truth. "Keep walking, we'll see if they're babysitting or delivering a message."

"Who besides SVR?"

"GRU, Russian CI, Langley, Norwegian Intelligence, Trondheim police." Phyllis swiveled her head looking for a sanctuary. "Any of those could be watching you. Every passing hour *Reformation* becomes more exposed."

From a trailing distance of a hundred meters, the car jumped forward until its slap, slap, slap of wiper blades became audible. Martell gave voice to an indisputable truth.

"If they plan to shoot us, it'll happen before the Old Bridge. See the *kafé*? Run as fast as you can."

Standing inside, hands on knees to catch his breath, Elias watched the car slow to a crawl. Poorly lit, he saw two men in the front seats. For an instant, twin spotlights on an oncoming snowplow filled the car with daylight. Disbelief filled his soul: Kirstin was the woman in the rear—they'd meant for him to identify her. Marta's conspicuous message shred his courage.

***

Screw-ups existed to be overcome; Raissa lugged a ski-bag and wore a backpack as she boarded the *SJ3000 Snabbtåg* fast-train to Sundsvall. Scheduled for three and a half hours, a jet awaited her arrival at Sundsvall–Timrå Airport.

***

Croatian, the former military pilot was an outlaw who specialized in transporting criminals and contraband. He'd get her to Trondheim regardless of the weather. His small truck's heater was inoperable.

"Change of plan…avionics in the Lear shit themselves. There's a fast two-seater…a little old but runs like a clock."

Painted white, the Cessna didn't look like much, although Raissa knew its production run spanned four decades.

Jakov anticipated her concern. "She's not the old, grey-haired, lady from the sixties. This baby is the T206H, manufactured in 2012…turbocharged Lycoming TSIO-540-AJ1A pumps out 310 hp. We'll cruise at two-hundred-twenty klicks including thirty to forty from a tailwind. Around two hours to Trondheim." Overmodest smile tossed her way, her pilot admitted, "Probably bouncy, since we'll be close to the trees."

Sundsvall–Timrå's runway 16/34 was crosswind critical as Jakov and Raissa heard Ground Control issue a stern warning. Brakes on full, the Cessna was buffeted by snow blowing sideways. Staring down a strip of pavement six thousand feet long, neither of them could see beyond fifty feet.

Jakov's voice was droll. "You said it was important, kiddo. Still time to call it a day and try tomorrow."

"What's it like in Trondheim?"

"Been snowing hard a couple of hours. This weather is heading for Trondheim. If things go well, we'll get there ahead of the worst."

"If things go bad?"

"It's a big lake…as long as we have enough visibility to clear the trees. So we maintain altitude until the trees disappear. Following the shoreline from over the ice shouldn't be difficult."

"Have you lost your mind? I can think of a dozen ways we wind up in the crapper." Raissa stopped short of aborting their takeoff. Stopped short of informing Jakov she'd become a licensed pilot since they last crossed paths.

Jakov pushed the throttle forward. Seconds later, with the small airplane's nose seeking the sky, they were airborne into a conservative climb. Jakov adjusted the radio to speak with ATC. As the altimeter settled at five hundred feet, he leveled off. Wind turbulence was moderate, and the plane handled well.

Raissa couldn't see the leading edge of high-mounted wings, so assuaged curiosity by asking, "De-icing okay?"

Jakov sought to ameliorate her nerves.

"Shouldn't be worried. System depresses the freezing point of ethylene glycol-based fluid. Works to -60°C. Dispersed on the wing's leading edges, wing strut, plus both horizontal and vertical stabilizers. Slinger-ring protects the propeller. Two on-demand pumps protect the windscreen."

Raissa nodded acceptance. Though she could fly well enough, getting down and dirty with an airplane's technical details hadn't been a priority until now.

"How far?"

"Four hundred fifty klicks, give or take."

"Sorry...I meant from the frozen lake to Trondheim's centrum?"

"Twelve klicks, if we get close to the eastern edge of Jonsvatnet. Vaernes would have been near forty klicks...assuming you got off the airport alive. Walking from Jonsvatnet will be safer by far."

"So five hours all-together to Nidaros Cathedral?"

Jakov failed to respond.

She felt the nose drop and the engine's RPM increase. When again level, Raissa noted the altimeter read three hundred fifty feet. Airspeed settled at two hundred twenty-five km/hr. Having never suffered motion sickness, she reached for her backpack and its thermos of scalding tea.

"Want some," she said, holding up a plastic cup.

"Doesn't smell like coffee. I'll grab mine later, thanks."

A rubber band held a map around the sun visor. Several lines were marked in grease pencil. Raissa checked the plane's navigation system; nothing seemed out of place. "What's wrong with the GPS? Dead reckoning...why rely on old-time voodoo?"

Easy enough to bite her head off, he understood why she asked: *Hope for the best, prepare for the worst.*

"Quick answer...we're flying through a snowstorm in the dark, at low altitude, with all the problems winter brings. You're a woman who doesn't show up in Norway with a ski-bag full of who-knows-what for no reason. So there's opposition out there. You're a woman who prepares because shit happens. I don't plan on dying today, so electronics are good, but my brain doesn't require electricity." He pointed at one of two ten-inch screens. "That's the big lake at Brunflo. Hundred eighty-eight klicks behind us. Two hundred sixty to go. Wind has dropped five knots in the last few minutes. Swung a few degrees towards the north." He put out his hand for a piece of Raissa's chocolate bar. "Jonsvatnet isn't the biggest lake, but it's not small...three klicks long on our intended course and two klicks wide. At a constant speed for a precise period, on a compass course altered only by wind-drift, I've computed several variations based upon the particulars of this storm. If we lose power, or the wind increases, the different colored plots provide guidance relative to what time we descend and the likely location of our landing. Electronics don't anticipate disaster...pilots do."

Jakov pointed at the most northwesterly plot, shown in black. "That's the line I'm flying…matches GPS pretty well. We'll adapt as needed."

"Highly advanced guesswork." Raissa challenged herself to keep a version of their progress in her head. "If you get it right, you'll turn left in a slow descent and hope to put the skis on the ice back into that north-northwest wind…have I got the plan?"

"Roger that, Raissa, if I get it right and visibility is anywhere near a hundred feet, you'll be safe and sound on thick lake ice."

***

Mannheim watched Mariah Ackerly's right hand, held behind her back as she opened the front door. Conflicted, yet as determined to resist as she was, Zachary was unwilling to begin their discussion under a Porte-cochère.

"There's no need for the gun, Mrs. Halvorsen. I'm no threat, however much you remember Marta saying otherwise. I'd be grateful if you put it away."

"I should kill you where you stand."

Zachary's eyes rose from the semi-automatic. "Why on earth would you kill someone who hopes Elias comes home alive? I'm wagering my life…" Mannheim nodded at her weapon "…to ask for help. Why don't you hear me out?"

Mariah stepped backwards and to the side. Ethereal, her emaciated presence hovered between cadaver and malnourished. High heel pumps made her seem fragile, not sexy. Nothing in front of him suggested the champion swimmer of her youth, or the high-flying spy of her early career. He followed into a kitchen more suited to a Michelin 3-star restaurant than a woman who never ate a full meal.

If words were bullets, Zachary would have died at the Ackerly's massive food-prep island. "What help? You're a has been. Kicked out of the Agency without benefit of a see ya later."

Bravado crumbled in bits of fine china as the teapot crashed to the floor.

In contradiction of his size, Mannheim ripped paper towels from their dispenser and knelt to contain the mess. Sensing her horror at an ordinary accident, he spoke without cessation of his efforts.

"Did anyone…even Elias…read-you-in regarding *Reformation*?"
Mariah's silence substituted for a denial.

How to tell this mother—her son was no more than a blunt instrument, intended to survive just long enough to be scapegoated as the American who assassinated Russia's most senior operatives?

"What did Elias tell you? Did Brantley come in person, or was Russell Tipton the messenger?"

"EJ Brantley is…was…a hero. Don't you dare…" Cutoff to avoid a flood of tears, Mannheim needed no further words to grasp the gist.

"Do you have a trash bag? The *Crown Derby* is hopeless, I'm sorry to say." Larger pieces of the teapot set aside, Zachary pronounced the floor and cabinetry neat as a pin.

"Come Mr. Mannheim, we'll try my husband's oldest Scotch." Small talk filled a temporary void before she again turned serious. "Brantley came to the house a year ago." Her hand gesture indicated the date was an approximation. "Told us Elias was an exceptional officer, and an undercover assignment of supreme importance was in the wind. Henrik behaved like a boor…challenged everything Brantley had done at CIA, since being enthroned on the seventh floor. Brantley admitted the dangers…how could he not, given my history. You're aware my so-called crimes were fictional…seventh-floor boys never admit going dark exacts a price. And still…there are days when memories overwhelm me. As for Elias, I cared about details and there weren't any."

Tumbler of Scotch placed on a doily, Mariah spent too long in search of a cigarette. Eyelids rimmed with tears; her fictional account of bygone years resumed.

"Not long-ago Elias materialized, without a text let alone a phone call. Told us less than Brantley. So try me out on the who, what, when and where? Start with the odds of Elias coming home in a box."

Dog with a bone, Mannheim would answer, but not until he learned more about Mariah Ackerly. "*Reformation* is, as Russell Tipton testified to the House Intelligence Subcommittee yesterday, intended to eliminate Petr Sillin, codename *Choirmaster*. Any chance you met Sillin in the bad old days?"

Cut glass raised to wet her lips, Mariah's satisfied expression melted into *if looks could kill.* "At least you're not selling shit and calling it chocolate ice cream. Yes, I had dealings with Sillin."

"So you'd recognize him?"

"God you've got balls. Aren't I the traitorous, broken-down mother of your human sacrifice?"

Pushed to relent, Zachary did so in a seamless shift of emphasis.

"Petr Sillin and Marta Hinrich Mannheim are the *who*...Sillin is the target. Marta is Elias's Field Director. *What* is Sillin's televised demise at the hand of your neophyte son, or his female, well-tested, Agency backup. *When* is either tomorrow or the next day. *Where* is Trondheim, Norway within *Nidaros Cathedral* during their Christmas Concert series. Langley's statistical geniuses give Elias a low-twenties percentage of killing Sillin and a single digit probability of coming home alive."

Zachary allowed a momentary hiatus for her mind to catch-up with heart-pounding emotion. "Because it's the Russians, there'll be alternate slants to the game."

Intense concentration writ plain, Mariah Ackerly tossed back her drink before leaning forward. "Would Zachary fucking Mannheim be the self-proclaimed author of the alternative theory?"

"Cynicism aside, the White House chose me to assess and, if need be, destroy *Reformation.* My wife, Marta, with whom you are well acquainted, is ever deceitful, so motives beyond the doctrinaire seemed prudent to consider. In their early stages of cooperation, Brantley agreed to Marta's terms. Petr Sillin would die in Norway; Raissa Ribeiro would be killed in her home. Brantley may have thought such terms lopsided in his favor."

Mannheim allowed a worried expression to grow into severe concern.

"Marta is more of a win-win kind of girl."

"Raissa the supermodel is CIA?" Mariah's use of the singular proved celebrity could intrude into even a used-up spy's misery. "What did Raissa do to Marta, I wonder?" Three fresh fingers of *Glenfiddich Janet Sheed Roberts Reserve* (1955) down the hatch, she grew antsy. An errant drop of Glenfiddich despoiled a starched white, tuxedo shirt of indeterminate heritage.

Is she dangerously unstable? Do I have any better choice of bait? Musings for another day, Zachary decided.

"Marta and Sillin will both die at the Christmas concerts…that's Brantley's wet dream. Elias and an officer named Leanne Crowder, both of whom will be featured in-the-act on live television, will be arrested or killed. It makes no difference; either way Russian Intelligence wins. Langley will suffer its worst-ever public calamity. You and I…we're going to engineer a contrarian's result."

Mannheim expected anything but Mariah's peculiar, yet calm demeanor. "Give me fifteen minutes to pack a bag and kiss my husband goodbye."

Chapter 17

Jakov's index finger adjusted the touch-screen's GPS range until it read one-hundred kilometers. Within minutes the Cessna's blip would cross the fifty kilometer circle. Raissa watched the clock tick-off eight minutes, felt the nose drop and their airspeed increase. Level at one-hundred-fifty feet, Jakov throttled-back until airspeed fell to one-hundred-eighty kph.

Out the windscreen visibility remained zero. "How high are the trees?" Regretful for sounding skittish, she added, "Ignore my rambling."

"Less than five minutes...we'll start a gradual descent to a hundred feet. Depending on my mood..." In a gesture of comfort his hand patted her shoulder "...and what the GPS suggests, we'll descend to land on the ice."

Every ounce of Raissa's self-control went into the simplest act: Breathe in, breathe out. Maintain a regular rhythm, like waiting to take the shot in a hostile environment. Influenced by a swirling wind, cloud patterns played tricks on her eyes. There's the ground; no that can't be true. Concentrate on the instruments; don't look out the window. Seventy-five feet—yes, there's the trees. I could touch them.

A small explosion on the ground, like a streak of lightning, erupted to be swallowed by winter's darkness. She screamed, "Missile. Get in the trees."

Jakov held the Cessna straight and level. Past training missions reminded him: *Evasive maneuvers against a MANPAD is a fool's game.* Raissa was correct: Terrain was Jakov's sole advantage: Put obstacles between airplane and missile.

Dead reckoning told him Mach 2 at low altitude would produce a missile velocity of seven hundred meters per second. Raissa heard Jakov speak to himself. "At a maximum range of five km, it'll take a hair over seven seconds to reach us." Resolve hardened into a frown he counted, " One one thousand, two one thousand, three one thousand, four one thousand." Pointing the Cessna's nose straight down, Jakov whispered, "Pray."

Out of the clouds, landing lights produced an ill-defined outline of trees and ice. Without time to appreciate a small gap in the forest, she braced for impact.

Jakov attempted to pull up from his dive to go through the exact hole identified moments earlier by Raissa.

Jakov's skill became irrelevant, when half the starboard wing was ripped from the fuselage. Each impact, as they pinwheeled through ever more trees, sent her head and chest hurtling against the seatbelt and shoulder harness.

Had it been seconds, minutes or an hour, when freezing cold made Raissa aware of their predicament? Upside down on the ground was bad. Upside down in a treetop would have been their end. Arms and legs functioned; would they hold her, when the harness released?

In the left-hand seat, Jakov's scalp pumped blood at an alarming rate; there wasn't time to triage the wound.

Missile launch's locale at five klicks from their crash site, whoever held the launcher would waste no time arriving. Torso twisted to reach the ski-bag, she listened for the high-pitched whine of a snowmobile at full throttle. Wedged against her seat, the outside pocket held her FNP-9 semi-automatic, SAT-phone, and a serrated knife.

She cut the seat belt and harness with her right hand while holding the welded end with her left. When asked to take her entire body weight, the left wrist collapsed in agony; she fell in a heap.

Ok, girl, what other body parts don't work?

She lay still to reassert a mind's dominance over its body—thirty seconds well spent when the plane's emergency kit, still secure in its webbing, served as reminder of struggles to come. Anything useful in the ski-bag retained, everything extraneous left behind, Raissa's attempt to exit the wreckage brought fresh challenges: Torn electrical wiring, strewn in a spider-like entanglement, delayed her exit. Gasoline drooled into snow, noxious vapor an inferno awaiting a spark. The door was a contorted ruin; a single hinge pinned the door against the fuselage. Its mournful protest kept time with wind gusts—in perfect harmony with Raissa's emotions.

Standing on one foot after the effort to pivot, her left sock was soaked in crimson. Would it bear weight? Years of surgery and pain, after being burned alive, taught tyrannical lessons about the dismissal of agony for a necessary purpose.

Limp closer to a controlled fall, she retraced the Cessna's torn path of wreckage. The Brügger & Thomet Rifle, an old friend in times of need, eased her nerves. Still carrying its Schmidt & Bender scope and GRS suppressor, the .338 Lapua Magnum rounds would be fine. Raissa would only be forced to calculate cold weather variables, if range became a factor. As far away from the ruined cockpit as practicable, she burrowed between two towering conifers in a foot of fresh snow.

High-pitched engine sounds ceased.

Stillness shouted a warning; the opposition's hunt had begun.

She estimated three-hundred yards as the range where she might identify a flashlight in the scope. Near enough to the lake, where heavily forested woodland thinned-out, cover for two hunters was readily available and an unobstructed target line hopeless for Raissa.

Have I abandoned Jakov to bleed-out?

One thing at a time, girl: Try to stay alive. You need to come up with something unexpected.

Snowfall accelerated; the worst of the storm directly on top of them. Soon nothing would give her position away but a dark knit hat and the all-seeing eye of the scope. Minute by minute she waited, knowing their priority would be clearing the Cessna and its immediate vicinity. Twenty minutes passed in Raissa's head.

In endless darkness and bad weather, with only two hunters, dislodging an experienced agent would give these hunters pause. At even odds she bet with herself; they'll leave Jakov and I to Norway's least merciful killer.

Forty minutes expired, Raissa heard a loud Russian voice.

"I am Tretiak, named after the goaltender of the Soviet Union's most famous ice hockey team. Not one of the team believed you'd risk coming by small plane...but Marta hates you enough to, how you Americans say it, *cover all the bases*. My compatriot is worried you'll kill us and drink our blood...every SVR field agent has been shown photos of Marta's disemboweled daughter. You'll be suspicious about how I tracked you. Did Jakov betray Raissa for money? Let me assure you, he did not. Unfair I agree, but Jakov will suffer the same fate as Beatrice Hinrich Mannheim; Marta's orders prescribe such a fate to anyone who assists Raissa. My compatriot will shoot him now.

Carving-out his guts won't be necessary…the bears or wolves will eat poor Jakov at their leisure."

Echoing through the trees, the aching sound of a single gunshot stressed Raissa's fixed purpose to the point of rupture. She acquiesced to grief for a brooding moment, then waited for the inevitable. An hour passed without movement in her direction—then a second hour. No matter how these Russians were dressed, they were cold, and their level of attention had diminished. Soon enough the *blue light* of Norway's winter will have them on a treadmill to despair.

A cellphone rang near the Cessna's carcass. In Raissa's cocoon of snow, conversation would never have been audible. An engine coughed to life, but the snow machine never moved. At idle, it was a lure, appealing more to pride than intellect. Did they believe I'd call-out in surrender? Shoot at *Julenissen*?

Covetous of Raissa's misstep, Tretiak waited fifteen additional minutes before his machine accelerated onto the ice. No longer the aggressor, retreat placed him in a weakened position.

Raissa ate from her stash of chocolate bars. Insulated from the wind by snow, the mouse was warmer than the prowling cat.

Headlight switched-off, eliminating Raissa's chances for a shot, the snowmobile on the ice returned at high speed. Tretiak's Russian transformed to mocking English.

"Should we come for you, Raissa? Are you badly injured? Do you even realize you're dying?"

Right elbow closer to a shooting position, Tretiak's amateurish effort revealed his weakness. Adrenaline flow slackened, Raissa yielded to a practiced stasis. Another hour passed.

One trick pony, that was Tretiak; Raissa responded when both machines broke cover. Awkward on a numb ankle, betting her life Tretiak and his partner were in retreat, she gained a hundred meters without incoming gunfire. At sixty-five kilometers an hour their machines would cover eleven-hundred meters in one minute. Raissa was fifty meters short of a poor probability of success.

Hand in pocket, a *Rocket Red* distress flare emerged. Designed to propel a parachute-flare three hundred meters high, it would burn for forty seconds. Even in low cloud its glow would be an assist. Flare on its way, limp exacerbated, she ran harder towards the Cessna. Rifle supported on its maimed door, the scope found the trailing snowmobile. Precious seconds expended to adjust the scope, Raissa squeezed the trigger three times as fast as her injured wrist could eject and reload. Twice the machine's headlight spun round.

Raissa hoped it was just the rider who was damaged.

Tretiak's machine out of sight and earshot, he'd abandoned a wounded comrade.

Hands raised in superficial surrender; Tretiak's compatriot understood they had provoked Raissa's careful approach.

Halfway, when Raissa fired a second flare, a last *Rocket Red* was reserved for the pursuit of Tretiak. At a hundred meters, the SVR agent's Makarov was visible. At fifty meters Raissa issued instructions in Russian.

"Throw all your weapons away. Slow, so I can see."

Arced over the snow machine, the Makarov made no sound as it sunk into snow covered ice.

"No other weapon," SVR's woman claimed in pathetic Russian.

Tretiak wouldn't have come without body armor and multiple weapons…and this woman will make trouble if she can. Raissa switched to English. "Show me your wound."

Spies, in Raissa's experience, weren't notorious for over-baked heroism. Spies were deceitful, slick-talking, creatures adept at milking a situation for the smallest advantage. Raissa considered whether this Russian spy was worth the effort of interrogation. Without warning, her rifle shot to the chest hurled the SVR agent backwards onto the ice. Survival without a first-class vest impossible, Raissa stated the obvious.

"Next one will break more than your ribs."

"AK-74 strapped to the sled."

"Show me your wound."

Right leg lifted to expose an ugly calf wound, Raissa felt fortunate to have brought the SVR agent down. What to do next?

"Roll the sled onto its skis."

"Not on one leg."

"I won't spill your guts in the snow, but you'll still be dead. Roll the damn sled." Delay irritated Raissa, who issued a final warning. "Now."

Upright, the sled started when Raissa turned the key. "Toss me your phone." Pocketing the Makarov along with the woman's phone, Raissa asked, "What's your name?"

"Kirstin Hansen...I'm Norwegian, not Russian."

"Doesn't matter...you're SVR." Raissa raised the rifle.

"I'm fucking Elias Thordsen, keeping him focused on Choirmaster. You're CIA...what I've done should matter. Or didn't anyone tell you we're on the same side."

"You came with Tretiak to leave me for the bears. You shot Jakov in the head."

One round shattered Kirstin's knee.

"Have a nice walk Kirstin Hansen, who's keeping Elias focused. He'll be thrilled to hear we met."

Spies weren't in a pleasant business. For the most part spies couldn't assess what was fair, moral or would pass muster with assholes who never missed a son's tuba recital, and never left the mother-ship's asylum in fear for their newest suit of clothes. Raissa had been recruited out of Rio's slums after turning fifteen, because she was beautiful. Recruited for an obvious purpose—she was a killer who killed people. Never did she feel sorry for herself; on rare occasions she appreciated the life lived by Raissa the supermodel.

Born in the favelas where self-reliance was inbred, she checked her phone for a compass heading, then increased the snowmobile's RPM to full throttle.

Chapter 18

Before his latest flight's departure, Mannheim invited Phyllis Martell to breakfast upon arrival.

Halfway across the North Atlantic Ocean, five hours after takeoff, he used the most recent of Randall's secure phones to reach-out to Nasha. His text read: *Throw Craig Hall out of your home. Take the children away to somewhere safe.*

David Nazarian read over Mannheim's shoulder as he typed. Curious as to Zachary's timing, he asked, "Poynter woman really in danger?"

Forced to construct a justification for impulse, Zachary loosed his demons. "She's smart, courageous and instinctual...heir to billions, when Jean-Louis dies. If our efforts go belly-up, long knives will be sharpened and victims will fall by the dozens without apology or vindication. Nasha and her children can't be among them. Mythical and real bodies will be strewn on the Capitol's steps before I let that happen."

Diet soda in a can, crackers whose composition was more air than substance, suit rumpled from professional failure and intentional weight loss, face lined with worry, Mannheim understood how he might appear vulnerable. Intelligence gathering and counterintelligence were galaxies apart in their demands. Spies enjoyed pressure relief valves: Undeclared bolt holes; all too willing bartenders and sexual partners; and governmental forgiveness for sins of omission or commission. Bought with the lives of assets—men and women who risked everything on a spy's promises and charisma—these were ineffective tools to ferret out second-rate traitors, cunning moles, or treasonous bastards.

Mannheim's failure, if *Reformation* blew-up in a public shitstorm, wouldn't soon be forgiven.

Seeking distraction, he queued video files from Emile Wright's home. Sent by Randall, they were the perfect distraction; he could power nap through dull segments.

Nazarian knew spies whose failure rate ran a close second to their glories. He'd spent an often-decorated career as a charm merchant, until Zachary Mannheim illustrated a narrower, but more rewarding path as a spy-hunter.

"Maybe a few hours of real sleep, sir," said David without apparent worry for his former boss and current mentor. Without permission he confiscated Mannheim's phone. On his feet, he asked the co-pilot, "Has Mrs. Ackerly eaten?"

"Yes sir."

"If either of my fellow passengers needs anything, wake me first. I'll give you a hand."

David sucked on a ballpoint pen under the impetus of solving more than one problem. Tapped 'play' to begin where Mannheim left-off. What he saw on Mannheim's phone, or what he thought he'd seen, sent shivers down his spine. A miniature drawing of the *Kremlin, Saint Basil's Cathedral* and *Red Square* erupted from a cheap note pad. David subdued a laugh; would events make the video critical evidence? Or would unexpected outcomes leave them dead?

Two hours prior to landing, Nazarian and Mannheim's phones vibrated with incoming texts.

Martell's message was short: *Breakfast OK. Uncertain whom to trust.*

Raissa's message came out of leftfield: *Weather diversion to Sundssval Sweden. Charter downed by MANPAD near frozen lake Jonsvatnet. Security leak...not charter pilot. 2 opposition w/ snow machines. Norwegian/SVR named Kirstin, honey-trap for Elias Thordsen, wounded and abandoned. Russian named Tretiak out of commission. Currently Kjopmannsgata 1...ankle and wrist injuries.*

Mannheim awake, he sipped from a steaming mug of tea. "Draft responses, David." Surprise and satisfaction in Nazarian's eyes, his mind drifted to Nidaros Cathedral.

Nazarian's text to Martell read: *Easy...trust Mannheim.*

To Randall he'd written: *Assess data for Raissa's flight-plan leak. SVR phone traffic referencing 'Tretiak'?*

His text to Raissa took care not to alienate her: *ETA 1 h 45 m. Injuries from crash or Russians? What does Tretiak believe...is Raissa alive or dead?*

***

Three Toyota Utes appeared through a mix of snow and rain. Armed agents deployed, taking-up positions around the jet aircraft. Einar Haugen, a senior official of the *Etterretningstjenesten* ("NIS") waited as the self-contained stairway descended. When the plane's door opened, he raised his voice over the wind.

"Hell of a thing, standing in freezing rain to protect a retiree who's afraid of his shadow. No Russians waiting to cut off your balls, Zachary. Let's get breakfast. Later we can arrange a proper celebration of an old friend's arrival for the Christmas Concerts."

Nazarian and one of Haugen's NIS agents were dispatched to *Kjoepmannsgata 1*.

Following the lead Toyota, Mannheim and Mariah Ackerly sat in back while Haugen gave directions to the driver.

"Vaernes Garrison, Bjørn…or wherever the food is edible for our guests."

Mannheim hid displeasure beneath a verbal barb. "That would be wherever the US Marine Corp eats, Bjørn, although Bravo Company, 1st Battalion, 2nd Marines, isn't a common topic of conversation here in Norway. NATO mustn't hurt Russian feelings."

"No need to poke me with a stick." Haugen's bland retort held no animus. "I've not said NIS can't help. We are brothers in NATO, but you are a civilian. You'll be less grumpy with food in your stomach. Then we plow through what is the problem, analyze how to fix it and resolve the devils laying in the details."

Mannheim snorted. Turned to face Mariah, he said, "Einar quoted me near verbatim. I taught him everything he knows about spy-hunting." In a serious vein, he introduced Mariah. "Einar Haugen, I've been rude to not formally introduce Mariah Ackerly, former CIA officer and loving wife of Henrik Halvorsen. Mariah's son Elias is a principal player in the Agency's Norwegian drama."

***

Good-natured bonhomie expended, after coffee, fruit and re-heated pancakes with near edible sausage, Haugen leaned his chair backwards.

"Start at the beginning, Zachary."

In thirty minutes Haugen and Ackerly learned more than they needed, or expected, to know about *Reformation*. Fingers steepled in front of his chest, Zachary Mannheim had one topic left to cover.

"We don't know how weapons will be supplied. It's also conceivable Leanne and Elias have been authorized to act independent of one another. Secure the Cathedral's interior, no weapons enter, no weapons leave, that's my request of NIS."

Haugen added a caveat. "Except for weapons already hidden away in the Cathedral's nooks and crannies. In your fanciful dream, Zachary, does NIS sweep the Cathedral before the concerts? If I undertake such a responsibility and fail, Norway takes the blame for the horse manure Einar Haugen stepped in…and Zachary's shoes are pristine."

Mariah Ackerly spoke for the first time. "I want Elias out of Norway before the concerts begin. That's why I'm here. The moment he leaves Trondheim, dead Russians are none of my concern."

Whether Mariah Ackerly noted Mannheim's reaction, Zachary allowed his stare to linger on her, hoping for another tidbit of insight or even a full-on mistake.

Haugen gave her a puzzled look; he was unwilling to suspend disbelief and wanted her to understand his position clearly. "Zachary didn't bring you to play Pollyanna, nor does he believe Elias's mother will succeed in de-programming her son. At a minimum Elias has spent months prepping this mission. What will you say to him, Mrs. Ackerly? What is your role in Zachary's dilemma, if your son refuses to go home? Is your husband planning to have Elias kidnapped? Henrik Halvorsen has money and influence sufficient to make a large splash."

Scanning both his guests, Haugen rolled his eyes.

"What a mess. Among many intransigent problems are the police. NIS doesn't do this sort of thing…Trondheim police carry the responsibility. But my friend Zachary won't ask the police, because he can't admit CIA's collusion with Russia, not when Russia's existential threat to Norway is a national malady. Our *Intelligence Service Act* states NIS shall procure, process and analyze information regarding Norwegian interests viewed in relation to foreign states, organizations or private individuals, and strictly in this context prepare threat analyses and intelligence assessments to safeguard national interests. Nowhere does it say we should disarm tourists from multiple countries during Christmas."

Mannheim's frustration was held in check; if Einar Haugen was looking for a veil to cover naked lies, providing gauzy fabric in a pretty color was a pimp's responsibility.

"Support for Norway's active defense alliances is the first item listed in your authorizing legislation. Wouldn't a joint operation...our Marines together with your Tactical Ops team, all in civilian clothes...meet that test? Then there's your mandate to procure information concerning proliferation of WMDs and the equipment and materials needed to produce such weapons. If an enquiry was convened in some distasteful aftermath, we can make the case rogue elements of CIA and SVR, plotting together, were primary risks for WMD proliferation."

"Do you possess authority to direct the Marine Battalion Commander?"

"Bet your ass I do." Zachary wore his poker face without flinching, but Haugen needed more reassurance. "What's worse, Einar? Two senior Russians assassinated in Trondheim...who knows how many civilian deaths...gory photos flooding Facebook, Twitter and Instagram...or an embarrassing kerfuffle where all parties walk away healthy? You don't have a good option...take the one where NIS and CIA get egg on their shirts but aren't seen as incompetent fools."

***

When Bjørn and a second NIS officer dropped Mannheim at Raissa's address, they heard a rehash of Einar's orders. "Mrs. Ackerly isn't to be out of your sight, gentlemen. Never out of her hotel room."

On an objective scale, *Nidaros Pilegrimsgård* rated somewhere between hostel and just-the-basics hotel—not the sort of place Raissa the Supermodel was accustomed to overnight. Greeted by NIS guardians designated to monitor the front and rear entrances, Mannheim found a skateboarder's brace around her wrist and a compression bandage on a bare ankle. Antsy about something, she would have anticipated Zachary's first question.

"I was fortunate to live through the crash."

Zachary compiled a mental list of nits to pick as he listened to a detailed report. When she finished, his inquisition began. "Who shot Jakov?"

"I didn't see, but I'd guess Kirstin. Does it matter?"

Mannheim wouldn't try to alter impressions formed during a life-or-death struggle. But, he thought, it might matter a great deal. Either way he wouldn't prejudice her explanation.

"The woman...she wasn't in your league?" His mind wandered in search for the right words. "This Kirstin...she fired the MANPAD and shot Jakov. Bit unusual for a macho Russian to sublet the kill-shot. Was Tretiak no more than Marta's odd-man-out?"

"Second string, I'd say. Admitted as much at one point. Poor tactician who never expended enough effort to roust me from cover. He did know when to cut his losses...give him credit for that. If they'd hung around...who knows what would have happened."

Mannheim wanted to sound like his next words were an afterthought. "Tretiak commented on Jakov betraying you. Were his exact words: *Did poor Jakov betray Raissa for money? Let me assure you...he did not?*"

Raissa exhaled and let memories expand. "Yes, that's the exact quote. I thought he accused Jakov of being a double."

"Either way, Tretiak considered him a troublesome loose-end."

"Jakov did everything right on the flight. He didn't sell me out."

Mannheim let Raissa see his doubts dissolve. "Where's Tretiak?"

"Ice-fishing shack, maybe two klicks from shore. Located him easily after finding his snow machine upside down. Broken leg, cuts and bruises...bastard should be well and truly miserable by now."

"But alive, without question?"

"Yes." Raissa's lack of elaboration spoke volumes. "Co-ordinates are on Tretiak's phone, along with his texts and e-mails. Phone was powered-off when I found it. Must have worried about it being recovered by the wrong team."

Pocketing the phone, Mannheim had what he needed. "Not much small talk between the two of you?"

Creeping over an angelic expression, a sardonic smile conveyed satisfaction—at least as far as Raissa's feelings for Tretiak were concerned. "Talk is cheap."

Maintaining eye contact with Raissa, he spoke to Nazarian.

THE LAST CHOIRBOY   177

"David, text Randall…first, I need the name of the Marine Battalion Commander at Vaernes Garrison; second, focus on Clarke Ludlow's digital footprint, and third sweep Swedish social media. Rule out incidental or thoughtless ways SVR could have deduced Raissa's travel plans. I need a result."

"I was clean. No mistakes." Raissa said, defensive at Zachary's implied criticism.

A paternal grin reassured her. "No doubt, my dear Raissa. It could have been the man fueling the Cessna, or a teenage boy unable to believe his good fortune…innocents all, whose moment with a cellphone camera led to what happened. You travelled on Raissa Ribeiro's passport absent disguise…it's one of the downsides of your legend." Mannheim switched gears. "Or Ludlow was sloppy, or miffed at being rebuked for Quebec City, and a loose tongue led to gossip about Raissa flying to Sweden. Let's rule-out these types of things before we turn our world upside down." Changing topics without notice, his tone darkened. "Where have you stashed the Turkish duffle we brought from Antalya?"

Crestfallen, her look pleaded for empathy. "In my ski bag." Reliving the crash, the exact moment when things went wrong played again and again. "No way I could carry it. Took my knife, 9mil, SAT phone and rifle…what I needed to survive. It's still in the Cessna, in the damn ski-bag…unless the crash site has been found. Shit Zachary, I'm sorry."

"Is the crash site visible on satellite or from, say, a helicopter?"

"Zero visibility…more than two hundred meters into big trees. Not obvious unless you've been told it's there…or know the GPS coordinates" Her meaning was obvious: Tretiak would've reported Raissa's crash location to Marta.

Mannheim searched his phone. Found a sightseeing company whose services were straightforward, and a corporate charter service whose web page featured a raven-haired beauty in a strapless dress. "Good morning, I'd like to charter your EC-130 for the afternoon, beginning ASAP. Is that possible?"

In five minutes, he strode towards the magnificent front entrance of Nidaros Cathedral. After a short exchange with Randall, he dialed Lt. Colonel Max Goodman at Vaernes Garrison.

"Colonel, my name is Zachary Mannheim, former Chief of Counter-Intelligence at Langley. I'm in Norway, and Trondheim, on special assignment reporting to National Security Advisor, Mr. Craig Hall. I've chartered a helicopter to interrogate a Russian spy on one of the nearby lakes. Your presence, and that of a medic with full kit, is critical to my task. Can you gather yourselves as-soon-as and meet me at *Trondheim Helipad*?"

Never suggestive of cooperation, the Colonel was dismissive. "Do you have formal Pentagon authorization, Mr. Mannheim?"

"Phone anyone you like, Colonel. Let me assure you, however, a challenge to my purpose or authority won't go down well at the White House. Time is of the essence, Colonel, don't mess me about."

"Five minutes out the door…less than fifteen to the helipad. On my way, sir."

Marines knew how to decide; Mannheim credited this Light Colonel with that much.

***

Zachary Mannheim was not beset by doubt. Self-questioning of his motivation wasn't just fair game, it was an intellectual precondition to an examination of a course of action. Listening to rotor blades make their signature *whumpf, whumpf, whumpf,* recovery of Korsakov's money wasn't a necessity. More like a wild card, keeping it from Marta presented him with options. Keeping the cash for himself never crossed his mind.

Twenty minutes after liftoff the chopper approached the lake's ice.

Goodman, his medic and a fully armed E-3 spoke among themselves without one question addressed to Mannheim.

Fifty feet above the ice, minutes from the Cessna and Jakov's corpse, Mannheim addressed them. "Next stop is the wreck of a CIA charter bringing field agents to a Top-Secret mission in Trondheim. One died after a Russian named Tretiak caused the plane to crash. There's a second Russian agent…a woman…dead somewhere on the ice. If Russians are present, we'll ask them to leave. If they're disagreeable, you'll use lethal force to dissuade them. Our task is to recover the pilot's body and collect proof of a missile strike."

Wind and snow dissipated, landing on the ice was no longer rife with danger. Two marines dispersed, taking position on either flank of the chopper.

Goodman pointed at Mannheim's left leg. "In your condition, climbing in, around, over and under the wreckage, seems like a job for both of us."

The reality of Raissa's estimate—two hundred yards from the ice to the Cessna—left Mannheim discouraged before they began. After a hundred yards, Mannheim leaned on Goodman's shoulder to clamber over fallen limbs and rotted trees. At two hundred yards, they rested.

Goodman inquired with discretion, "Bullet wound?"

"Yes, Colonel, courtesy of SVR days ago."

"Surgery go well?"

"So they said."

"Where else? You're listing to starboard."

"Through and through my ample mid-section."

"Why don't you stay here…let me find the aircraft. I'll bring back a full report."

"A man died in that plane, Colonel. On most days my profession is callous, if not worse. I've promised a colleague to retain any shred of humanity left in these old bones. With your help, for which I'm grateful, we'll continue."

Jakov's body unfit to move, which animals feasted on him remained a stomach-churning mystery. Burial of scattered remains impossible, Mannheim and Goodman stood in solemnity more than a minute after a whispered prayer concluded. History taught Mannheim certain truisms; a spy's peripheral assets suffered more than the main players on the stage. Not for a pittance did these unknowns sacrifice so much—fifty pieces of silver more the province of self-absorbed politicians. Photos of the airframe were taken with as much care as a cellphone camera allowed; a missile strike wouldn't be a challenge to corroborate. Raissa's ski-bag was collected without explanation to a Marine Lt. Colonel.

As the chopper settled at their second stop, no signs of life broke the horizon in any direction—just a windowless, six by eight wooden structure on skids, suitable for towing by snowmobile.

"Colonel, the shack should contain a single Russian with at least a broken leg, one or more AK-74s, one or more Makarov 9mm pistols and one or more MANPADs. Please clear the shack and confirm an inventory. Bring Mr. Tretiak to full consciousness, by whatever means, so I can speak with him. I need specific information and there's a tiny window to obtain it."

Goodman wore suspicion like a cilice. "From whom did you obtain the Russian's status and an inventory of his weapons?"

"Basic deduction, Colonel," Mannheim lied.

Dissatisfaction evident, Goodman nodded at the Lance Corporal and turned towards the shack's entrance.

Wearing a field agent's mantle was unappealing on many levels—getting shot was the least of them. What passed for a door creaked on rusted hinges, when the Lance Corporal kicked it with his boot. Less than a minute later, Mannheim was summoned to witness Tretiak curled in the fetal position, lumped in a corner next to a cold pot-belly stove. Two rusted folding chairs stowed against the opposite wall, Mannheim lowered himself, prepared to wait a short time before drastic steps were taken. When the medic stepped away, Mannheim slid to Tretiak's side. Holding the man's fraudulent credentials, he offered a critique.

"Too much throttle, Tretiak. Sensitive creature the 800cc Arctic Cat. Your leg's broken badly...you're aware of that much, hmmm? Speak up, so I'll understand."

"Too fast," he lowered his voice to avoid further embarrassment. "Raissa the she-devil chased me."

Mannheim decided this Russian could be treated as aware and functional. "You're not a field agent, why were you sent to intercept the aircraft?"

"Marta said my projections were crap...flying through snow was the last thing a spoiled American would do. Told me...go to the lake and prove what my algorithm predicted. Told me to take the missile and the Norwegian slut...shoot the plane out of the sky. Marta's muscle-bound sociopaths laughed at me."

"*Muscle bound sociopaths* sound like regular Russian army. Why not her SVR Special Ops team?"

Mannheim puzzled over possibilities: Would Marta consider it more expedient to lose regular army teenagers, if events turned against her?

"The army boys will pose as tourists at the concerts. Drinking and sex is what they think about. Only four SVR agents...true professionals like myself...came with us to Trondheim."

"Your analysis was correct about flying in a snowstorm. Proves how valuable you are, Comrade Tretiak."

If the Russian cyber-specialist noticed Mannheim's use of his name, he failed to react. "My analyses are always correct, unlike pathetic Americans."

"Aren't all you hackers fans of each other?"

"Tretiak is not a hacker. SVR has elevated cyber-skills to high art. Hackers have no purpose, no plan." Tretiak shifted in search of a more comfortable position; his face was colored chalk-white under a fresh onslaught of pain.

Accidental pain, the unexpected variety, most often loosened tongues. Artful examination of a captive agent, when turning that person, involved a proportional yet unscientific mix of pain and fear.

"You're a scientist, not some game-playing fool?"

"Yes, I am a scientist."

"As a scientist, your laptop is critical. What have you done with your laptop?"

Pride was thick in Tretiak's bravado. "Destroyed. Nothing can be recovered."

"Doesn't a rigorous scientist send data to the cloud…and keep its encrypted address on his phone. Did you destroy your phone, Comrade Tretiak?"

Cognizant of error, SVR's cyber specialist fell silent.

When he spoke to the Medic, Mannheim managed to sound hesitant, if not sympathetic. "Is it critical to amputate the leg here on the ice?"

"No. No. No. Please, God. No." Each protest grew louder as Tretiak absorbed the reality of an untenable position.

"Colonel, would you and your team wait outside, please? Tretiak won't want his tears to be seen. Nor will he key his phone's password for anyone other than me."

Goodman wasn't happy. About to lodge a protest, he assayed the look on Mannheim's face and complied.

Mannheim returned to the distasteful job at hand. "Comrade Tretiak, I won't amputate your leg, not this minute. But I'll remove the leg before you die from blood loss, hypothermia or a combination of the two. Or I could tell Marta how you cooperated…Marta is kind and understanding. A thorough explanation of how you were coerced will satisfy her."

Mannheim paused almost too long before issuing a one-time demand.

"Dictate the password to me. I'll enter it and we'll see where a careful scientist has secured his operational files."

Panic overwhelmed logic, a sad event for a scientist. "Amputate my leg. Kill me…do it quickly."

Breaking into a wide grin, the table was set for Tretiak's recruitment. "Perhaps you're unaware, Tretiak. I'm Zachary Mannheim, Marta's husband." Pausing for effect, he studied a young Russian whose face had turned to jelly.

Raissa was correct; Marta pumped her team full of hatred for Zachary the Barbarian, who defiles his victims. Without time for a patient approach, Zachary's thigh throbbed where Marta's toe probed his fresh bullet wound.

"Watch me, Tretiak."

Exposed bone poked through Tretiak's pants. Mannheim's boot loomed six inches above Tretiak's *Tibia shaft fracture.*

"I bet you've heard Marta rail about the bastard she married. She told you…I eviscerated my own daughter. What could I do to a computer scientist…a genius named Tretiak with his whole life to live? What if I amputate your fingers and thumbs? Are you skilled in the use of voice actuated keyboards, Comrade Tretiak?"

Smarmy smile fixed in place; Mannheim placed a stack of €100s next to Tretiak's right hand.

"Or you can receive hospital treatment provided by the United States Marines and keep half a million for recuperation, perhaps in Florida working in a high-tech laboratory. Which shall it be?" Within minutes of promising every promise Tretiak could dream-up and having received and tested the Russian's data-access code in return, Mannheim exited the shack.

A text to Randall was quickly tapped: *Link to Russian data trove attached. Rent self-storage unit nearest Clarion.*

With his phone set to record, he called to Goodman. "Colonel, could I have a word?"

No longer thrilled to be a spook's errand boy, Goodman approached Mannheim out of earshot. "We'll take this fellow with us. Can you keep him out of sight?"

"No hospital?"

"Not until I finish what he started." Mannheim saw Randall's return text and offered the Cyber-gods thanks for Randall's talents.

"You're not providing much incentive for continued cooperation. What's going on?"

"Colonel, my request to hold this man incognito was a courtesy. Right this minute, you haven't sufficient clearance to be read in. Clearance is what you crave to sort out a situation which repels and attracts you at the same time. Be careful what you wish for, Colonel…sooner than you know your status will change. With that in mind, let's get Tretiak loaded."

Returned to the helipad without incident, Tretiak and his gear were catalogued and secured in a JTLV. Mannheim's text to Nazarian was self-explanatory: *Self storage "OK Minilager," Trondheim-Lade, Haakon VIIs gate 23." Meet Marines in 30.*

Phone passed to Goodman; Mannheim became collegial. "Colonel, have your Marines deliver those munitions to David Nazarian at the address shown. They should ask to see Nazarian's passport as surety."

Mannheim slumped a little, vulnerabilities close to the surface. "I'm grateful for your assistance, Colonel." Turned to two marines, Mannheim offered appreciation. "We're done for today. You marines will transport the Russian hardware, then take Tretiak to Vaernes Garrison. Make him as comfortable as practicable. No questions, no gossip, no stories to your buddies. We've done a miserable, stressful job, one I couldn't have accomplished without you. Thank you for your professionalism."

While he drove, Goodman spoke with noticeable reticence. "If I might say, sir, and with not an ounce of satisfaction, you sound like a man settling his affairs."

"What you saw at the crash site, Colonel, never ceases to sadden me. You've seen war up close without too often questioning your commanders' motives. Spy-hunters tire of sifting through the detritus of humanity in search of betrayal. In this case, sad to say, Judas Iscariot has a surfeit of modern-day disciples."

***

Parked close by the Cathedral, Mannheim's choices winnowed to nil. Craig Hall would prove himself rational—or a national disgrace—in the next minutes of a precarious day.

"All right, Colonel, we've crossed an unspoken line between the USMC and the National Intelligence apparatus. It's my intention, with your cooperation, to commandeer an adequate number of marines to provide security, in tandem with NIS, at the Christmas Choral Concerts at Nidaros Cathedral. Your Marines would be dressed in civilian clothes with one job: Enforce a strict ban on weapons…confiscation mandatory from Norwegian citizens as well as foreign tourists. Commandeered firearms from Norwegian civilians will be turned over to NIS at the end of the concert. You'll need reassurance…I agree you should have it. So let's start with my version of a commanding officer and see how we go."

Inside Mannheim's wallet, next to his driver's license, was the business card without a name or address. Dialing the embossed number, he expected a phone-mail message.

Craig Hall's voice suppressed disbelief. "Zachary, been looking for you. Where the hell are you?"

"Working on your behalf, Mr. Hall. How's your health?"

"Can't believe it, but I feel pretty damned good thanks to your network of miracle workers. I'm in the office…what's the news?"

Taken aback by Hall's upbeat voice, Mannheim checked his phone's clock.

A text from Randall marked *VIP Concert Guests* contained the original Cyrillic list and a translation. One name stood out.

Hall wouldn't use the word *Reformation*, so Zachary issued an ultimatum. "We've arrived at the moment we spoke about. Time to thank POTUS, excuse yourself from the White House and never return, if throwing ourselves into the abyss is unappealing."

Sober and zealous, Hall was succinct. "Time's passage has simplified my position…what do you need?"

"I'm with Lt. Col. Max Goodman, USMC, Commander of a Marine battalion in Trondheim, Norway. I've asked more of him than any sane officer should provide absent higher command approval. Can you arrange the appropriate order from USMC HQ, on my phone, ASAP? My task hangs by a gossamer thread."

Hall responded without equivocation. "Keep your line open."

Fixing Goodman with a hard-edged stare, Mannheim said, "We'll wait, Colonel, and see what transpires."

In the tumult of his mind, Mannheim marveled at Hall's daredevil audacity: Sex with a congressman's wife; shot in the chest, decides against a world-class hospital; back on the job, when most politicians would be jetting-off to lick their wounds. Spy-hunters were cynics, so giving Craig Hall his due was followed, without hesitation, by suspicions: What trade has been made; what lives bargained away on the cheap; is the light at the end of the tunnel a MANPAD launch?

One question was beyond palatable, though denial proved impossible: Was Hall lying to POTUS, or was it the other way round?

Less than a minute ticked away before Hall spoke again. "Zachary, is Col. Goodman on speaker?"

"Yes."

A new voice joined the call. "Col. Goodman, this is Jack Givens, Assistant Commandant of the Corps. You got a grip on what this civilian needs from you and your Marines?"

"Yes, sir."

"Then your orders are simple...do the job. Show appropriate initiative. You got that, Colonel?"

"Roger that, General."

***

Phyllis's icy voice uttered a meager, "Hello."

"Phyllis, you've waited patiently and I'm unable to offer an excuse. You are Chief of CIC. I represent no challenge to your authority over counterintelligence operations. *Reformation*, however, is a different beast. We have little time to sort out our views on how to proceed. Mariah Ackerly, Elias's mother, is with me. If you, Elias, Mariah, David and I can't agree on a course of action, Langley and the FBI will move to prevent an act of aggression against Russia by Agency personnel. Speak with Elias...let's meet on your turf on your schedule."

Noncommittal though Phyllis had been, he felt confident there'd be one opportunity to tow Elias back from the cliff's edge.

A text to Randall Carter read: *Evaluate data belonging to SVR cyber-agent. Tweek data to partially corrupt and make useless. Download corrupted files to Nazarian's laptop. Determine whether you can, with lives on the line, and with a high probability of success, assume this agent's on-line identity.*

Chapter 19

Held close since his dinner at the White House, misgivings gave way to outright accusations. Too tightly scripted. Too detached. Too easy. Too cute by half. In a hall of mirrors where every image is distorted, Zachary Mannheim's inner cynic screamed curses into the Norwegian darkness.

All wrong—all of it—was what he decided.

Zachary saw empty sockets where Jakov's eyes once burned bright. Listened to Raissa's warnings from not so very long ago. Start over, he told himself or walk away. Can a spy-hunter walk away? How about a used-up spy-hunter who'd soon be tossed into a shallow grave, without so much as a fare-thee-well? He looked sideways at Goodman, trying to decide how the blow might be softened. It was the Colonel's expected reaction—and his own cynical expectations—which made Mannheim queasy.

"What would you think, Colonel Goodman, if you discovered my assignment is being undercut by Mr. Hall?"

Two men, with not so different aspirations and convictions, stared at and through each other.

"I'm a Lieutenant Colonel in the Corps. General Givens has issued my orders. I'll follow those orders. Whatever obstacles you face, Mr. Mannheim, are above my pay grade. Marines obey orders. When, or if, General Givens or a higher authority rescinds or modifies my orders, I'll comply with those updated orders."

Mannheim wouldn't cling to broken limbs and parsing the Colonel's response was pointless; both men understood Goodman's assistance was ephemeral, hanging on Goodman's definition of *appropriate initiative* and/or *higher authority*.

More from habit than conviction, Mannheim abandoned the metaphysical and returned to practicality. "Two things, Colonel. We're attending a meeting where the dialogue may strike you as duplicitous, treasonous or plain weird. Calibrate your bullshit meter. Don't answer questions unless they originate with me. I'd appreciate a full debrief, upon our departure."

Mannheim watched impending events wash over a professional soldier. Decided he couldn't afford to give the benefit of doubt or underestimate the allure of conspiratorial insurrection.

"Our ice-fishing friend disclosed the Internet address of SVR's Op Plan. Langley will send a decrypted copy of that data here to Trondheim. I'll transfer a data-stick to you for safekeeping."

***

Trondheim Kunstmuseum hosted temporary exhibitions of international and regional art in addition to Norway's third largest public art collection. Of the Kunstmuseum's two locations, Mannheim assumed Martell selected *Bispegata 7 b* because of its proximity to Nidaros Cathedral.

He pushed through the entrance door as his phone vibrated. A glance at the Washington Post's headline told him the rules of the game had changed: *Aydan Fetisov, Senior Counselor at the Embassy of the Russian Federation in Washington has been found dead of a heart attack.* One foot heavier than the other he climbed at a turtle's pace towards the second floor.

Brain spinning at maximum RPM, he stopped to examine a corner of the Cathedral visible out a window. Being powerless bred desperation; the situation in Trondheim was slipping away. With little appetite for wholesale carnage, should he summon a pay-as-you-go killer? Mannheim hated himself for these thoughts, but they persisted despite very visible stop signs.

A text to Raissa copied to Randall read: *Get out of Trondheim now-USMC taxi to airport imminent. Trondheim-Oslo-JFK Air France. Make a splash…hide in Raissa's skin. Radio silence.*

"Colonel, there's been a troubling development in DC." Mannheim showed Goodman the news about Fetisov. "Fetisov was a competent diplomat, whose death complicates my efforts to stymie Marta. He and I worked to calm the waters between our countries. He'll be missed." Mannheim disliked being in anyone's debt, but Raissa's injured ankle put her at risk. "Because the timing of Fetisov's death is transparent, could your Marines deliver the woman waiting at

Nidaros Pilegrimsgård, Kjøpmannsgata 1 to the airport…and protect her until she boards the flight to Oslo. Avoid confrontation, but no one gets close to her."

"How will they know which woman?"

"Trust me, Colonel…young Marines will recognize this particular woman."

Goodman dialed his phone.

Mannheim settled himself before entering the meeting room. Stale air and harsh light greeted Goodman and Mannheim when they entered a room furnished with a cheap, plastic table surrounded by a hodgepodge of mismatched chairs.

Phyllis Martell, sitting erect as a headmistress, occupied one end of the well-used table.

Defiant in posture and expression, Elias fidgeted near rebellion, sandwiched between his mother and Russell Tipton.

A petite, young woman—Zachary assumed this was Leanne Crowder—sat opposite Phyllis, wearing the face of a zealot imitating an anarchist.

Devoid of enthusiasm, David Nazarian pointed at three empty chairs. Informed by the seating arrangement and body language, Mannheim's strategy was reduced to stirring a boiling pot. His monologue was aimed at Elias, at the price of confounding Goodman.

"Elias Thordsen…I'm Zachary Mannheim, Marta's husband. I imagine you're feeling a bit out of control so close to your first live attempt at assassination. Regardless of the bullshit Tipton's been shoveling in your direction, *Reformation* is illegal. There'll be no parade. You won't have saved the Republic. More important, Elias, your treason and life will end in the Cathedral. To die…is what you were brought here to do, whether Petr Sillin, codename *Choirmaster,* is killed or not. One old woman, assisted by old men on both sides, intend to manipulate the balance of power in both countries. Whomever you've allowed yourself to become, whatever men who promise anything when promising is easy, promised you…none of it is true."

Phyllis tried to butt-in. "Sit down, Phyllis and, please, shut up until I'm finished." Turning back to Elias, he continued.

"Leanne will shoot you herself, if SVR's thugs don't finish you. There's a nasty rumor she killed a congressman's wife…in the woman's own bedroom. In the process of running from law enforcement, our innocent Leanne acquired a fresh bullet hole in her chest. She'll show you, if you ask nicely. How about your mom? Will she let you become CIA's second family victim? Mariah is a professional victim, so don't assume your best interests are in her heart. Think for yourself. Run away, live to fight another day."

Nazarian stared at Leanne Crowder with wary eyes. Everything he'd seen of her fieldwork, if you called murder-for-hire fieldwork, told him this woman was unstable. Moments after Mannheim began speaking, both her hands eased onto her lap. Whether provocation or the real thing, he wasn't prepared to wait and see. He motioned with his Glock: *Put your hands on the table.* A small handgun appeared, her finger in the trigger guard.

Without raising his voice, David demanded, "Slide it to me, butt first."

Mannheim never removed his eyes from Elias.

"By the way Elias…has Marta, or your mother, informed you of Kirstin's death? Marta thought you'd be susceptible, if the right girl happened your way. Marta arranged Kirstin's death, Elias, because Marta didn't think of Kirstin as a real person. Doesn't think of you as a flesh and blood man. You are a tool of her ambition. You are a tool of Tipton's bargain with Satan."

Head rotated away from Elias towards Tipton and Martell; Mannheim's opinions slashed through air like a Samurai's Katana.

"You've been consistently lied to, Phyllis. When a spy-hunter can't see an egregious lie, she's in the wrong job. Mr. Tipton, it's a bad end you've made for yourself. How will you avoid the fate of Aydan Fetisov, whose fatal heart attack this morning exposed Marta's intent to leave no witnesses to tell their tales. With that, ladies and gentlemen, give my best to Marta…and to Minister of Foreign Affairs Taras Sluchevsky and his lovely wife Oksana. Quite the coincidence, don't you think…Sluchevsky attending the Nidaros concerts this year of all years. Marta always believed she'd make a good and proper Minister of Foreign Affairs."

Wearing a broad smile of indeterminate essence, Mannheim exited.

***

Goodman's silence broke as their vehicle entered the gates at *Vaernes Garrison*. "Was I a witness? Someone to testify to what you said, if it comes to that?"

"Not at all, Colonel. It's my hope the theater you witnessed will prompt a mistake by one of our own…any mistake by my wife is unlikely. One or more mistakes by others could benefit the country we both serve. Your presence, if you continue under current orders, will assure a neutral party's testimony describing what I *did not say or do* at today's meeting."

"Wouldn't Mr. Nazarian serve that purpose?"

"David works for Ms. Martell. If her misguided behavior leads to the assassination of two high-ranking Russians, David will at best lose his job and at worst lose his life. Either way, he'll not serve as a character witness for me."

"Tipton sure seemed shocked, when you mentioned Sluchevsky…why?"

"Information sways battlefield outcomes…be it a Marine's style of warfare or mine. Tipton is an ideologue who, along with the former head of CIA, bought into a trade…a Congressman and an undercover Agency operative in return for an impediment to Marta's career advancement. Dead or discredited, in either case, makes no difference. That's a simplification, but as the battle nears its climax one sees the metaphorical living and dead more clearly."

"Is Sluchevsky metaphorically living or dead?"

"Neither. He's the ace up my wife's sleeve."

"Jesus Q, Mr. Mannheim…how do you know all this?"

"I wouldn't have known without your assistance, Colonel. Tretiak, you see, is SVR's cyber-specialist. He exchanged data stored outside Russia or the USA for a change of address to a laboratory in Orlando. Analysis of Tretiak's data yielded a trove of real-world Intelligence: Marta's goal is to see Sluchevsky dead in addition to Petr Sillin, her leading rival within the Kremlin. Leanne Crowder is here to kill Sluchevsky; she's amoral, ruthless and has killed high profile targets before. Elias is here to kill Sillin. Tipton agreed with his Russian counterpart, the now departed Aydan Fetisov: Elias will be proven the assassin. CIA will be left holding a large bag of dripping feces. In Marta's perfect world, voila…my wife slips into Sluchevsky's chair while chaos descends on CIA, the American Intelligence Community, and possibly our entire government."

"I need a scorecard."

"No, Colonel. It's a question of whether Marta's true goals correspond to my informed guesses. It's a question of how we react to her planned actions. It's a question of whom you decide to believe. I confess believing no one is my personal preference."

"When is all this happening?"

"Tomorrow evening. Sluchevsky and his wife are visiting the Christmas Concerts as private citizens…one performance and they'll be gone back to Moscow."

"What will you do?" Goodman wondered whether Mannheim would invent an answer.

"Not a clue at this moment."

"Why not have the Concerts cancelled?"

"Can you hear it now, Colonel. *Mr. Prime Minister…there's an American lunatic saying multiple assassinations will occur if we don't cancel tomorrow's concert.*" Zachary laughed as an alternate to weeping.

"Why not call-in a bomb threat?"

What's the human equivalent of a bomb threat? Zachary sorted a short list of candidates who preferred darkness to light, fetid to sweet, and cash to all other things.

"Excuse me, Colonel, while I make a short phone call."

Before he settled on a number in Croatia, Zachary tallied the time available versus the job's requirements.

"Guten Tag, Gräfin."

Dead air lingered while a woman of a certain age, most certainly not German and decidedly not a Countess, tallied the reckoning. "Fünfmal den letzten betrag."

"Plus ein Charterjet nach Trondheim, Norwegen, ASAP."

"OK. Ich werde text bei der ankunft."

***

Raissa's replacement ski-bag held nothing more than her knife, FNP-9, SAT phone, rifle and loathsome clothes purchased for her by Nazarian. When Marines arrived one rifleman exited, weapon at the ready, while another sheltered Raissa as she crossed an icy sidewalk. Without a word exchanged, the JTLV pulled away from the curb in the direction of Trondheim Airport.

"Change in plan, guys..." Raissa insisted "...can't fly commercial, so I need an hour or so for my plane to arrive. Where's best to wait?"

Lance Corporal Martinez, trying not to sound like a robot, answered. "Colonel's orders, ma'am. Got to check-in with Col. Goodman to deviate."

Stern gaze directed at the marine seated next to her, she offered an explanation they'd all understand. "Marine, open the bag. Tell the Lance Criminal in the driver's seat what you see."

Shrill whistle of approval abated; PFC Winship complied. "Custom sniper rifle with scope and suppressor. Some kind of cool shit."

Raissa asked, "Think they'll let me put the weapon above my airline seat?" Hearing no response she said, "I'm OFP, guys. Don't call your half-bird...I cannot, repeat cannot get caught in a cluster-fuck."

From the front seat came, "You're the boss, ma'am."

Two hours later Raissa's Gulfstream broke through cloud cover into endless Norwegian darkness. Her contradiction of Mannheim's edict mattered little. Having traded a public presence in Oslo for sleep and security while flying, her tactical instinct prevailed. Zachary wanted me out of Norway with an airtight, full-on celebrity presence over at least the next thirty-six hours—it was his prerogative to issue the directive—looking like something the cat-dragged-in wouldn't serve his or my purpose.

She tried to walk on a torn-up ankle: Heels of any height were out of the question. Seat reclined after a series of texts, answers to a multitude of questions were hours in a future where Randall Carter and Clark Ludlow were awake and on the job. She perused recent texts among Mannheim's support group, which led to minute examination of video from Emile Wright's home.

***

Mannheim stood away from prying eyes, in the South Choir Doorway of Nidaros Cathedral, awaiting the arrival of Einar Haugen.

With a view into the Romanesque transept blocked, he adjusted position to cover both the doorway and transept with his handgun. Neither a field agent nor a marksman, he fidgeted, fractious nerves countered by assessing the Cathedral for an assassin's nest. A combination of medieval architectural styles illustrated the genius behind a simple 11th century basilica's transformation into a 12th century Grand Pilgrimage Cathedral. Early gothic carved corbels, the 13th century Nave and Choir and an impressive wall of sculpture-filled niches adorned the West Front with its twin towers and central Rose Window. A shooter would benefit from multiple advantages and face an equal set of challenges: Wondrous acoustics would enhance the grand organ and conceal a suppressed gunshot. Dozens of choir voices, in perfect harmony, would deflect screams of fear and agony. A skilled shooter would like his/her chances: Good news for Leanne Crowder or any of Marta's sniper-trained agents. Worse, from Mannheim's perspective, the Tower stairs allowed access to an excellent field of fire over the Cathedral's contiguous neighborhoods.

Hearing the door open behind him, he filed negative thoughts in a mental wastebasket and turned towards Haugen, hand extended.

Einar Haugen disliked Mannheim's text but was ready to admit intercepted communications from Göran Berglund to Marta Hinrich Mannheim were unfortunate.

"I appreciate your willingness to consider alternatives, Zachary. Under current circumstances you must be feeling strong pressure to solve problems with a dose of old-fashioned American muscle." Haugen's busy smile struggled for sincerity, hidden as it was behind disingenuous solidarity.

Patience shrunken with ticking of the clock, Mannheim demanded, "How long has Berglund been under your nose?"

Haugen went for the jugular. "You should've told me, Zachary. You knew Grover Norris was here, in the flesh, asking the Prime Minister for my head."

If Grover intends to marginalize me, Zachary thought, taking away NIS and Einar Haugen's tenuous cooperation seemed a perfect start. "Stop and think, Einar. ...if I wanted to ride roughshod over NIS, would Grover Norris be the best way? If Grover's in Norway, there are bigger fish to fry than a Russian stringer in charge of a Cathedral choir. Göran Berglund, if his wildest dream comes true, will be seen on television, grace and decorum maintained, baton conducting his choir in the face of egregious tragedy." Inundated with conflicting thoughts, Mannheim began to triage Einar's wounds. "Is Grover in Trondheim, or still in Oslo?"

"From what I hear, he'll be landing later tonight."

"Let's concentrate on breaking Berglund. It's what we came for."

Low ceilinged entrance abandoned for the Cathedral's magnificent interior; their footfall reverberated in still air. To Mannheim it felt like an empty, dreaded edifice.

Göran Berglund turned from the Monarke organ as a last thundering note was swallowed by ancient stone, stained glass and gold altar adornments.

Mannheim and Haugen marched in lockstep past the solid silver statue of Jesus crucified, and between massive stone columns which, in a trick of perspective, appeared to lean towards them to identify their purpose.

Berglund radiated no outward signs of distress.

Haugen's remit left little wiggle-room: How much to threaten versus pander was an enduring issue, when dealing with a man without loyalty. Leverage favored Berglund until whatever would happen tomorrow happened.

"You've been found out, Göran. In bed with SVR isn't a good look for you. Would you care to see transcripts of your conversations and e-mails with Marta?"

Swagger, a knee-jerk reaction for the artistically inclined, worked for an indeterminate length of time. Berglund needed hours, not days, weeks or months.

"I am a patriot, Einar, quite different from you. Sleeping with the Russian Bear is required to keep our American friends up to date on Marta's plans." Berglund wore the smarmiest of grins, failing to appear wounded by Haugen's accusations. "Do you know Grover Norris, Einar? More important than our Prime Minister, he's a wealthy investment banker with the ear of the American President. Göran Berglund, not Einar Haugen, is Grover Norris' eyes and ears. I'm the one who fought to award a soloist position to Elias Thordsen. Took slings and arrows for my fortitude, I did. The boy is a beginner, though under my tutelage he's shown promise. So no, I'm not SVR's rent-boy. Nor, for that matter, am I a stooge for NIS." Berglund snorted. "Norwegian Intelligence Service…more like minor bureaucrats who wouldn't contaminate their horrible suits with the dirty work of real spies."

Mannheim moved just his eyes, expecting Grover to emerge from some smaller, shadowed chapel to throw his weight behind Berglund.

So like Grover it would be—ego uber alles. After seconds ticked away in anticipation, he took aim at Berglund's self-admiration.

"I represent the President's National Security Advisor, not some investment banker parody of a spy. Be assured this tragic comedy of assassinations in Nidaros Cathedral hasn't been authorized by the President. More importantly are the long prison terms, or quiet disappearances which await its planners and participants. Men like you, Mr. Berglund, are extraneous. You won't know whether a Russian or American bullet ended your involvement. But a bullet it will be...not Kruggerands, Euros, adulation or whatever bright-colored paper your ambition is wrapped in. Tell me what types of weapons SVR is providing and by what methods they'll be smuggled into the concert."

Nestled in his right hand the Pug revolver weighed heavily in Mannheim's personal equation. Would shooting Göran Berglund between the eyes produce the desired result? Or would the show go on—including Elias's prominent solo—without notice of Göran's absence? Surely an understudy artistic director, hungry for opportunity, would rise above trepidation.

Zachary allowed his lack of skill to enter the equation. If unable to shoot Göran dead, where to shoot the pompous twit was a vexing millstone?

Berglund issued a reckless challenge. "Arrest me. Let's see who is shoved aside...Einar the spy or Göran who makes beautiful music."

Drained of color Berglund took two steps towards the organ, when he stopped to look at Mannheim with something approximating pity.

"I know what you are, Zachary Mannheim...no match for your wife, Marta. No authority. No allies. No chance." The opening notes of Mozart's *Laudate Dominum* rang out in accompaniment of the verbal caricature he'd drawn of Mannheim.

Zachary retreated to a row of straight-backed wooden chairs far from where male and female choirs were gathered for a final dress rehearsal. He would procrastinate—linger in hope of an opportunity to convince Elias to abandon *Reformation*. Wait for Grover Norris' arrival in the hope prudence might prevail over raging ambition. Dawdle long enough to allow even a mediocre strategy to fully reveal itself.

Undone and overwhelmed, no intercession or miracle appeared on his horizon; a mental signpost pointed in one direction to perdition, and in its opposite to abject failure.

Without consideration for the time differential, a text to Greg Riley read: *Increase personal safety for yourself and Randall. Consider further relocation.* A text to Tom Nichols read: *Relocating Gregory and Randall. Transport?* Addressed to Randall, a text read: *Grover's location? Re-assess encryption on all friendly devices…run threat algorithms. Record all conversations within range of my phone.* Annoyed with himself, Mannheim recognized his messages as the machinations of a petty bureaucrat.

The girls' choir began rehearsal, filling the Cathedral with magical voices. Mannheim's mood darkened. Unaware his fingers were steepled against the chair in front of him, renouncing the idea prayer would improve his situation, an inspired strategy was needed.

Riley's response was short: *Roger that.* Nichols text was terse: *Awaiting plan.* Randall's text was clinical: *Sustained regular SVR hack-attacks. System coping. Re-doubling security. Encrypted devices OK. Grover Norris arrived your locale sixteen hours ago. Arrived specific co-ordinates forty-five minutes ago. Recording your phone and peripheral phones.*

Dialing Raissa on his Sat phone, Zachary chastised himself for ill attention. "Raissa…where are you?"

Neutrality prevailed in Raissa's voice. "Lovely to hear from you too, Zachary, although your stress levels are too high. Get a grip."

"If only that were possible…things aren't optimal here and the situation will deteriorate. I'd like to send Randall and Gregory into your care for the duration…your boatyard friends have done yeoman's duty and suffered enough in the doing. What do you think?"

"Tell me, Zachary, what does David think?"

Raissa's question struck Mannheim odd; he chalked it up to concern for a colleague.

"David and I will soon be isolated and alone. Grover landed within the last hour…he's not here to provide support. Identification of Marta's soldiers is David's difficult and perilous chore. We haven't seen each other in hours."

"David needs to know what you're thinking, Zachary. Share your thoughts, you two…eat something. Give me an hour…I'll be in touch with a plan for things on my end."

***

Berglund was in a foul mood.

Tension was palpable for every member of the assembled choirs. Gone were references to singing with joy and having fun. Tongue-lashings were dispensed with enthusiasm for minor and major errors.

Kirstin was dead at Marta's hand, so said Zachary Mannheim. Was the former Agency spy-hunter to be believed?

Elias reached-out to Marta with no success.

Was the vacuum created by her silence dispositive? Was abandoning *Reformation* and its goals the correct and professional course of action? Mystified by the jumble of thoughts running through his brain, Elias listened to Berglund scream.

"No, Elias. No. No. A hundred times no. Why do you lose concentration? Why not strive for perfection? Why settle for bungled mediocrity? Perhaps you are afraid to succeed."

Defiance on the tip of his tongue, Elias watched his mother slip into a row of chairs accompanied by Russell Tipton and two men he couldn't identify. It took a lengthy moment to realize Zachary Mannheim occupied the chair in front of his mother's foursome. Obvious from near two hundred feet, Mannheim squirmed under their presence.

"Mr. Thordsen, are you still a member of this choir or do you wish to visit mommy?"

Behind Berglund this snide rebuke brought a smattering of laughter, cut off at its root when the artistic director's hand slammed the lectern. Sheet music fluttered lifeless to the floor. Berglund observed what he'd wrought; considered the effect on tomorrow's program. Emphasized a pleasant tone to complement a smile.

"Could we give it another try Elias, please, from the beginning."

***

"Zach, you look like warmed over dog shit."

Changing gears from what passed as social rigor, Grover Norris ignored Russell Tipton and instead pointed at Elias's mother.

"You know Mariah Ackerly. Have you met Lt. Col. Goodman of the local Marine contingent?"

If he hadn't been overtired, if putting up with Grover's distilled arrogance wasn't so tedious, Mannheim might have opted for finesse—see whether Goodman was still possessed of his testicles. As a sop to ill temper, Zachary elected farce.

"No, Grover, do you require a Marine in full regalia to babysit a well-regarded friend of POTUS?"

Pissed-off was Grover's go-to retort. "Never a team player, Zach...always been your problem. Col. Goodman is going to escort you back to Vaernes Garrison, where you'll stay until I let you return home, back to the oblivion of a defanged spy-hunter and his meager retirement."

Mannheim's list of options—Hail Mary passes that they were— would always have contained alternatives custom-tailored for a man with Grover's level of self-admiration.

"Has POTUS decided to support *Reformation,* or have you convinced him the Great Grover can turn Petr Sillin into an Agency asset?" Before Grover could respond, he added with a dollop of incredulity, "Quite the coup, if you pull it off."

Irritated at Mannheim stealing his dramatic pronouncement, Grover left no doubt about his plan. "We'll give the bastard Hobson's Choice...isn't that one of *your* top-ten techniques?"

"So a Russian hard man, known for resourcefulness and political survival, can either defect, or be shot dead on the spot. Is there a fallback position? What will you do if, somehow, Sillin should turn things around...will you defect to Moscow or take a bullet to the brain for POTUS? Or is Mr. Tipton to be your sacrificial lamb? If it was my selection of victim, Mariah would make the better missionary. She, at least, was on the Russian payroll in the bad old days. You were D/CIA back then. Surely you haven't bought her newly minted protestations of innocence. From a mission critical perspective, let's be honest...among the three of you Mariah would be deemed most credible by Sillin."

"Fuck you, Zachary." Mariah Ackerly said in a voice that echoed through Nidaros loudly enough to be heard by her son.

Tipton's retort was barely audible. "I'll make the approach to Sillin." Whether as antidote to Mariah's outburst or reflecting his understanding of how Hobson's Choice could apply to more than one side in a defection, he provided rationale. "I've been point-man on *Reformation*. It was me who met regularly with Fetisov to iron out details. Marta won't be surprised by my appearance."

Mannheim shook his head in consternation. "Dear, dear, Mr. Tipton, hasn't anyone told you Fetisov is dead? Let's hope you won't head the list on Marta's Top-Forty."

Grover responded with heavy cynicism. "You've been a great help, Zach. Bringing Mariah along with you made my life easier. Tipton and Elias's mother will be our emissaries. I'll enjoy seeing whether Sillin appreciates the irony...defect to Mariah or die at the hand of her son."

"Then it's settled, let's each retreat to a neutral corner." Zachary's airy-fairy words conveyed a kind of scorn which hinted at acceptance—his imitation of Grover's dogmatic tonality a final fragment of insurrection.

***

Elias stopped mid-passage as his mother's outburst faded.

Berglund's reaction was to turn round, searching where Elias's eyes were pointed. The gathering that included Elias's mother was no more: Mariah walked towards the West Front entrance; Russell Tipton approached the choir, although such action made no sense to Elias; Mannheim and the uniformed Marine used the South Choir Doorway through which Zachary had entered; the man called Grover was joined from the shadows by a man and woman easily taken for bodyguards. Elias stared until those final three passed through the North Doorway into the cold, dark afternoon.

Berglund's expression confirmed Elias's initial instinct: Berglund was up to his neck in *Reformation's* implementation. Tipton's conspicuous attempt to gain Elias's attention ignored, he refocused on the sheet music. Waited for Berglund. When the conductor's wand brought organ, choir and soloist to the ready, Elias filled his lungs   and   opened   his   mouth   to   sing.

Chapter 20:

Settled in Goodman's vehicle, Mannheim let out a long sigh.

"It was kind of you, Colonel, to spare me going over and over the efforts we've invested. As you no doubt noticed, Mr. Norris and I have history." Mannheim's phone vibrated. He wouldn't chance missing a call from Raissa; with the stubborn streak of independence she exhibited, it happened too seldom. "I apologize for the interruption. Give me just a minute, Colonel."

Raissa had dedicated considerable mental energy to sidestepping Mannheim's instruction to maintain an up-tempo social profile. Establish an alibi, protect her cover and her career from association with *Reformation,* those were Zachary's methods to minimize his guilt or seek forgiveness in advance. Not interested in self-preservation, she ransacked the smallest bits of memory for something, anything, incongruous with *Reformation.* Successful, she considered a text, but knew rejection would be harder, when Zachary listened to her voice.

"Not a particularly good moment, Raissa. Can we speak later?"

"Thirty seconds. Listen to me."

Rebuked and stung, he acquiesced. "Go ahead."

"Remember the green laser...the beach shooter who helped the hostages escape? Who could it have been but Louis Phillips? Explains why he was on the scene so soon, giving Tom Nichols a raft of shit. You described his testimony to the Subcommittee as absolute support for Brantley, Tipton and *Reformation.* So ask yourself, why would he help Raissa? He's at Langley, in detention. I want to talk to him. Can I call Jamie, and if not Jamie, who'd be better?"

"Let me think on it. I'll reach out."

"No, Zachary. I don't want approval. Give me the best person to arrange an off-the-record chat. "

Mannheim's frustration won out. "Grover Norris thinks he's going to stage-manage Petr Sillin's defection. Every bloody American spy in Norway has gone round the bend. We'll be lucky if any of us leave Trondheim alive."

"Take a breath, Zachary. You'll see I'm right."

Taking advice wasn't the easiest thing, not under pressure. Not when it was the eighth inning and the scoreboard showed crooked numbers in favor of the opposition.

"Yes, I can see where you're headed. Call Jamie but be prepared for him to be flummoxed. Not every day he bluffs the opposition with stakes this high. If you can't reach Jamie, go to Ian Riddick. Call when you know."

"Zachary, listen up, add me to the loony bin next to Grover. Would hijacking Sillin, or Sluchevsky for that matter, be the worst thing? Sure as Hell would tilt the field. Talk soon."

***

A bit of rogue danced in Goodman's eyes.

Mannheim saw him interpolating what he'd heard, adding it to his earlier conversation with Grover Norris.

Goodman swallowed a smile before he spoke. "Mr. Norris took pains to update me up on his curriculum vitae: Former Director of CIA; legendary investment banker; close friend of POTUS; father of a senior Agency executive; and raconteur par excellence. Man has a high opinion of himself."

"So where do you plan to incarcerate me, Colonel?"

"Whoa there, Mr. Mannheim. If you're chasing Mr. Norris, you can hardly be incarcerated. Perhaps you might want to inquire about the status of my standing orders."

"*Appropriate resourcefulness*...wasn't that the gist?"

"Mr. Norris never suggested I speak with a higher command authority. Never said anything more than, *I'm in charge*. You're the best man for the job in my judgment, Mr. Mannheim. And I bet you'd like to get on with it. So hop out and know Marines will do what we can."

"Grover enjoys the good life, Colonel. Make the next right and drop me halfway down the block. I'll track his cellphone from there."

Goodman keyed the ignition and began to roll. "Tracking a cellphone in real time, thousands of miles from home. It must be true; you are a spy."

"You bet, Colonel. Wrote the algorithm's code myself, don't you know." Grim smile in place, he bet on *Kjøpmannsgata* as the street Grover would have taken.

***

Mannheim's text to Randall read: *Grover's location?*

When the blip showed on his screen, his instinct was justified: Grover would head for the best hotel in the city. At the blip's apparent speed, the hotel would be less than six or seven minutes away. Middle of the workday in Norway, the street in front of the Cathedral was nearly deserted. A snow-throwing machine hurled a mixture of snow and ice into piles as tall as streetlights.

Pushed to concentrate, his first question was unanswerable: Who's transporting Grover? A dues paying member of the limousine set, Grover Norris didn't use taxis.

Reminded of Raissa's gentle criticism, he texted David: *Where are you?* Cold wind bit into his cheeks. He turned away as his screen glowed: *Across the street.* Mannheim called himself a fool for ignoring the skills and dedication of those he recruited.

Pavement rutted with unpredictable patches of snow and ice, he avoided falling twice by the smallest of margins. A spy must appreciate conditions on the ground; that was one of the ten commandments for a field agent. Neither Russian nor American will be nimble, quick or reliably upright in Trondheim, not today and not tomorrow.

Safe in the warm interior, Nazarian listened to Mannheim admit what was incontrovertible. "Randall suggested you rescue the old coot?"

"Something like that."

Finished with his mea culpa, Mannheim presented the news. "Grover's in town, David…planning to make Petr Sillin an offer he can't refuse."

David's face presented a puzzle.

Zachary realized—David needed immediate direction. He concentrated on his phone's map while he spoke. "Stay on *Kjøpmannsgata* till the roundabout, take the second spoke onwards to the next circle. Straight-on to the third, then left on *Brattørkaia* to the *Clarion*."

With the car ten klicks over its best, safe, speed, David volunteered a report on Marta's support team. "Half dozen SVR first-stringers. Three, maybe four, gofers. Hard to tell about local stringers, though your buddy Berglund is a burr under Marta's saddle. They're a man-down on cyber-tech…Marta's unhappy about that, to say the least."

Wary, Zachary inquired, "How do you appraise Marta's state-of-mind?"

Kjøpmannsgata, on their left side, consisted of sidewalk, curb and two primary lanes for vehicular traffic. On its right side a tree-lined median with a bike-path shared space with deciduous growth twenty feet in height. Further to the right, a third lane served as local access to a series of four-story housing units. No streetlights lit the roadway, but a warm glow from window lights pockmarked apartments where normal people lived normal lives. A quarter mile ahead on the median strip a dull glow burst into orange flame, where a car burned in malignant phosphorescence.

Not an explosion associated with a bomb, Mannheim decided, but a gasoline fire. "Pull over, David. Near as you can get." Wind direction and velocity estimated by a contrail of black smoke, Mannheim texted Randall: *Grover's location?*

David stopped the car, left its engine running and exited as close as possible to the burning vehicle. Certain this fire wasn't an accident, he observed the driver and front seat passenger consumed by the inferno. Absent emotion he shielded his eyes with his right hand: No rear seat passenger was apparent.

Randall's text: *1.5 km north of your position*

Nazarian stripped off his parka—waited for a gust which would push flames even a few feet away. Seeing opportunity, he grabbed at the door handle with the parka. When the door creaked open, it was instantly propelled by the fire's overpressure. David tumbled backwards. His head hit the curbstone as the dead passenger flew from the burning seat, landing in a heap across Nazarian's legs.

With no urge to assess risk, or wait for the inevitable arrival of fear, Mannheim lurched over the curb, grabbed David's bare hands/wrists, and pulled the dazed field agent from under the corpse and a safe distance away from Hell's own inferno. A nearby tree burst into flame, its lowest branches fully engaged. Soon the conflagration would spread further.

How badly David might be injured impossible to determine, waiting for local fire and police would be a tactical and legal error.

Zachary hefted David over his left shoulder. Twenty-five yards would have been fifteen yards to far without ramped-up adrenaline. Inelegant in the passenger seat, snow filled handkerchief pressed against David's bleeding skull, Zachary told a disoriented Nazarian to hold the compressed snow tight. In the rearview he saw traffic queue in both directions behind them. Sirens could be heard coming from the direction in which Mannheim drove. Approaching the wide, highway-style bridge over the *Nidelva*, he saw a significant increase in pedestrian and vehicular traffic. Trapped and delayed would be their fate on his planned route. To be identified with the car fire would be worse. *Fjordgata* offered the sole option; he turned left and parked in the first spot available. Sweating from exertion, uncertainty and concern for David, Zachary opened a window and closed his eyes to compose himself.

It seemed an hour before he heard David ask, "Did you see his ID?"

Mannheim closed the window; Nazarian would be in shock. "Any sign at all of a woman passenger?"

Nazarian shook his head.

"How badly are you hurt, David?"

"Bleeding has stopped, I think. Gonna have a lousy headache later. Hands don't feel bad at all. How do they look?"

Removing his winter gloves, Zachary gingerly took hold of the fingers on David's right hand. Under the car's dome light hair was singed, but nothing like a severe burn was apparent.

"Looks like you got away with that foolishness. What were you thinking?" Mannheim's flash of anger vented a delayed reaction of concern and irritation.

"He wasn't SVR and didn't die in the fire." A grim smile of vindication appeared with David's elaboration. "Marine. Bullet in his forehead."

Disbelief diluted everything Mannheim believed true. Caught off guard and played for a fool, having drunk Goodman's Koolaid was a hard blow to recover from. Mannheim tried and failed to comprehend the myriad implications of a dead Marine, a reinvigorated Grover Norris, and multiple warts sprouting from the reasoning suggested to David.

"So either SVR or GRU managed to eliminate Grover's babysitters, cause a diversion and vanish leaving no discernible trace."

Nazarian issued a stern look of disagreement; his injuries contributed to a prejudiced indictment. "Smells more like Tipton's psychopathic Girl Friday. Could be we'll find Grover's body next."

One thing at a time, an overused elixir meant to restore emotional and physical balance still meant they needed to reach Grover's hotel. Multi-tasking, a self-accusatory label attached to inexcusable miscalculations, was rejected after one bitter remonstration: How could I have accepted any of it at face value?

Leery of a dive into self-pity, Mannheim consulted the map and headed west on *Fjordgata* toward *Krambugata*. River crossed on a parallel bridge to his intended route, he took the 2nd exit of a roundabout, crossed over the main railway lines and completed a one-eighty where *Fosenkaia* became *Brattørkaia*. In one kilometer they squeezed into a space near the front of the Clarion Hotel and Congress Hall.

Nazarian looked worse.

***

Raissa found a willing audience in Jamie Norris, whose suspicions regarding his father's whereabouts and reckless intentions were confirmed in the first minute of their phone conversation. Jamie agreed with the emergent nature of her request, as well as the wisdom of Raissa's refusal to appear at Langley. So Ian Riddick, Louis Phillips, Jamie Norris and Raissa Ribeiro, as diverse a foursome as might be convened under the Agency's tent, found themselves occupying a booth in an Indian restaurant off Chain Bridge Road. Not ten minutes from where they were all employed, or not employed as future circumstances would determine, pleasantries were not on the menu.

Phillips wore a guarded, suspicious, mask. Earlier in the parking lot Raissa witnessed how the fear of being handed over for more visceral retribution could eat at a man. No longer Chief of Police in a Cape Cod town, an active duty NCS Field Director existed in limbo following the Subcommittee's discussion of treason. Spared a quick demise, he refused food and wouldn't touch coffee ordered on his behalf.

Jamie hoped to balance an olive branch with a stout stick.

"You were present on the barrier beach during the attack on Raissa's home. Not only were you present, but you fired numerous times in support of the hostages. Yet you transported a member of the assault team to Joint Base Cape Cod, where that person was exfiltrated by Leanne Crowder. Anything inaccurate in what I've said?"

Phillips' face deformed into blank misery. Several different reactions followed like parade horses, one after the other. It took more than a minute before Phillips could answer.

"Field Directors live and die with their agents. I'm called upon to provide accurate, useful data regarding mission status and the agent's future movements. I provide funds, weapons, transport, medical care, and on a rare occasion informal burial. After Langley's in the rearview, I lie, cheat and steal to support my agent's mission. But not one damn thing in any Agency manual or directive tells a Field Director to allow his agent to murder another agent. Yes, Tipton told me to exfiltrate Thordsen...little shit lost his lunch when I suggested he walk away on his own. Wish I never picked him up...wished I never used my mission pre-planning to enter the Base and locate the airplane. No freaking idea who the pilot was. Don't know Leanne Crowder. Shouldn't have been detained for doing my job. Field Directors are the punching bag, when things go tits-up."

Jamie wasn't in a forgiving mood. "Did you expect trouble? Did Tipton tell you to support Raissa, if all the tits were up?"

"Since Afghanistan, Tripoli, Syria, Yemen and the rest of those hell-holes, no Field Director goes into the field without every weapon he or she can carry."

Left hanging was Phillips's ability to hang Tipton out to dry

"How about Tipton...come on, man, there's no recording. *Reformation* will consume a whole bunch of folks. We're looking for a way out."

Phillips turned his hands over in supplication. "My assignment ended when Little Lord Fauntleroy got on a single engine antique. Never told where he was going. Didn't ask. Not by the book, but Tipton was Brantley's Golden Boy. I defended my Op, when questioned by Nazarian and Mannheim. I obfuscated, avoided and changed the subject. *Protect your field agent*...look it up in the manual...not unusual or unprofessional." Phillips issued a world-weary laugh. "Mannheim's retired...what a phony. Acts like he owns a patent on Agency principles. You had me locked up on nothing more than Mannheim's say-so. Why were politicians allowed to interfere in a Langley field operation?" Moving his finger to Ian Riddick, he expanded his disgust. "You, Ian, should have asked a shit-ton more questions."

Ancient history this was—Raissa knew they could go round and round and wind up back where they started. More than that, she endorsed every word Phillips said. More important than belief was an ongoing reconsideration of everything she'd been told, or come to believe, about *Reformation*.

"Lots of water under the dam, Louis. For you. For Jamie and Ian. For all of us. Hours from now *Reformation* could go so wrong it defies my ability to explain or comprehend. Tipton has two agents primed to assassinate two very senior Russians...supposedly a quid pro quo for SVR's assault of my home. One of Tipton's shooters is Thordsen. Second is Leanne Crowder, who's no virgin at killing. White House believes Marta Mannheim will permit the assassinations, but with a twist: Thordsen and Crowder will be shot dead while television cameras broadcast Nidaros Cathedral's famous Christmas Choral concerts. If this sounds nuts, your conclusion could be a thousand percent correct. Mannheim and Nazarian are on the ground, trying to defuse or disrupt the entire shit-show."

Collaborative demeanor misread, Phillips prodded. "What's your involvement, Ms. Ribeiro?"

Jamie Norris caught Ian Riddick's partial nod of agreement out of the corner of his eye. It was all too easy to forget: Raissa's role at Langley was highly restricted. Of the few Agency officers with superficial knowledge, less than five were read-in on the truth.

Raissa's tone turned brutal. "I'm the one who would have died, Mr. Phillips. To you it would have been another mission accomplished...another young agent shepherded through a baptism of fire. Would you have given a second thought to some blonde bimbo's mutilated corpse?" Catching her breath, Jamie's wink was reassurance. "So I called the President of these United States to demand an explanation. If you're a big enough celebrity, and pretty enough, this Commander-in-Chief takes your call. Anything further is irrelevant, because you're going to Norway tonight...to talk your agent down, or take him down, or do any other damned thing asked of you. Fuck up and some SVR heavy will end you. Or I will."

***

A final text to Randall confirmed the nearby presence of Grover's phone, if not the man himself.

Architecture from the warehouse school of modernism, the *Clarion* featured a main entrance constructed of mirrored, triangular structures in blue and gold. Its front desk mural of seabirds soaring under blue skies jolted Mannheim, fresh from depressing darkness and the smell of incinerated flesh. Using Euros from Stefan Korsakov's retirement fund, Room 508, with two double beds, came with a staffer's apology for not providing two rooms. Over-booked as they were for the Christmas Concerts, Mannheim accepted the keycard with indifference.

Neither *Skybar*, the main restaurant, nor a wraparound outside deck revealed Russians, Norwegian Intelligence, CIA personnel, or Marines.

Zachary retraced his steps to collect David, who attributed his limp to stiffness not pain. Aspirin administered and over-the-counter salves applied, Nazarian fell asleep before hitting the pillow. Tretiak's 9mm, grip wrapped in a clean handkerchief, added to the Pug revolver in his pocket, Mannheim switched off the lights—let the door close and lock behind him.

Identifying where Grover would meet Sillin was Mannheim's priority. Text to Randall: *Grover's location?* Randall's reply demoralized him: *No movement since prior update.* Grover and his phone were separated. Mannheim texted back: *Other phones present when Grover's first located?* A single word summarized their situation: *Negative*.

Zachary sighed—it had become a shabby habit.

Faced with no car to trace, no witnesses to interrogate, no police to assist, no Agency resources to rely upon and, one might argue, no options, he would abandon a carefully polished, individual code of morality. Field agents, not unlike politicians, broke laws, shattered societal norms, betrayed friend or foe, fornicated with or abused whoever was in their way to achieve a mission's goals. After-the-fact justification was a contortionist's specialty, unavailable to a spy-hunter whose prey would, in order to achieve a conviction, be entitled to Due Process. Paper thin veneer this code was everything which separated spy-hunter from field agent.

As he abandoned intellectual discipline, any semblance of Mannheim's better self was left to bring up the rear.

A careful examination of front desk employees caused him to enter the door marked Managing Director. Her look of sharpened disapproval brushed aside, this Assistant Managing Director had grown inured to younger men and women advancing, while she remained stuck in corporate mud stewing in the privacy of well-mannered ill will.

"Ms. Svendsen, my name is Zachary Mannheim, a colleague of Mr. Grover Norris, one of your guests as well as a senior official with the Central Intelligence Agency of the United States." Mannheim slid a business card across the desktop within her reach. "Mr. Norris is working with Norwegian Intelligence to prevent a major terrorist attack. An hour ago he was involved in an attack where two agents were shot and killed. Mr. Norris' car was wrecked and burned...you may have seen news reports. In the aftermath Mr. Norris has gone missing. I've a list of possible guests at your hotel who may assist our search. I'd be grateful for your assistance in checking guest records against my list."

Her face contorted, first showing pique, then irritation and at last passive rejection. "Entirely impossible, Mr. Mannheim," she said, eyes scanning his card. "Contrary to *Clarion* corporate policy as well as Norway's privacy laws." Her thumb and forefinger fondled the card's embossed print.

"It's impossible to overstate the importance of this matter, Ms. Svendsen. If you'd be willing to assist our efforts on a larger scale, on your own time of course, I'd be more than willing to compensate you as a consultant to CIA."

Eyes widened. Surprise at this turn of events evident, the idea of being a spy sparked Ms. Svendsen's imagination. Fingers on his business card ceased their back-and-forth motion. She frowned in hesitation.

How much was the all-important hocus-pocus, when recruiting civilians to a local spy network. Some joined out of a sense of patriotism. Very few sought life or death adventure, but fascination with adrenaline was known to happen. A large majority were mercenaries of one kind or another. Mannheim would make a single offer; negotiation was always a mistake.

"It's quite possible you'll incur expenses…compensating a messenger, using off-duty employees as watchers. Really anything you, in your complete discretion, deem important to locating the people on my list. In cases like this one, both our governments understand the importance of saving lives over crass concerns with money. I'd suggest ten thousand Euros to cover the next three days."

"My sister is a staff member at NIS…with whom are you collaborating on this matter?"

When a bluff was at stake, there could be no vacillation. "Einar Haugen."

Eyebrow arched in pleasant surprise, their arrangement was sealed. "Could I examine your list, please?"

Extending a single-sheet of A4 stationary with names neatly printed in capital letters, he held-on firmly when she reached to take it.

"Time is of the essence, Ms. Svendsen. It would be best if I used a Master Cardkey…for cases where you or your associates could be at risk. I can't have civilian consultants becoming fodder for unpleasant Russian spies."

Tonje Svendsen showed no distress at Zachary's test of her backbone, but rather nodded her head in affirmation. Marching in lockstep to the Front Desk, Mannheim blessed the fates for providing such an unexpected accomplice. Moments later, with more than all his needs arranged, armed with the keys to the kingdom, he entered the elevator opting to start on the top floor.

Chapter 21

Eduardo's text presented stark reality: *Flight plan approved. Estimate IAD to HYA to TRD at 15 hours all-in…departure @ 20:00 today, arrival @ 11:00 tomorrow. Expecting 5 passengers.*

Should there be any type of delay, be it air traffic, weather, or whatever, their ability to assist Mannheim would be diminished. Scheduled at 20:00 hours Trondheim time, the Cathedral Christmas concert schedule was fixed by contractual conditions between the Norwegian Broadcasting Corporation, international networks purchasing distribution rights and the Cathedral Choir's leadership.

Nothing would delay television; the audience would arrive, and the show would begin on-time.

Raissa examined her phone. Added forty-five minutes travel-time to Dulles. Texted Eduardo: *ETA Dulles 19:30. OK?*

Eduardo: *Barely.*

"Let's get going, gentlemen. Ian, thanks for your help. There's cold weather gear for both you, Jamie, and Louis on the airplane. Regardless of the outcome, we'll be on the way home in less than forty-eight hours." A gray cloud of disquiet descended on a face devoid of makeup. "Or we'll be in Norwegian custody. Or one or more of us will be dead."

***

A Bright moon, rising in the east, lit the way as the Gulfstream crossed Martha's Vineyard before traversing Nantucket Sound to land in Hyannis. When parked, the copilot deployed self-contained stairs. Greeted by a thirty mile per hour northwest wind accompanied by temperatures in the twenties, Jamie Norris' sarcasm rang-out as the cabin's comfort level plummeted.

"Shame to give up summer on Cape Cod for winter in Trondheim."

Two figures ran towards the plane, followed by a baggage cart with a light load. Jamie laughed. "How come cyber-genius gets to bring luggage?"

Greg Riley, first up the stairs, stamped snow-covered feet before dropping into one of the custom blonde-leather seats. He caught Raissa's eye. "Nice way to travel."

"Not just comfortable…" Raissa said, teeing-up a dark punch line "…final meals for the condemned come with the seat."

Randall Carter dragged digital devices in canvas bags up the jet's stairs. Stern look directed at Raissa, he wanted to know, "Will we be connected the whole way?"

"Great to see you too, kid. Want me to warm-up some old pizza? Might even have warm beer, if you'd prefer. But internet at forty-five thousand feet? How could a wee girl manage that?"

***

Room 730, entered as if Mannheim had every right to do so, was marked on Svendsen's list as Grover Norris' suite. To find it empty wasn't much of a shock. Purple nitrile gloves in place, he examined the sitting room, bedroom and bedroom closet without disturbing Grover's personal items. About to exit, rigorous habit made him tug at the coat closet to the left of the suite's entrance. A thud from inside startled him; he jumped aside as if avoiding a snake's fangs. Throat tightened with expectation, he gripped tight and yanked. Gruesome to look at, the Marine appeared to smile above a neck wound made by a garrote.

Nauseous, Mannheim was too familiar with that wound. Years might have passed, but the memory of Fulton Bennett's near decapitated body was imprinted on his retinas. A glass of tap water prevented a loss of innards. Each time his stomach rebelled, he squeezed the Pug's grip tighter.

Have I lost perspective? Are there teams and players unaccounted for?

Eliminating three United States Marines wouldn't go un-noticed by anyone paying the slightest attention. If Grover's alive, who is his guardian-angel? If not, where has the opposition deposited his corpse? Who's on first, second and third?

Mishmash though these thoughts were, they protected him in the short term from a higher probability: Grover Norris would be ransomed for an impossible price to pay. Shaken to the core, Mannheim walked down to the fourth-floor elevator lobby. The car at Mannheim's eleven o'clock pinged arrival; its doors spread apart, revealing a crowd. Jammed with tourists, Mannheim forced a smile. "I'll take the next one," he said, with feigned affability. He caught a glimpse of Mariah Ackerly—managed a nod of recognition as the doors closed to begin its descent.

Zachary stared into a black hole.

Another ping. Open doors revealed a woman holding an oval makeup mirror, examining her reflection. Undeterred by fear or circumstance, his subconscious identified a face from Raissa's Quebec City fashion show. His shoe preventing closure, her eyes snapped up then back to the mirror in clear distress.

Mannheim watched her right hand close the compact and lower it towards a purse hanging by a delicate chain.

"Your *Dior* bag won't last long used as a holster. Marina, isn't it? You're a long way from the Russian Consulate in Quebec. Still on loan to my wife?"

"Marta's husband isn't known to carry a weapon." Smug satisfaction struck Mannheim as misplaced confidence.

"Does it puzzle SVR's foot-soldiers, when your ranks suffer more than predicted fatalities? Marta is a zealot, untroubled by the sacrifice of others. Perhaps my bride's favorite aphorism has crossed your mind …*Dead men tell no tales?*"

"You and Nazarian are alone…opposed everywhere by superior Russian operatives. Grover Norris, Einar Haugen and, with a certain irony, the United States Marines, have been removed during the initial skirmish. Nazarian suffered first-degree burns. You, Zachary Mannheim, could have been killed ten times over in Quebec. Do your bullet wounds argue the battle is over? Or do you still insist the world is flat?"

Arrived at the second floor, Mannheim eased himself out. Marina from Quebec allowed a superior smile to crease her lips. Game's not over till the fat lady sings—he should have reminded her. But he'd done no such thing. While wounded pride hemorrhaged, he marched towards Russell Tipton's room. Little more than ten feet separated him from Tipton's door, when it opened. Back facing the corridor, Tipton checked the door's lock.

"Not facing the opposition…good way to get shot dead, Mr. Tipton." Mannheim knew he shouldn't but acknowledged a bitter reality. "Weren't you meant to be in detention at Langley?"

"Weren't you meant to be puttering away in your garden? You'll excuse me, if I don't stay to chat."

Zachary stiffened, making it clear he'd block Tipton's path. "Why would EJ Brantley, with your informed advice at hand, conclude a thick-headed deal with SVR?" Pug pointed at Tipton he answered his own inquiry. "Trading a vague opportunity to kill Raissa, in return for an equal and opposite opportunity to assassinate Sillin…under no circumstance, Mr. Tipton, was that ever tit-for-tat. You and EJ traded the deaths of Sillin and Sluchevsky straight-up for what, in baseball, are called future considerations. What did you and Fetisov decide to recommend as the final deal? Aydan Fetisov died earlier today. Scuttlebutt says he suffered a fatal dose of integrity. There's some twisted deal with no winners, or none of us would be stuck here in the endless snow and ice."

Tipton responded, "I'll bet the farm you won't blow-up your reputation and life's work on uninformed, desperate guesses. Let me pass."

"What if I shoot you where you stand? Who'll give a dollar or a donut whether Russell Tipton bled to death in some godforsaken Norwegian hotel? Not Grover Norris, I promise you. Is it possible Grover intends to blow up the deal with Marta? Blow it up over your strong objection. Blow it up, if need be, over your cold, dead body. Is it possible you've over-valued your continuing involvement?"

Edging along the wall Tipton passed Mannheim, two sets of eyes meeting in mutual interrogation for less than a moment. Face drained of natural color; it wasn't ghost-pain from Tipton's missing limb causing the grimace on his face.

Mannheim called after him. "Lives in the balance, Mr. Tipton…who should decide?" Seeing Tipton shake his head, he tried a final time. "Do you know who's standing in the shadows?" In desperation, he shouted, "How come those shadowy men never lose a leg? How come it's never one of them in a body bag?"

Zachary accepted the results of self-recrimination: A younger man might've chased Tipton and shaken him silly; Nazarian might've followed Tipton to discover whom he met. A defeated man slumped to the floor, where spillage from a hundred room-service trays soiled his pants. He admitted a visit to Sillin's room would serve no purpose. What would I do, were Sillin and Grover negotiating the Russian's defection? Tail between his legs, Mannheim returned to find Nazarian asleep. Fully clothed, he lowered himself on to the bed nearest the door.

***

Unsure whether he'd slept, a keycard scraped in the lock mechanism; it brought Mannheim to full attention. Makarov in hand, he slid into a chair offering momentary advantage over an intruder. When a gloved hand flicked the light switch, an overhead fixture bathed the Countess in its blue, unflattering, glare. Mannheim's hand relaxed, letting the 9mm settle into the seat cushion.

Legendary acidity undiminished by the late hour, or time's slippage, she pointed a varnished nail at David Nazarian, who'd risen to a seated position.

"Zachary, you old queen, have you always been gay? I admit you've fooled everyone." With a minimum of kinetics, she repositioned herself to where the younger man could be engaged, if this was a trap.

"David was burned identifying the corpse of a United States Marine. He's resting in anticipation of tomorrow's..." Viewing the time on his phone Zachary corrected himself "...I should say today's festivities in the Cathedral. Let me get you a chair, Elise."

Back straight, legs crossed, jacket of a tailored wool suit buttoned, she offered Nazarian a frozen-fish smile. "Could I see your hands, please, Mr. Nazarian? It's an ugly request, but one inspired by our shared profession. Not intended to offend I assure you."

David complied. "Elise is from the Hebrew Elisheba? Are you Mossad?"

"Half correct, my scholarly new ally. Elise can be Greek, American, Hebrew or even French. In every case, it's a shortening of Elisabeth...and, of course, a paean to whichever God you worship. We who carry Elise through life are visionary and versatile. We strain against rules and conventions. Sometimes we are rebellious. On rare occasions we kill other humans for great gobs of money. But it's late. Give me what I need, Zachary."

Mannheim handed over a thin manila file folder for examination. After doing so, he retrieved the red sports-bag embossed with the Turkish crescent.

Half-moon glasses slid from forehead to nose as a forerunner of disappointment. "Too many names, too many photos, Zachary. You know better. These can only be background...people to be aware of, to watch, even to fear. Nowhere among them can I find a definitive target?"

Caught out for an inadequate briefing, Zachary answered, "No one, Countess, but everyone. That's why your fee is one million Euros."

"You are surrounded by uncertainty yet prioritize survival." Stated as fact, it was at once shrewd and, in the way of someone with a lifetime of success, imperious.

Mannheim took his time. Holding her gaze, it was age driven contradiction which provided encouragement. Wrinkles and liver spots covered by an attentive regime hinted at decay. Dove grey eyes blazed defiance, cauterizing doubt.

"My situation demands simplicity. In part because I lack resources. In part because, on my wife's part, we're dealing with ego gratification absent a whiff of national interest. Marta's success requires the young man...Elias's picture is first in your order of files...to die a violent death on live television and be accused post-mortem of murdering one or both of Sillin and Sluchevsky. You're familiar with both those men, Elise. I'm paying you to keep Elias alive until I remove him from the Cathedral grounds."

"Regardless of who dies other than young Elias?"

Mannheim handed Elise a second file. "With these exceptions."

Photos and biographies sifted with professional curiosity, she said, "Be pleased Mr. David Nazarian. Second on the list is a stature to be cherished." An arched eyebrow prefaced a second question. "Raissa cannot be what this file claims, not unless she is a triumph of deceit. Is she your creature, Zachary? Or, God forbid, how long has she been my replacement?"

"Not really a concern, since she shouldn't be in the Cathedral, or for that matter, in Norway."

"Your list suggests otherwise."

"Raissa is unconventional."

"The best compliment you could offer an assassin, Zachary. I'm impressed. Do I choose my methods?"

"Yes."

"No ifs, ands or buts?"

"Cell phone communication will be down beginning with the concert's broadcast schedule. Trondheim's electrical grid will go down upon my signal. The airport's backup generator will suffer a simultaneous electrical fire. Candles in the Cathedral will provide adequate operational lighting. Clouds will lift, revealing bright moonlight to interdict opposition personnel outside the Cathedral. You, Elise, will position yourself in the front row nearest the choirs, or perhaps near the television cameras…as your judgment dictates and in your discretion. No one besides David and I will know of your presence. The Cathedral is open to all until 19:00 hours Trondheim time, so reconnoiter as you prefer." From his pocket, Mannheim passed her an admission ticket as well as two cell phones, one encircled in green electrician's tape.

"Until the outage, text and voice on the all-black phone will be fully operational intra-team. You'll receive real-time text updates, as will we all, regarding opposition plans and movements…although we believe Elias's attacker will be American and included among the data I've provided to you. Should events prove us wrong, eliminate any clear and present danger to Elias, regardless of gender, religious preference or nationality."

Elise examined the second phone and its gaudy green adornment. "What purpose does this serve?"

"Cell phones will be re-activated upon the first hint of violence. Contact David or myself with that phone. Our numbers are preset. No other numbers will be accepted."

Heavy with inquisition, grey eyes mixed suspicion with a jigger of pragmatism. "Was there always a surrogate when I was primary, Zachary? I learn something about your evolution each time we meet."

***

Curtains swept aside a morning habit, what should have been dawn stared at Nazarian with hostility. Obvious tension in his shoulders and neck communicated without sound, David was on edge, primed and, although diminished by the burns to his hands, operational in every way which mattered.

Other than self-indulgence, Mannheim saw there was no reason to inquire after his well-being. "Shall I have coffee sent up, David?"

"Why leave the impression she could walk off with Korsakov's gym-bag?"

"A simple reminder, David. There's no such thing as a pre-paid kill. Only on occasion is a partial payment made as a sign of good faith. When money changes hands before the deed is done, it's a last resort...from a position of weakness"

Pained as David's face was, Mannheim wanted no protestations of innocence to weaken their shared, fixed, purpose. "We demonstrated our capacity to pay the agreed upon fee. No payment for failure. No payment for betrayal, although if I'm outbid by another player, no claim of betrayal will hold water. Elise and I last crossed paths quite some time ago. It was important that we test each other for signs of depleted resolve."

"She didn't like Raissa being involved."

"Elise fits our needs. She's a wild card who will look the part next time you see her...assuming you are able to identify her. Marta has never met Elise, which was a prerequisite to her presence. Besides David, beggars can't be choosers...we're not suffering an over-supply of qualified killers."

Nazarian shifted to a bitter tone. "Does every briefing contain a lie? Do you ever tell the exact same story to more than one player?"

"Spy-hunters...and Deputy Chief/CIC makes David Nazarian Langley's lead spy-hunter...are a mistrustful lot. We may or may not give our targets a fighting chance to prove themselves innocent or, in a lesser circumstance, not complicit with the opposition. Develop the tactical lie, David. Keeping track of all one's lies is part of the job and isn't as simple as it may seem."

A myriad of emotions raced across Nazarian's face. His battle for acceptance resulted in three words. "Breakfast sounds good."

Chapter 22

To pass time before choir members would assemble in the Cathedral, Elias sought the comfort of his peers. Gaggles of male and female singers, bubbly and nervous about such a big performance, formed, amused themselves, disbanded and reformed in hotels and restaurants throughout the morning hours.

Simplicity is best, when feeling overwhelmed. Buoyed by a shred of wisdom from his trainers at the *Farm*, he was still surprised to see Leanne Crowder sitting alone in the window seat of a popular kafè. Boots, jeans, a heavy sweater and woolen beanie made for a common denominational outfit. No makeup and stringy hair, common enough among Girls' Choir members, Leanne fit any profiler's expectation, lessening the probability of being identified as an outsider.

She crooked her finger at a second chair, arranged so they'd be close together backs to the wall. Unobstructed views to the street, where the kafè's gas lamps spilled into ovals of subdued light, worked against their being surprised. There could be no ambiguity about whether Leanne Crowder was armed.

Elias observed a change in Leanne, the fly anything, anytime, anywhere daredevil. This altered Leanne was crossing-off items from a to-do list. Perhaps not memorialized on her phone, this accidental meeting ticked-a-box.

"Why couldn't you give me straightforward answers on the plane? What difference…"

Leanne hissed him into silence. "No one expected you'd live long enough to matter…that's one reason. If Marta's mad dogs stressed you hard enough, beat you unconscious days on end, you would've broken. Every spy breaks. Every spy who breaks tells every secret they ever knew, including my identity."

In a sudden movement, Elias twisted her wrist enough to remind her who'd been frozen, hung upside down, beaten bloody, and forced to kill a trained killer. Angry spittle flew in the wake of his words.

"Stupid nonsense spouted by phony spy. Hope you never pray for death. Hope you never find out how much you can suffer, for how long. What are you here for?"

What Leanne thought of Elias left nothing to the imagination: Nonsensical bravado from a child pretending to be a hard man. Glaring at a bruised wrist, any sense of shared effort evaporated.

"I won't suffer or die for you, Elias, so listen up. There's no super-slick spy shit involved in what we do tonight. Under the table is a shopping bag. Inside is a sketch of the Cathedral marked to show where Berglund deposited five suppressed Glock 17s. Find one...whichever is easiest to access...hide it under your cassock."

Amused by the irony, Elias's casual inspection of the room proved Leanne twin to a dozen other young women. Elias realized her advantage in the run-up to their assigned assassinations: Leanne could be anyone in the Girls' Choir. No fancy technology would subject her to suspicion.

"A photo of Sillin, taken this morning, just hit your phone. He'll be on your left, near enough to the first row, as you begin *Laudate Dominum*. Take a few steps toward him and empty the clip. Center mass, like you were taught. I'll take Sluchevsky on your first step. Run for the Choir exit. Don't look around, no matter what you hear or see. I'll find you. Then it'll be a long, roundabout trip home."

Drained of affection Leanne patted Elias's cheek. As she sashayed towards the exit, Elias knew better than to reach for the shopping bag. Chair leaned back on its rear legs, he spent thirty minutes cataloging those in the kafè who were unfamiliar. Determined to be professional, there would be no hesitation. No second thoughts. This Op wasn't about his mother's hatred of Langley. Or Mannheim's pathetic plea to end *Reformation*. Or Leanne's juvenile need to prove everything to everyone. It was a job with hurdles to overcome, no different from defeating Kazimir.

When two different women, whose ages varied by more than twenty years, and who'd occupied two different tables, rose to follow Leanne, Elias dismissed them from concern.

Of those two women, the one employed by Norwegian Intelligence entered a generic description of Elias into her phone for distribution.

***

Eduardo put the Gulfstream on the ground twenty minutes earlier than his ETA predicted.

Raissa busied herself identifying tail numbers of aircraft whose presence could be related to the job at hand. Feeling the big jet stop, she texted Nazarian: *Randall OK on cell phone shutdown; power grid shutdown TBD. Greg Riley monitoring opposition and supporting Randall. Sending Luis Phillips (don't ask) to identify flights scheduled to depart today and their location on tarmac. Phillips then to corral Tipton and Martell. Sending Jamie and Ian to find Grover…should you join Jamie or let him go it alone? Sillin's current location? I'm headed to Vaernes to conscript Marines, then deal with Leanne. Zachary OK? How about you, David? You OK?*

David's response took Raissa's breath away: *Three Marines dead; two burned to death in car fire, one garroted in Grover's suite. Glad you're here.*

Raissa found a taxi outside the Arrival Hall. With full realization Vaernes was less than a ten-minute drive, she pushed two-hundred Krone towards the driver accompanied by an apology.

"Would you wait, please? I'll be less than ten minutes."

At the Vaernes Garrison gate, she left the cab to approach the guard shack. Met by a double-take from one of four Marines on duty, she played her request straight.

"I'd like to speak to Lance Corporal Edgar Martinez."

Tongue-tied and unclear how to address a supermodel, the young Marine responded. "I can find out whether he's on duty, ma'am."

Her phone's clock ticked past ten minutes. Raissa returned to the taxi, passing the driver another two-hundred Krone without a word.

Five minutes later two vehicles pulled-up just inside the entrance gate. Raissa watched an officer lead the way. She offered her hand. "You're Colonel Goodman. I'm Raissa Ribeiro, I work with Zachary Mannheim. I'd like to borrow some Marines."

Max Goodman couldn't help a look of bemusement. "Mannheim's a man with a lot of nerve, Miss Ribeiro. If memory serves, he wanted you anywhere but here in Trondheim tonight. Corporal Martinez delivered you to your flight. Oslo on to JFK, isn't that right Martinez?"

The Corporal's face turned to stone.

Goodman continued in the same deliberate manner. "We don't make a habit of loaning-out Marines. What were you planning to do with them?"

Raissa didn't enjoy condescension. "We don't live in a perfect world, Colonel. In an imperfect world, any Marines I'd borrow could expect to be killing Russian Intelligence agents before today turns to tomorrow...if killing Russians meets your definition of *appropriate initiative*."

Brought up short by Raissa's familiarity with General Givens' orders, Goodman stared hard at a woman he underestimated. "What does a fashion model know about killing?"

"Ask Martinez what luggage I carried, when your grunts played Uber."

Goodman nodded at the Lance Corporal.

"Nothing but a ski-bag, sir. Inventory limited to a SAT phone, Kbar, FNP-9, custom-made sniper rifle, scope, suppressor and .338 Lapua Magnum rounds. Entire kit wrapped in dirty laundry."

Goodman wasn't satisfied. "Mannheim wants Marines in civvies, set up at the Cathedral's entrances to discourage SVR. Doesn't sound like what you've got in mind. Come up to my office, we'll hash this out."

The last thing Raissa expected was her warning antenna to twitch, when listening to a USMC Battalion Commander in a NATO country. She would've preferred not to feel leery, but there would be no denial of a well-tuned bullshit meter. Under an assumption Goodman wouldn't escalate, she spit intolerance. "I need help, Colonel." Turned towards the waiting taxi, chills running down her spine, Raissa tried to find words which fit her intuition. "Right this minute you've filled two body bags. There's another dead Marine in Grover Norris' suite, garroted by a professional."

Goodman's face fell. Caught short about the fate of the third Marine, all three deaths counted against his future promotion.

Raissa's sympathy was non-existent. "Three too many for an officer in your position to explain. If you're content to sit your ass on the fence, keep your Marines home tonight. I wouldn't want them confused between a concert and a battlefield."

Disgusted by unexpected losses, embarrassed in front of Marines hyped-up and looking for revenge, Goodman managed no more than, "I'll decide what's best, Miss Ribeiro. Marines aren't likely to be confused on any battlefield."

Raissa let disdain show. "Trondheim city streets and a Cathedral full of international dignitaries, children, wives and husbands…sounds like anything but a battlefield. Enemies who live in shadow, so-called friends lurking under a rock, two jarheads burned to death in broad daylight, another nearly beheaded from behind. No forgiveness, no mercy, Colonel…that's how SVR operates. That's what we're up against, if you've got the balls for a nasty fight."

The taxi's door slammed, punctuating an unsatisfactory waste of her time. In an answer to the driver's question, she told him, "Clarion Hotel."

***

Phillips's first assignment should have been trivial: Ferret out the tail-number of Marta's airplane and determine whether its pilot filed a flight plan. Tail-number in hand, the airplane's physical location on the tarmac could be determined with field-glasses. What he came up against was a wall of silence from airport officials and unusual resistance from less official sources.

With less than ten jet-bridges at Terminals A & B, Louis assumed no flight would be permitted to park longer than needed to turn the aircraft around for its next departure. Nevertheless, he walked the length of the Terminal to find a Lufthansa A320 and an SAS 737 in the process of boarding passengers.

Trondheim's General Aviation parking area proved a challenge. Security denied him access to Raissa's Gulfstream where it sat among nine other aircraft and a single helicopter. Next tactic under evaluation, Phillips watched a sleek Sukhoi 100 roll to a stop. Three Mercedes sedans arrived within seconds of its forward door being opened. Taras Sluchevsky, in the flesh and a perfect match for his photograph, was the first passenger to exit.

Phillips texted: *Sluchevsky arrived. He and wife plus four-man detail and six miscellaneous (3 men, 3 women late thirties early forties) aboard a 100-seat Sukhoi. A Ka-62 chopper (700km range loaded) - 14 passengers plus 6 stretchers - is sole candidate for SVR's departure. Advise.*

Raissa responded: *Photo passengers. Move on.*

Louis Phillips was an experienced Field Director, a position which required significant powers of anticipation: He'd departed the Gulfstream with a 35mm digital camera fitted with a long lens but missed Sluchevsky in the well-lit area of the jet's exit door. Displeased with himself, he moved away from the double-doors where the Sukhoi's passengers would enter the Terminal. Long lens exchanged for a wide angle, he snapped two security-men, Mr. & Mrs. Sluchevsky, two additional security-men and what appeared to be six bored staffers. When the main Russian group exited the Terminal out of earshot, one of their pilots broke towards him. Phillips checked his position—saw the door to the Men's toilet. In the process of stowing his gear in its shoulder bag, he looked up to find the Sukhoi's pilot standing way too close.

Five seconds was all it took for the pilot to deliver his message. Phillips focused on the pilot's Intel and managed only a profile shot as the pilot rejoined the Sluchevsky's entourage. Phillips crossed to a coffee stall. Texted Raissa: *Photos uploaded. Approached by Sluchevsky's pilot, verbal message as follows: 'My name is Andrei Fetisov. Tell Zachary Mannheim - Grover Norris and Petr Sillin to meet at 15:00 in St. Saviour's Chapel.'*

Raissa's return text was curt: *Move on. Confirm.*

Her internal clock hit one minute; there'd been more than adequate time for Phillips to confirm his instruction and exit the General Aviation Terminal without drawing further attention to himself.

"Shit," she said out loud, drawing a subdued laugh from the taxi driver.

Her text to Randall: *Last text from Phillips—hacked?*

Randall's response: *Encryption intact—text secure.*

Raissa: *Enhance photo of Andrei Fetisov. Distribute. Delete Phillips last text.*

Randall: *No need.*

Phillips's silence made her edgy. Her text barked at Randall without provocation: *Phillips dead or SVR. Block Phillips's phone.*

The idea of Grover meeting Sluchevsky was Machiavellian, particularly under an anonymous Russian icon depicting a beady-eyed Christ surrounded by a golden halo. Nicknamed *Savior of the Wet Beard,* the icon was famous for peering straight into the eyes of the viewer regardless of the viewing angle. Raissa pictured Mannheim as a fragile moth burnt to ash in one of the Cathedral's banks of Offering Candles. Not a woman to allow a chimera to rule over logic, she chased away obvious questions. Distilled from the self-evident would-be Zachary's first concern: Whether Andrei Fetisov, a Russian pilot claiming to be Aydan Fetisov's son, could be a credible messenger.

She texted Mannheim: *Andrei Fetisov credible? Who will go with you to Grover's meeting with Sillin?*

Mannheim, in complete agreement regarding Phillips, expressed exasperation: *Didn't we agree you'd stay away?*

Raissa: *Answer the question.*

Mannheim let go of unproductive agitation: *Jamie to meet David and I @ 22:45 - West Front of Cathedral. Your chat with Col. Goodman wasn't pleasant.*

Raissa: *Sit on the fence - get splinters in your ass. What's Goodman gonna do?*

Mannheim: *What chance Marta bought him?*

Raissa texted: *Time will tell.*

Troubled by Mannheim offering no opinion as to Andrei Fetisov's credibility, she wondered: Did Aydan Fetisov even have children?

Confined spaces occupied the bottom rung of Raissa's operational preferences. Deep within a stone edifice, in a chapel with one entrance/exit, protecting Mannheim would be as much a matter of good fortune as skill.

For less than an instant an explosion of automatic weapons fire overwhelmed her. Shell casings flew past her face from a shooter's Kalashnikov. Deafened by the cacophony, the smell of death caused her stomach to rebel. Emerged from a recurrent purgatory, she pored over who would acquiesce to a meeting where every participant could be killed in seconds?

Who in their right mind would have chosen *St. Saviour's Chapel?*

Her phone vibrated. An enhanced photo of a man claiming to be Aydan Fetisov's son could be anyone. She hoped the image would mean something to Mannheim, who would attend the *Grover − Sillin* meeting without her. Her text to Nazarian would puzzle everyone on Randall's private network: *David - vehicle location?*

His return text caused Raissa to grimace: *Vehicle compromised. Plan B?*

***

David Nazarian's vehicle was not, to the best of his knowledge, compromised in any way. His text to Raissa reflected a growing sense of operational malaise and the reduced effectiveness of decisions made under threat of betrayal. Why, David demanded of himself, had Randall's mimicry of SVR's internal communications continued apace, while real-time Russian content dwindled to mundane generalities? Why had Marta's clamorous, categorical, demands of her agents faded? Yes, David allowed, SVR's operational plans could have been simulated and practiced to supersede an exchange of orders, or interpretation of events during implementation.

Or not.

If we are compromised, how did it happen? No, that's not relevant any longer. Assume we are compromised.

Who can be trusted? This way leads to insanity, David told himself.

Trust Mannheim.

Trust yourself.

Be cold-blooded. Don't pray; shoot first, assess righteousness at another time in another place.

Trade money for lives.

Trade goodwill for another breath.

Trade your last breath for what you've valued most.

Chapter 23

Mannheim intended to walk the Cathedral's perimeter, examining each nook and cranny of its ancient stones for concealed points of access. His point of origin, at the King's Entrance on the North Front, exuded light and warmth from the interior, which would heighten the audience's anticipation of the Christmas Concert. Stopped in admiration, he examined details of stained-glass windows depicting the Old Testament. Jarred back to the present, he turned east, switched on a flashlight and adjusted its beam to throw a narrow, intense cone of light. As east turned clockwise to south, scenes from the New Testament emerged in the windows high above him. In an act of procrastination, as the distance from *St. Saviour's Chapel* diminished to yards, he slowed his forward progress. Depleted by ambiguity he stood still as a sculpture. Somewhere inside thick walls was the High Altar and not far away, if a door was secreted in rough-carved structural stone, *St. Saviour's Chapel.*

In the adjacent private car park, a car door closed, its telltale thud penetrating darkness thick as congealed blood.

Seconds passed.

Movement conjured by a restless psyche, processed in a different fashion than other emotions, raw fear bypassed Mannheim's sensory cortex. Friend or foe cluttered his amygdala, the almond-shaped origin of fear. Flashlight extinguished, a minute passed without visible or audible signs of whomever slammed the door. His left leg cramped as he embraced the Cathedral's wall where it made a sharp angled turn. Masked to anyone in the car park, he chided himself: Excessive nerves reveal you as an amateur. Still he delayed, cursing the absence of late afternoon daylight commonplace in other parts of the world. Flashlight switched on his heart jumped into his throat, when a strong grip pinned his right hand against his back.

"Relax, it's me," David hissed without freeing Mannheim's hand.

Mannheim made a pro-forma attempt to extract his hand. "Release me, David, before I lose my wits." Freedom re-established; he extinguished the flashlight.

Neither man could interpret the other's facial response.

Nazarian spoke with certainty he couldn't feel. "Marta knows Tretiak isn't running cyber-ops. Anything we hear on the SVR feed is a trap."

"It was never going to last, David. Tretiak fell into our laps with a short sell-by date…we can't pretend ignorance. We'll go our own way as planned…let events at the concert dictate our response."

David hesitated a moment too long.

Mannheim didn't need more than one guess. "You're wondering whether Tretiak has been released by our friend Colonel Goodman?"

"No, sir. With Phillips out of action, it's obvious…Marta intends to take us one by one. Whatever fate she's dreamed up for you will arrive at her leisure."

Cold penetrated Mannheim's fingers. A northwest wind swirled, stinging his right cheek as a reminder: Hiding was a waste of effort with today's rules-of-engagement writ plain.

Nazarian melted away.

Zachary continued to hug the wall, probing for what proved non-existent. Satisfied, he picked-up the pace, intending to enter via the West Front under its famous Rose Window depicting the Day of Judgment. Aware its center panel symbolized Christ, flames radiated outwards ending in angels trumpeting judgment's imminent arrival.

What could have been taken for a convivial circle of churchgoers shunted two of its brethren in his direction; neither was Jamie Norris or Ian Riddick. One wore a fedora, winter coat and black dress shoes. Three steps to the rear lingered a Marine rifleman in winter uniform wielding a suppressed M-27 automatic rifle—the gift he'd once hoped-for from Einar Haugen and Lt. Col. Goodman, just when Mannheim changed his mind about its efficacy.

Raised hand not subject to interpretation, an NIS officer bathed Mannheim in light before issuing his demand. "Could I see your identification, sir? Routine security check for the concert tonight."

Mannheim, without any sort of official ID, decided against officiousness in favor of Einar's attention to detail. "Mannheim's my name. I'm cooperating with NIS and the American Marines on security measures for the concert. I'd planned on making the first of several sweeps of the interior. You'll find my photo on your phone." Eyes never leaving the lethal M-27, Mannheim believed the odds of survival improved with deployed Marines in support. SVR wouldn't have brought heavy weapons and wouldn't engage in an unrestricted exchange of gunfire. He inquired of a serious young Marine, "Are you deploying the 50 Cal?"

Without change in expression, or movement of any kind, the teenage Jarhead responded, "Above my pay grade, sir."

Phone reversed to confirm Mannheim's photo, the NIS officer's hand indicated Mannheim was free to enter. Ten steps took Mannheim away from prying eyes to where a text to Randall would be private: *Take down all cell phone networks ASAP. No less than five minutes no more than fifteen. Reactivate at first indication of violence.* He watched the unencrypted phone's timer tick off 1:23 before the device lost connection.

Mannheim felt nothing like those angels depicted in the Rose Window. With the magnificent bronze door closing, his right hand tested the added weight of the semi-automatic's suppressor.

Across a gap too wide for certainty a large, well-muscled, man was distracted by a failed cellphone. Mannheim forced his right leg to move forward, then the left and the right a second time. Groomed tight to this fellow's cheeks, from sideburn to sideburn, a new beard was inadequate to prevent recognition of Marta's Chechen agent. The driver of Vehicle One in Quebec City held the uncooperative phone in his gun hand. Advantage not to be wasted, Zachary pulled the trigger three times. From less than ten feet, three bullets aimed without expertise left the mercenary staggered. The Cathedral's vast interior swallowed what little sound escaped Mannheim's 9mm.

At a range of less than five feet, Mannheim demanded, "How many others?"

A man in his late forties, who'd survived a long time in a younger man's game, saw what non-compliance would mean. He would offer a lie, but not an egregious one, in a fool's expectation of mercy. Perhaps mild deceit wouldn't cause Marta's devil to apply the coup de grâce.

"Two."

"Are these two inside the Cathedral? Are we talking about two dozen? Or some other fictional number? Two men? Two women? Be explicit. Five seconds. Four...three...two...one." In an eruption of fear and anger, Zachary pulled the trigger. He recognized a grievous error while his eyes searched for an inevitable response. When the SVR type, dressed in faux Armani, was seen advancing through the Nave's thicket of wooden chairs, Mannheim's supposition was proven correct. Fifty meters separated him from a qualified field agent whose face wore a look of impudence. Seven worshippers were seated close enough to make them candidates to suffer unintended consequences.

Why not wait? Let the slow-walking Russian come closer. Mannheim took the aisle chair on the right side of the last row.

"Yevgeni Popov, Mr. Mannheim," the Russian announced in a worthy expression of composure. "An unarmed intermediary sent by Marta to seek accommodation. May I join you?"

Zachary's silence interpreted as license, the Russian sat in the penultimate row. A sideways glance at the dead man produced a spy's requiem.

"Our dead Chechen had no appreciation for his tactical situation."

"Popov...is your father a Russian Orthodox priest as the name suggests? You are surely aware the Church of Norway is Lutheran. In 1537, or thereabouts, the Lutherans broke ties with the Holy See resulting in a church integrated with the state. Marta broke all ties with the Vatican, but without any intention of integrating religion and politics."

"My father isn't a priest, although some suggest he worships at the Cathedral of Jim Beam. He's an oligarch according to CNN, who disapproves of his male offspring and my profession. As to Marta and the zealot Jesuit, the Gleinicke Bridge's tragicomic prisoner exchange is over the hills and far away. Your wife invites you to discuss ways in which all parties might declare themselves satisfied with their efforts in Trondheim."

Mannheim was disinclined to accept. "Are there alternative choices?"

Popov's smile overflowed with self-gratification. "Exactly as I predicted. Zachary Mannheim is a man driven by analysis." Face full of irony, he continued. "For a troglodyte like you, all data is excessive. I've won our inter-office pool: Marta predicted you would shoot me rather than appear in her presence, cowed by a woman."

Mannheim's phone vibrated; Randall returned cell service at a propitious moment. Device raised on an extended arm, he photographed Yevgeni Popov. Without regard for any threat Popov might represent, he transmitted the photo accompanied by a request for facial recognition.

Burdened by a seed of doubt, the Russian's face turned sour.

"Are you unnerved, Yevgeni? Is SVR suffering technical difficulties with its communications?"

"No, not at all. Service in Norway is infected with intermittent reliability."

Mannheim ended their charade. "Marta awaits her husband in *St. Saviour's Chapel.* Who else will be in attendance?"

A knowing smile greeted an expected question. Popov was back on script and intended to cleave the old bastard's neck with a dull blade.

"Neither Norris the elder or younger is available, but your former protégé, Phyllis Martell, will join us along with SVR's long-serving double, Mariah Ackerly, and your President's National Security Advisor, Craig Hall."

"Will you be in attendance, Yevgeni?" Mannheim's question served to provide a respite from body blows delivered moments earlier by the smarmy Russian.

"I'll be on the lookout for David Nazarian, lest he be given the opportunity to prove himself worthy."

Mannheim stood. "After you, Yevgeni."

As the SVR agent retraced his steps, Zachary's priority was to identify Popov's backup. Unable to pick out a single soul who appeared interested or capable, innocent worshippers lingered as targets for misdirected bullets or ricochets off stone walls, floors and columns. A rapid inventory identified six women and one man, each a senior citizen.

Apart from his and Popov's footsteps, which echoed through praiseworthy acoustics of the majestic Main Choir, Mannheim felt rather than heard the Cathedral go silent. Eyes drawn back to Popov, Zachary heard nothing of a high velocity bullet, but witnessed Yevgeni Popov collapse in a heap. An old woman dressed head to toe in black screamed. The man next to her, wearing a suit several sizes too large, rose from where he knelt and pulled her close to provide comfort. Enveloped by his sympathies, her gaunt face turned to Mannheim in triumph. Zachary examined her male companion and found recognition under professional makeup. Mannheim's earlier best option—shoot Yevgeni Popov dead—faded to irrelevance. He stepped over Popov's unmoving body. Curiosity about the fellow's deserved demise was a million miles distant from what he suspected would, in less than a minute, strain mind and heart.

Behind him the Countess and Nazarian maintained their positions until Mannheim disappeared from view.

David Nazarian began a running tally of the evening's body count.

***

Mannheim accepted his weakness. If he hesitated, if he thought too much about outcomes, if he remembered too little, if he imagined death, if he totaled the cost of hubris, then cowardice would prevail. If a coward could admit his nature, the Chapel door could be opened against the instinct to flee. With a fleeting look backwards in the direction of the High Altar, he walked faster. Surprised to find himself alone, he grabbed the brass door handle, rotated it clockwise and took one step inside *St. Savior's Chapel.*

Grover Norris was dead, an observation which required no forensic examination.

Mariah Ackerly's head lolled over her right shoulder, then, robbed of neuromuscular control flopped onto her chest. A drug cocktail administered against her will was anything but a tricky assumption. Elias Thordsen, christened Elijas Halvorsen by his mother and father, knelt and wept by Mariah's side.

No Marta.

No Craig Hall.

No Russell Tipton.

No Phyllis Martell.

No Jamie Norris or Ian Riddick or Louis Phillips.

No Göran Berglund.

No Einar Haugen.

No Lt. Col. Max Goodman.

No Raissa.

No *Choirmaster.* Had *Choirmaster* always been a ruse? Window dressing meant to suggest and distract?

A pair of chairs were arranged so their occupants would face the chapel's Russian icon away from human death and suffering.

Mannheim elected the one leaving his right hand and arm free to move.

"Your sorrow won't help your mother. Were you already here, when they dragged her in? Did they administer the drugs while you watched?"

"Fuck you," Elias screamed without a change in position. "You did this."

"That's so tiresome, kiddo. I've heard every kind of accusation. There's no need to play games inside your head. I can read your mind."

If looks were fatal, Elias would have felled Mannheim where he sat. "Pathetic old man. I killed a real SVR thug...sailed the North Atlantic alone...just to get here. You wouldn't be much challenge."

"Don't let the fire in your belly rush to your head. Giddy for the chance to be a big-boy, you've known from the beginning...this is how it goes, when you drink the Kool-Aid. Where it goes from here, what you do next...is what matters."

Elias pushed himself erect. Four words cost him a trove of emotional currency. "Will you help her?"

"Don't whine like a simpleton. Grover Norris isn't coming back from the dead...you're not dealing with fools. Give me a good reason. Or if not a good reason, give me one reason I can believe."

In desperation, Elias chose disingenuous over sincere. "I'll do whatever you want."

Mannheim pushed himself upwards into a position of equals. "I don't need to see or hear any more from you, kiddo. Cling to those false illusions Tipton fed you. Believe the prettiest of Russian lies. Don't cry when your mother dies. Don't cry for yourself. Don't believe in me...I'll cheat you blind."

Mindful of time passing, there was nothing more to do in *St. Savior's Chapel*. Repercussions failed to weigh on him. Zachary's end, if or when it arrived, would last the wink of an eye fixed on eternity.

***

Mannheim walked the length and breadth of the Cathedral. His purpose, clouded by too much death and too little relevant data, included who would enter and leave *St. Savior's Chapel* in the immediate future.

Nazarian and the Countess were no longer an elderly couple at prayer; the dead Chechen's corpse had been taken away by persons unknown. A creature of gloom, Mannheim's text was concise: *Jamie, call Einar Haugen of NIS to arrange removal of Grover's body from St. Savior's Chapel. Hold on tight—mourn your father tomorrow, do your job today.* Five minutes passed without a response before he tapped: *Ian, where's Jamie?*

A long delay ended with Randall's text: *Jamie and Ian's phones located Clarion Hotel Trondheim.*

Mannheim considered the impacts before he issued a response: *Phillips phone?*

Randall: *Phillips phone powered off. Last location Trondheim Airport.*

One text remained: *Raissa, where r u?* Mannheim felt his blood pressure rise as minutes ticked away.

Punctuated by clatter and chatter attending the arrival of television technicians tasked with pre-broadcast preparations, the Cathedral's aura brightened. Klieg lights and special effects turned the main choir's background into a snowstorm of clear, sparkling crystals then transformed the stone encapsulated space into a multi-colored forest. Left hand held up against glare, Göran Berglund stood in the center of the choir. Head rotated to survey where the audience would be positioned, he marched on a direct line towards an unidentifiable objective.

Mannheim vacated the shadows, resolved to intercept the Artistic Director of the Boys Choir.

Berglund turned towards *St. Savior's Chapel,* where two police officers escorted two ambulance attendants and their rattling gurneys. Riveted, Berglund made eye contact with Elias, then, consumed with unknown emotion, turned away exhibiting reluctance.

Mannheim counted rows of chairs, a half-measure to fix Berglund's position in his mind. Then like a ship taking-on water, the Cathedral's entrances sprouted a half-dozen synchronous surprises as small groups of choir members poured into the Cathedral's interior.

Four cautious steps had restored Mannheim to obscurity, when the closure of the West Front's bronze door intruded. A party of five stood in a half-circle; were they listening to a docent? They meandered towards the Choir and Main Altar, arms of their guide sweeping upwards to illustrate Nidaros' architectural features. Russian Minister of Foreign Affairs Taras Sluchevsky and his wife,

Oksana, committed full attention to a vast expanse of stone and stained glass, filled with the promise of a Christian god's love and forgiveness.

Mannheim censured himself: *Don't grab at straws, you old fool. Offense or defense, you must choose.*

Filled with the organ's demands, choir members organized themselves. Berglund abandoned his earlier search in favor of his baton and the final touches to the evening's program.

Elias took his front row position in the Boys Choir.

Marta extended her hand to Oksana Sluchevsky; the two women took seats reserved for VIP guests. Two senior SVR agents assumed defensive positions. Taras Sluchevsky stood behind and to the left of his wife.

Even as he wondered whether two SVR agents were Marta's last and best, Mannheim accepted a zero probability of survival from an uninvited approach.

Each choir finished one selection with restrained praise from Berglund. Elias completed a portion of his first solo before Berglund, in exasperation, cut him off. On their way to makeshift dressing rooms in the bowels of the Cathedral, choir members heard Berglund's full-throated reassurance.

"Butterflies are normal. You've worked hard. This evening will bring out your collective best. I'm very proud of each of you."

Mannheim believed Marta's opinion would mirror his own: Elias would be suffering qualms of mistrust and fear. The lad had become unreliable—little more than a wild card. For an Op in which his wife had invested so much political and career currency, decisions about Elias's reliability would suffer from delay; the concert's broadcast would begin in a haze reflective of a precarious future.

Chapter 24

Grover Norris' credibility would have meant everything to Petr Sillin in the most forbidden discussion between men close to Presidents.

Russell Tipton's personal credibility nonexistent, it was more than possible Sillin wouldn't recognize his name. As he used a cell number purported to belong to Sillin, *Reformation* appeared fated for a footnote in the unwritten history of CIA.

A suspicious voice answered in American accented English. "Who is this?"

"My name is Russell Tipton. I'm a serving officer …"

Irritated, the voice interrupted. "I know who you are, Mr. Tipton. What do you want?"

Several options cycled through Tipton's test of ethics versus equity. From near desperation came a frantic response. "Grover Norris has been executed. Every Russian and American in Trondheim is a Free Agent until the Christmas Concert begins. I'm offering what Mr. Norris would have offered you." Tipton choked-off a witless sales pitch; Sillin knew the framework of Grover's proffered defection agreement.

"Mr. Norris's death is unfortunate. Although we never met, Russia and the United States will be damaged by the loss of his diplomatic experience. In minutes I will leave for this evening's concert. Goodbye Mr. Tipton."

Tipton didn't find Petr Sillin's aloof dismissal credible. He pushed doubt away, firm in belief of what he'd told the Russian; all parties, regardless of prior commitment, could make deals in good faith until the massive organ filled the Cathedral.

His missing leg craved relief available in the *Clarion's* bar. Resistant defiance accompanied Tipton as he hurried out the hotel's main entrance.

His taxi pulled away half a minute prior to Raissa's arrival.

*****

Raissa's circuit of the public rooms provoked a critical decision: She would not attend the Christmas concert. Skill set unsuited to close quarters and crowds, she would invest no more than half an hour searching the hotel for Jamie Norris, Ian Riddick, Louis Phillips, Phyllis Martell, Russell Tipton and Leanne Crowder.

Her immediate enterprise centered on gear stored at *Nidaros Pilegrimsgård;* after its collection a tactical position on the periphery of Trondheim Airport would support a rear-guard action capable of saving Mannheim. Selfishness, about her opportunity to save others, or not, was deadweight to be ignored.

Photos on her phone, together with enough folding money to sweeten a doorman's memory, suggested Martell and Tipton took separate taxis, at different times, to *Nidaros Cathedral.* Neither doorman identified any of four Agency officers. Jamie's room was empty as was Ian Riddick's. Louis Phillips had never checked in. Nor had Leanne. A search for definitive data rendered null and void, Raissa's working classifications included: Phillips—dead; Leanne—operational; Jamie and Ian—neutralized possibly dead; Martell—irrelevant.

As the taxi pulled away she considered those classifications a less than fifty-fifty proposition. Storage unit's address retrieved from encrypted texts, she showed the screen to the taxi driver—*OK Minilager, Trondheim-Lade, Haakon VIIs gate 23.* Shoved a wad of cash into the front seat accompanied by further instructions.

"You wait at the mini-storage. Then we'll go to *Nidaros Pilegrimsgård.* Okay?"

Raissa caught the driver examining her via the rearview. Watched him count the cash. Saw him nod as the taxi accelerated. Disliked his scrutiny of her more than a half-hearted exploration of twenty-dollar notes. It was undeniable; every taxi in the hotel rank could be driven by an NIS agent or a local stringer purchased weeks ago by SVR. Paranoia wasn't sufficient to condemn a man outright, when his features matched the license photo on the sun visor.

Furtive glance down and to his right, was it a phone, two-way radio, or weapon he sought?

Raissa racked the slide on her 9 mil. "If that's your phone, hand it to me slowly." She braced herself in anticipation of some surprise aggression. When he stiffened, she added, "You'll be dead before we crash." His phone in hand she scanned recent calls. One number repeated several times.

"Who answers this number?"

"My daughter. She'll be excited to know Raissa is in my car."

"You're betting your life on it."

"Her name is Ella. Please don't hurt me."

Raissa would've preferred to let Randall vet his claim of fatherhood but couldn't deny a nagging insistence comms were no longer secure. Her left thumb highlighted the number and initiated the call.

A woman's voice answered with one word. "Hello." This gatekeeper's voice was similar to a hundred others Raissa had heard.

"Phyllis Martell, CIA/Langley. Connect me to Einar Haugen at Nidaros Cathedral."

"Where are you, Ms. Martell?"

"Are you the evening desk officer?"

"Provide your location, Ms. Martell."

Raissa ended the call. Spoke to the driver in an even-handed tone. "Want to try again."

"Doing my job. Jockey in the queue; try to drive any American who needs transportation. Monitor where they go. Identify who they meet."

The taxi slowed to a stop in front of the storage unit. The driver turned round, hands empty and extended.

"Show me a picture of Ella," was Raissa's version of a fair demand.

His left hand returned his wallet which held half a dozen pictures of a wife and daughter who looked pre-school.

"Genuine or cover?"

"Not senior enough for undercover."

"Leave the key in the ignition and get out. You can load my stuff, then we'll see what comes next."

Two MANPAD missiles, two Kalashnikov AK-74 assault rifles, one Makarov 9mm, two cellphones without a SIM, an unopened bag of packaged food and water, and a ransacked first-aid kit were the residue of Tretiak's capture. Loaded in the taxi, those missiles and the bag of packaged food and water formed the basis of a contingency plan. She shot a look at the driver, who lingered in anticipation inside the storage unit. Checked her phone for the time.

What to do with her ersatz chauffeur?

"Pull down the door. Do it now." She snapped the padlock and tossed the key.

Twenty-five minutes expired in the retrieval of her ski-bag from *Nidaros Pilegrimsgård*. Reassured by the rifle's readiness she counted .338 rounds. Set her phone's GPS for the airport and began the thirty-minute drive. Inconspicuous the goal, she never exceeded the posted speed limit or passed another vehicle.

Focused on the unforeseen, Raissa felt contradictory but familiar emotions erupt from the history pages of her specialized expertise. Taxi abandoned, she accessed historical data from flight operations to determine wind direction and takeoff/landing headings.

The rifle would be best while the opposition walked the tarmac to board SVR's Ka-62 chopper or Sluchevsky's 100-seat Sukhoi. Her expertise with the rifle second nature, a MANPAD was a different beast. Based on the experience with Jakov, Tretiak's missiles would be either *Strela* or *Igla*, both able to engage targets head-on, from behind or from the side. Both systems utilized infrared, UV seekers which made them difficult to elude.

With no effort Raissa recalled the terror a missile caused its target. All things being equal, she preferred launching head-on as Tretiak had done against Jakov's Cessna. Mental calculations estimated the distance to an optimum location at near two miles. The range to parked Russian aircraft would be six to eight hundred yards. An aircraft on takeoff could be engaged in-flight at under two miles. Destination established, her intention was to ignore both incessant pain from unhealed wounds and the missiles hundred pounds of extra weight.

Near the bottom of her tank of energy, she sheltered in the welcome asylum of deep snow.

Raissa searched for the broadcast of the Christmas Concert on her phone. On its screen she watched both choirs' joyous procession proceed single file through the aisles. Girls carried flowers, gifted to children throughout the audience. Boys distributed brightly wrapped gifts as a remembrance of the occasion.

***

Nazarian felt audience anticipation grow, charmed as they were by the choir's manifestation of the holiday. Individual blessings were conferred upon choir members in whispered voices belonging to enchanted children. A living organism, the assembly manifested its pleasure in time with organ music.

David hadn't caught sight of Mannheim in over thirty minutes.

There would be no sighting of the Countess; she was everyone and no one. David's intention was to do his best, whatever such a nonsensical goal might mean.

As two choirs reassembled, deep bass tones from the organ trumpeted the introduction and welcome by Göran Berglund.

Back pressed against stone, Nazarian inched closer to dark, cordoned-off areas behind the choirs. This position offered an ideal view of semi-circular VIP seating in front of the Artistic Director's reading-stand, countered by an on-again-off-again line of fire through male and female choir-members. Focused on targeting Marta's two SVR agents, David worried about his exposure to live television cameras once *Reformation's* assassinations began.

Berglund raised his arms, right hand tight on the baton's blonde wood. Cathedral silent, the background burst into a snowstorm of clear, sparkling crystals. With a nod to the Boys Choir, and a sharp movement of his baton, the concert began.

***

In the cocoon of Raissa's Gulfstream, Randall Carter and Greg Riley were slaves to the Program Guide and live performances within the Cathedral. *Laudate Dominum* would be the first solo of the evening; Elias was scheduled to step into a spotlight thirty-two minutes after Berglund's opening movement. Timed to Elias's presence in the limelight, Randall would cut electric power to Trondheim's grid.

Antidote to tension and boredom, Riley's laptop ran multiple facial recognition algorithms on screenshots pulled from the High-Definition broadcast. Reclined in one of the Gulfstream's leather armchairs, he watched photos flash-by on his screen.

In a hack of an entire power grid, Randall would've expected Mannheim approval for localized, pre-concert outages designed as QA/QC for the full-scale attack. Such minor interruptions wouldn't reach near a blackout or brownout, but two requests had received sharp denials. As a poor substitute, Randall and Greg spent the prior twenty-four hours running multiple simulations of the real thing. They both understood risks inherent in an unproven digital intrusion. Failure would provide a significant advantage to SVR. Success was more amorphous in nature; without power Nidaros Cathedral would be candlelit, except for television lights and cameras which would broadcast via a 20KW standby generator. Within the artificial world of the choir stage nothing would be altered by the outage. In the Cathedral's vast interior, chaos might or might not smile on Langley's diminished contingent. Outside the Cathedral a mixture of Russian Regular Army, US Marines, NIS, SVR, CIA and a horde of Norwegian civilians could collapse into a morass of indefensible casualties.

Greg and Randall were aware of Raissa's instructions to Eduardo, pilot of the Gulfstream. As soon as fire was reported in the airport's standby generator, operations would cease, and Eduardo would taxi to the on-deck position for the main runway. Unless contravened by direct voice communication from Raissa, Eduardo was authorized to exercise his judgment to prevent loss of aircraft, passengers or crew.

Greg felt excited apprehension when he spoke his first words in over an hour. "One minute countdown initiated."

At the thirteen second mark facial recognition's electronic voice stated: *Leanne Crowder - Girls Choir, second row, third from the left.* Riley devoted precious seconds to confirmation but couldn't validate facial recognition's conclusion. Terrified by the thought of unintended circumstances, he texted the result to Mannheim's team. His phone timer buzzed. No time to think, he acted.

"Randall, take it down."

Randall Carter's glance at Riley conveyed a hundred meanings. He pressed *Enter.*

***

While the Cathedral's already dimmed electric lights faded to black, Elias unscrewed the pistol's suppressor; his assignment called for noise. Alone under the spotlight, alone in a crowded Cathedral, he stepped forward. Organ and violins filled listeners' ears, as Berglund's baton urged lyrics from Elias's vocal-cords. In an extemporaneous hope of throwing his enemies off balance, and with a controlled intake of breath, Elias began.

Laudate Dominum omnes gentes
Laudate eum, omnes populi

Elias allowed the music's required pause to lengthen, then continued.

Quoniam confirmata est
Super nos misericordia...

Eyes centered on Petr Sillin, the fingers of his right hand closed on the Glock beneath black cassock and white surplice. In one continuous motion Elias raised and aimed the weapon.

Nazarian caught sight of a Girls Choir member aiming her semi-automatic at Elias. Focused on Elias and Sillin, he never saw a second Girls Choir member aim at Taras Sluchevsky.

Elias fired twice as a sledgehammer struck his back. Loss of control over his legs ruined an attempt to return fire. Knees buckled, Elias saw Sillin's hands clutch at his chest. An awkward fall left Elias in a heap unable to breathe.

In surrealistic choreography David Nazarian and Leanne Crowder sighted on different targets. Driven by divergent fears neither fired.

Leanne felt her vest absorb a bullet. Near her partially healed wound, searing pain caused a cessation of thought. She managed to gain partial cover behind a pillar and dropped to a knee. One or more ribs bruised or broken, she began a mental regimen designed to diminish pain and maintain operational functionality.

Two SVR minders failed to move fast enough. Four suppressed shots came out of nowhere to make twin impacts upon each man's body armor. Stunned, their deaths were delayed not prevented by a false sense of preservation. Each man took an additional suppressed round to the head.

Minister of Foreign Affairs Taras Sluchevsky grabbed his wife Oksana's elbow. Her scream drew his attention to a neck wound oozing blood. He half carried her from the stage in the direction of the high altar.

Cell phones all over Trondheim returned to life.

Less than ten seconds had passed from the moment Elias's weapon became visible.

To the horror of the Girls' Choir, two members settled into lifeless forms. Makarov 9mm semi-automatics released from dead hands clattered upon the stage.

Nazarian watched Leanne struggle to stand. Her scrutiny of *Reformation's* outcome incomplete, choir dress ripped off, she limped in the direction taken by Sluchevsky's entourage. David delayed further movement in favor of a survey of the actors in Mannheim's drama. Zachary was alive, tucked away in dark shadow. Marta Mannheim, Deputy Director of SVR's First Directorate, vacated the Cathedral for an unknowable location. Einar Haugen emerged from obscurity, accompanied by armed NIS officers, to usurp Göran Berglund's microphone to calm the audience.

Illustrative of failure, a mass retreat showed signs of uncontrolled panic. Among those frozen in fear were surviving members of both Choirs. Those whose fates remained indeterminate included Raissa Ribeiro, Russell Tipton, Phyllis Martell, Jamie Norris, Ian Riddick, Lt. Col. Max Goodman, and Andrei Fetisov.

Nazarian could discern no police presence: Would Haugen try to curb Norwegian media's coverage of events?

One of Haugen's officers approached his superior, pointing towards the High Altar as they spoke.

David read Haugen's text to Mannheim on the NIS network: *CIA shooter took two in the right lower back. Stable. Surgeons awaiting ambulance.* Unhappy with the intermittent encrypted signal, Nazarian texted Randall: *WTF, genius? We need good comms.*

Greg Riley responded with understandable pique: *Comms up. Game over…we lost.*

Disingenuous it was, but Greg made a point. So what if SVR monitored his comms? David typed: *Team check-in.* The text generated no responses.

Riley appeared to be wrong; a version of the game would continue under alternate rules.

By the time Nazarian's focus returned to the Cathedral, the Nave was, for the greatest part, abandoned. Through an aisle of scattered chairs, pausing only to don gloves and grab one of Berglund's stashed Makarovs, David crossed in search of Mannheim.

A different searcher's movements paralleled Nazarian's: He recognized Andrei Fetisov from the airport photo sent by Phillips. Candlelight sparse in the Cathedral's geographic center, certainty suffered. Friend or foe—in what category did Fetisov the Younger reside?

Nazarian slowed his pace, keen to improve his assessment of the Russian.

Mannheim's dissection of events recoiled between pleased and confused. If Sillin and Elias proved the only significant deaths, Trondheim might yet be submerged under brighter, shinier stories excavated during the 24-hour news cycle. If both survived, the inevitable claims and counterclaims by the Kremlin and White House would smell like rotted fish.

So what outcome should an old spy hunter root for?

Why do I feel elated, defeated and let down?

"Mr. Mannheim, it's Andrei Fetisov. May we speak?"

Mannheim raised his head from his phone's screen. "Good evening, Andrei, shouldn't you be preparing to fly Sluchevsky home to Moscow?"

In short-circuited words, Fetisov showed his jitters. "My father shared info with you in the hope peace would prevail over war. I'd like to continue his efforts."

Mannheim maintained his grip on the Pug revolver. "Your father was intelligent and courageous. Not a combination often found in troubled times."

Fetisov ignored a specious request to validate himself. "Russell Tipton, Jamie Norris and Ian Riddick are SVR prisoners; they will be offered to you for repatriation, perhaps in a three for one exchange for Raissa Ribeiro. Tretiak is assumed to be in US Marine custody at Vaernes Garrison. Marta won't bargain for his return."

Focused on a man he'd never met before, Mannheim waited. There was more to come in this opening offer from Marta.

Andrei Fetisov shifted from foot to foot, then relented. "Sluchevsky's wife sustained a serious wound. Sillin's life is threatened by his injuries. The CIA assassin is expected to succumb or at best survive as a vegetable."

Zachary grew weary of the dance. "Where is Sluchevsky, Andrei? Why are you Marta's messenger?"

"Sluchevsky approached your Marines, seeking protected diplomatic travel status to Trondheim Airport and the Sukhoi...the aircraft is fueled and ready to either return to Moscow or to an agreed upon destination."

"Are discussions under way between Foreign Minister Sluchevsky and representatives of the United States government?"

"I cannot speculate about such things, Mr. Mannheim."

"You'll need more than speculation, if called upon to fly Minister Sluchevsky to a black site chosen by the White House. How about further hostilities here in the Cathedral, Andrei? Are we finished shooting for the evening?"

"I am unarmed, Mr. Mannheim."

There was something in Andrei Fetisov's eyes, something akin to treachery but short an ounce or two of sufficient depravity. Mannheim ignored the waiting Russian; Marta's contrivances could not be allowed to proceed on an expedited schedule. He texted Nazarian's burner: *Take charge. Locate Countess and Tretiak, update Raissa.*

All-knowing expression fixed in place, he told the Russian, "I'm ready. Is it Russell Tipton we're meeting? Or possibly Lt. Col. Goodman?"

"I assure you, Mr. Mannheim, my role as intermediary precludes deception or harm to participants in this attempt by both sides to disengage." Andrei took a confident first step in the direction of the South Choir Doorway.

***

Nazarian examined the phone's green tape as he would an IED's detonator—pressed the hot-key for Elise and listened to six rings before ending the call. Goodman answered David's call from the unencrypted CIA phone with suspicion.

"Who is this?"

"David Nazarian, Colonel, Deputy Chief of Counterintelligence at Langley assigned to Zachary Mannheim while he's in Trondheim."

"Where's Mannheim?"

David's training taught the value of truth, when uncertainty prevailed. "Last I saw he was headed for the Cathedral's South Choir exit with Andrei Fetisov."

"Fetisov…Sluchevsky's pilot?"

Nazarian wondered how long this bullshit would continue: Goodman didn't give a rat's ass about Andrei Fetisov.

Goodman ignored Nazarian's silence. "Any of CIA's team injured?"

Nazarian offered a strategic half-truth. "Elias Thordsen was shot twice in the back by members of the Girls' Choir. On his way to surgery." Tired as he was of Goodman's phony superiority, David would go along to get along.

"Where's your boss, Mr. Nazarian?"

"If you're referring to Phyllis Martell, her location is unknown. Maybe you could tell me?"

"Is that why you phoned, Mr. Nazarian?"

"No sir. I phoned at Mr. Mannheim's direction to confirm Mr. Tretiak remains in your custody."

"Where's Raissa, Mr. Nazarian?"

David sensed the charade coming to an end. "Have you released Mr. Tretiak, Colonel?"

"I am a United States Marine officer, Mr. Nazarian, subject to the chain of command. Spooks aren't familiar with the concept."

"Didn't you receive an order from General Jack Givens, Assistant Commandant of the Corps to *do the job* requested by Mr. Mannheim and to show *appropriate resourcefulness* in so doing?"

"Yes, Mr. Nazarian, those were my orders from General Givens until they were superseded by higher authority. So, with all due respect, the status of Mr. Tretiak is none of your business. Beyond that, you ought not to approach any Marine with requests for assistance. You, Mannheim and any other CIA types have, to put a pleasant face on messy business, used up your welcome."

Nazarian texted Mannheim using the Mannheim-Countess-Nazarian three-way phone: *Tretiak released. Location unknown.*

***

Follow the money—one of Mannheim's ten commandments when hunting foreign or home-grown agent provocateurs—caused

Nazarian to hurry towards his rental. Caution exceeded, it took minutes more than he could afford to return to the *Clarion*.

Ms. Svendsen was only too pleased to confirm Ms. Marina Aslanov, from the Russian Consulate in Quebec City, inquired for Mr. Mannheim minutes ago at the Front Desk. Ms. Aslanov indicated she'd wait in the bar for Mannheim's return.

Marina, who claimed diplomatic status at Raissa's Quebec City fashion show, was nowhere to be found in the Clarion's *Skybar*. David walked to the bank of elevators, racking the slide on the Glock 17 with Berglund's fingerprints as he went. From inside Room 508, in heavily accented English a Russian yelled, "Where's Mannheim's money-bag?"

David couldn't conjure a face or name to match the voice. He stepped to the left of the door—rapped hard three times. Guessed how long to wait. When half a dozen seconds expired, Nazarian stretched the Glock's suppressor onto the door's peephole and fired twice in rapid succession—heard a body slump to the floor, then fired a third round into the lock mechanism. Half falling into the room after slamming the door with his shoulder, David watched Marina fumble in her purse. Caught a glimpse of Elise's pistol-whipped face. Put a fourth round into Marina's chest. Small semi-automatic in hand, she fell and lay still.

Priorities clear, Nazarian nodded at Elise as he dialed Ms. Svendsen's extension. Heard the Deputy Managing Director's voice convey controlled concern.

"I'm Mr. Mannheim's Deputy. Would you join me as soon as possible, please? There are immediate decisions to be made."

Towel applied to Elise's eye to staunch bleeding, he asked the Countess, "How long ago?"

"Less than a few minutes. Not the brightest bulb, the greedy younger man would have slit my throat after the Russian bitch found the bag full of cash in the closet"

"You let them in," David suggested, inflection padded with disbelief.

"No other option," Elise claimed, leaving a lie as its own explanation.

"How'd they know about a sports-bag embossed with a Turkish crescent?"

Elise the Countess, concussed as she was, appreciated how Zachary's Op was closer to the end than its beginning. Mistakes would invariably have been made; no plan ran without flaws and blunders.

"Marta made it her business to know…doesn't matter how. Broken ribs, broken teeth and possibly a cracked skull, Mr. Nazarian. My contract with Mannheim has been fulfilled…five SVR dead by my hand. Get me out of Norway with my fee."

Arrived in the doorway an out of breath Tonje Svendsen's face gave every thought away.

David spoke in a quiet, urgent tone. "The shooter is gone, Ms. Svendsen, weapon left behind. Fingerprints should provide an identity." Finger pointed at the Glock 17, he suggested a plan of action for Svendsen's consideration. "The woman on the bed, a guest in your hotel, suffered a serious concussion during an invasion of Mr. Mannheim's room. Evacuation, from her room on the fourth floor to a local medical facility, would be most beneficial. Transportation arrangements for her return to Italy, paid for by Mr. Mannheim, should be arranged in advance: Night train to Oslo before a flight to Milan. Allow your staff to discover the dead Russians in 508 without intervention. When your staff alerts you, call the police. By now you've heard about the shootings at the Cathedral. Police won't be shocked to hear violence spilled over to your hotel." David pressed a three-inch stack of 100 € notes into Tonje Svendsen's hand. "Seventy-five thousand for your expenses, as per your agreement with Mr. Mannheim." He smiled with genuine warmth, when her face showed grit and determination. Svendsen had cast her lot with NIS and CIA; two dead Russians weren't reason enough to falter.

"Can you assist Elise to her Room…retrieve her passport from the Front Desk…and get the Concierge started on travel arrangements?"

"We pride ourselves on Customer Service. Your instructions will be implemented immediately." Tonje Svendsen made a mental note to inform her sister at NIS before notifying the police.

Nazarian assisted the two women to the elevator. Upon his return, he soaked a sheet and pillowcase stained with Elise's blood with bottles of vodka from the mini bar. Left both his and Mannheim's clothes and personal effects where they'd been. Threw the sports-bag weighted with Korsikov's Euros over his shoulder. At Reception, he tipped the concierge twenty Euros to arrange a taxi and driver well-known to the Clarion staff.

David assumed his comms were open secrets. What impact his texts might have upon Marta, other Russians, or Americans with multiple loyalties was a legitimate mystery. It didn't matter—like Ms. Svendsen, David was all-in with Zachary Mannheim. He texted Mannheim on the three-way: *Countess battered not beaten*. Texted Raissa: *Tretiak on the loose*.

Her lack of response was a good sign in David's opinion, because Raissa Ribeiro was most dangerous when alone and at long odds to succeed.

A text to Mannheim's charter pilots directed their immediate return to the aircraft.

Chapter 25

Whatever control software Randall's hack interrupted, Trondheim's power grid continued to suffer random dysfunction.

Mannheim sat next to Andrei Fetisov in the rear of a sedan driven by Russell Tipton. Headlight beams were streaks of light across a dark canvas, giving the appearance of an impressionist world gone mad. Thirty kilometers without a word spoken brought them to Radisson-Blu Airport Hotel, ablaze in light courtesy of its backup generator.

A glass table, eight modern pale-pink chairs and subdued lighting created an atmosphere thought by designers to enhance corporate meetings. Phyllis Martell appeared queasy sitting at attention in one of those chairs, on the table's longest side. Seated at the head of the table, Taras Sluchevsky puffed on a cigar. Tipton chose a chair next to Phyllis, closer to Sluchevsky. Fetisov selected a position opposite Tipton, loyalty to the Russian center of political power declared by his decision. Congressman Emile Wright and National Security Advisor Craig Hall were visible in High Definition on a large, wall-mounted television screen.

Mannheim remained standing.

Emile Wright sought to lessen the turmoil on Mannheim's face. "Please Zachary, there are more than enough phones recording this meeting. Take a seat. This meeting could represent a new beginning."

Loutish riposte repressed, Mannheim sat opposite Tipton and Martell next to Fetisov. "Is this a gathering of the willing or a meeting among survivors?" His rhetorical question went unanswered but altered the mood for the worse.

Wright deferred to Craig Hall, who intended to introduce a single topic and say no more. "In discussions between Foreign Minister Sluchevsky and Grover Norris an agreement in principle was reached governing Minister Sluchevsky's request for political asylum in the United States. Grover, as you all know, has passed away. We're gathered to discuss the agreement in light of recent events in Trondheim. Let's begin with a summary of those events. Minister Sluchevsky, would you please begin?"

Mannheim raised his voice to demand, "Who killed Grover Norris?"

Face drawn tight with intensity, Sluchevsky insisted, "I had nothing to do with Grover Norris' death. At no time was I a participant in the planning or execution of an operation codenamed *Choirmaster*. If Petr Sillin dies of his wounds, the Russian Federation will be the better for his demise. Marta Mannheim created the chaos which enveloped each of us tonight. Her maniacal contrivances, collusion with groups who advance her views, and willingness to butcher those who stand in opposition to her ambition are an abomination. I can no longer participate in a government which tolerates her. I seek political asylum in the United States. I am willing to serve in any capacity the White House deems fit to my experience and talents."

Prodded into silence by a patently reasonable statement, Mannheim watched Phyllis Martell with interest. Sluchevsky's various denials, claims of Marta's witchcraft or tongue-licking by Greg Hall and the President meant nothing to a spy-hunter. If Sluchevsky proved to be democracy's most famous Trojan Horse, not a word said this evening, nor the volume of words in a subsequent legal agreement, would carry water to the fires burning Hall's government down. Eye contact established, he urged Phyllis to break the spell of what he believed a pre-ordained result.

Free of tone, Phyllis asked, "Mr. Hall, what do you want from CIC? As of this hour there is no counter-intelligence investigation of Mr. Sluchevsky, Mr. Sillin or Mrs. Hinrich-Mannheim. What do you want from Mr. Tipton? *Reformation* has run its course; Mr. Tipton is either up for re-assignment at Langley or the subject of a criminal investigation by the FBI. Neither he nor I make Agency policy. Neither he nor I can execute an asylum agreement with Mr. Sluchevsky. As for Mr. Mannheim, he's a civilian with no governmental authority. What could you possibly want from him?"

Tipton broke into Martell's train of inquiry. "Mr. Hall...are you aware Grover Norris discussed defection with Petr Sillin? How could

that have happened under the agreed upon parameters of *Reformation?*"

Hall wouldn't engage in a back and forth with Agency employees, not when he didn't like their questions or attitude. "Whatever Grover did or did not discuss with anyone, including Petr Sillin, was made irrelevant by his death. Ms. Martell, CIC might be well served by an arrest of Mr. Tipton. Lt. Col. Goodman's Law Enforcement Unit is prepared to take Tipton into custody and arrange his transport to Langley."

Martell held her ground. "Besides Mr. Tipton's arrest, sir, what do you expect CIC to provide the White House?"

Hall smiled at the closed-circuit camera to hide exasperation. "You're last man standing, Ms. Martell. Grover's dead. Nazarian, your Deputy, wanders in the wilderness. Tipton is responsible for this mess. Thordsen is in critical condition. Petr Sillin is less well off than Thordsen. Raissa Ribeiro has been seen in a dozen locations in Europe during this evening. Leanne Crowder is wounded and missing-in-action. Several Agency officers, including Jamie Norris, are missing and presumed held against their will by SVR. Tonight, the government of the United States doesn't care about the right and wrong on either side of *Reformation*. CIC should have nothing on its plate more important than recovering those CIA officers and securing the life and liberty of Mr. Sluchevsky and his family. I'm interested in what you, as Chief/CIC, intend. Without a D/CIA in place, you have the authority and resources to act as your best judgment dictates."

Martell saw no way out of an impossible assignment. "Or die trying, is that how you see it, Mr. Hall?"

"Risk goes with the job, Ms. Martell. Col. Goodman will liaise with you as you require. The Colonel received updated orders from the Marine Commandant earlier."

"Use of Force against SVR and the Russian Military is authorized by the President...will you confirm that position for the video record?"

"Absent an order from the President, which is not anticipated, Use of Force is within your purview, Ms. Martell. Make good decisions and all should be well."

"Has Col. Goodman made travel arrangements for Foreign Minister Sluchevsky and his wife?"

For Zachary Mannheim a slow-motion farce shifted into a parody of Intelligence work. In a momentary lull he injected a dose of reality.

"Mr. Hall, you hired me to assess and, if need be, destroy *Reformation*, which turned out to be more your creation than EJ Brantley's. After you joined negotiations, the deal negotiated by Brantley and Marta was altered. Marta vanished in favor of Aydan Fetisov. You and Aydan Fetisov traded the lives of Sillin and Sluchevsky straight-up for next to nothing. Then Aydan died from an overdose of rectitude...and Marta reappeared here in Trondheim." Puzzled by why Hall allowed him to speak without comment, Mannheim watched Sluchevsky's expression of satisfaction grow into one of dominance. "Will Marta be the victim of an accident in Trondheim tonight? Or arrested and shot upon her return to Moscow?" Mannheim waved a hand in dismissive fashion at Hall's obvious intention to contradict his claim. "Rhetorical question, Mr. Hall, nothing worthy of this august gathering. Is it fair to say my assignment has come to a close? If so there's nothing to keep me in Norway."

Hall visibly relaxed. "Yes Zachary, *Reformation* has run its sad and unfortunate course. Travel home safely with my thanks."

Congressman Wright seized the last word. Exasperated, he asked, "What about Carol's murder, Mr. Mannheim. What's to be done?"

Where Mannheim categorized the National Security Advisor's voice as disingenuous, Emile Wright sounded midway between whimper and moan. "Leanne Crowder hasn't been apprehended, Mr. Wright. It appears Col. Goodman and Ms. Martell have assumed responsibility for her capture."

Wright looked astounded. "I'll issue a subpoena for your testimony."

Mannheim would've appreciated more intellectual flexibility from Wright, so answered consistent with the bureaucratic double-speak used by Hall.

"The Subcommittee has my attorney's contact information."

Martell left a path for appeal. "Come with me, Mr. Tipton. Col. Goodman's people will be waiting outside."

Zachary gathered his phone and a cheap hotel notepad where he'd jotted random thoughts—moved towards the conference room's exit without need of, or interest in, a discussion with Martell or Tipton.

When he reached the door, it was opened by Goodman in winter warfare gear. Mannheim stuck out his hand.

"Good luck, Colonel. Big Brass have hung you and Phyllis out a fourth-floor window. Are you enjoying the view?"

Goodman's response sounded rehearsed. "I could place you under arrest."

"But you won't, will you Colonel. As soon as my aircraft is cleared, I'm headed home, while you're stuck with the bronze medal for 3rd place. Don't make policy or grant clemency...that's above your pay grade. Do your job." Mannheim strode down the hallway, anxiety rising in anticipation of betrayals not yet anticipated.

***

An hour passed after Eduardo taxied the big jet to the far end of what would have been the active runway, if airport operations were normal. His nerves were well frayed.

"Mr. Riley, how much longer can we wait?" Neither Mannheim, Nazarian or Raissa had responded to Riley asking the identical question.

Out the pilot's cockpit window, Riley caught a glimpse of Marine combat vehicles parked by the gated entrance to General Aviation. Last in line was an AFV carrying a M2HB .50 caliber machine gun. Fearsome to contemplate, the M2 could fire 450–575 rounds per minute. Even in single shot mode, 40 rounds per minute would ruin the Gulfstream in under five seconds.

"Eduardo, takeoff now. Declare an emergency on climb-out. Terrorists on the airfield...shootings at Nidaros Cathedral...whatever. Request vectors for Oslo."

***

Minutes after refusing David Nazarian's latest text, Raissa heard the engines of her Gulfstream screaming at maximum power immediately prior to takeoff. She smiled as cabin lights winked-off; Eduardo was doing his best to eliminate the jet as a target. Watched through the rifle's scope, the beautiful machine leapt forward and in seconds disappeared.

Aware of the Marine vehicles, Raissa recognized Goodman and Sluchevsky in an intense private conference at the front of the column; their body language suggested neither friendship nor alliance. She prepped a solution for a head shot on Sluchevsky, when a single stretcher was unloaded onto a gurney.

Was its occupant Sluchevsky's wounded wife? If not, who was worth evacuation alongside the sitting Foreign Minister of Russia? Perhaps an intra-Russian exchange was in the works.

For what conceivable purpose?

Perhaps it was Tretiak, although he was Marta's creature not Sluchevsky's.

In a high-risk gamble she texted: *Goodman with Sluchevsky near Sukhoi and Ka-62 chopper. Gurney carrying Tretiak? Advise.*

Two responses appeared within seconds.

No longer certain of his encryption's status, Randall texted: *Destroy SIM. Power off phone.*

Opportunity at hand, Mannheim texted: *Tretiak and Sluchevsky radioactive.*

Raissa removed the SIM, mangled it with the Kbar and powered off the phone. There was no preferred place to hide. On foot there was no escape from mechanized pursuit. If Goodman had been authorized to demonstrate goodwill towards Marta by concluding *Reformation* with the elimination of Raissa Ribeiro, she would play by the Marine Colonel's rules of engagement.

In suspended animation Raissa glued her dominant eye to the rifle's scope.

***

Mannheim, joined by David Nazarian, entered the Terminal to await a takeoff notice from their pilots. Amidst continued uncertainty and cancelled flights, David ticked-off reasons why Mannheim would insist SIMs be removed from every phone. In plain view of CCTV, airline employees and Norwegian security personnel, one piece of logic stood out: Mannheim was establishing a verifiable assertion of innocence for any violence yet to come.

In a whisper David asked, "Why do we care about Tretiak?"

Mannheim's answer demonstrated vulnerability. "Find yourself a coffee, David. It's been a long night. Miles to go before we sleep."

An answer without meaning pointed David towards food kiosks, where he peered into the abyss through plate glass. Ordered two coffees and a pastry. Added sugar, cream to the coffees—and four SIM cards to the trash—with practiced sleight of hand.

***

When three cars passed through the General Aviation entrance gate, Raissa anticipated Marta's emergence with Jamie Norris and Ian Riddick in tow. Through the scope, she watched Marta approach Sluchevsky. Two of the most powerful aides to Russia's President moved away from Goodman's Marines—a transaction which suggested *the enemy of my enemy means I have two enemies.*

One of Sluchevsky's minions pushed the gurney away from the Marines towards Marta's sedan. The starboard engine on the Sukhoi 100 came to life in a cloud of whitish gray exhaust. Rotors on the *Ka-62* began to turn.

Raissa's doubt eliminated, Tretiak was being exchanged for Norris and Riddick.

Minister Sluchevsky, his wife's stretcher and their surviving retinue entered Russia's latest regional passenger jet.

Marta and her SVR team delayed their departure, protected from the Sukhoi's jet blast as it taxied for takeoff.

Goodman, joined by Phyllis Martell, Russell Tipton, Jamie Norris and Ian Riddick, would have issued Hall's ultimatum. Behind the AFV, the M2HB was manned and ready to thwart SVR aggression. Marta had played and lost. Would she be found dead from a single gunshot in a miserable Moscow alley?

Unconcerned with Marta's future, Raissa's target priority was determined first by National Security: Taras Sluchevsky's intended defection, like Iraj Rashidi's defection a few short years ago, stunk of a False Flag Op. With the elimination of the threat posed by Sluchevsky, blame would find its way onto a Russian missile operated by Marta's First Directorate bad boys.

Less critical, in her world view, was the nature of the *Strela* or *Igla*: MANPADs were ground to air missiles and the Ka-62 sat on tarmac. If time allowed, a second missile could be fired in hope it would lock-on to the infrared signal of the chopper's engine. Grip-stock held firm Raissa listened to twin jet engines roar; the big plane would soon be airborne. Wait, she told herself, until the Sukhoi lifted off. More guess than science, when the jet's left wingtip navigation light rose Raissa pulled the missile's two-step trigger while elevating the launcher tube. Ignition of the rocket's engine hurled a twenty-four-pound projectile at six hundred meters/second. Impact on the jet with fully loaded fuel tanks occurred at less than one thousand feet of altitude. A warhead of less than three pounds produced a primary explosion and a secondary fireball. Remnants of the Sukhoi rained into Trondheim Fjord

Raissa paid no attention to post-crash turmoil; she tossed the empty launch-tube against the fence and acquired the gurney's occupant in her scope. Crosshairs aligned forward of Tretiak's left ear by two inches, she fired one round. Primary tasks compartmentalized, she re-packed the ski-bag, consuming cello-packs of Russian crackers as she worked. Drank a half liter of water, eyes peeled on the Marine column for signs of movement. Regretted her inability to target Marta Mannheim.

Sirens from the airport fire brigade filled the night.

Trondheim's electric grid, fully restored, was reactivated.

Disorientation and agitation among Russians and Marines settled into practiced order. Goodman approached Marta and spoke in animated gestures.

Within half a minute Tretiak's gurney, abandoned during the height of the Sukhoi's explosion, rolled towards Marta's helo. Goodman spoke to the driver of a JTLV, pointing in the direction where the missile launched. His next decision positioned the AFV, with its M2HB, behind Marta's vehicle: the Marine Colonel would make no attempt to protect SVR.

Mannheim's coffee in-hand, Nazarian witnessed the sky glow orange over the Fjord. He was convinced Raissa was responsible for whatever aircraft had been destroyed. David sent an open-source text to Einar Haugen: *Russian missile destroyed aircraft. Sweep perimeter for perpetrators. Exercise care, CIA has agents on the ground. Request pick-up at baggage claim.*

***

The JTLV's headlamps were pinpoints without effect as Raissa pushed herself to climb the ten-foot wall of snow left behind by plows. On the far side and invisible, in a full sprint for a count of twenty, she dropped the ski-bag, stuffed the FNP-9 into a rear pocket and reversed course. Back on the airport's perimeter road, respiration normalized, she walked towards the oncoming JTLV.

At the passenger window, bravado replaced angst. "Edgar, nice to see you man. You too, Winship," she added, smiling across at the driver.

Martinez was blown away. "What you doin' out here by yourself, Ms. Ribeiro?"

In for a dime, in for a dollar went one old saying about gambling with your life. "Looking for Russian agents to kill. How about you?"

Martinez absorbed the simplicity of her answer. "You saw the missile light-off?"

Raissa pointed at the fence. "Shooter set up by the fence, fifty or sixty yards back the way you came. Rider came at me on a dirt-bike without a headlight. So fucking dark out here...emptied a clip before she almost ran me down."

Martinez showed signs of regaining equanimity. "How about you show me?"

"You bet, Corporal. Shouldn't be hard to find...wasn't carrying the empty tube when she bolted."

Martinez's flashlight found the empty launcher and second missile. Winship stowed the unused weapon. "Everything's in Russian, Edgar...missile, food wrappers and water bottles...all Russian except Norwegian water."

"Collect it all, Private." For Raissa, Martinez had a single question. "Does my Colonel know you're out here?"

Raissa answered with a question of her own. "Less than five people in government know my real job, Edgar. Should I send your Light Colonel a Christmas card?"

Before Edgar's questions could press harder, a sedan skidded to a stop, blue and white lights making patterns on the snow. Its driver glared at Raissa and Martinez absent the slightest sign of goodwill.

"CIA and US Marines here to save poor little Norway...an unholy alliance. Ms. Ribeiro, come with me. Corporal, give Einar Haugen's regards to Colonel Goodman."

Raissa saw David Nazarian in the back seat of the NIS sedan. Watched Edgar Martinez consider his available options. Climbed in with David as Martinez spoke into the JTLV's radio.

Nazarian waited for the NIS agent to arrange himself behind the wheel. "Nils, let's use one of the other gates…Goodman isn't much of a team player. Hate to give him a chance to be a pain in the ass."

Haugen's second in command cared not the smallest bit about Americans and their political pissing contests. "Yes, Mr. Nazarian, I'll take you to your rental, but please plan to travel independent of Mr. Mannheim. Einar told me the old man lost his government's support when the Nidaros shootings went viral."

A mile further from Marine vehicles, Marta's Ka-62, and Mannheim's charter, Raissa announced, "Stop here, I'll walk." When Raissa was no longer visible in the rearview, Nils Lund quizzed Nazarian. "What was that about?"

Nazarian's response was nothing akin to his private thoughts. "Dead bodies aren't good publicity for a world-famous lady."

***

Raissa dug into the ski-bag for one of three expensive wigs. Platinum hidden under mousy brown curls, face wiped clean of grime, she walked to the Radisson Blu. Agreed to five times the normal taxi fare to Hommelvik Station where she used Kirstin Hansen's phone to text Eduardo: *Göteborg-Landvetter - 16 hours.*

Purchase of a series of one-way tickets on the 11pm train took Raissa to Storlien Station (Swedish Norwegian border), Sundsvall Centralstation (Sweden), Stockholm Centralstation (Sweden) and Gothenburg CentralStation (Sweden). Raissa woke at each stop prepared to exit; hunker down within the station and re-schedule; re-board her original train; or implement any opportunity which came her way.

No contingency plan needed, she climbed into the Gulfstream's cabin without incident. Mousy Raissa deplaned in Hyannis to find one of the boatyard boys waiting to drive her home. Randall and Greg continued to Dulles.

Chapter 26

Mannheim grew antsy sitting in a plastic airport seat.

Electricity restored, all around him travelers, airport workers, airline employees, security forces and Norwegian Military engaged in an emotional free-for-all. Rumors grew like summer weeds: A private jet crashed into the sea; a Russian politician's Sukhoi exploded after takeoff; missiles were fired from a Russian SU-24 fighter bomber; US Marines shot and killed Russian Army soldiers; Russian spies assassinated CIA agents; Norwegian NIS agents arrested CIA agents; a Russian helicopter was confiscated by NIS agents; a Russian helicopter was destroyed by a shoulder-fired Afghani missile; Norway's Prime Minister accused the American and Russian Presidents of covert operations intended to destabilize Norway's sovereign status.

Truth was a needle in a haystack.

A contingent of media entered the Terminal from the first post-outage arriving flight.

Ignored by the mob, Zachary kept close watch on the General Aviation Gates; Marta would use one of those stairways, when primed to manipulate her husband. In the middle of an hour-long lull Max Goodman slid into a chair next to Mannheim.

"Thought you'd want to know…I put Martell and Tipton on your charter. Nazarian's on-board. Pilots are ready to go. Something holding you up?"

Mannheim wore a wry smile, when examining a Minor League right-fielder sent to the Show for one playoff game. "My wife."

"I think you've delayed departure long enough."

"Mr. Hall mixes a potent brew, Colonel. Have a care before your career dies from an overdose."

Under the direction of an unheard, unseen cue, Marta entered the Terminal striding straight towards her husband. She stared through Goodman at four combat-ready Marines.

"Are you a Marriage counselor, Colonel, qualified to mediate my differences with Zachary? Go play with your machine gun…leave statecraft to the adults."

Obstinacy deployed, Goodman held firm.

"Are you pleased with the evening's outcome, husband?"

"I've been here in this chair for what seems hours, Marta. Catch me up."

"I'm recording on my encrypted phone. Feel free."

Mannheim turned his suit jacket pockets inside-out with tepid sincerity. "No phone, Marta. Vile devices. I don't object to any recording you make."

Marta looked around the Terminal in a gesture of mockery. "Where is your pathetic hacker?"

"Randall is on vacation. Never set foot in Norway. Will your post-mortem include a review of every player's role and status?"

Marta acknowledged none of Zachary's snark.

"Petr Sillin died of gunshot wounds, a victim of Elias Thordsen, CIA assassin. Thordsen's wounds will kill him long before his trial for murder in a Russian law court. A Russian airliner was blasted from the sky by an American Stinger fired by Russell Tipton, a CIA officer and US Marine. Taras Sluchevsky, his wife and several Russian citizens died in the crash. Details of these travesties have been provided to media outlets worldwide. You, husband, shall be prosecuted in absentia for the wanton killing of two Russian tourists inside Nidaros Cathedral."

Mannheim's muted facial reaction gave way to an irritable snort. "A narrative of histrionic fiction, Marta. Will the Kremlin put you on television to scream these colorful accusations? Will Craig Hall gift-wrap Tipton for you, or bury a decorated war veteran in some dark corner of Langley's mailroom never to be seen in public again? Will the Kremlin take this opportunity to rid itself of a post-menopausal American woman who bungled a foreign policy coup, and in its ashes outstayed her welcome?"

Goodman couldn't remain quiet. "No one will believe her lies. There'll be evidence to show the truth."

Mannheim clucked. "Whose evidence, Colonel. Whose truth? In today's world, if there is no video there is no truth. Is there video on either side, Colonel? You abstained from tonight's events. Be satisfied, Marta may yet take your name in vain." With a firm look of disinterest, Zachary cut to the bone. "You are to be congratulated, my dear spouse. Two powerful adversaries gone in a single stroke. Are you convinced the missile was a Stinger?"

Not a vestige of concern flashed across Marta's face.

A flicker of hope danced behind Mannheim's eyes. There were complexities to overcome, manipulations to chance, snares to deploy and IED's to bury by various roadsides. With multiple ways to lose, would there be time enough to win in extra-innings?

"We shall see, Marta. What you paint in silver and gold this night may resemble a water-color under a harsh Moscow sun." He held her gaze before speaking his last. "Who could've guessed Leanne loved Carol Wright?"

Voice raised, Marta tossed a carrot to a pet gelding. "Hall won't survive in the White House. Leanne is a minnow with no teeth. Give me Raissa, husband. Nothing ends until my daughter's butchery is avenged."

**

Deputy Assistant Director Wade Tisdale would've declined the Subcommittee's invitation, but a drumbeat of media coverage in Norway and Russia accelerated Chairman Wright's threat of subpoena.

Chairman Wright brought down the gavel with Mannheim's intractable refusal to testify ringing in his ears. "Mr. Director, would you prefer to update your earlier testimony to the Subcommittee or respond to questions?"

Tisdale responded with relief, "An update of earlier testimony, in my opinion, will be the most efficient way to put Members on equal footing."

Former Vice Chairman Lester Morgan, present under countenance of the Subcommittee's unwritten rules, rattled a cough of admonition.

Chairman Wright stared in Morgan's direction. "Proceed Mr. Director."

Tisdale checked his notes a final time.

"When the Subcommittee last met, the video from Chairman Wright's home security system had not been forensically examined. As a result, the Bureau was unable to certify the video as authentic and unmodified. Today the certification is complete in both respects. Operated on a twenty-four-hour loop, events relevant to Mrs. Carol Wright's assassination begin early in the evening, continue through the unimpeded arrival of an intruder, the fatal shooting of Mrs. Carol Wright and the subsequent shooting of National Security Advisor Craig Hall.

"I'll summarize what Members will see. The first relevant event is a sexual encounter between Mrs. Carol Wright and Ms. Leanne Crowder, a CIA officer seconded to Special Projects Director Russell Tipton. Ms. Crowder departs the residence after this encounter. Within minutes of Crowder's departure, NSA Craig Hall arrives. Carol Wright and Craig Hall engage in a sexual encounter which ends in a furious argument. Mr. Hall fires a single shot into the chest of Carol Wright. Bureau specialists recovered a .22 pistol from the bathroom with Mr. Hall's fingerprints. Within another half hour an unknown party accesses the residence through the unlocked kitchen door. Approximately two minutes later this intruder arrives in the second-floor hallway and, without a word, fires a single gunshot into Carol Wright's chest...and a second gunshot into Craig Hall's abdomen. Both these shots came from a 9-millimeter semi-automatic. No such weapon was recovered from the Wright home or during an extensive search of the neighborhood. Analysts identified the intruder as Ms. Leanne Crowder, who fled after a verbal exchange with Mr. Hall.

"Mr. David Nazarian, Deputy Chief /CIC, observed both shootings during real-time monitoring of Congressman Wright's cameras. Mr. Nazarian communicated situational facts and requested the Bureau's presence...then traveled to and entered the home, determined Carol Wright deceased and applied external pressure to Mr. Hall's wound.

"Coincident with events at the Wright residence, I was interviewing Mr. Zachary Mannheim, retired Chief/CIC, about the murders of two Bureau Agents in his home. At my request, Mr. Mannheim accompanied me to Chairman Wright's home. After an examination of the scene, I notified appropriate Bureau personnel. Mr. Hall was conscious...his mental faculties never in question. I told Mr. Hall of my intention to call an ambulance. Mr. Hall declined in favor of a private medical facility. Bureau personnel later confirmed

Mr. Hall had been removed from the residence by attendants from said private facility.

"Bureau personnel gathered evidence and made a record of the scene. Congressman Wright's recording device and its memory were secured in accordance with permission granted by Chairman Wright. Chain of custody was established and remains unbroken. Pathology confirmed either or both bullets would have, and could have, caused Carol Wright's death. NSA Hall recovered from his wound and resumed his duties in the White House. Mr. Hall remains a prime suspect in Carol Wright's death. Ms. Crowder has not been taken into custody, and, per Mr. Nazarian's eyewitness account, was on-duty as an active CIA officer during recent events in Trondheim, Norway. Ms. Crowder remains a prime suspect in Carol Wright's death.

"Given the sensitive nature of these events, National Security concerns have delayed a final determination related to criminal charges."

***

Mannheim handed Tisdale a plate filled with take-out barbeque. "How did Wright handle accusations from his Committee Members?"

"Kicked everyone but principals out of the room. Never budged on the video's authenticity. Kept the Subcommittee focused on what comes next. Refused to hear voices demanding advisory opinions from White House Counsel or buddies of the President. Refused to hear the hue and cry for Zachary Mannheim's scalp."

"How soon will it leak?"

Tisdale forked baked beans on top of chicken. "You listening?"

"Not this time, Wade."

"You figure POTUS knows?"

"Best to assume he does. Who's waiting in line for your job?"

Tisdale chuckled. "Line forms around the block. No one can figure whether I'm a hero or villain."

"How about the *Times* and *Post*? Anyone jockeying for a Pulitzer?"

***

Days slipped away.

In thrall to February's short days and damp cold, Mannheim dripped sweat on his new exercise bike. Intervals of hill-climbing better tolerated with an active cell phone, he answered an expected call.

"My condolences, Jamie. I apologize for not attending the service or funeral."

"May I come see you, sir?"

"Carol Wright's murder rots on the vine. Wade Tisdale has received no prosecutorial decision from the FBI Director, the U.S. Attorney General, or the White House janitor. Henrik Halvorsen's attorney sent a process server: I'm a named defendant in Henrik's lawsuit, filed in Federal Court, against a laundry list of agencies and individuals. Among a paucity of real news is Elias's survival...unwelcome to Russian and American Presidents...but relished by a father who lost his wife. At this rate, Grover will never be comfortable in his grave...come to talk whenever you like, Jamie."

Mannheim checked his vital signs and sighed. Through the rigors of Grover's assassination, Jamie Norris had been thrust into situations which required the velvet glove of diplomacy and iron fist of a spy's secret world. Four miles of hills awaited as his headset brought Phyllis' sycophantic voice to his ears.

"Hello, Phyllis. Not a social call, I'd expect. What can I do for you?"

"Breakfast next Tuesday?"

***

Jamie knocked on Mannheim's door late one afternoon. They sat in the kitchen, old affection and new stations in life set aside.

"Who killed Grover, Mr. Mannheim?" Grief raw, Jamie held anger and revenge in an identical embrace.

"I don't know who shot your father, Jamie. Marta didn't pull the trigger, but there's no doubt she gave the order."

"Is it true you shot SVR thugs in the Cathedral...like the Russians claim?"

"Not much point in extending *Reformation's* headlines, Jamie. Very little of what happened in Trondheim has been reported with accuracy. Your detention by SVR is a perfect example. Russian accounts claim it never happened and CIA's response has been a curt *No comment.*"

Jamie examined Mannheim at close range. "Leanne Crowder reached-out through an emissary."

Zachary fought the urge to speak, substituting a poker face accompanied by a distinct nod.

"She was doubled from *Reformation's* earliest days. Nothing but excess weight around Marta's neck, Crowder survived a first attempt on her life. Wants to go on the offensive. What do you think?"

Mannheim contemplated who, besides Jamie, would hear his response. "Who carried the message?"

Jamie Norris, interim Deputy Director/NCS, stared into the great void. "Congressman Jedediah Sewell, veteran in-fighter and a politician not to be trifled with."

Mannheim let his eyes smile at a boomerang of his own words. "Crowder isn't stupid. She made a good choice in Sewell. EJ Brantley and Jedediah Sewell always shared a wavelength." Zachary pondered another, more troublesome, prospect. "Any chance Sewell is your next D/CIA?"

Jamie answered too fast. "From what I've heard, Sewell is on the white House short list along with Lester Morgan and Craig Hall."

"What did Sewell ask for, Jamie?"

"Wants Leanne in from the cold under my protection."

"Did Leanne tell Sewell about her intention to target Marta?"

Jamie Norris' face went blank.

Zachary wasted no words. "Sewell won't tell you bedtime stories, Jamie. Morgan or Hall will give you nightmares. As for Leanne, do not let her disappear. Leadership carries burdens…and you must always do what's best for the country, Jamie. Always."

***

Inside the Toolbox Café a second time, Phyllis Martell found Mannheim in the last booth opposite the deli counter. Her demeanor exhibited signs of rehabilitation.

"Good morning to be alive, Mr. Mannheim."

Mannheim would suffer no small talk. "What did he want?"

Martell smiled at the waitress who filled her coffee mug. Waited until the Café's din would distort any audio. In a slight adjustment of position, turned towards the wall to foil a lip reader.

"Hall wants you detained somewhere unpleasant...he's spoken more than once to Marta. Lester Morgan met with David...offered him the Chief's job, if he arrests every Agency employee who went to Trondheim. Morgan also met with Elias Thordsen...very off the record."

Zachary wouldn't be coy. "Smart lad, your David. Morgan has no credibility at the White House." News of Elias Thordsen would be ignored; lawsuits hindered communication. "Heard from Leanne?"

"No."

With enthusiastic curiosity Mannheim asked, "What was David's response to former Congressman Morgan?"

"Haven't heard from or seen David."

"Who provided the Intel from Hall?" Zachary felt himself hold his breath.

"Craig Hall himself. Besides his babble, he asked whether I could arrange a private meeting with your wife. Claims Marta opened a backdoor to defection."

"Who told him such a thing?"

"You won't believe it... Aaron Frankel called the NSC with Khalid bin Rahman on an encrypted line."

Mannheim's eyes burned with excitement. "So you accepted Hall's task after a tête-à-tête with two outlaws."

"Hall is the National Security Advisor. What else could I say?"

"What do you want, Phyllis. I'm nobody these days."

"In Hall's narrative, Marta insisted on Zachary's arrangements and Zachary's presence at every stage of negotiations. You run the show or there'll be no show."

"When will you communicate with Marta?"

"Whenever you say, but not without your instructions."

Aaron Frankel and Khalid bin Rahman represented distinct complexities. Bin Rahman, the author of each detail of Fulton Bennett's death, lived the life of a Prince while funding terrorism with efficiency and without conscience. Frankel enjoyed the nom de guerre of *The Terrorists' Banker* until his betrayal of the Sheikh catalyzed CIC's theft of bin Rahman's billions. Each man hated the other. Frankel lived under the Agency's protective shield. Bin

Rahman had become a ghost, or perhaps a zombie. If their hatred has been put aside in support of Marta's defection, Mannheim would have one opportunity to anneal old wounds.

***

Zachary Mannheim wouldn't make a sacrificial lamb of Nasha Poynter, not under any circumstance: Her counsel would be sought, her active assistance limited. To accomplish competing goals required persistence, blind faith and an aptitude for desperate action embodied in Yusef Schwartz.

What facts were available came from Nasha.

Born from a love affair between an Israeli and a Palestinian, cultures and religions surrounding Yusef confused a young boy. After his mother died in a terrorist's bomb blast and his father on a desert battlefield, Yusef became Nasha's first friend in the refugee camps. She stole food with Yusef, shared her one and only book with a boy who couldn't read, and cried on his shoulder when nightmares plagued sleep. Nasha threw herself at the feet of Jean-Louis Michani, the billionaire banker who would save her, begging for Yusef to be her brother as Michani would be her father. Tears burrowed tracks in filthy cheeks as her crusted nails dug into Michani's wrists. Until he relented.

Mannheim's perceptions of Nasha's adoptive brother were limited to Yusef's significant participation in Fulton Bennett's execution, offset by his out of nowhere support in saving Nasha and her children from Hamas radicals. The first precedent indicated zealous obedience to Sheikh Bin Rahman, the second an unpredicted devotion to family.

Against the insistence of reason and the passage of years, Mannheim kept both Yusef's secrets.

Nasha rejected any accusation of Yusef as terrorist; she believed Yusef a Mossad operative.

Mannheim's opinion favored Yusef as a proselyte of situational ethics—a rare ideologue who rejected ideology. Still employed in CIA's mailroom, as he was prior to Bennett's death, one question dogged Zachary: How had the passage of time hardened or softened Yusef Schwartz?

***

Mannheim sat in his old BMW and shivered. Darkness arrived without Yusef.

A knock on the window shattered unwanted sleep. Mannheim saw Yusef's face and heard him laugh. "Some kind of spy you are. Unlock the door."

"You left Langley hours ago."

Yusef hesitated. "Decided to run home."

"Does your bullet wound from the night of Bennett's murder cause problems?" Yusef offered no response. "Fifteen miles from Langley...less than ninety minutes for a marathon runner. Where were you the rest of the time?"

Finger pointed at Mannheim's forehead, Yusef demanded, "What are your intentions with Nasha?"

"I'm in love with Nasha, Yusef. She's taught me humility and compliments my cooking."

Yusef felt himself relax.

***

At BWI Zachary Mannheim and Yusef Schwartz boarded a Jet Blue flight to Boston, where they took an El Al flight, in coach, to Tel Aviv. They sat apart and never interacted. At Ben Gurion Airport they were joined in an armored limo by Nasha Poynter, who arrived earlier on Michani Bank's G600. Pressed for time, Nasha's unexpected joy at seeing her brother was dwarfed by the magnitude of their joint effort. In a non-descript house maintained by Michani Bank, they slept, ate and engaged in the strained, pre-operation conversation known best to spies who flaunt probability.

At first light Mannheim and Randall Carter climbed into a hired shuttle. The battered VW bus drove them two hundred twenty-five kilometers north, then east across the Jordan River, and south on Jordan Valley Highway to Amman.

Yusef travelled hours, marked by diversions, switchbacks and vehicle changes, to rendezvous with Bin Rahman's representative, who himself completed a roundabout course through *Kefar Menahem* and *Kiryat Gat* before he stood on Route 4 outside *Ashkelon*.

In strict accord with the representative's directive, Yusef walked southwest parallel to Route 4 until met by an old woman, who guided him to one of Hamas's concrete tunnels into the Gaza Strip. Hamas's representative drove Yusef along the Mediterranean before turning inland to *Az Zuwayda*, southwest to *Khan Yunis* and finally to the *Rafah Crossing Mosque* at the Egyptian border.

Yusef waited until approached by a small Egyptian boy. Perfect English marked a partial quote from Rudyard Kipling. "*...sooner or later your man will come: the docks of London and Port Said.*" With the *Rafah Crossing* closed more often than open, Yusef followed the boy to a different concealed tunnel, this time into Egypt.

Once GPS co-ordinates of the entrance were transmitted to Gavriel Rabin, a taxi covered two hundred fifty kilometers in five hours.

Outside offices of the Suez Canal Authority HQ, Yusef found himself approached by a man in a bespoke, navy-blue suit.

Yusef was greeted in English, not Arabic. "I never expected to meet Yusef in the flesh. Years have passed...I'm told you remain loyal. You watch over Nasha and her children, but not once have you spoken with her or entered her home. Why would that be?"

"I serve Sheikh Khalid bin Rahman above all else in this miserable life."

"Do you visit Fakhir?"

Jet lag caused Yusef's error. "Fakhir is less than nothing."

In Arabic Bin Rahman's voice resembled a jackhammer. "Fakhir killed Bennett."

Yusef responded in Hebrew. "I was wounded. Fakhir abandoned me...he is a coward." In Yusef's heart, the Sheikh's words were an omen; Nasha's children were in peril. In equal proportion the Sheikh's words revealed weakness: Nasha's children were beyond Khalid bin Rahman's reach.

The flare of a lighter allowed an examination of Yusef's face. Bin Rahman looked satisfied before he switched again to English. "What do you wish of me, Yusef Schwartz?"

"Marta Mannheim wishes to defect to the United States. You could serve as intermediary to negotiate terms. I recommended such an arrangement to Nasha."

"Marta's husband is no longer a man of influence." Statement of fact, the Sheikh's statement dismissed the idea out of hand.

"Marta has told Craig Hall her defection is to be arranged in every detail by Zachary Mannheim."

Spit on the ground was a gesture of disgust; Sheikh bin Rahman started to turn away. He caught himself long enough to probe, "What benefit to our cause, Yusef?"

"Hall will make redress for the Sheikh's three-billion-dollar loss."

"Who establishes our terms with Hall?"

"Jean-Louis Michani, whose bank held the funds after the theft from your accounts."

Bin Rahman switched to Hebrew. "Who is the author of these intrigues?"

"Zachary Mannheim."

"What does a man who has been so demeaned gain from his efforts?"

"Bennett's murderer."

A hint of Machiavellian pleasure crossed bin Rahman's face. "A result which would also please Yusef Schwartz. Fakhir has served the cause well. Should I be suspicious, Yusef? Why would I not believe myself the one at risk?"

"An American poet and philosopher named Thoreau said: *We are always paid for our suspicion by finding what we suspect.* Vigilance overcomes suspicion. I serve Sheikh Khalid bin Rahman in all things."

"Is there a timetable, Yusef. Americans are always in a hurry."

"Zachary Mannheim has arrived in Amman. You have a long-standing relationship with SVR. The timetable is yours to create. As is the location of any meeting."

"Mannheim will want a dozen sycophants."

"If a meeting is agreed, it will have three participants: Marta Mannheim, Zachary Mannheim and Sheik Khalid bin Rahman."

"Mannheim is in Amman. Where is Marta?"

"If you decide to participate, text the number I give you and wait for Marta to respond with an encrypted number.

"What will Mannheim do, if I refuse?"

"I cannot see the future. If my Sheikh refuses to participate, Yusef resumes his existence with no debt or obligation to any man."

Yusef found a gypsy-taxi at Port Said's bus station and negotiated a price to *Al-Arish*. Several texts conveyed data, opinion and conjecture to Zachary Mannheim. A simpler text conveyed a more discrete assessment to Mossad via Gavriel Rabin.

***

Mannheim's text to Hall read: *No meeting without your presence. Arrangements on hold—text arrival Amman ASAP.*

Hall needed a big splash to scrub away talk of a murder indictment: Marta's defection would fill the bill.

No White House jet would deliver him as the President's National Security Advisor. Hall would fly commercial and pay with personal funds, then disappear into an unadvertised three-day vacation.

***

Yusef's optimism centered on bin Rahman's hunger to regain status and influence within the greater world of terrorist organizations. Readmission to their sanctum of sanctums could be purchased with nothing less than hard currency—American dollars.

Lined with concern, if not cold feet, Nasha's face predicted her words. "No way I transfer three billion dollars to the Central Bank of Lebanon...not without assurance the funds never actually leave my father's bank. Zachary, you of all people should appreciate my position. Rig a better mousetrap. Come up with something more clever."

Zachary aimed a bitter appraisal at himself. Off balance, the room spun: After Trondheim can I ever again escape careless assumptions?

"Yes, Nasha, a better mousetrap it will be."

Chapter 27

Khalid bin Rahman was married with children. Sex with women of power, title or wealth—sometimes all three—gave lie to a proscription against adultery preached by every major religion. His paramours were married with children. By the Sheikh's measure, these affairs improved the lovers and so improved their contributions to spouses and offspring.

Imams, priests, rabbis or clerics would ridicule his logic as self-indulgent and blasphemous. Religions would spend epochs into the future building walls of ignorance to enslave the sheep, while shepherds ate lamb. Popes kept mistresses. Priests their secret boys. Imams stoned women. Rabbis were Imams with less authority. Christians wanted a chance to be like the others, to slurp at the trough of ultimate authority. All religions shared one common need: Revenue.

Much the same could be said of governments: Sheer the sheep for the benefit of the ruling class.

Bin Rahman favored government by religion and for religion: God and devil rolled into one. Would that Jesus and Muhammad could have negotiated a merger. See, he laughed at himself, you're finally and irrevocably a revolutionary. If your thoughts became public, Muslims would behead you, Catholics would condemn you to Jesuit inquisition, Jews would nail you to a cross as a currency hedge and the Church of England would ransom you in order to crown you King.

He slapped the bare rump of a minor Saudi princess. Rose from his bed at the Intercontinental Amman and entered the shower. He wouldn't show anxiety to Marta or Zachary Mannheim. With sufficient good fortune his coffers would be filled once again. Wrongs would be righted. The end for these sheep would not be bloodless.

As he touched the phone its screen awakened. Marta's text remained clear and bright; there had been no superseding missive. Rafa would play host to a gathering of Intelligence giants. Razor in one hand, he issued a short response to each Mannheim: *Two days from today @ 1100 hours. Land of Fish restaurant, Rafah, Gaza. No electronics. No staff or security. No audio or video.* To Craig Hall a more important text set out the Sheikh's demand: *Bank representative to repatriate funds stolen by CIA, in person and alone, @ 1000 hours two days from today. Bank representative to travel via Tel Aviv by car to Ashkelon, Israel. Text this number for final instructions.*

***

Relief swept over Bin Rahman when he saw the Ihsan Mosque a block inland along Al Rasheed Coastal Road. A discrete nod went unanswered by either of two men leaning on a taxi nearby Alleight Beach Resort. A battered pickup turned right onto the unnamed road where his billions would be reclaimed.

His phone showed 09:48.

Including the three Hamas fighters he'd acknowledged, twenty more were dispersed in and around *Land of Fish*.

At 10:02 Fakhir Khaldun's skittish disposition gave him away. Bin Laden sat next to Fakhir and said, "No need to be apprehensive, Fakhir, I assure you."

"I serve Sheikh Khalid bin Rahman in all things."

Bin Rahman fought to maintain equilibrium. "For what tasks did the Bank select you, Fakhir? Details, please."

"My Managing Director summoned me. Jean-Louis Michani joined us. He provided an encrypted device whose purpose is to transfer funds to an account of your choosing. Michani gave me a written list of conditions which must be met before the device will accept input. Once you are satisfied with the device's operation, my task will be complete."

Bin Rahman's brain demanded answers. Had the restaurant's co-ordinates been entered into the computer of an American drone? How many seconds until a Hellfire missile ends my life? Rational thought strained to intrude upon incipient panic. Too much effort had been expended for the Americans to destroy a civilian site in Gaza.

"Show me."

Larger than a phone, smaller than a tablet, Fakhir set the device in front of the Sheikh.

"Power on the device. When prompted, enter the encryption key which consists of the full legal names of Person1, Person 2 and Person 3 without spaces. Each participant will enter a password and allow scans of their left and right thumbs. When data collection is complete, the device will prompt you, Sheikh, to enter a routing number and account details. Funds transfer will commence as soon as each password is re-entered, which can occur remotely from any phone until 17:00 hours today, after which time the device will not function."

Doubts caused anger to rise in the Sheikh's eyes. "Too complicated, Fakhir. When the meeting concludes, my obligation to CIA and SVR will be met. Payment should be immediate and without conditions. What else does the device do? Is there a tracker? Are there explosives?"

Fakhir stood and bowed out of respect. "I am a messenger, my Sheikh, nothing more. Michani gave his assurances in respect to the device. There are no alternate instructions."

"You, Fakhir, will meet me at these coordinates, when the meeting concludes. Your responsibility is to assure the device performs as advertised."

Bin Rahman's phone indicated 10:21 as the banker Fakhir Khaldun shriveled in dread.

***

At 10:50, with no remaining customers, shades were drawn. No longer could the Sheikh see sunshine sparkle on the sea. Sad for its loss, sounds made by a Russian GAZ-Tigr ceased and the front door opened. Four SVR soldiers dressed in dark blue suits stood guard outside; Marta Hinrich Mannheim entered alone.

He took several steps toward her before extending his hand. A restrained tone accompanied his greeting. "How pleasant to see you again, Mrs. Mannheim."

"Should I guess how an invertebrate like you was selected to intercede, Khalid?" Marta found a chair and filled a glass with bottled water.

Bin Rahman's smile was warmed by a wish to put a full clip of 9mm bullets into this woman, ending his endurance of her acidic tongue.

"Restrain yourself, Mrs. Mannheim. Soon you'll get a second turn on the American merry-go-round.

Marta felt a wisp of breeze.

Bin Rahman rose to greet a second guest. "Welcome to Gaza, Mr. Mannheim."

Mannheim adopted a fatigued inflection. "Shall we begin, Sheikh? Sooner begun, sooner concluded."

Delighted to oblige, the Sheikh explained the encrypted device's operation without comment or objection from either Mannheim. A good omen, two of the world's highest level Intelligence executives needed no coaching; he pulled the bank's device back across the table with his right hand.

Bin Rahman was formal. "Mrs. Mannheim, state the terms to be met by the government of the United States to implement your defection."

Marta handed two sheets of common A4 copier paper to each man. "The list is prioritized top to bottom."

Bin Rahman examined Zachary, whose reading glasses were buried in his wife's demands. "Take as long as you need, Mr. Mannheim."

"No need. Marta's demands are standard fare in a high-level transaction. There are, of course, details to iron out. May I state the requirements of the United States?"

"Please proceed."

"First and foremost, the defector's benefits of citizenship, title, employment, income and so forth will be conditioned upon a complete debrief which may last up to a year from the date of any agreement. Completion of the debrief rests in the sole discretion of the United States. Benefits from defection shall become null and void should Marta disparage the current, past, or future governments of the United States. Defector waives the right of due process and agrees loss of benefits and deportation to a third country shall be the sole remedy for any such disparagement."

Marta's inelastic laugh conveyed no amusement. "Too many words, husband, for what would be a quiet bullet. We all understand something of value is being traded today. I put my life in your hands in return for every useable bit of information I possess about Russia, its adversaries and friends. It's an arrangement not unlike marriage." A different kind of laughter accompanied acknowledgement of one specific marriage's wreckage. "I brought my normal security contingent, dear Zachary. Will they return me to Cairo in one piece? Or will I be black-bagged onto one of CIA's unmarked jets."

Husband and wife went back and forth over fine point after fine point with no triviality ignored. Their slog lasted long enough for an optimistic morning to dim with the blinding sun's last resistance against nightfall.

Five o'clock less than thirty minutes away, Bin Rahman intervened. "We reached agreement twenty minutes ago. You would both benefit if we call a halt...and agree to agree. Mr. Mannheim, please tell me the United States is satisfied."

Zachary nodded. "Send your security to Cairo, Marta. You and I will drive to Amman. A day, perhaps two, for you and Mr. Hall to get to know one another. Then you travel on Hall's airplane to a new life in Virginia."

Marta issued the two men her first genuine smile.

Personal passwords re-entered without objection; Bin Rahman felt three billion Goosebumps travel down his spine.

The restaurant owner opened the shades before two Americans, or one Arab, could shade their eyes.

Blinded, each heard rather than saw glass shatter from a first sniper's bullet. Mannheim's skull impacted; it tore out a piece of ear as it passed. Arms thrown in the air immediately after the strike, head twisted hard to his right, a second bullet slammed into Zachary's exposed left armpit. Hurled backwards into the legs of chairs and underneath a table, blood gushed from his head wound. A deep stain spread down his side and pooled on the filthy floor. Conscious for seconds, head hammered by pain and unable to breathe, he listened to the irresolvable *dialogue between spirit and dust.*

Outside the restaurant, staccato outbursts from automatic weapons drowned-out Marta's thoughts. No speculation was spent on her husband's prospects for survival.

Khalid bin Rahman gripped the bank's transfer device and waited for Hamas fighters to destroy whomever the opposition might be. His phone declared 04:41; adequate time remained to implement the funds transfer.

***

Nasha Poynter's military field glasses filled-in the obvious portions of a landscape strewn with disingenuous behavior conjoined with confusion and death. Yusef's ultimate objective remained buried in obstinacy, fed and watered by Zachary Mannheim's zipped-up professional demeanor.

Hamas fighters, SVR agents and unknown others created a zone of destruction from the beach to the restaurant.

Soon enough her experience in Lebanon's Intelligence Service would be tested. She hunkered down unable to alter inconvenient truths.

***

View of the restaurant obstructed, Raissa gauged the effect of rifle-fire from the beach on Marta's security team. On the sand, a hunger for revenge was on display in all its absurdity. She triggered her comms.

"What a shit-show. No discipline, no tactics. SVR security was unprepared. Not long before Hamas will be inside."

Nazarian responded with no view of the field of fire. "Stay with the plan…support father and son." Raissa's instructions from Jamie Norris centered on providing cover to Henrik and Elias Halvorsen, as necessary to assure survival.

David added, "Where's Mannheim?"

"Still inside."

"Roger that."

Raissa cradled a dirty rifle fitted with a 50-round magazine of 7.62 ammunition. "Not the ideal weapon."

Nazarian offered a platitude. "Ours is not to reason why."

"You're not Tennyson and this isn't the Light Brigade. No good guys should die today."

Barrel supported by the low parapet, she wounded three Hamas fighters with ambitions to enter the restaurant. Four more, who approached the Halvorsens's beach position, dropped onto sunbaked sand.

Who could've thought Elias's wheelchair qualified the lad for guerilla-warfare? Who could've thought his seventy-something parent a suitable foxhole buddy?

Nine rounds expended to drop an eighth and ninth Hamas fighter, Raissa prayed for rain in a land where it never fell. She observed Marta, sheltered by a single SVR survivor, clamber inside the Tigr and lay behind armor plate as the IAV accelerated towards *Al Rasheed Coastal Road*. On three wheels it turned south, away from diminishing gunfire from the beach and towards dozens of Hamas tunnels into Egypt.

Scope again rotated towards the restaurant, a lone figure clutched something against his side and on foot turned left to parallel the beach. Earlier reconnaissance informed Raissa the unnamed road ended in a stand of trees and open plots of land. If this was Khalid bin Rahman, his escape route could not be extrapolated.

"Working in the dark here, David. Sheikh just walked away. What the fuck?"

Nazarian was too calm. "Status on the beach?"

Raissa thought this situation couldn't get worse. "Unknown SUV loading two Halvorsen males. No apparent damage to daddy. Hard to tell about Elias. God watches over fools."

"Leave the weapon. Exfiltrate as planned." David never believed in keeping team members in the dark; believed even less in team members being exposed to prosecution.

"Zachary Mannheim has not exited, repeat, Zachary has not exited."

No time for argument, David reacted with, "Not your job. Go."

Raissa left the rooftop dressed head to toe in black, a narrow slice of skin showing around her eyes. Consumed by guilt, she started towards the battered old Vespa—skeptical seemed a better description of her secondary emotion. Suicide by Hamas wasn't Raissa's wish for Zachary Mannheim. Regardless of semantics, without her presence a bad outcome inside the restaurant was certain; Raissa turned back towards *Land of Fish*.

***

"Status, David?"

Jangled nerves a bad symptom, Phyllis Martell wiped sweating palms on her rear-end. Barefoot at the edge of a calm Mediterranean, Phyllis and Leanne Crowder each wore a black Abaya and a neutral color Hijab. Mother and daughter holding hands, they'd drawn no attention since being dropped by Nazarian an hour earlier.

"Fifteen seconds. Start towards the road." David's firm voice encouraging, they complied. Neither woman examined southbound traffic.

Yusef stood mesmerized by the Tigr's high-speed approach. As it passed a rusted bicycle, left as a guide when he buried twin IEDs during the dregs of last night, his cell phone detonated the first shaped charge. Right-side tires blown out, the Tigr shimmied as the driver fought for control. A twin explosive shattered the drivetrain and left the motor inoperative and smoking. Dust settled everywhere on everyone.

Bicycle retrieved, Yusef pedaled towards the restaurant.

Nazarian yelled into his microphone, "Finish it." Seconds from arriving on the north side of *Al Rasheed* road, he scanned the beach for opposition.

Phyllis stopped. Leanne's right hand lifted Sokoloff's Makarov, once hidden in a red sports-bag full of Euros. Loud as a blacksmith's hammer blow, two shots rang-out. A small fire took root in the Tigr's engine bay.

An old taxi stopped. Less than ten beachgoers, inured to Gaza's violence, paid attention when two women crossed the road. Half the sun disappeared into the sea—Marta Hinrich Mannheim and her SVR driver were dead. Sokoloff's pistol, left next to a corpse, would tell its story to anyone who cared enough to listen.

Nazarian returned Martell and Leanne to their vehicle.

At the *Erez Checkpoint,* Leanne would use legitimate diplomatic documents to effect clearance.

David navigated the stolen taxi to University College of Science and Technology in Rafa. Communications needed to be re-established and odds against re-computed. On foot he connected to Randall in Amman.

"Location of Mannheim's phone."

Seconds brought Randall's reply. *"Land of Fish."*

"Notify team of any change in status."

***

Nasha's best choice, as she stood in the dark a hundred yards from *Land of Fish*, was to run away and await Yusef's return. "How will I live with myself," she muttered, before sprinting towards the restaurant. Through the door without breaking stride, she slipped in blood before reaching Mannheim's side.

"Alive…" she yelled at a man frozen into a pillar of salt "…he's alive."

Voice rediscovered, the owner threatened in English. "I know you…Lebanese Embassy whore who spreads her legs for the British and Americans." A Karambit's hooked blade in hand, he halved the distance to Nasha.

A black clad figure stepped through the doorway. "Drop the knife." Raissa shot him in the foot. "Drop it. Sit on the floor."

Nasha cleared away the wicked-looking blade and returned to the task at hand. Life and death was a crapshoot for ambulance medics anywhere in the Gaza Strip; whether they would come wasn't a given. She spoke Arabic to *Red Crescent* ambulance dispatch.

"A tourist has been shot in *Land of Fish* restaurant. People are shooting everywhere. Please help him. Please." She heard a bicycle clatter to the ground.

Raissa aimed her 9mm at the doorway until Yusef entered. Each tasked to act alone; this lack of discipline was a bad indicator.

Ragged silence prevailed until the ambulance arrived. Nasha found the woman ambulance-jockey while two medics examined Mannheim.

"Where will you take him?"

Tone dismissive, the woman stated, "*Nasser Hospital,* it's closest."

"Is a good surgeon on duty tonight?"

Opportunistic greed jump-started, the driver said, "Dr. Hassan trained in England. Can you pay?"

Nasha nodded. "I'm coming with you."

Raissa's and Nasha's eyes met; a thousand words wouldn't have conveyed a clearer message.

Nasha told Yusef to set off after Bin Laden.

Raissa caught a last glimpse of Nasha closing the ambulance doors from inside. There were times, Raissa understood too well, when money was the most effective weapon.

"You're alive. Give thanks to Allah," Raissa said to the swarthy owner as the door slammed behind her .

Across the street an SUV dumped two men and a wheelchair before racing away.

Secrets and spies be damned, Henrik cursed Marta, who had manipulated the lives and deaths of a double-agent mother and her doomed-from-birth son. Henrik would shed no tears for another man's son. Soon to be dead, eyes fixed on an Arab woman across the street, Halvorsen spit in defiance.

Raissa left him in despair.

The Vespa leaned against an unpainted fence. On its seat ready to go, Raissa glanced at a text from Randall: *Mannheim's phone offline.* She responded: *Mannheim shot. Ambulance to Nasser Hospital with Nasha. Yusef on foot. Halvorsen, father and son, dead.*

***

Yusef's pursuit continued at a punishing pace; the Sheik's head start would not easily be overcome. While minutes spun out of control, he shoved doubt into a dark closet. When his left foot found a hole, Yusef fell hard. Blood dripped onto a surface which never looked unsafe. For sure this was a lesson; did it represent precognition?

Course changed in an instant, he would bet on a specific tunnel into Egypt. In pain and limping, he texted Gavriel: *F-16 status.*

On station jump-started a marathon runner's competitive drive.

***

Nasha strained to hear the exchange between ambulance driver and a *Nasser Hospital* triage nurse. Every syllable of the nurse's reaction negative, she went back to the driver's side.

"Dr. Hassan isn't here?"

Middle-aged in appearance, on close observation the hardened face was no older than thirty.

"Your friend will die here. I heard the stupid bastard at *Land of Fish.* You work for the Americans. All the decent doctors are in surgery at *Shifa* tonight." Hand extended, she added, "A thousand Euros gets your dying friend to *Shifa's* Emergency Room alive. Demand to see Dr. Hassan. Promise him medicines and equipment."

Nasha found a wad of twenties and hundreds. Fanny-pack turned inside-out she pleaded, "Almost eight-hundred dollars."

Nasha texted the team: *ETA Shifa Hospital 40 minutes. Mannheim stabilized. Best available surgeon prepped. Owner of Land of Fish recognized me. Advise.*

***

It would be the middle of the workday at Langley, but with no viable options left Nazarian dialed Freddy Medina's unencrypted phone.

"Who's this," Medina demanded.

Nazarian didn't know the current code-in. "BusStop rifled an MI-24 to save me."

A snort of laughter punctuated recognition. "Ass in another crack?"

"Any birds orbiting Gaza…maybe from Kuwait or Umm Al Melh?"

"Target?" Medina's question signaled Nazarian: *Give me a blue-chip name.*

"Khalid bin Rahman and Fakhir Khaldun, Fulton Bennett's murderer."

A high-pitched whistle prefaced Medina's answer. "Dangerous and low probability. No guarantee, but I'll do my best."

***

Raissa believed Jean Louis Michani's assistance riven with bureaucratic and logistical bullshit. She texted: *You and I, David, if all goes to hell. Meet ASAP. Randall, put my real-time location on Nazarian's phone…his eyes only.*

In need of options, which meant weapons, Raissa added: *Randall, copy Jean-Louis Michani and Gavriel Rabin as follows: Nasha attempting ground exfiltration of Zachary Mannheim from Shifa Hospital, Gaza, after life-threatening GSW. Opposition aware of Nasha's presence & identity. Yusef in active pursuit of Sheikh Khalid bin Rhaman.*

On an open line she called Gavriel Rabin.

His verbal outburst related exclusively to Nasha. "I'll come myself."

Raissa made her position clear. "Nasha won't leave Mannheim. Mossad's presence will be a pox on both houses. Supply what's needed against an Egyptian Mi-8 out of Almaza AB...Egyptian air crew plus guests. More than an hour we'll all be dead."

A broken connection provided Rabin's response. Her bag of tricks reduced to the last and least desirable recourse, she waited for an infamous gunrunner known as Hamid to answer.

"Gunther Probst died long ago. What does his devil's spawn want with an honest man?"

Hamid's genetics lacked purity; how much Egyptian blood coursed through his body mattered not at all. Dark skin matched to a dark heart, his soul belonged to the Kremlin. Hamid would manipulate Raissa's worsening tactical situation to maximum advantage.

Raissa was matter of fact. "The American President's National Security Advisor will come to Gaza tonight. Two Russian RPGs, two Strela missiles, two IWI DAN .338 rifles and a pickup truck...one hour. Terms?"

"All but the rifles...one hour and two-hundred thousand Euros."

Raissa was not inclined to barter. "Not without substitute rifles."

"How about SSG 3000s, twenty-four-inch version, shoots .308?"

"Two-hundred thousand in dollars, you deliver in person and alone."

"Three-hundred thousand buys you concierge service."

Raissa consulted her phone. Any meeting with Hamid would be as far as practical away from Mannheim's ambulance. "Three bricks it is...sending you co-ordinates now."

Hamid poked Raissa with a stick. "Between *Maghazi* and *Bureij*, Raissa the atheist chooses ground near an anonymous mosque. Expect two trucks and two men."

"No. One truck. Just yourself, Hamid. Bring a bicycle." Raissa believed the exchange would take place without third-party intervention—three-hundred thousand US dollars was still real money. Once Hamid departed, the real outcome would be up for grabs.

***

Yusef felt nothing, when Khalid bin Rahman walked into the kill zone of the Israeli F-16's smart-bomb. Confirmation transmitted, he focused on whether Fakhir would arrive for his rendezvous with the Sheikh. A small spike of anticipation bloomed; Fakhir's disembowelment would be a fair and proper resolution of an ugly, unresolved quandary.

When it came, the explosion was an anticlimax. A hundred feet of tunnel destroyed; one purveyor of death gone to a just reward.

From the rubble of a bombed-out home, fifty meters to the south, Fakhir's arms and legs accelerated to a killer pace. Egypt would be his sanctuary. Yusef sprinted in pursuit; Rafah Crossing, less than ten klicks south by southeast, negated Fakhir's advantage over longer distances.

***

Zachary Mannheim awoke to sounds and vibrations indicative of a small truck. He worked hard to reconstruct short-term memory. Yes, he'd been shot; by whom and for what purpose were unknowable. Yes, he'd had medical treatment; intravenous bags provided positive evidence. Pain's absence indicated drugs; his brain would be a weak link. Sandpaper in his throat, leftover from tubes and anaesthetic, produced a raspy voice.

"What time is it?"

From the passenger seat came a murmured reply, "Time to repay my debt."

"Are we alone, Nasha?"

"David is behind your head. Raissa is nearby."

"Opposition?"

"Restaurant owner recognized me…so the opposition is hunting us for sure. No sightings since we left the hospital." Zachary's next question anticipated, Nasha continued, "No comms from Raissa."

"Can we stop, please?" He felt brakes applied with care. Waited for Nazarian to offer crushed ice. "What are my limitations?"

David was blunt. "Two hours of surgery before they assured us you'd survive the trip to *Erez Checkpoint*. Notes of surgery, x-rays and scans are on my phone. You need more surgery, so flat on your back is where you stay."

Mannheim insisted his mind moderate its frenetic pace.

"Casualties?"

Nazarian kept to a quick summary. "Marta and her SVR agents dead. Henrik and Elias dead. Multiple Hamas fighters perished. Leanne crossed into Israel. Phyllis is missing. Last we knew, Yusef was on-foot in pursuit of Sheikh bin Rahman and the Lebanese banker."

"Weapons?"

"One 9mm and one Karambit."

Never had Mannheim submitted to his highest order fear. Before Hamas or SVR or his injuries killed him, klieg lights would shine on Craig Hall's world. Smoke the bastard out. Damn the consequences.

"David, type on your unencrypted phone as I dictate…text to Craig Hall, blind copies to every politician, every reporter, every television and radio station, every person or entity of any kind in the address book Randall maintains for me."

Nasha rambled, "Why reach out to Hall?"

Mannheim's fingers touched David's hand until mutual recognition clarified the moment. *"Marta's Defection Agreement signed, conveyed to Phyllis Martell as Director/CIC, copy to Jamie Norris, Deputy Director/NCS. Imagine the fallout when everything Marta knows about Craig Hall becomes grist for the 24-hour news cycle. Defection negotiation attacked by Hamas at Hall's behest. Marta's entire SVR protection detail killed (witnesses are troublesome). Marta and I (more witnesses) are wounded…exfiltration blown…on the run. Marta will testify Craig Hall is the ultimate SVR Sleeper…promised Marta's job, when all who might stand against him are eliminated. Hall manipulated the deaths of Sillin and Sluchevsky. Hall sent Bulgarians and FBI/SVR sleepers to kill Mannheim. Hall shot Carol Wright, an SVR asset with second thoughts, to cover his plans. I'll bleed to death before Marta expires, Mr. National Security Advisor. Worry about Marta…revenge fuels her. I've predicted your location. You can easily predict our location. Come find us. All our futures depend on what you do before the sun rises."*

David hesitated; the ramifications of Zachary's intended result too painful.

"David, turn on your personal phone, locator algorithm enabled. Send the message." Mannheim crunched the remaining ice; cold and wet, his throat felt renewed.

"Nasha, after half an hour David and I will leave you and the driver by the roadside. Keep the handgun. Phone your Papa for assistance after our taillights disappear. David, please send an encrypted text to Raissa with the latest details…then we'll await Mr. Hall's pleasure."

***

David's text allowed Raissa to synchronize the relative timing of events. Hamid's honesty wasn't the issue; everyone in Gaza could be bought. Would he need to leave Raissa for the animals?

Headlamps from a single vehicle approached where Raissa lay prone on flay desert sand. One man exited a black pickup.

Hamid spoke at a conversational volume. "Gunther believed in caution. How long will suspicion delay you?"

Still dressed head to toe in black, Raissa stood straight and tall, eyes focused on Hamid at a distance where the gunrunner would die first. "Step away from the truck, you know the drill."

Raissa lowered the bicycle onto the ground. Cast her eyes over four camouflage-painted tubes consistent with her specifications. Took note of two rifles with scopes and a rusted ammunition box. Shuffled back to the driver's seat and checked for the key in the ignition. Three bricks of hundred-dollar bills, wrapped and sealed in gold plastic by the U.S. Treasury, were placed in the bicycle's front basket.

She told Hamid, "One brick is rigged to blow your intestines into Israel. Tell me what happens next…I'll tell you how to keep the cash and stay alive."

Hamid's face twisted into unrestrained horror. "Or you'll shoot me…and keep the bricks. Not how Gunther operated."

"Odds in your favor are one in three. Figure it out on your own." Raissa reached in to start the engine.

"Stop woman, I surrender. Two trucks identical to this one. Kord-12.7 heavy machine gun in the rear bed. Four Russian Army on each, dressed like Arab fighters, with RPK-16s. I don't know where they're going or who are their targets. Leave me in peace. Go with God."

"Look for a text after breakfast…if I'm alive." Raissa shifted into first gear and left Hamid and the Mosque behind.

***

David watched Nasha and the ambulance driver walk in the direction of the Mediterranean Sea.

Nazarian texted Raissa: *Nasha and driver on foot northwest from my location. Ambulance to continue original route in parallel with the garbage dumps of Wadi abu Qatrun and the polluted waters of Nahal Hanun. Hall will come via helo, one hour from now or not at all.*

Raissa texted Randall: *Sat photos David's location plus or minus 20 kilometers. Set parameters for vehicle ID.*

***

David was focused on navigation, when a ninety-degree jog in the route caused him consternation. Lost progress recovered, as the road deteriorated and headlights shone on open desert, the GPS map showed the ambulance closer to *Wadi abu Qatrun* than ever before.

Randall's first satellite photo showed their situation in stark relief. Ten klicks behind, a single pickup followed the exact route taken by the ambulance. Two klicks further behind, tandem pickups were making-up ground. A second photo, clear enough to an expert in photo interpretation, showed the populated outskirts of Gaza City fifteen klicks further on. From there the Erez Checkpoint, and safety, was less than five klicks in the distance.

David believed the single truck belonged to Raissa: *Sat photos? Who's behind you?*

Raissa responded: *Regular Russian Army. Heavy machine gun mounted each pickup. Slow down, we need open ground. I'm coming.*

Three minutes passed before Raissa texted: *David, stop. Russian pickups slowed to a crawl. Hall's helo imminent.*

***

Off-road by a half-klick, Raissa unloaded two Russian missiles. In the distance she heard the deep thrum of a freight train.

Randall's last photo showed little separation between the ambulance, her pickup and the Russian pickups. Her last text read: *David — ask Zachary whether the Kremlin will abandon Hall?*

David responded: *Give them a chance.*

Out of the dark Raissa heard too many rotors battering Gaza's cool night air.

Two Mi-8s appeared.

Tracer fire from Kord-12.7 heavy machine guns raked the helos with 700 rounds per minute at 2,800 feet per second. Faced with annihilation, the lead Mi-8 turned to engage the pickup trucks with pod-fired S-5 rockets and its nose mounted machine gun.

Response from the pickup trucks dwindled to nothing as the Mi-8 pitched forward. In a cataclysmic fury the main rotor spun off, impaling wounded Russian Army soldiers on chunks of shrapnel. Ordnance on board the Mi-8 exploded. Fire consumed the machine.

Raissa assumed Craig Hall's hubris precluded Mannheim's destruction by anti-tank missiles fired at the ambulance from a glacially impersonal distance. Opportunity accepted with cold calculation; she pulled the double trigger on the Strela aimed at the surviving Mi-8. Impacted below the engine, its main heat source, the helo spun towards the ground. Flames licked at a less than agile contraption, while its battered and bloody crew, and single passenger, crawled an unsafe distance away from the machine's death-throes.

Obvious to Raissa, the public story of Craig Hall's death would be Russian on Russian violence. So no bullet to the brain, or another fitting coup de grace, was acceptable.

Truck in low gear, she approached the helo to a range suitable for a Russian RPG-7. Three-foot launch tube on her shoulder, she fired. The helo shook, glass disintegrated, doors spun away like mad Frisbees—yet the ubiquitous, old whirlybird refused to detonate. Certain she'd identified Craig Hall's arrogant smirk, Raissa fired the second RPG. Higher than the first Mi-8, the resulting funeral pyre engulfed all mechanical things and every human's flesh, blood and bone.

After all was said and done, SVR's leadership was decimated.

Raissa appreciated the irony: the Kremlin placed its bets on younger, nimbler, successors to Zachary's wife. Zachary, she knew, would consider what happened and conclude it wasn't any kind of victory, but rather a temporary suspension of hostilities.

She followed the ambulance in the black pickup.

Halfway to *Erez Checkpoint*, David spotted Phyllis's exfiltration vehicle. In response to his request, Raissa found Phyllis Martell without a pulse, cold to the touch, shot through her left ear.

"Phyllis is dead, David. Nothing to be done. Keep going."
Raissa's thoughts about Leanne Crowder would remain private.

Chapter 28

Zachary looked out over the crowd in Michani Bank's largest, most ornate, conference room. Stage-managed to perfection, Nasha's press conference would soon conclude. Her answers and explanations, as the bank's new owner and one of the world's wealthiest women, met his every expectation.

An elegant woman columnist, more silver in cropped dark hair than the last time she questioned Nasha Gemayel Poynter, raised her hand. Nasha nodded at her.

"What role will your adopted brother, Yusef, play in the bank's management?"

"Yusef's charitable efforts in the Middle-East occupy his time and commitment. My love and the bank's financial support will follow Yusef wherever he travels."

"One follow-up, please, Nasha. With the death of your father, and your ascent at Bank Michani, in the streets of Lebanon they demand the daughter of Bachir Gemayel return to campaign for President. Will you comment?"

"My name may be Nasha Gemayel Poynter...whether Bachir Gemayel was my birth father cannot be known. I make no claim to his lineage. Now let me introduce Mr. Zachary Mannheim, former executive at CIA and the new Chief Operating Officer of Bank Michani."

Mannheim hoped the 5th Estate would be less combustible than House and Senate Intelligence Committees. He should have known better.

"You've been living in a supermodel's beach home for months...what's an old spy got that Raissa needs?"

"I must confess..." Mannheim paused for rather too long "...to a serious involvement with Ms. Ribeiro's roommate, Agatha."

Another journalist spoke over excited mumblings. "Agatha is Raissa's black lab, Mr. Mannheim. Don't play games with the media."

Mannheim offered a grin intended to remind this journalist of his long memory. "Recent surgeries necessitated a long recuperation. I bought an older cottage...in need of substantial renewal...nearby Ms. Ribeiro on Cape Cod. She's often away doing what a supermodel does. Raissa offered a roof over my head. My monthly rental payment includes the care and feeding of Agatha, a new and welcome best friend."

Hands raised with insistence; Zachary selected a different media representative at random.

Her first question was a verbal grenade. "You accused Craig Hall of treason in a text sent to the entire world. Your charge was based on the testimony of your wife, Marta Mannheim, a traitor to the United States and a ruthless official in Russia's infamous spy services. Your text disappeared behind a stonewall of politician-speak. Neither Marta Mannheim nor Craig Hall has been seen in public since your memo was published. Is Marta Mannheim dead? Is Craig Hall dead? If either or both are dead, what was your role in their deaths?"

"Craig Hall assigned me the task of negotiating Marta Mannheim's defection from her position within Russia's SVR. Marta's signed defection agreement, sent from Gaza to Langley, includes charges against Mr. Hall. Whether Marta Mannheim or Craig Hall are alive, dead or abducted by aliens, I cannot say with certainty and will not offer idle speculation. Social Media across the world overflows with conspiracy theories. In your individual investigative efforts, your ethical stance would benefit from consideration of the following. Has the Russian government issued any kind of protest? Is there a reliable Russian source who claims skullduggery by the United States? Has Hamas or the Arab Street produced a shred of evidence in support of one conspiracy or another? How about Mossad...what do they say happened? For my part I'm convinced, by hard evidence, of one simple crime: Mr. Craig Hall assassinated Mrs. Carol Wright and will, if apprehended, be convicted of the acts set forth in my text."

Thank you for reading!

I enjoyed every minute of researching and creating the characters and their circumstances in **THE LAST CHOIRBOY**. Stay tuned— their world of spies and politicians will be the subject of a new book to be published for the Christmas and New Year's holidays.

Reader reviews have the ultimate power to influence a book's acceptance and sales. Whether you loved my story or found it a disappointment, please take a few minutes to give me and other readers your opinion.

Here's a link to my author page on Amazon, where you can find all my books:

https://www.amazon.com/JohnHayden/e/B002MN7358%3Fref =dbs_a_mng_rwt_scns_share

Select the book you've read and its format. Scroll down to the Customer Reviews section and then click on the "Write a customer review" button.

Thanks again,
John

INVITATION TO SAMPLE:

The fourth book in the Zachary Mannheim Series is titled
**A SPY'S BURDEN
OF LIES**.
The first two chapters begin below.
I hope you'll enjoy the sample and continue to read Zachary Mannheim's stories of a life in Counterintelligence

A SPY'S BURDEN OF LIES

A Novel of Espionage & Deceit

Zachary Mannheim Book 4

John Hayden

CHAPTER 1

His reflection, captured in polished Brazilian Walnut hardwood flooring, brought his rapid stride up short. Could it be the bank's subtle lighting scheme? It certainly was not the morning May sun, long ago risen into the sky above the Washington D.C. head office of Michani Bank. Could the face revealed truly be himself, Zachary Mannheim, formerly Director of CIA's Counterintelligence Center ("CIC") and now Chief Operating Officer of the aforementioned Michani Bank?

Any number of official documents would serve to identify Mannheim. Each would disclose his age. A hoary number, he allowed, although no longer an arbitrary societal limit which sentenced a man to idleness and gradual decay.

A smile began at the corners of his brown eyes, worked its way in businesslike fashion on to the entirety of a face which could have been the badge of a younger man. Nine months after a final restorative surgery; eighteen months after being returned aboard a Medevac flight from a near-death, illegal, and deniable undertaking in the Gaza Strip; and twenty-four months after setting goals related to his long-term health and physical appearance, Zachary looked away from a momentary aberration. With nods to employees on his left and right, he took up a position several feet inside the Bank's main entrance.

***

Apprehension caused doubt, a hungry virus which, once attached to Yusef's psyche, would, under the stress of interrogation, eat its way from the inside out. Emerged from his eyes in a river of bright red blood, when exposed to the stale air of the train station, the virus's color and form could morph into any of the men and women waiting for the train's departure from Baghdad to Fallujah.

After a four-year hiatus caused by the armed incursion of the Islamic State, rail passengers today could transit Baghdad to Fallujah in just over an hour. By car the journey could take several hours under even more dangerous conditions. Through thirty miles of Iraq's war-torn western desert, once infamous as a Sunni insurgent stronghold, Yusef's future would remain beyond his control.

The train was Chinese-built, air-conditioned, with a power car at each end. Built in 2015, dust from the desert and maintenance difficulties had taken its toll. The driver and conductor assured its riders the tracks running through Anbar province were clear of mines planted by ISIS (or "ISIL" as some preferred) and of collapsed bridges blown-up when ISIS marauded through western and northern Iraq in 2014. Police in combat gear roamed corridors, fingers on the triggers of automatic rifles. Iraqis had learned the concepts of safety or security were risible and subject to horrible re-definition without notice. Outside the windows were hopeful signs of rebirth as well as the wreckage of multiple armies, whose blood and hubris had torn Iraq asunder. Sleek sheet metal no longer offered this train a favorable comparison with the French *Train* à *Grande Vitesse* or the Japanese *Bullet Trains*.

Yusef Schwartz's life would, once upon a better day, have appeared to an outside observer little different from a hermit's existence. To abandon rigorous mental discipline would have been the emotional equivalent of throwing himself off a bridge. Product of a love affair between an Israeli and a Palestinian, fluent in English, Arabic and Hebrew, as a boy Yusef had been confused by the cultures and religions in his life. Today, more than two decades after his mother died in a terrorist's bomb blast and his father on a desert battlefield—eighteen months after his failure to outrun and kill his terrorist target on the streets of Rafa, nearby the Rafah Crossing into Egypt—Yusef had fallen hardest and furthest in his own harsh estimation. Despite what months of self-recrimination burned into the tall man's consciousness, ego's prickliness mocked his inability to accept the truth, acknowledge the high price paid and move on.

In every aspect of a spy's nature, invisibility to the opposition—the ability to move as an innocent among friend or foe—was paramount to an operation's success and the spy's survival. The train journey to Fallujah, by itself, would never be dispositive: it was the equivalent of a dead-drop initiated by a stranger Yusef might not meet, but who could end his life from the black shadows of a burned-out building. Exposed as he was in the grand hall of a half-empty station, a spy accustomed to status as a lone wolf catalogued dangers both significant and trivial in the hope of avoiding a tragic, perhaps fatal, error of omission.

A particular Russian made no attempt to disguise his origin or intent. Greasy hair, a cheap suit too small for large shoulders, knockoff sunglasses and worn-out shoes heralded a minor agent who would slit a throat as soon as drink warm beer. A paper bag full of Kleicha dripped crumbs on a light sweater then on to the floor as each pastry was added to the half-chewed remnants of its predecessor. He is here to impede me, guessed Yusef with no rationale for the conclusion. How many other Russians will be on the train? Of those, how many will be SVR?

A particular Iraqi was out of uniform and uncomfortable in its absence. White sport shirt above a pair of lightweight tan trousers, he wore a dark blue pair of expensive hiking boots purchased online. An ankle gun was a certainty, bulging through the pants for all the world to see. A knife would be secreted somewhere near at hand. The Iraq National Intelligence Service ("INIS"), successor to Saddam Hussein's IIS, or the Iraqi Police Service ("IPS"), would be this officer's employer. Yusef considered this fellow a Watcher, possibly even off-duty and a non-combatant.

The young girl—could she be older than twelve?—stared with eyes of stone. Not once did they blink. Not once did they indicate recognition. Not once did they suggest she would apply a merciful coup de grace, if Yusef lay at her feet as arterial blood spurted from the effect of a bomb's shrapnel. The dog at her side slept, curled up to half its undernourished size.

As the announcement of boarding raised four or five dozen travelers from their seats and private concerns, an older Jewish woman with conspicuous intent, maneuvered herself into position behind Yusef. Dressed in a long, bright red skirt, long-sleeve white shirt embroidered with blue flowers, and worn-out sandals, peripheral attention showed how she stuffed her right hand—with its bleeding fingernails bitten to the quick—into one of the skirt's patch pockets.

Yusef chose a seat behind the young girl and the now attentive mongrel.

The woman Yusef tagged as Mossad elected a seat opposite the girl and offered the dog something with her left hand. By the time the train jerked to a start, none of the other identified threats were present in a car weighted better than seventy five percent with grandparents and males travelling alone.

Yusef sighed. He'd done as the encrypted email, received six days ago, demanded. Uncertain what awaited in Fallujah, he increased surveillance of passengers moving between seats and/or cars. Unarmed other than his Janbiya, its double-sided, curved blade sheathed on a leather belt worn around his lower abdomen, the anxiety created by a spy's exposure to the world at large struck home with an ominous thud.

Ten minutes outside Baghdad the rubble left over from war—burned out hulks of tanks, armored personnel carriers, and every other vehicle on which a machine gun could be mounted—delivered grief and heartache to every Iraqi traveler. Recent wars, which had engulfed Iraq, identified no winners. Losers were adults and children alike. Losers were dead, deformed or disabled. Yusef's single, unintentional, tear tracked across his cheek. When two children standing by the train's raised roadbed hurled rocks, one went through the window four seats to Yusef's rear. Struck on the forehead, a man cried out in pain. Behind the rock-throwers, an older child aimed an AK-47 or AKM, Russian assault weapons indistinguishable from one another under the stress of the moment.

"*Rashasha*," screamed Yusef, as a burst impacted the train's skin and shattered the window where Yusef's eyes had met the shooter's gaze a fraction of a second earlier.

Falling to the floor with no grace, he felt the sting of glass fragments in his scalp. Instinct sent his hand to explore for damage. Retrieved from his rucksack a clean cotton cloth, ordinarily used as a bandana, was pressed against the dribble of blood. He heard a cold voice state the obvious in fluent, idiomatic, English.

"An American in Iraq is always a viable target. Even Yusef Schwartz, refugee from the CIA mailroom, should expect no better. Just last night three 107 mm rockets struck an Iraqi base in Irbil killing one non-U.S. civilian contractor and injuring five U.S. service members. The rockets, part of a volley of about twenty, hit areas between the civilian airport in the Kurdish-run region and the base where U.S. troops were wounded. Terror never stops, Mr. Schwartz. To counter its influence requires serious diligence. It does not benefit from your ill-considered, reckless, vendetta against Mr. Fakhir Khaldun, an international banker well known to intelligence services in this troubled corner of the world. Israel supported your prior incursion to end the life of Sheikh Khalid bin Rahman, despite the concurrent and regrettable loss of life among Palestinians, senior Russian diplomats, American intelligence officers and the former President's National Security Advisor. Your success has faded…old news, related in a most insignificant manner to Mr. Khaldun, who will not be hectored or harassed through any cooperative effort of Israeli Intelligence. You should be a thousand miles away from this place, Mr. Schwartz."

"Who exactly are you?" Yusef responded in Hebrew. "Whose interests do you represent?" His questions came out rather too loud, caused by outcries of distress in the damaged rail car. The Israeli woman and the young Iraqi girl with the dog represented the exception to fear and panic dominating other passengers after the assault rifle's ear-splitting attack.

"All you need to know, Mr. Schwartz, is that Gavriel Rabin hasn't been connected to any Israeli government agency or entity since the death of Jean-Louis Michani. Promises made by Rabin or any random emissary claiming to represent Rabin, which you might think meaningful or substantial, are empty and worthless. If you'd died moments ago, no one in Iraq or Israel would have taken official notice of your passing. To hazard a guess, my government believes your sister, Mrs. Nasha Michani Poynter, to be shocked and saddened to hear of your misadventures in a part of the world where you have no financial or political interests."

"What is the significance of '*a thousand miles from here*'?"

"An oratorical figure of speech, Mr. Schwartz. Your very expensive private education covered such usage, did it not?"

Yusef made a mental list of significant locations in the vicinity of a thousand miles (1,600 km) from Fallujah. Incirlik Air Base, a NATO stronghold in Turkey, qualified at 1,800 km. One of the vehicular routes to Tabriz would transit Irbil, mentioned with specificity by

Mossad's woman. What would Fakhir be doing in Irbil? Port Said, Egypt, was 1,600km from Fallujah. Port Said was where Yusef recruited Sheikh Khalid bin Rahman to negotiate Marta Mannheim's defection from Russia's SVR to the United States of America. Riyadh, Saudi Arabia was a possibility at 1,300km. Tabriz, in eastern Iran, checked-in at 900 km. Jerusalem was also 900 km.

Mossad's woman turned away from Yusef to offer murmured words of comfort in Arabic to the young girl across the aisle. To Yusef's surprise, the girl's demeanor exhibited no signs of the prevailing pandemonium. Cynical though it was, he chalked-up her uncommon calm to a life exposed to gunfire and its resultant carnage. Her dog's reaction was visceral and instinctual; on the floor where the pup quivered, its poop made a grand mess. A paper towel appeared in the woman's hand along with wordless instruction to Yusef: Remove the offensive excrement.

***

Mannheim examined the threesome as they entered through revolving doors, one after another. First in line was Congressman Emile Wright, of Texas's 19th District and Chairman of the House Subcommittee on Terrorism, HUMINT, Analysis, and Counterintelligence.

"Good afternoon Congressman, it's been too long."

With a silly, almost embarrassed grin, Wright stepped aside to allow former Congressman, and current Director of CIA ("D/CIA"), Jedediah Sewell, space to enter. A veteran in-fighter, and a politician not afraid to employ ethics as a cudgel, Sewell wouldn't be trivialized by supporter or adversary. Zachary Mannheim and Jedediah Sewell weren't strangers.

"Jedediah, good to know a New Englander is at the Agency's helm."

Warmth in Sewell's voice was legitimate, without hint of a hidden agenda. "You know how it goes in Maine, Zachary. Massachusetts is a foreign country even if Cape Cod is a second cousin, twice removed."

Behind Sewell came Jamie Norris, Assistant Director of the National Clandestine Service ("NCS") at Langley. "Hello Jamie, are you and David making life miserable for Director Sewell?"

"Doing our best, Mr. Mannheim. How are you feeling?"

Norris's approach to any meeting with Zachary Mannheim involved high levels of concentrated discretion and his full attention. Jamie would wait and see whether old affection and new stations in life would be set aside to mutual benefit.

Settled in a small conference room off Mannheim's ornate office, Zachary noted a luncheon spread with an informal invitation. "Better than average is the chef's target. Nowhere near as good as the food in the White House…where I'm assured you gentlemen are greeted as friends of our new POTUS."

Congressman Wright responded. "I remember accusing you of being too much a political animal. My exact words weren't much on tact. *'Friends in high places, Mr. Mannheim, make you a man not to be ignored.'*" Wright's composure strained; his tone remained neutral. "Your advice brought me through a tough time. Our new POTUS might not pick me out of a thin crowd."

A stylistic open door wouldn't always present itself so elegantly, so Zachary accepted the opportunity to walk through. "Jedediah doesn't have that problem. Old friends with POTUS, he is. I hope you're still old friends with an old spy"

Sewell was a fellow who preferred fewer words than flowery rhetoric. "We came to offer you temporary employment, if you'll submit to some preliminary questions."

"Not much Jamie doesn't already know…if your questions involve former NSA Director Craig Hall."

Sewell seemed to appreciate Mannheim's backhanded invitation to drop any pretense or subterfuge.

"*Perspective is everything. To be effective, seeing the world through a narrow lens will not serve an intelligence officer well. Effectiveness suffers when facts have become a matter of personal opinion.* Sound like something you've said a time or two, Zachary?"

"Vaguely familiar, Jedediah. I can be pompous when under pressure from smaller intellects. Why don't you begin. If I don't satisfy you three gentlemen, or if I tire of an attempt to meet your expectations, we can agree to a halt."

Jamie Norris cleared his throat, indicative of discomfort. "Chairman Wright asked me to bring along an immunity agreement. Would you like to give it a once over?"

Mannheim was tempted to laugh but held tight to the nature of this odd meeting among men growing more uncomfortable by the minute. "No Jamie, I'm in no need of immunity. But thank you for the consideration. Proceed, Jedediah."

Sewell had no need of notes prepared by staff. "Is Craig Hall dead or alive?"

Mannheim, in every public utterance for two years, had held firm about Hall's fate. "Craig Hall is almost certainly dead."

"Did you witness his death?"

"No."

"Who killed Hall, if he died in whatever manner you believe true?"

"Regular Russian army troops, operating under a wink and nod from Moscow, in the desert of eastern Gaza less than fifteen miles from Erez Checkpoint."

"The Russians deny involvement at the highest level of government. Specifically they deny Hall was on their payroll. Was Hall our highly placed mole?"

"Please Jedediah, must we use the narrow lens I so abhor?"

"My apologies, Zachary. Old habits, etcetera. Were the Russians responsible for your gunshot wounds in Gaza?"

"The bullets recovered during surgery...and in the restaurant during the subsequent investigation, such as it was...were Russian. The shooters were either Hamas or SVR. Too many rounds fired by too many shooters to know the answer with specificity."

"So you were targeted?"

"Not in my opinion. Bad luck seems a better explanation given the range from the beach and, because of the uphill slope, no line of sight into the restaurant."

"The Agency's after-action report strongly suggests your team in Gaza included Nasha Poynter and her brother, Yusef Schwartz. True or false?"

"False as to Mrs. Poynter. She was not involved other than providing the bank's Gulfstream for my use. True as to Yusef. He played a key role in recruiting Sheikh bin Rahman to serve as referee in the negotiations of terms and conditions governing Marta Mannheim's defection."

Sewell fingers, set to tapping on a yellow legal pad, illustrated the first signs of unease.

"Reports have circulated about a woman, matching Mrs. Poynter's description, arranging an ambulance in response to your gunshot wounds...your triage care at Nasser Hospital in Rafa...subsequent surgery at Shifa Hospital in Gaza City...and an eventual ambulance trip to Israel. Are these reports a cover story, disinformation, a total fiction, or something else?"

"Have these reports been authored by verifiable eyewitnesses and vetted by people who would know...people who CIA's Director trusts? Or are the reports the sort of unreliable, make-believe chatter resulting from sources who've been paid or own axes in need of a sharper grind?"

Zachary rose, turned away from the three men at the table, and poured a cup of steaming tea. Added lemon and stirred, waiting for further accusations softened by bubble-wrap.

Sewell understood his next words could end the discussion before it began. "Yusef Schwartz, Zachary, would you describe his contribution in more detail?"

Mannheim returned to his chair, wearing a look which conveyed his inclination to disengage.

"The Agency, Jedediah, you'll remember from Subcommittee briefings after Bennett's assassination, confiscated billions belonging to Sheikh bin Rahman. My arrangement with Craig Hall, granted wide latitude to arrange suitable restitution for Bennett's death. We negotiated a bargain destined to remain verbal yet binding. One of the unexpected outcomes was an opportunity to destroy the troika sitting atop Russia's State Security apparatus. As it happened, Marta's baby-step towards defection needed a bold response. At my suggestion, Yusef offered to arrange repatriation of the funds as the Sheikh's fee to facilitate Marta's immediate and unconditional defection. Tough deal to make happen given intense suspicion on both sides. But Yusef delivered the Sheikh...and the Defection Agreements were signed."

"Payment was never made, is that correct?"

"Not a penny changed hands...and here I must rely on the account of David Nazarian, because I was unconscious, and more than halfway dead, from those gunshot wounds you referenced. Sheikh bin Rahman sought to escape the carnage in Rafa via Hamas tunnels into Egypt. Yusef followed...at the tunnel's entrance he targeted the Sheikh for an Israeli F-16. Bin Rahman was killed by the

F-16's missile. In a decision comprised of wisdom, restraint and inter-governmental collaboration, CIA, IAF and Mossad have managed to keep the Sheikh's fate secret. Bin Rahman's status, thought alive and well by your enemies, suits the strategic purposes of your Agency, Mr. Director."

"Schwartz is Mossad?"

"Yusef's motivations can appear obtuse. It's certain he has straddled or muddled the out-of-bounds line. I'd judge him driven by family and an elevated sense of morality. He is not Mossad and not for sale."

"How confident are you of those facts?"

"I'm one hundred percent confident. But you, Mr. Director, would, could and should know better than myself. I'm similarly confident David Nazarian passed every polygraph and stress test administered by Agency officers with no loyalty to David as Interim Chief/CIC. Or he wouldn't be Chief of CIC as we speak."

"Who killed Marta Mannheim?"

"I did."

"How was it done?"

"IED."

"What role did Phyllis Martell, Leanne Crowder, Yusef Schwartz, Elias Thordsen and his father, and/or David Nazarian play in Marta Mannheim's assassination?"

More than two decades ago, Zachary became persuaded there were infrequent times, when despite the best intentions of all concerned, a spy better served his agency and government by coloring or withholding the whole truth and nothing but the truth. At this moment he believed CIA Director Jedediah Sewell to be engaged in a witch-hunt, wrapped in fancy red, white and blue bunting, tied with artistic bows of reflective silver ribbon.

"I hired a local operative who planted two devices of Israeli design, on the beach road. My plan involved Phyllis as a spotter; she maintained line of sight with the bomber. After detonation overturned Marta's SUV...and proof of death was acquired, David drove both women to Phyllis's rental vehicle."

Mannheim preference would have been to leave his answer without further adornment.

Sewell's face clouded over.

Before Zachary ceded the floor, he offered further insight.

"Marta was brilliant, daring, and willing to play the long game…already had one high level CIA scalp on her wall. Ted Granholm's assassination, as you'll remember, employed the Agency's own drone, let alone its hellfire missiles. Through her successes in Trondheim, Marta's path to control of Russia's entire security apparatus might have been unobstructed. SVR, FSB and all the other apparatchiks might well have been asleep at the switch. I believed the Kremlin would be unnerved by her actions. What good and loyal Russian man would, upon reflection, allow an American woman so close to the seat of ultimate power. The offer of defection was designed to leave an impression the Agency knew more of Moscow's level of comfort than did Marta herself. Leanne Crowder was doubled by Marta before any of these events took place. Leanne was Marta's insurance policy inside the Agency. And yet Leanne, competent, well trained, ambitious and without conscience, couldn't provide insight into David's and my plan. Leanne worshipped Marta, remains very dangerous and is beyond anyone's direct authority. If you've met in private with Crowder, Jedediah, count yourself lucky to have survived."

Deep lines across Sewell's forehead were transparent, a tribute to a politician's artfulness. Jedediah was trying to piece together competing timelines; Zachary's critique of Leanne Crowder smelled of rotten fish.

"Have you heard the recent rumors about Crowder?"

"No. Nor would rumor contribute to a reassessment of her."

Sewell's silence extended to his next question, asked in a dissatisfied tone. "Concurrent with Marta's death by IED, both Halvorsen males were killed by Hezbollah gunfire. Is that correct, Zachary? Why were Henrik and Elias Halvorsen on scene?"

Mannheim stretched-out a response by peeling an apple. Why, he wondered, would Sewell care about the Halvorsen males in the context of this discussion? Zachary's answer was an informed guess.

"Again I wasn't conscious when Elias and Henrik were shot dead. It's still a puzzle how they came to know some details of my operational plans for events in Gaza. But no matter what they did or did not know, the outcome was suicide by Hezbollah. Neither man wished to survive. They'd come to hate Zachary Mannheim, in part because of the death of former Agency officer Mariah Ackerly, wife and mother respectively…and coupled with Elias' crippling injuries incurred in Trondheim. Their presence in Gaza and their eventual deaths are a heavy burden for which, of those still alive, I bear responsibility."

"Did Yusef Schwartz kill anyone in a direct manner?"

"No one died by Yusef's hand."

"You're certain?"

"To the extent I can be, yes."

Sewell, determined to align two disparate versions of events, asked, "Crowder was on scene with Martell. What role did Leanne Crowder play in all the deaths?"

"Leanne was no part of my team. Her presence was by the personal choice of Phyllis Martell, then Chief/CIC, now deceased. For reasons of her own, Phyllis wanted Leanne in Gaza. Phyllis and Leanne attempted the identical exfiltration route David used for my ambulance but were ahead of us by more than half an hour. David found Phyllis's body, one bullets in the chest two in the forehead, less than fifteen miles from safety in Israel."

Mannheim aimed a question just beyond Sewell's willingness to answer. "When you met with Leanne, who, as I've just explained, is an SVR operative without a handler or a future, how did she explain Phyllis's death? What are these new rumors about Leanne Crowder?"

Sewell took a sip of water. Debated for the thousandth time the optimal way to preserve his options as the Agency's Director.

Mannheim was certain of the next name to be lined-up for passive aggressive denunciation.

Sewell ignored his prior interest in Leanne—and Mannheim's questions. "Where was Raissa during the Gaza operation?"

"Raissa left Trondheim on her personal aircraft. She wasn't assigned to, or present during, the Gaza operation."

Sewell's expression twisted into lethal miscalculation. "Your answer was a boldfaced lie, Zachary. Want a second try?"

Mannheim's reaction was immediate. "No thank you, Mr. Director. I've told you the truth and you've chosen to prefer Leanne Crowder's more captivating and useful Russian fairytale...written by Marta's successor, whomever may turn out the winner of a no holds barred contest. You're not a Congressman any longer, Jedediah. Random accusations, made against private citizens, aren't productive or polite outside the rarified bubble of Congressional hearings."

Astounded by how, in seconds, the meeting had gone off the rails, Congressman Wright intervened. "Director Sewell, have you met with both Ms. Ribeiro and Ms. Crowder, assessed their statements, and sought corroboration from all credible sources? If you have, why has the Subcommittee not been briefed?"

In the face of Sewell's failure to respond, Wright turned to an examination of Jamie Norris, whose disposition revealed an officer who would strive to avoid conflict. "Let me have your thoughts, Mr. Norris, or better yet, any firsthand knowledge you've come across at NCS or within the Agency at large."

Jamie was firm. "Not my place to offer insight or advice to D/CIA, unless requested. But Director Sewell has been at the helm more than long enough for a honeymoon period, or a claim of unfamiliarity with Agency protocol, or culture, to have expired. What I can offer is my professional assessment of Leanne Crowder. She is a chameleon, a liar, and a ruthless Russian assassin. Her bullet killed your wife, Congressman, under orders from Moscow…not orders from Craig Hall. Those who've held the position of D/CIA are never at ease when they allow themselves to get down in the weeds of a field operation. They struggle to maintain perspective. Granholm couldn't let go of first impressions…and paid for nearsightedness with his life. Grover often stepped-in at Langley at the request of the former POTUS, including several stints as Acting Director. He handled senior staff conflicts badly and shot from the hip regarding Intel from field officers. Grover's specialty was modification of field operations to satisfy his ego. No legitimate debate exists about how these tendencies and multiple prejudices impacted operations at Langley. For what it's worth in today's context, I believe Leanne Crowder killed my father, in Trondheim, under a direct order from Marta. I never saw Raissa Ribeiro in Trondheim or Gaza. Raissa remains a considerable asset at NCS."

Jamie settled into contemplative silence, prepared to watch how Zachary Mannheim reacted to a D/CIA who challenged his integrity, persistence, and tenacity under adverse circumstances.

Emile Wright, in the weeks before and after his wife's death, had learned never to assume Mannheim cowed or defeated. He poked a fork at pieces of fresh pineapple and awaited Sewell's decision.

Jedediah smiled a distressed grin at Jamie Norris. "Pretty good advice, Jamie, for a guy who only speaks when spoken to. Zachary, I apologize. Not for any actions I may have taken as D/CIA, but for the presumption of how others could and would interpret those actions. For damned sure I apologize for an insufferable derogation of your integrity. Inexcusable, really. We can call this meeting closed if an alliance seems irretrievable."

Zachary added the pros and cons. Decided to paint delay and deferral in a bright, genial color. "Let's put acrimony aside and continue with what must be next...your questions about David Nazarian, Randall Carter and Gregory Riley."

Sewell's sincerity would be measured by his continued dissection of the Gaza operation espoused, ordered, and paid for by the office of former NSA Director Craig Hall.

"Thank you, Zachary. As to Nazarian, was he with you during the ambulance rescue from Gaza...and Hall's death? How did Hall die?"

"For David and me, our exfiltration proved a fatal convergence between Craig Hall elevated ego and Moscow's decision to eliminate a sitting National Security Advisor, who, after Marta's demise, was their best remaining source within the United States government. It took no flash of brilliance to predict Hall's reprisal against those who destroyed his unprecedented rise to a position close to the Russian President. For over two hours, as the ambulance bounced along a dirt road, and I slept off the anaesthetic, David and Randall maintained satellite surveillance of two Russian helos from Egypt, tasked by Hall with our destruction. Randall, a clever lad with a suspicious nature, located two jeeps on a vector which would bring the ambulance, two helos and two jeeps to a point of close contact. David checked with Freddy Medina at Langley...no UAVs were close enough to destroy helos and/or jeeps. Coincident with our situation in the ambulance, Yusef was tracking the Sheikh for the IDF F-16. When my brain began to clear, David updated our status. Here's what he told me, word for word: *Marta and her SVR agents dead. Henrik and Elias dead. Multiple Hamas fighters perished. Leanne crossed into Israel. Phyllis is missing. Last we knew, Yusef was on-foot in pursuit of Sheikh bin Rahman and the Lebanese banker.* David and I gambled on the Kremlin's decision to let Hall twist in the wind...and baited the hook. The entire world read my text. Its publicity in the media ended Hall's already shrinking value to Moscow. Hall's anger assured our destruction by the helos, without intervention by the Russian jeeps. Ten miles from contact, I ordered David out of the ambulance. When the ambulance driver reached the projected intersection, she ran like hell. I made peace with the coming death. It's impossible to describe my elation when the jeeps opened fire with heavy machine guns. The first helo exploded. I heard the second helo increase speed. Its blades battered the air, sounding like a freight train under heavy load. Nothing for me to do but wait for its missiles to immolate the ambulance. I heard, but didn't feel, a second massive explosion...fuel and ordnance generating a considerable ruckus. Quiet settled over the ambulance, deafening by contrast with what came before. Jeeps withdrew towards Egypt. David walked ten miles back to the ambulance, directed by Randall's guidance. End of story. David, together with all those at Gregory's consulting firm, are gifted members of your Agency extended team, Mr. Director."

Sewell estimated it could take weeks to absorb and read between the lines of Zachary's harrowing Pas de Deux with death. For now, Mannheim's one reference to Fakhir Khaldun presented an invitation to the task at hand.

"Fakhir Khaldun, the Lebanese banker...what happened to him?"

"Fakhir is a competitive marathoner. Yusef tried to run him down on the streets of Rafa but faced with a choice between Khalid bin Raman and Fakhir he chose to refer the Sheikh's position to the F-16."

"Yusef is in Iraq as we speak, searching for Fakhir," Sewell said with reluctance.

Jedediah Sewell wished himself able to invent a palatable solution out of whole cloth. Practical alternatives to deal with Yusef Schwartz were non-existent. In many ways Zachary Mannheim's negatives outweighed even an optimist's optimism. But Mannheim's record of success remained unassailable. His persona could be, might be, enough to allow the Agency, and its new Director, to escape public humiliation.

"Yusef is on his own. Not on the Agency's dime, and without the knowledge of anyone we've discussed today...apart from Leanne Crowder. Zachary, we'd like to retain you, with whatever volunteers agree to assist, to locate Yusef, appraise whether his presence is a significant positive to our government's interests, and recommend a course of action. I'd provide a detailed Op File with the usual estimates and fallback positions, but no such file exists.

Eyes narrowed by lowered eyebrows; Zachary had heard glossier versions of a kill order.

"Here's something I once said to Yusef, Mr. Director. *Walk the tightrope at your peril, young man. Decide to whom Yusef Schwartz belongs. Not the terrorists…choose the terrorists, you become every man's enemy. Not Mossad…they see double agents around every corner. CIA is paranoid and Yusef is Arab first, Jew second. Choose family, Yusef. Find a way to shine light into your shadows. Nothing will be different. Nothing in the life of an improbable spy ever will be.*"

Mannheim saw no reason to hesitate or delay. There would be no worthwhile explanation of Sewell's true goals—just pretty lies wrapped in a bloodstained coat leftover by Jedediah's predecessors. "Is there an agenda for this task which overlaps with Russia's invasion of Ukraine and the ongoing war which the invasion began?"

Sewell's expression was grim. His face had twisted into an unrecognizable complex of emotions. His voice strained to retain an even tone. "Give me an example of such an improper agenda."

Mannheim never used 'improper' as a qualifier for Sewell's agenda but would not dispute Sewell's interpretation. "Russia built the Crimean Bridge across the Kerch Straits. If Yusef should be involved to make the bridge unusable, and I deem his involvement within the Agency's interests, may I proceed as I see fit?"

"You will proceed at your own risk unless in receipt of Jamie Norris's approval in whatever electronic format Jamie determines acceptable."

"With an unlikely situation dealt with, how is the overall assignment to be administered? Black-Op rules? Black budget? Perhaps an extension of Craig Hall's Trondheim Op? No questions asked or answered until the Op is completed or blown.

"Exactly, Zachary…Trondheim redux. Encrypted emails will transmit details from either side. Don't send an SOS under any circumstance. You and your volunteers are on your own."

Teacup and saucer pushed away, Mannheim's fingers twitched with the compulsion to scratch the wide scar where a Russian bullet had torn through scalp and ear. An itch which never went away, it served as a permanent reminder: To save the nation fell not to the high and mighty. Or to those dangerous brokers of disruption who lingered in the shadows of which the high and mighty were so fond. To save a nation falls to those who suffer risks and consequences in equal measure. It had been a different itch; one Zachary could afford to ignore until the events of Fulton Bennett's assassination. Fate handed Zachary an unwanted baton in a competition where winners won another day to draw breath. Losers lay in Flanders's Fields.

Where and how John McCrae's poem came to mind unknowable, Zachary remembered each of its final lines. "Not all poetry is sufficient to a particular moment, Jedediah. Are you familiar with this one? *We are the Dead. Short days ago we lived, felt dawn, saw sunset glow. Loved and were loved, and now we lie in Flanders Fields. Take up our quarrel with the foe: To you, from falling hands we throw; the torch be yours to hold it high. If ye break faith with us who die, we shall not sleep, though poppies grow in Flanders Fields.*"

CHAPTER 2

Yusef waited until all but stragglers left the train. Among those who lingered on a new concrete platform into the Fallujah Station were a bedraggled congregation of unemployed young people, whose unsuccessful search for employment in Baghdad was easy to identify.

A clean-cut lad in his twenties managed to catch Yusef's eye. Greeted in English, not Arabic, he told Yusef, "I'm a recent graduate in medicine. I had a job interview with a new clinic this morning, but there's not much hope. I work the occasional construction job here in Fallujah, but it doesn't pay much." Circumspect, with eyes darting everywhere danger could lurk, Ammar hesitated until he could safely initiate the agreed upon code sequence. "I never expected to meet Yusef in the flesh. Years have passed...I'm told you remain loyal."

Yusef issued the code's response. "I serve Sheikh Khalid bin Rahman above all else in this miserable life."

From ten meters distant, Yusef saw the young girl wave and his intended agent in Iraq wave back in a gesture of obvious affection. Led by the dog, the girl ran into Ammar's arms. The dog licked Yusef's hand, nose sniffing for food.

"I am Ammar Jawad. This is my sister, Sawa.

"Sawa and I, we almost met on the train," Yusef replied, "until an AK-47 ruined the trip."

Motivated by the train station's sieve-like security, Ammar grabbed his sister by the elbow and urged her into a normal walking pace. As they walked he whispered, "Did you see the shooter, Sawa?"

In Arabic the girl demanded, "Let go of me, big brother. The kid with the machine gun was not from Fallujah. A street rat from nowhere and everywhere, he'll someday graduate to wearing a bomber's vest. But there was an Israeli pretending to be a grandmother, who hoped to leave your new friend a fresh hole in his chest." Sawa pointed at Yusef with a grim expression, her thumb and forefinger a comic book imitation of a handgun. Dead serious, with a look thirty years beyond her age, she switched to English. "This fellow is a half breed, like you and me. A dead half breed is less trouble to Mossad than a live one with questionable loyalties."

"Yusef's sister is one of the wealthiest women in the world, little Miss Know-it-All. Her name is Nasha Michani Poynter. You and I, we are poor; our options are few and unattractive. Yusef wants to find Fakhir Khaldun...he will pay for our assistance. I know you remember Fakhir."

Sawa turned to Yusef. "This Fakhir fellow showed up outside my school. Followed me to the train. Stayed close until Ammar met me. Pulled my arm away from Ammar on our walk home. Begged my brother to drive him across the border into Turkey near the Black Sea. The quickest route...though never quick...goes through Samarra, Tikrit, Telol al Baj, Mosul, Duhok, Zakho and over the Ibrahim Khalil Border Crossing. Even a man who has never served his country, like you, has read the accounts of battles fought in those places. This man whom you seek, told us he was the successor to Sheikh Khalid bin Rahman."

Ammar's face told of contempt for a certain type of man, whose sense of personal entitlement was nothing to do with prayers to God.

"Fakhir offered the blessings of Allah as a substitute for hard currency. If a girl of fourteen can see through Fakhir the Impostor, if Fakhir the junior banker, living a middle-class life in Washington D.C., is to become principal fundraiser for the Sheikh's interests, there remains a steep learning curve to climb."

Stopped closest to Ammar, feigning examination of a map, the bulky Russian thug showed scant interest in an aide memoire. Yusef noticed how lopsided the FSB rough boy's face appeared. Saw how his left hand clutched at an area between his nose and left ear, where blood spread through constricted fingers.

"Come on Ammar, let's get out of here," Yusef said, while nodding in the direction of the Russian.

Ammar pushed Sawa forward and the threesome exited onto a street-oriented north to south from the train station. After a kilometer at a healthy pace, they approached Furqan Mosque. When opposite the mosque's main entrance, where the Iraqi intelligence agent from the train caught up with them, he addressed himself to Yusef in Arabic.

"Mr. Schwartz, I am Agent Khalaf, tasked by General Sherwani of Iraq State Intelligence to assure your safety while you are here in Iraq. Our Russian friend from the train...I assume he managed to attract your attention...will be otherwise occupied and present no trouble to your visit."

Troubled by Sawa's assumption of the Sheikh's death, Yusef decided to take the temperature of the Iraqi intelligence officer.

"What does Fakhir Khaldun say about Sheikh Khalid bin Rahman?"

No hesitation or purposeful delay preceded the Iraqi's reply. "The Sheikh has demonstrated care in all his ventures. Never has he sought or attracted public attention. Mr. Khaldun suggests the Sheikh is unable to continue as a counter-balancing force to the expansionist tendencies of the Great Satan. My General supports the Sheikh's efforts today as he has done without interruption for years."

Khalaf's words, enhanced by the hint of a grin, sounded like an election campaign handout, printed, and read aloud as the official INIS HQ position. His words, neutral to Sunni and Shia rhetoric, left wiggle room for whatever outcome proved to be the new political reality in Baghdad. In the subtext of a careful spy, Khalaf's warning to Ammar and Sawa Jawad had but a single interpretation: Spend your accrued trust with great care.

Unaware how INIS might have hypothesized Yusef's purpose in Iraq, he chanced a more direct query. "Do General Sherwani and Director Sewell know each other well?"

"I've often heard Americans use the phrase *Above my pay grade*. I think it applies in this case."

"Can I intrude on your hospitality to ask the best route by car to the Ibrahim Khalil Border Crossing?"

"Rely on Ammar would be my advice, Mr. Schwartz. He knows how to reach me, day or night." The INIS officer nodded at Ammar Jawad; entered a car which pulled-up alongside just as it was needed.